NOT SO PRINCE CHARMING

LAUREN LANDISH

Edited by
VALORIE CLIFTON
Edited by
STACI ETHERIDGE

PROLOGUE

GABRIEL

*T*he pre-dawn sunlight peeks through the window, and faintly, I can hear the train rolling through town though the tracks are miles away.

I sit on the edge of the bed, my mind whirling and my back to the cause of my breakdown.

Will you, or won't you?

It's not that simple, though. When I'd accepted this job, I hadn't known the possibilities, couldn't have anticipated what was going to happen.

I hadn't planned on her beauty, her full lips puffed out as she softly snores, her head turned sideways on the pillow and her face so innocent.

I hadn't planned on the way her hair spreads out on the pillow, rich chocolate waves that, even in her sleep, flow around her like a messy halo. I curl my hand to stop myself from reaching out to stroke them, feel their silken threads against my rough palm.

Looking over my shoulder, I watch her, hating that I've been forced from the warm paradise of her embrace by nightmares of who I am, of what I've done. Of what I'm supposed to do.

I'm chased by the monster I've become.

If you're a monster, then why not be a monster? Why not do what you were hired to do? You've done it so easily before, time after time.

But I'm not sure if I can do it any longer.

I can't help myself as I slowly peel the sheet back so as not to disturb her. I need to see her, need to commit every curve and angle to memory. Because one way or another, I will lose her. I know that already.

She's an angel. A sleeping beauty whose glamour pulls me toward her, regardless of the dangers she represents.

Then why are you continuing to stay here? Why not just walk away?

Because I know if I walk away, then someone else will do the job, and I can't let that happen.

Unable to wait any longer, I reach out to see if she's real or just a hallucination caused by my own tortured conscience finally snapping.

She doesn't stir as I run my fingertips over her shoulders, brushing a stray lock of hair away from her cheek and allowing me to see the graceful swan-like curve of her neck.

My fingers keep going, tracing the light knobs of her spine as I descend, my own arousal growing with every inch of flawless skin I touch.

Somehow, despite all the years of hard work and struggle she's faced, her skin's still silky soft and flawless.

It's lightly tanned just enough to tease at the naughty side of my mind because I want to trace those tan lines with my tongue, revel in being the only one to see the natural creamy paleness of her breasts and ass.

I find the tiny dimples at the base of her spine and the tattoo she's got there. She calls it her *tramp stamp*, but she couldn't be anything further from that.

She has this daintiness and dignity that can only come from a well of great inner strength. A strength I admire, a well I wish I could tap into to find some fortitude of my own.

I leave the sheet over her hip, tracing back up her body as my cock rages in my boxers, but she doesn't move, doesn't stir as I feast on her curves with my touch, holding back on my desire to roughly take her.

That's the other side of me. The ugly side that wants to be purged, to violate her purity with my darkness.

To do your damn job.

But despite my nature, I want to treat her the way she deserves to be treated, like a queen.

Perhaps that alone shows that this ugliness is not my nature, but rather a depravity I've nurtured and let bloom inside my soul.

But this is no pretty flower, more like a weed that refuses to die and instead grows mightier each day, changing me, weighing me down, and strangling any attempts I might make to be better or do differently.

She hums, and a small smile forms on the pink bow of her lips. "Lower."

She doesn't open her eyes as my hand strokes lower, pulling away to slide under the sheet by her ankles and run up the outside of her legs. I find the swell of her hip, and she sighs softly, a breeze on the air that tells me that she's enjoying this.

I run my fingers inward and am rewarded by the warmth of her cleft, already wet and waiting for me. "Were you having a good dream?"

"Mmm-hmm," she whispers, gasping lightly as I slide a finger into her. Warm, slick velvet envelops me, and I slide deep inside her, pulling out just enough to find the nubby ridge of her inner spot and massage it.

She loves it, lifting herself and arching her back, all the while keeping her eyes closed as she playfully pretends to still just be waking up.

That stops, though, when my thumb finds her clit and her dark brown eyes fly open, already alight with arousal as she gasps.

"Oh, my God."

"Shh . . . just let me," I whisper, my fingers and thumb rubbing all the right places inside her.

But she can't seem to stay quiet now. "Yes . . . oh, fuck, yes. Right there, Gabe," she says.

She's moaning my name over and over, her hips pushing back to meet my plunging fingers as I fill her deeper and deeper.

"Do you want to come?" I ask, and she shakes her head.

She knows what she wants, and she lies flat on the bed, arching her back to lift her ass tantalizingly in the air, trusting me to give it to her.

But I don't deserve it, even if she does trust me. I shouldn't be this attached to her.

Somehow, in the weird alchemy of the universe, I've found the one I'm meant to protect and keep safe for the rest of her life.

But how am I supposed to protect her . . . when I'm the one who was hired to kill her?

The question floats away as I hover over her, holding my weight off her. Lining up my rock-hard cock with her slit, I push into her, slow and easy.

Letting her heat envelop me.

Letting her honey anoint me.

Letting her pussy absolve me.

But I can't be saved, not even by her. As she clenches around me, I wonder if the reverse is true. Can I save her, even from myself?

CHAPTER 1

GABRIEL - WEEKS EARLIER

ou know why you're doing this.

It's not about the girl.

There is no girl.

There is only a target.

I repeat the mantra in my mind as I get out of the shower, my body freshly scrubbed and my skin tingling with the exfoliating scrub I always use in preparation for a situation like this.

It doesn't totally eliminate shedding skin cells, but I don't get paid to take chances, so I take all the precautions I can.

Looking in the mirror of the cheap motel room I'm currently renting, I get dressed on auto-pilot.

Remember . . . in, out, and don't think. Just do.

First is a cotton T-shirt, black, Hanes. You can get these at any discount store, and that's why I wear them. I don't need some hotshot CSI finding a scrap of cloth and somehow tracking me down based on my clothing purchasing habits.

On top of my undershirt is my long-sleeved blue hoodie

pullover. It's fashionable enough that I won't stick out here in Roseboro, with its working-class population, while at the same time, it's dark enough that I will blend into the shadows.

It's just like they taught you in the Boy Scouts. Be prepared.

Black jeans, a basic pair of bootcut Wranglers, and underneath, a pair of common, run-of-the-mill black leather workboots.

Everything I'm wearing is commonly available at ten thousand stores around the country, and nothing is over fifty dollars. Considering I'm burning all of this after tonight, there's a good reason why.

On the bed are my main tools for tonight. First, a pocket knife. I've used this Leatherman for a very long time, the multiple tools and attachments being more useful than a lot of people would recognize.

Next, my lock picks. I'm prepared to break a window to get in if I have to, but I'd prefer not to.

The fewer details I leave behind, the greater the chance that I'll be sipping beer and watching the game before the Roseboro police even know something's wrong.

Finally, tonight's weapon of choice, a snub-nosed .38 Special revolver fitted with a silencer. Not the highest power of pistols, but accurate, and no shells will be left behind for forensics.

I finish up, tucking my ski mask into my pocket, knowing I might need it later, and put black leather gloves on before walking out to the plain-Jane Ford truck that I'm using for this job.

Time to go to work.

The house isn't exactly in the best part of town. It's maybe one of the oldest in Roseboro.

Once upon a time, it was probably considered rural, but as Roseboro expanded, the plot of land with a short row of near-matching houses is now on the edge of the industrial district. The cheap galvanized chain-link fence that surrounds the tiny two-bedroom 'mill' house is a product of a bygone era, back when the biggest employer in this city was Cascade Cider House.

But the national expansion of the big beer chains closed Cascade Cider by the seventies, and now the only things left are a few of these tiny breadbox-style places that used to be filled with people who smelled of fermenting apples nine months out of the year and fresh apples the other three.

It's a miracle any of these places still survive, but this house is one of the few, and while it's old, and nowhere near what anyone would call a dream home . . . it's been loved and cared for.

I see it in the way the trim is painted, not always in the same shade of blue, but carefully done anyway.

Or in the way the little brick flower garden underneath the tiny living room window is still bordered in tightly-fitted bricks, although the flowers are now replaced with hardy herbs that don't take nearly as much care as petunias.

I park across the street underneath an old, twisted scrub pine that's shed a thick blanket of needles all over the uncurbed grass that lines the backstreet. It's the sort of neighborhood where your parking space is the chunk of dying grass next to your mailbox.

I sit in the shadows of my truck, waiting and watching. The first step is to make sure my target's there, that she's alone, and that I'll be uninterrupted.

I know her schedule. She got out of her last class twenty minutes ago. She should be home soon to drop off her books before heading in for a late-night shift at The Gravy Train, where she'll work until the last of the late-night barflies get their greasy plates eaten.

Then she'll come home, crack the books until her head drops onto them, and do the whole thing again tomorrow morning.

Whether now or after her job, it ends tonight.

I see her pull up on her scooter, a little 50cc thing that a lot of people around here call a 'DUI bike' since you don't need to insure them.

She has a car, a beat-up twenty-year-old Honda that she inherited from her aunt when she passed away, but insurance and gas mean the scooter's her vehicle of choice more often than not.

I'm tempted to just take the shot here. It'll be easier and faster, although riskier and less controlled.

But I do have a few rules to my work, an honor code, even though what I do is less than honorable by anyone's standards, including my own.

First, be patient, hence my learning her routine and doing my research. I'm good, not because I'm the fastest, or the nastiest, or the strongest. I'm good because I take my time and do it right.

Second, absolutely no bystanders. I won't take a shot on anyone if there are innocent people who could get hurt if something goes wrong.

The last thing my conscience needs is me accidentally shooting some eight-year-old kid because I didn't see them or a bullet bounces off a lamp post.

Third, don't get too close. But I don't want to think about the third. Because I'm pretty sure I'm breaking the hell out of it with this job.

As I watch her shake out her long brown hair, nearly black in the deepening dusk, I grip my steering wheel a little tighter.

I know she doesn't try to be, but Isabella Turner is uniquely striking in her beauty.

Her hair falls simply, nearly halfway down her back, waving in the air like a dark curtain that frames her lean face.

Her eyes are large, almond-shaped and framed with thick lashes, like she's a princess hiding in this working-class setting, just waiting for her chance to be restored back to the throne that's waiting for her.

Of course, I'm being foolish, maybe a little whimsical. But I do this with every target.

Usually, I'm trying to make them go the other way. Paint them with a brush that pushes them fully into the 'evil' category.

So, the drug dealer isn't just a guy selling drugs but someone who's stealing kids off the streets, carelessly taking their potential future by hooking them on his poison smack to fund his criminal empire.

The stock broker isn't just a shady trader but someone who's laundering billions of dollars of crime money while robbing poor, innocent grandmothers of their retirement savings.

It helps me sleep at night, and quite honestly, isn't that hard to do. Not with the contracts I've accepted.

I've killed a lot of bad people. Hunted them down, snuffed out their miserable existence, and not felt much remorse about it.

Occasionally, I even feel like I'm doing something darkly noble, protecting those who can't do what I do from the evil in every corner of the world.

But no matter how hard I try or how much I look into her past, I can't make Isabella Turner 'bad' in my eyes.

But if I don't do this, I'll never get the answers I need. Blackwell hired me for this job, making it very clear that this is a tit-for-tat-only negotiation. I do this, and he gives me what I want . . . a chance for justice.

Considering carefully if this is the moment, I scan the street, looking for potential witnesses. As my hand reaches for the door handle, I freeze, seeing a man approaching the house from down the street.

His hair's long and greasy, the two-day-old growth of beard on his gaunt cheeks making him look even scuzzier than the ripped long-sleeved Nirvana T-shirt he's wearing.

"Hey, Izzy!" he yells, and I shrink deeper into the seat, willing myself to be invisible, my eyes narrowing as I rest my hand on my pistol. Something about this puts me on edge. "Izzy Turner!"

The look on her face tells me everything that Miss Turner feels about the man calling her name, and mentally, I quickly go through my research on this mission to place a name to a face . . . Russell Carraby. Thirty-five, single, currently listed as 'self-employed' according to his most recent tax records. And Izzy's landlord of sorts. He doesn't own her house, but Russell inherited the land Izzy's house sits on.

Seems the Carraby family got along quite nicely with the Cascade Cider people and that's how these houses came to be built out here. Back then, it was probably a sweet deal all the way around. But now, people who own their house, like Miss Turner, still have to pay a small fortune to sharks like Carraby because of where their home sits.

Meanwhile, Carraby gets paid doing jack squat.

But the financial data I'd run on Isabella Turner had seemed dry and unimportant, just a list of bills she paid off each month like clockwork. This moment with Carraby feels decidedly more threatening than a monthly invoice.

"What do you want, Russ?" Isabella asks, her shoulders slumping as Russell gets closer. "I already paid you for the month."

"No, you paid me catch-up money," Russell says, his ferret-like eyes clearly undressing Isabella even as he smacks the large wad of gum in his mouth. "Not all of it either. Late fees can be such a bitch." He shakes his head like he's sad, but even from across the street, I can see the joy he's taking in this moment. "Long story short, you're still behind."

Isabella isn't ready to back down, though. "You need to check your books. I paid you extra last time."

"Nope . . . you still owe," Russell says, smirking. "I got it all in my computer back at my place. If you'd like to come see?"

"There's no way in hell I'll ever go inside your house, Russell," Isabella growls, her anger flaring. "And trust me, I keep my own records too. Of every single red cent I give you. So you can stop looking at me like that. I'm not going to whore myself out over a damned land lease I've already paid."

"Just being neighborly. If you can't pay in cash, I'd be open to letting you pay another way," Russell threatens with a shrug and a smile, like he'd be doing her a favor. "Hell, it might even be fun. And I know you haven't had a man in a long time."

Even as that intel does dangerous things to my cock, my hand tightens on my pistol. I'm about ready to shoot Russell on principle when Isabella pokes a hard finger into the front of his dirty shirt, denting the doughy skin of his chest. She takes several steps forward, and like the coward he is, Carraby backs up under the weight of her fury.

"The next time you mention something like that is the time I call the cops on your ass," Isabella yells.

The threat, combined with her pushing against him, causes Russell to take another half-step back.

"I'm gonna give you one week, and if I don't have my fuckin' money by then, I'm going to take you to court," he says. "Don't fuck with me, Izzy. I know the sheriff. You might just have more problems than looking for another place to live."

But he's adding to the space between them, already walking away without giving her his back. Coward. Smart man, considering the balls on this girl, but still a gutless way to try to intimidate her.

"I bet you do know the sheriff . . ."

She pauses dramatically. "Since he's arrested you twice before," Isabella calls after him. "As for court, you bring your records and I'll bring mine."

She's taking aim at his every threat, but I can see it in the way her shoulders slump a half-inch that the fire's dimming. Still, she fakes it pretty well until Russell's disappeared around the corner, and she goes inside her fence.

This is the time I should be moving, taking advantage of her shaken state, but I can't do anything but watch as she fumbles, trying to get the keys to her house into the lock before giving up.

She drops her bag to the concrete stoop and collapses into the small, cheap plastic chair, discount lawn furniture at its finest, next to the door, burying her face in her hands.

She doesn't sob or cry loudly. Instead, she just sits there, her shoulders shaking quietly, her body looking like she's exhausted. She's carrying the weight of the world on her shoulders and she's tired out from doing it. I can almost see the scrabbling grip she has on the end of her rope, but still, she fights to hang on.

I watch, my soul touched. I want to go to her, to take her into my arms and tell her that the world isn't so hard and cruel, even if it's a lie. I want to . . .

Do your fucking job!

I clear my throat, blinking slowly as I pick up my ski mask, slipping the breathable Lycra over my head and then down my face, leaving just my eyes peeking out.

I pull up my hoodie, but I'm frozen, unable to move as she finishes her moment of weakness.

Then, in a show of resilience that makes my mouth dry, she stands up, wipes her face, and glances at her watch before opening up her front door enough to drop her book bag off and leaves immediately.

You need to finish this.

No.

I rip the mask off, stuffing it in the console. I need to find out more. I can't risk violating my most cardinal rule, that I don't kill the innocent. This is something that I could never come back from if I'm wrong.

Ever since I was given the contract to end Isabella Turner's life, I've broken myself trying to find something she's done wrong. She's not perfect, but she's done nothing deserving of death.

And Blackwell's reason for hiring me doesn't carry enough water with me. I know everyone is a pawn in someone else's game, but I refuse to the be the Grim Reaper for a soul that doesn't deserve it in some way.

My gut is telling me there's something more here, a puzzle piece I don't have yet. And I won't make a move until I have the full picture.

Isabella gets on her scooter, tucking her hair into her helmet again before taking off. I let her get a good block away before following. The streets in this neighborhood aren't busy and I already know where she's going.

The Gravy Train is that rarity to find anymore, an honest to goodness old-fashioned diner. The long silver bullet-shaped building resembles an old train car, and the inside decoration is a color I swear only comes when you take white paint and expose it to ten years' worth of fried onions, splattering greasy meat patties, burps, belches, and other bodily emissions.

I park in the lot, watching through the huge windows as Isabella goes inside and talks with another worker, who nods and clears away a spot at the counter for her. She brings her what looks like a grilled cheese while Isabella consumes it in four large bites before heading to the back, and I make my move.

So far, I've never gotten close enough to actually let her notice me, but something about her is calling to me, promising answers.

I push my hoodie down, not wanting to look suspicious, and my hair springs free, sticking up every which way, but I don't give a shit. I lock my pistol in the truck and head inside.

Taking an open booth, I pull out my cellphone, pretending to be obsessed with the screen while I surreptitiously watch for Isabella.

"Hey, honey, you orderin'?" a waitress asks, all sass and big hair and saucy attitude. She looks like she's about to tell me I need to order or move along, but one look at my face tempers that.

I'm used to women softening at my looks. I'm not arrogant, but I know that I'm easy on the eyes, and I've used it to my advantage more than once.

"Just a coffee for now," I order. "Decaf, if you have some ready."

"Honey, of course we've got decaf," the waitress says, turning around.

She gets me my cup before Isabella comes out, the two obviously swapping out as one goes off shift and the other comes on.

I nurse the coffee for a good half hour, watching Isabella at work. She's exhausted, almost sleepwalking through her shift, and while she keeps a smile on her face, it looks nearly painted on.

Still, as she keeps working, I find myself drawn to her more and more. It's not just physical attraction. I felt that the first moment I saw her picture in the office of the man who hired me to kill her. No, this is more than that.

How could he? How could he hire me to kill a pretty woman who mostly seems to be desperately struggling despite working her fingers to the bone?

She can't have any bearing on a man like that's life, they're literally worlds apart. There must be something I'm missing. There must be something he's not telling me. Surely, even he's not this cruel, this reckless.

"Hey, Izzy!" the cook in the back yells, banging on the little chrome bell next to the pickup window. "Come on, you got plates waitin'!"

"Yeah, sorry, Henry," Isabella says, grabbing them.

She hands them out to the three guys waiting at the old-fashioned sit-down counter before going over to the register, where another waitress, an older woman in her fifties who looks like she's done this her whole life, is tallying up a bill. I'm close enough that I can hear them.

"Hey, Elaine, I'm gonna grab another coffee. You mind?"

"I don't say nothin' about drinking the mud," Elaine says. "Don't let Henry get on ya, honey. Just his ulcer acting up again."

"No . . . no, I've been shit so far," Isabella says, yawning. "I can't keep going on three hours of sleep a night. But I don't know what else to do."

"You keep busting your ass, you're gonna end up like me, fallen arches and all," Elaine says encouragingly. "Seriously, what could have you scraping for every dime like you are?"

"Russ came by my place again," Isabella says quietly, recounting the confrontation at her house briefly. "I've got enough to pay the bastard but—"

"But then you won't have enough to live on. Don't say anything else," Elaine says. "Next week, you come in, you order what they allow us, and if it magically turns into a full chicken-fried steak and gravy dinner, well shit, I guess I just need to get my eyes looked at."

I see Elaine give a huge wink, like it's a brilliant conspiracy, and Isabella smiles. "If you do your studying here, you can have my shift meal too. That'd get you two per day at least. Make one of them the Country Plate Special and you can take the toast and little peanut butter packets and get a sandwich later too."

It's a kind gesture from the world-worn waitress, and with how quickly she throws that idea out there, I can tell she's been through some rough times too. Isabella nods quietly, touched, but I can tell her pride is stinging that she needs to take such charity. "You know if it was just any old house, I'd say fuck it, move into an apartment or something, but—"

"I know, honey," Elaine says. "I know."

15

Isabella clears her throat and finishes off her coffee. As she comes around the counter, I clear my throat and she looks over.

Our eyes meet . . . and inside me, I feel more conflicted than ever.

Because in the first meeting of our eyes, I feel what I've thought doesn't exist.

The Spark.

CHAPTER 2

ISABELLA

"*H*appy little clouds," I murmur to myself as I swirl my finger along the top of my touchpad, wishing for the millionth time that I could do this again with real paints and canvases.

But real art equipment costs money, and money is something I don't have. So instead, I use GIMP, which is free, and pray my laptop doesn't die again before I finish college.

Right now, I'm working on my own version of the *Mona Lisa* . . . if Gal Gadot were posing for the famous painting. Well, that and my color choices are a little surreal, but I sort of like the idea of putting light green clouds in a lilac sky behind the eternally smirking diva.

It's a lot more colorful than my real life, and I can go for a little bit of that before I have to slog my way through another day.

An insistent *meow* on my left gets my attention, and I look over to see Nirvash, my cat.

Technically, it's my best friend Mia's cat, but her former apartment lease didn't allow pets, so when she brought me the little ball of fur and begged for me to watch after it, I couldn't help myself.

Now, the miniature monster is mine, and I probably wouldn't give her back even if Mia begged. Not that she would. She knows what this cat has come to mean to me.

Sometimes, I wonder if Mia didn't plan the whole thing to trick me into getting a pet for my own good.

"Thanks, Vash. It's that time?"

Vash *meows* again, and I get up off the couch, stretching a little. Vash takes the opportunity to climb onto the keyboard, though she knows she's not allowed, and looks at the screen before turning her nose up and walking away.

"Humph . . . everyone's a damn critic. Well, I'm not done with it yet."

Meow.

"Yeah, yeah. I know, feed you before you get angry," I reply, heading into the kitchen and picking up the quarter-carton of nondairy creamer on the counter.

It, like a lot of the food I've got, is scraps from The Gravy Train's kitchen, since they can't keep opened containers overnight. I'm not sure that's a real rule, but Elaine had vehemently insisted it was true as she foisted the creamer and a large to-go bowl of soup on me.

She means well, and though it was a hit to my pride, I had taken it, knowing it'd help. The creamer is Vash's little treat and she loves it. "Is this what you want?"

Meow.

"Fine, fine . . . but you only get a little along with your real food," I reply, filling the shallow bowl Vash uses for food.

I check my clock and see I've got five minutes to be out the door before I'm late for my first class of the day. I toss the carton back in the fridge and hurry to the bathroom.

It's my own damn fault, really. When I'm painting, I'm able to escape, let my mind relax, and not worry about all the crap that's weighing down my life, even if only for a few minutes.

But that also means I let time get away from me, and as I quickly brush my teeth and pull a brush through my hair, I'm rushing.

"Okay, Vash baby, be good and keep the mice company!" I toss over my shoulder as I grab my bookbag and rush out to my little scooter.

The morning air's chilly, but until we get snow or rain, I need to be frugal, and using my scooter instead of my car saves me several dollars a day on gas.

As the wind blows in my face, numbing my lips, I curse myself for forgetting to use Chapstick before leaving. I've got some in my bag, but it'll have to wait until class. I just don't have time.

Like a lot of my life, I just don't have time for a lot of things. I barely have time for friends. I don't have time to take care of myself. I don't have time for anything except work and school.

I don't have any family left. The closest thing to family I have is Mia, my other bestie, Charlotte, and a cat that earns a good portion of her food through keeping the neighborhood rat population under control.

Other than that, my life's empty.

No time for self-pity though. I console myself with the idea that soon enough, I'll be able to take the next step after I finish my degree. Just one more year like this and then everything will be better.

The thought doesn't comfort me much when I hear an approaching truck motor and see Russell driving up in his Chevy. "You're up early," I mutter, tugging on my helmet and palming my keys. "Must really be running low on meth."

Russell comes to a stop next to me, putting his truck in park but leaving the motor running. "Izzy, where's my money?"

I growl, buckling my helmet. "You told me last night that I had a week, Rusty."

I've known Russell since I moved into this house, and I know for a fact that he hates that nickname.

Still, I'm just too tired and too hungry to think clearly about poking the bear, or honestly, to give a rat's ass about his bullshit this morning, especially since I've got class soon.

Russell's face reddens at the name, and he rubs at his cheek, where it looks like he's been doing the junkie shuffle all over his face. A shiftless kid who spent most of his teenage years trying to score beer and terrorizing the neighborhood middle-schoolers, he hasn't improved with age.

He scored his first drug conviction at twenty-two, but Russell's father got him out of those charges. Russell Senior had owned a lot of land on the outskirts of Roseboro, and as the town grew, he flipped a lot of the flat, empty pastures that weren't worth much to housing developers who needed easy plots for subdivisions. It'd made him bank, and money makes you powerful.

By the time Russell's parents died five years ago, a heart attack behind the wheel that resulted in a fiery crash that killed them both, Russell had inherited over a million dollars.

And he's burned through it all. Literally. A certified smoke hound, if you can put it in a pipe and smoke it, Russell Carraby's put it in his lungs. Quite a few rumors say he's moved on from smoking to straight up injecting poison into his body. All in all, it makes him unpredictable and desperate, which worries the shit out of me.

But money buys you lots of friends, and since Russell hasn't yet shit where he eats in terms of drug violence, the local cops don't do anything to stop him. I have a feeling the influence his money has bought is coming to a firework-worthy finale though.

He's down to his house and the deed to the land that my house and a few others sit on. He's like the slumlord of outer Roseboro, but with only the small pool of our row of old homes to dip into.

And he's digging in with a damn shovel, trying to squeeze out every last drop he can get.

And that's what I owe him, a freaking land lease that I never had to pay to his parents. They had charged a small annual sum, more for show than anything, but when Russell inherited it, he used his connections to get a court order saying I have to make up for back payments. Stupid me never had a contract with Russell Senior, having just continued the deal they'd always had on the property and trusting that would always be the case, an honorable verbal agreement between all involved parties.

Russ isn't nearly the reasonable businessman his father was though. He's desperate for money, and I know it. He probably doesn't even remember telling me I had a week just last night, whatever memory he once had ruined by chemicals. The fact that he's back here so quickly tells me he's looking for a fix before the next payment is due.

Danger warnings ring in my head. Technically, I'm meeting the agreed-upon court ruling with my monthly payments to him, all documented carefully because I'm no fool. But the fact that I do owe him the money, at least legally, does cloud matters because if we go back to court, they could order me to pay it in one lump sum. And I'd be done for. So keeping him at bay is imperative, even if it means making smaller weekly payments rather than a monthly sum.

Because he still holds a lot of the cards in this little scam he's trying to run on me. And for all his drugginess, he's still smart. Sometimes.

Like now, he's technically not on my property, staying outside the fence, but the intimidation is just as effective and even more of a threat than taking me back to court.

"I said, where's my fuckin' money, bitch?" Russell says again, slapping the hood of his truck. "What, you want me to fuckin' go in your place and just take what I need to even us out?"

I see the blinds across the street twitch, and know the neighbors are watching this showdown. But they're just as scared of Russell as I am because he holds the land lease on their homes too. In a perfect world, we'd all band together and fight the evil slumlord. The reality is, they'll happily leave me to the wolves if it means the wolf isn't trying to blow down their house.

So I'm on my own. As always.

"You take one step through that gate and I swear I'll call the cops!" I yell back, reaching into my pocket and pulling out my phone. "I'm sure they'd love to offer you a field sobriety test, maybe search your truck?" I toss out the threat, hoping it's enough to scare him off because sure as the sun sets in the west, there are drugs in that beat-up ass truck of his.

He presses right up to the fence, hands on the top like he's considering vaulting over it. I measure the distance between me and the front door, deciding that my better bet would be to bean him with my helmet if he comes over the fence. "You owe me, and one way or another, I'll collect!" Spittle flies from the corners of his mouth as he yells, his eyes narrowed and mean.

"I'm calling, Rusty. Nine, one, one." I press at the black screen, feigning that I'm dialing because I know that even if I call, no good will come of it.

He throws his hands up, backing off. "Fine, but your bony little ass better get my money. Or else."

He drives away, and my hand shakes as I put my phone back in my pocket. As I do, I have a moment of hysteria that a junkie just called me skinny. Looks like Elaine's help isn't doing as much good as I'd thought. Vaguely, I wonder how Russell manages to stay so soft and round when all he does is smoke, putting every dollar to drugs and none to food.

My mind clears and I realize just how badly that whole interaction could've gone. Don't get me wrong, yelled threats and almost dialing 911 are serious. But Russell is escalating and I need to watch out for that. He knows I'm here alone, he's getting more desperate for money, and it's reaching the point where he has nothing to lose. The thought that he could get worse terrifies me. I'm so frightened that I nearly run my scooter into the fence, and it's only a last-second jamming of my brakes that prevents me from not going to class today at all.

My scooter stalls, and I push it a few steps back, looking around to make sure things are clear before I restart it. As I do, I do a double-take, swearing I see Russell's truck again, but despite them both being the same shade of silvery-gray, this one's a Ford, not a Chevy. I haven't seen it before and it's parked in front of Old Mrs. Petrie's house. She never has visitors other than her son, who lives a few towns away and drives a red Camry. I remember seeing the blinds twitch at her house and wonder if maybe she has someone over.

But the blinds are in place now. Still, I feel like I'm being watched, and as the hairs on the back of my neck stand up, I try to get a better view of the truck since it's the oddity in our same-shit-different-day neighborhood. The sun's at the wrong angle, though, and I'm forced to ride by it slowly to see inside. When I do, I see it's empty, and while that should relieve me, for some reason, it doesn't.

THE GRAVY TRAIN BECKONS LIKE THE VAMPIRIC TEMPLE THAT IT'S been for the past three years for me. The long, train-car-like exterior glimmers in the late afternoon sunlight, and after four hours of classes this morning and some study time at the campus library, I'm not looking forward to slogging through another six hours of waitressing.

But if there's any chance that I'm going to keep Russell off my ass, I need to hustle and bust my butt for the tips. Dinner's the best time to get tips too.

Still, the next six hours will require me to keep my mind in a special place, clicking along as I work and provide smiling service even to surly customers—because trust me, the customer is definitely *not* always right—while simultaneously not focusing on the looming thundercloud of debt over my head. As I walk in the door, I'm not sure if I can keep it up.

The smell of the grill and the fryer, which probably makes most people's mouth water, smacks me in the face, making my stomach roil. In hunger or disgust, I'm not sure which. After three years, six days a week of that smell permeating every pore of my skin, it oddly feels like home, but some days, I swear I'd give anything for a salad. Unfortunately, fresh produce is a luxury I can't afford. Not if I'm going to keep Russell at bay and my school payments up to date.

And there I go already, letting the storm take over. I take a deep breath, letting the French fry-scented air fill my lungs as I shake my head, willing the dark thoughts away.

Smile, Izzy. You can do this. You always do.

"Hey, Elaine, order up!" a big voice hollers from the kitchen, and I sigh. Henry's the head cook at The Gravy Train, and while normally, he's an overgrown teddy bear, for the past month or so, he's been increasingly short-tempered. He says it's an ulcer, and I guess if I were a forty-year fry cook who had an ulcer, I'd be upset too.

"Hold yer horses, Henry, I'm comin'!" Elaine, the head waitress, tosses back as she throws me a wave. "How're you doin', Izzy?"

"Is that Izzy?" another voice calls from the back. "Tell her to come back here!"

Elaine rolls her eyes, since obviously, everyone in downtown Roseboro heard it. She tilts her head at me, adopting a faux fancy voice like she's a phone operator at one of the big skyscrapers downtown.

"Martha'd like you to stop by her office."

I grin at her over-the-top antics, appreciating the levity, and head back to the office, which is more like a storeroom closet with a desk, where I find Martha. Short and heavyset, she's the business manager while Henry's technically the owner . . . but we all know who really runs the show, both in their marriage and around here.

"What's up?"

"Hey, I just wanted to tell you I put you down for a double on Sunday," Martha says, typing away at her computer and not bothering to even look up at me. "Apparently, the new girl decided the Taylor Swift concert this weekend is more important than her job."

I sigh, nodding. I don't feel any pity for the new girl. She was here so short a time that I didn't even have a chance to learn her name. And I did tell Martha to let me know if she needed coverage for any extra shifts so I could make some more money.

Unfortunately for me, that's meant Martha penciling me in without really consulting me. It's fine, I need the shift, but the thought of another Sunday double, with cheap tippers after church and a basically dead dinner rush, doesn't sound like a worthwhile investment of my time.

"Is that a problem, Izzy?" Martha asks, sounding concerned. "I can always ask someone else, but you told me you wanted as many hours as you could get."

"No . . . no, I did say that, and I do need it," I reply, trying to keep my voice cheerful and utterly failing. "Thanks, Martha."

I get changed quickly. Thankfully, The Gravy Train did away with the ridiculous skirts for uniforms a long time ago, and black jeans, a diner T-shirt, and an apron are all I need. Coming out, I double-check that I've got my order pad and my two pens ready before sagging.

I just can't take this anymore.

No . . . no, I have to.

Why? So Russell can take all your money and still take the house?

"It's all I've got left," I whisper, wiping away a stray tear. I know I shouldn't be crying. It's just a broken-down old house that probably isn't even worth the wood it's made of anymore, but it's my 'inch.'

"Izzy, don't tell Mommy we're watching this, okay?"

Daddy smiles and hands me the bottle of lemonade, and I grin as I take a sip. Of course, Mommy knows that Daddy sometimes lets me watch 'grown-up' movies, but she says it's okay because they're on cable.

I don't quite know what she means by that, but that's okay. It's just a reason for me to hang out with my Daddy.

And on the screen is one of his favorite movies. A tired-looking old man in a red shirt and black jacket is talking to a bunch of football players, and as he talks, the players get more excited.

"On this team, we fight for that inch," the man says, and the players cheer. He keeps going, and while I don't understand all of it, I still giggle as I hear where the bad words were changed for TV. There's a lot of them in this movie.

"I am still willing to fight, and die, for that inch. Because that's what living is! The six inches in front of your face!"

In my head, I can see my daddy on the couch, eyes on the screen and mouth moving along with the famous speaker I later learned was Al Pacino. *Okay, Daddy, for you, I can keep going.*

Even if those six inches seem impossible.

"Izzy, you okay?"

I look over and see Elaine with her head through the swinging door, a concerned look on her face. She's a diner lifer, and I've appreciated her sassy, occasionally foul-mouthed mentorship.

"Yeah, I'll be okay, Elaine. Just got offered a double shift on Sunday."

Elaine whistles, but her face is still lined with concern. "You sure? You came in looking like you were ready to pack it all in already, honey. You need a break, at least a solid day to do absolutely nothing but laze around with cucumbers on your eyes and conditioner in your hair."

A sad smile twists my lips as I think about wasting a cucumber that way. If I had one, I'd probably just bite right into it, maybe with a little Tajin seasoning.

I follow Elaine back out into the main diner area, nodding. "Yeah. It's not only the work. Rusty's being a jerk again."

"What? Didn't you say that boy gave you a week just yesterday?" Elaine asks, her brows knitting together. "You know, his parents weren't exactly what I'd call the best apples on the tree, but ooh, he's just a rotten one."

"Yeah, well, Sunday'll help," I reply. "I'll figure it out. It'll be fine, always is." I'm trying to convince myself as much as her.

"Hmph. What you need to do is kneecap him with a Louisville Slugger the next time he comes around your way," Elaine says. She lowers her voice. "By the way, seems you've got a fan."

"Huh?" I ask, following Elaine's pointed gaze.

It's *him*. The guy from yesterday. He only ordered a plain meal, burger and fries, but in the few moments that we talked and our eyes met . . . I swear I'd felt human for the first time in ages, not like an automaton going from one job to the next.

No, not human. I'd felt like . . . a woman. Something I haven't had a moment to be in way too long. Elaine's chatter breaks into my daydream of what a man like that could do *with* and *to* a woman.

"Mmm, mmm, mmm . . . and I used to think the mud pie was the yummiest thing in these four walls," Elaine says teasingly. "But that man looks so good I wanna just sop him up with a biscuit."

My eyes are locked on the man, but I can hear Elaine making smacking sounds like she's devouring something delicious.

"Come on, he's just a customer," I murmur, but I sound fake as hell and I know it. The man's so handsome that my heart's already hammering in my chest, with piercing brown eyes, a boyish curl to his lips that seem to promise an eager smile even when he's looking serious, and just enough scruff on his cheeks that he looks . . .

Well, to steal one of Elaine's weird sayings, like I'd love to sop him up with a biscuit.

"Uh-huh," Elaine says. "The man came in a half hour ago, ordering just coffee . . . *again*. I bet if you go over there and bat those pretty brown eyes of yours at him, though, he'd order a meal. Or if you're lucky, make a meal of you. I'm just sayin'."

Just saying. Meanwhile, my brain and my primal urges are saying something else, that it's been a long, long damn time since I've looked at any man and felt more than a tired toleration of him.

But this guy, I don't even know his name, and I'm feeling fluttery inside.

I feel like a teeny bopper at a Justin Bieber concert just looking at him. I swear I have to hold my arm at my side so I don't hold it in the air, waving around as I yell, "Pick me, look at me!"

I'm not that girl, never have been, but suddenly, I think I could be if only for a moment. Which is a sure-fire sign that I need to slow my roll. Guys are the last thing I have time for. Even for a one and done.

"Elaine, I—"

"You're going to go over there and take his order," Elaine says with a laugh, pushing me lightly. "Go on now, git!"

My heart in my throat, I nod and approach the man with my pulse roaring in my ears. "Hi. Can I take your order?"

He looks up, and again our eyes meet. *My God . . . he's gorgeous.*

"Yes, *you* can."

It's only three words, but in those words I can hear a promise. Maybe Elaine was right, that he was waiting for me. But why? No matter. The way he's looking at me right now makes me feel something . . . something I haven't felt in far too long.

CHAPTER 3

GABRIEL

*S*he's absolutely stunning, even on this second mini-conversation, and as she holds her pen and pad in her hand, I feel myself almost split in two.

Charm her . . . get her off guard, lure her in, and get the job done.

But that's where the divide is. One part of me is screaming the 'job' is to touch her, mark her, fuck her, and claim her as my own. All the basal, primal urges she draws up in me with the barest of smiles.

The other part is reminding me of the job I was sent here to do and my blood runs cold.

"So, what would you like?" she asks, a pink flush overtaking her cheeks that makes me wonder what's going through her mind right this instant. I'd like to imagine it's something dirty, something involving the two of us and sweaty sex in the bed of my truck.

But probably not. She's a nice girl, I think, likely accustomed to taking a lover in her bed, gentle and sweet after dating for a while.

She smiles expectantly, and I realize I've been staring wordlessly for an awkwardly long time and not answering her question. The smile is a little brighter than what I saw yesterday when she talked with other customers. She's smiling for me.

"A burger again?"

She remembers. Then again, I remember everything that happened between us yesterday as well. And how that bastard Russell harassed her this morning as I watched from across the street. Luckily, I hadn't had to intervene and then was able to duck down behind the wheel of my truck in time when she rode by on her scooter.

"What's your favorite on the menu?" I reply, painfully aware of the way her uniform is hugging her body.

She's not voluptuous but rather lithe and lean, and the slim shirt and tight jeans show off her every slight curve and angle. Again, I'm struck by the image of her being a princess. She should be wearing a tiara and a ballgown, not worn-out and faded rags.

Even exhausted, her cheekbones are high and proud, making my palms itch to cup her face. The precious bow of her lips makes me want to trace it with my tongue.

As I watch, her lips twitch upward at the corners, like she's actually enjoying talking to me. Even though I know I can talk my way into anything, and could probably sell porn to the Pope, it doesn't seem like work with Isabella.

I just want to see her smile for me, to know that I gave her a moment of joy.

Dammit, how can I even consider killing such a beautiful creature? It'd be like double-tapping a unicorn.

"Well," Isabella says, biting her lip in a way that makes my cock twitch in my jeans, "I gotta be honest, I usually get the big plates if I can around here. If you're hungry, that means the Country Plate Special. It's an eight-ounce chicken-fried steak, hashbrowns, eggs any way you want 'em, two slices of toast, and two sausage patties."

"Phew, that sounds like a lot," I reply, chuckling. "And you can eat all that?" I let my eyes trace down her body quickly, judging her reaction.

"I usually have to doggie bag it," Isabella says with a laugh. "Actually, it's so big that when the Roseboro High football team's coach wants to fatten up some linemen for the season, he sends them down here before summer workouts. Now, I'm not bragging or anything, but that little high school's sent three kids to Division 1 schools in the past three years. So take it for what you will."

I laugh. She knows how to turn on the diner sass while still sounding authentic. "And if I don't want to be a linebacker?"

"The Reuben," she assures me automatically. "With or without the gravy dip. It's the best sandwich in town, hands down."

"Hands down?" I ask, smiling. "You sound like someone who's speaking from personal experience. Perk of the job?"

"Sometimes," she admits. "But more often than not, I stick with a grilled cheese with bacon. I'm too worried I'll get a mustard seed stuck between my teeth in the middle of a shift."

"Ah," I intone wisely. "The dreaded mustard seed. Nearly as deadly as that dastardly bastard spinach. Nowhere near as painful as its cousin, the popcorn shell, though."

Isabella laughs, tucking a stray lock of her beautiful hair behind her right ear. "True. It's a hard part of the job, but I deal with it. What about you? Any dangers lurking about in your daily life?"

Experience keeps me from freezing, even as my mind calculates whether she knows who I am and what I'm doing here. But the flirty smile lets me know she's just making conversation without any ulterior motives, so I answer accordingly.

"My job? Oh, there are all sorts of dangers and threats," I reply, grinning though I sound dire. "I mean, paper cuts can make even a tough guy cry."

She laughs again, and it's like listening to angels from above. Her laugh is musical, genuine, and pleased, and when she looks at me, I feel that same *spark* I felt yesterday pass between us.

But this time, it's not just a spark, it's damn near a flowing current, white-hot in the air between us as I look up at her from my bench seat.

"I don't mind it if a man cries . . . for the right reasons," she teases. "Paper cuts might make the list, under the right circumstances. Big paper?"

"Oh, the biggest," I tease back, a moment later realizing how naughty that sounds.

I see the flash in Isabella's eyes when she gets the unintentional innuendo too. She looks down at her order pad, twirling a toe against the floor nervously. "So, what'll it be?"

Too far, man. Don't scare her off. Not yet.

Returning to the innocuous conversation, I say, "Hmm, such a tough decision. How about this . . . you bring me one of each, and I'll brown bag whichever my stomach feels like not eating?"

"Deal. You know, if you're going to come in all the time, I'm going to have to start remembering your favorites and your name. Personalized customer service is kind of our thing around here."

It seems like a big step for her to ask my name, like she's not used to doing that. And I wonder if it's because guys follow her like the Pied Piper or if it's because she doesn't date at all. Either way, I'm glad she set us back on course, leaving the awkwardness of a second ago behind.

"Gabe . . . and when I find what I like, I'll make sure you're the first to know," I reply, smiling easily as she writes my order down and walks away. "Wait, what's your name?" I ask, remembering to cover my ass even though I already know the answer.

She stops, looking over her shoulder with a smile that nearly stops my heart. "Isabella, but everyone calls me Izzy."

While she's gone, I watch her interact with the other customers, the cold, ruthless part of me cataloging the ways I could do the job without leaving a trace. I already know so much about her . . . her routine, her vulnerabilities, and even a way to make it look like Carraby did it. Maybe a little posthumous justice for Isabella, and punishment for a bastard like Carraby is always warranted.

But I . . . I can't find that detachment.

I can't judge her as evil.

No matter what I do, what mental gymnastics I've twisted through my head over the past couple of weeks, I can't.

It's never been a problem before. Clean or messy, I get it done before disappearing like smoke in the breeze. I've never felt guilty about it.

Not since . . .

"Okay, I talked with Henry, our cook, and he says the sauerkraut isn't good today," Isabella says, interrupting my thoughts and actually surprising me a little. "So would you maybe like to change that into a grilled club?"

"No, I'll just tackle the Country Special," I reply, smiling. "As long as you don't mind me sitting here for a couple of hours afterward, letting it settle."

Isabella blushes a little, nodding. "Not at all."

"It'd be a lot nicer if I could have someone to share, say, a slice of that mud pie I see behind the counter with. Maybe?"

I can see it in her eyes, a flash of excitement, and I can see she's just about to say yes when there's a dinging sound from the kitchen window, jangling and cutting through our talk.

"Hey, Izzy! Order up!" Henry yells from the kitchen, and Isabella's eyes pinch down a little.

Jolted back into reality, she sighs, looking tired again, more docile. It pisses me off, because watching her eyes light up when I flirted a little with her . . . it was like discovering a treasure that nobody's ever discovered before, a diamond in the rough unearthed in front of my eyes.

Now it's hidden again, buried under minutiae and unimportant details.

By the time she comes back with my Country Special plate, the fire in her eyes is just a dim ember, barely flaring when I give her the patented heart-stopping, panty-dropping smile that I've had since long before I got into this line of work.

"Here you go," she says, setting the admittedly huge platter in front of me. "Anything else, Gabe?"

I like the sound of my name on her lips, would love to bend her over this table right here and make her scream it. "How about that mud pie?" I ask instead, raising an eyebrow. "Or better yet, your number? It's less embarrassing than coming in for lunch here tomorrow."

I have the number already—it was part of my background check —but I would absolutely do it, come in day after day just to see her. As I look at her expectantly, every little detail comes into sharp focus.

Not just her beauty but her exhaustion. It makes me feel like a shit for thinking obscene thoughts about her, and suddenly, I imagine myself caring for her, laying her in a hot bath, rubbing the knots out of her shoulders as she soaks away the stress weighing her down, and curling up around her and holding her as she sleeps.

She's mulling it over, and I can see her pen moving toward her order pad like she's going to write her number down when her face falls and with a frown, she looks down.

"Ah . . . I shouldn't. I'm sorry. I need to check on the other customers." The words are mumbled, disappointment woven through them.

She scurries off, and as I watch her go, I can't tear my eyes from her. She glances at me again before taking an order from a young couple obviously here on a cheap date, her flawless skin flushing before she turns back to her work.

I look at my Country Special, and I realize I've got a problem in front of me. There's no way in hell I can eat all of this. The plate's nearly as wide as my shoulders and covered in about a week's worth of food. No wonder the football coaches send their players here to get hefty for the season.

I also have a professional problem. Because no matter how much I twist it, no matter how hard I try, there is no way I can justify killing Isabella.

But the most powerful man in the Pacific Northwest hired me to do just that.

CHAPTER 4

BLACKWELL

Roseboro Community Health Fair! Sponsored by Goldstone Health. With special thanks to Thomas Goldstone!

I turn away, growling at my driver. "Get us out of here."

He responds immediately, no questions, no hesitation as he accelerates, turning right at the next intersection to remove that hated name from my sight.

A year ago, I had the world in the palm of my hand. Well, maybe not the world, but at least the city of Roseboro, and with it, the linchpin of the entire Pacific Northwest. If you wanted to make an impact anywhere between San Francisco and Vancouver, you came to me.

While I never greeted anyone with *buona sera*, and nobody called me it, I was *the* Godfather.

Until he came along. Thomas Goldstone . . . the usurper, the upstart . . . the *Golden Boy*.

At first, I was content to let him build. I found his forays into business amusing as he made choices I would never consider, stepping left when I would recommend right. He'd been like an experiment playing out before my very eyes.

As out of sorts as I found his style to be, he was successful, shockingly so, and at first, I'd been delighted, like he was my own personal dog and pony show. But he wasn't supposed to be *this* good, *this* fast.

I'd assumed he'd be the one to take over the mantle of Roseboro after I'm gone, not that that's on the horizon anytime soon.

But I thought I'd pass along my empire to capable hands, ones that would laud my brilliance and impact on Roseboro and beyond. He was supposed to be just a caretaker, maybe add a little few pebbles to the mountain that I'd built . . . and now he's eclipsing me.

I can't have that. I *won't* have that. My legacy will live on.

One weakness Thomas Goldstone has is that while he's smart, and he's nearly as ruthless as me, he won't go as afoul of the law as I will. I can't believe he's totally innocent. No man with as much money and power as he has is totally clean, but he's never cultivated the connections I have.

So I started hamstringing him. At first, it was subtle, using my backdoor connections to take profits away from him, hobbling him through several projects he'd planned.

Yet still, he rose.

I stomped his dreams into the dirt. I destroyed his attempts at expansion.

Yet still, like a phoenix from the ashes on a mighty wind, he rose.

Finally, I had to take direct action, and through a bitter, angry employee, I conspired to break him, to destroy not just his business, but his mind, his very soul.

I had him. I was so close . . .

And yet he rose.

Now, he's more successful than ever.

He's gone from one of the most well-known men in this part of the country to the darling of the entire *nation*. There are already whispers that when the next election rolls around, Thomas Goldstone would be a shoo-in if he chose to throw his name in the ring. Senator? Representative? Governor?

There've been whispers that the governor's mansion wouldn't be his last stop, either.

He's untouchable. I've spent millions trying to find more skeletons in his closet. Yet my best attempt, the most direct intervention I could try . . . and now he's actually *gained power* from it.

I could cry over the failure, beseech the gods to grant me this demand, or I can change direction and try again. I already know my course of action.

I'm going to teach Thomas Goldstone about the nature of power. Power isn't just money or fame. It's fear. It's pain. It's about being willing to go all-in and do the ugly deeds truly required to intimidate and inspire those around you.

And I'm going to give Thomas Goldstone a very educational lesson.

Reaching into my jacket pocket, I pull out my phone and dial. It's my normal phone—no reason *I* should be the one buying 'burner' phones.

"Hello?"

"You're taking too much time."

On the other end, the man hums. *"You knew when you hired me that I do things at my own pace. I don't rush."*

"There is such a thing as taking your time, and then there is wasting *my* time," I remind him. "*Do not* cross the line between the two. I want to see results. Soon."

"As in?"

"You have seven days. Or else . . . I will be upset."

The line goes dead, but I don't mind. My message was received.

Up ahead, a flash of white and silver catches my eye, and I wince as I see the building we're approaching. The Gravy Train Diner.

Where *she* works. Isabella Turner.

The woman who took my carefully-laid plan using Goldstone's employee, a man I'd manipulated for months, and demolished it in a single conversation.

She thought she'd been doing her friend a favor, but favors have consequences, and I have seen to that personally.

Within a week, she'll get her comeuppance. I have hired the best of the best to see to her punishment. And the happy byproduct is that it will devastate Goldstone and his woman, crumbling their very foundations and insuring that they understand just how vulnerable they truly are.

Though the thoughts race through my mind, I whisper them to the window, giving them power by declaring them aloud. "Soon, very soon, my little waitress, you will be doing *me* a favor of sorts."

My limo slides past The Gravy Train and we start to approach my building, my tower . . . my home. "You'll help me send The Golden Boy a very important message—don't interfere in my business. This is still *my town*, and your death will prove it."

It *almost* makes me smile.

CHAPTER 5

ISABELLA

The music plays on the TV, and I feel a wave of energy fill me. It's not the tune, a tired old piece of trumpet fanfare that's been used by this station since I was a kid. It's what the music represents . . . the hour it represents.

"Tonight on *News at Ten*—" the voice in the background says before Elaine turns it down.

"I don't need to listen to the organ grinder of doom three times a damn day," I say, putting the remote back down. "Anyone wants to find out what's going on, they can read the captions." I say it like I'm daring the handful of customers to argue about it, but no one so much as blinks at me.

I nod silently as I take a late-night order for pork chops from a delivery driver who just got off shift, but my brain's on cruise control.

It's him. *Gabe*.

I know it's stupid. I mean, I totally chickened out when he asked me for my phone number, reminding myself again that I don't have time to get involved with anyone.

But still, I'd gone home last night to an empty house and kicked myself in the butt for not at least considering. I mean, even if it didn't lead to much, a slice of pie with a hot guy or maybe *more* would be the highlight of my week.

All right, more like my year. But I'm focused, determined . . . and lonely.

Hot dreams had kept me tossing and turning all night, and in the light of day, he's been on my mind constantly. The way he smiles, the little twinkle in his eyes as we tossed a few double entendres back and forth . . . the dimples on his cheeks that highlight his perfect teeth.

I mean, how weird is that? I'm getting heated up thinking about a guy's *teeth*.

For the first time in I don't know how long, I've gotten through the day without feeling like hundred-pound weights are tied to each ankle.

I've felt lighter and brighter, like my lungs are full of helium and there's a glimmer of sunshine warming my back. It's been like this all day, through classes and the first four hours of my shift here at The Gravy Train.

Glancing over at the table where he sat last night, I remember the note he left on his bill, along with the tip, and I swear my belly floats up to the rafters.

Bella . . . gotta be out of town tomorrow, but I'll see you Wednesday. Gabe

Yeah, it's stupid, but I can't stop thinking about him. Even the fact that he called me Bella. I've been Izzy ever since I was five. Almost everyone calls me Izzy. But the way Gabe wrote it . . .

Well, to quote my besties, I left work moister than an oyster. I shiver at the word *moist*. There's always been something about it that makes me cringe.

But more than that, in the few minutes I've talked with him, I've been able to forget about the shit storm that is my life. I felt almost . . .

"Hey, you alive over there? Bueller? Bueller?"

I look up, realizing I've been spacing a little as I wipe down an already clean salt shaker. The delivery driver who wanted the pork chops is trying to get my attention, full-on snapping at me with his dirty fingers.

He seems to have missed the lesson on rule number one of diner life—don't ever snap at your waitress. Fixing my best coolly professional smile on my face, I walk over, clearing my throat.

"Did you need something?" I intentionally don't apologize because fuck his rudeness. I might've been off in la-la land for a moment, but he got his dinner in less than five minutes and looks to have been shoveling it in Hoover-style.

"You can start by answering the question," the driver challenges sarcastically, his mouth twisted in an ugly sneer. "You alive?"

"Sometimes, I'm not even sure myself," I answer honestly, blanking out my face.

I know this guy's type. He's been dealing with shit all day, probably been stressed out by half a dozen things that have forced him into having dinner here at ten at night. So of course, he's going to try to make me share the pain.

Misery loves company, they say, but I ain't visiting the Sad-Lands tonight. Not with Gabe on my mind, even if it's just a pretend fantasy where I'd given him my number and we'd gone out on a date.

"Can I get you something?" I ask with faux pleasantness.

"These pork chops . . . they're overcooked and dried out," he says, poking a fork into the small amount of meat left on his plate. "Unacceptable."

I can hear that it's a word he probably uses often. I do my best to limit my eye roll and pick up his plate.

"Can I get you something else instead?"

It's a pretty common scam for someone to eat half their plate, complain, and then want a replacement. Sometimes, I call them on it, but right now, I just want this guy to eat and not kill my happy buzz.

"Burger. Well done," he barks. But I see the tiny uptilt of his lips as he internally celebrates his successful schtick.

I head back to the kitchen. "Henry?"

"Yeah, I heard the asshole," he growls quiet enough the customers don't hear, a fresh burger patty already sizzling on the grill. "Son of a bitch should be glad I don't serve him a fried shit burger and make him choke on it. He sure as fuck ain't getting fries though."

"How's the ulcer?" I ask, and Henry grumbles again. "That bad, huh?"

"No, what sucks the most is that the doc's got me on the special diet," he says, sticking his tongue out to let me know exactly what he thinks of his modified menu.

"Prilosec and yogurt, but no milk or real cheese. Kimchee, sauer-kraut, any sort of cabbage until I'm swimming in the shit, but no way can I have a sausage to go with it. All this weird frou-frou hippie dietary crap, no real food. And no booze. How the hell am I supposed to get the eight hours they say I'm supposed to get if a man can't have a post-work beer before bed?"

"Don't know," I answer honestly. "Hope you get back to normal soon. You're more fun that way."

"Yeah, well, tell Happy McAsshole out there five minutes and I'll have him another round of dinner," Henry says, giving me a pained smile as he rubs at his bothersome belly. "At least it ain't the big C, am I right?" He kisses his fingertips and holds them up, looking beyond the ceiling. Henry's not particularly reli-gious, but I guess he figures a bit of prayer won't hurt.

I nod, going out to Delivery Driver and passing along the news. "Five minutes? I'd better be getting a discount."

"I'm sure we can. I just have to ask my manager," I reply sweetly before going back to the register to help someone with their bill. After ringing it up, Elaine comes over, smirking.

"You're so busy with the UPS guy that you didn't see Red come in," she says, pointing to the far corner table where one of my besties, Charlotte Dunn, is sitting. "Go take a break. I'll handle everything for a bit, and I'll have two slices of mud pie over there lickety-split."

"You're the best, Elaine," I murmur, handing her my order pad. "Thanks."

"I know it, and you're welcome," Elaine says, shooing me off when I warn her about the grumpy delivery guy.

I walk over to the booth and drop in, suddenly feeling the long day. "Hey, Char, what're you doing here this late?"

"They had me on late shift at work for a special project," Charlotte says, smiling that happy smile she always has.

Seriously, Char's like the chirpiest person I know as long as you're not talking about men. She's had an especially bad run lately, and even her usual mantra of 'there's no such thing as Mr. Wrong, only Mr. Right and Mr. Right Now' has been trashed. But you could dump her in the middle of the Sahara in August with nothing but a ski outfit and she'd be happy about how the goggles help keep the sun out of her eyes.

"Another girl called out sick and the copies had to be made and filed today."

"Ah . . . Blackuenza?" I ask, using my made-up term for when people who work in the Blackwell Building just say fuck it and quit with no notice. "I seriously don't know how you put up with it, babe."

"I don't work for the man directly, remember?" Charlotte says with a smile. "I honestly can't think of the last time I saw him even come inside the building. And the pay's okay for now."

"For now . . . how'd we end up in this fucked up cul de sac of life?" I ask, shaking my head. "I mean, Mia found her way out, but I feel like I'm circling the drain most days."

"Yeah . . . you were ready to castrate her man not that long ago, remember?" Charlotte asks, and I laugh. That's true. I was.

But Mia's guy, Thomas, came through in a big way for her, like grand gesture style, and I'd happily watched from the sidelines as she got her fairytale ending. And I am thrilled for her, truly and completely, but it is a reminder that while people around me are making leaps and bounds, I'm drudging along with baby steps.

Forward, but at a snail's pace that's basically killing me most days.

Today was different, a voice whispers in my head.

"Okay, okay . . . so what brought Roseboro's most vivacious ginger in tonight?"

"Redhead, not ginger. I got a soul!" Charlotte teases. "Mostly just wanted a little comfort food and to catch up with you. Been a few days."

Elaine comes over with two of the biggest slices of mud pie I've ever seen on each plate. Seriously, she had to have hand-sliced them.

"You should tell Red about your Prince Charming hottie."

She doesn't wait for me to say a word, turning straight to Charlotte and spilling, "He came in the past two nights in a row. Whoo-wee, that man is a good two hundred pounds of pure American beefcake if I've ever seen it."

She closes her eyes, grasping her hands at her chest and moaning, "Mmm-hmm."

"Oh, God, don't start," I groan, dropping my head as Elaine laughs. "Seriously?"

"Beefcake, huh?" Charlotte asks, eyes ping-ponging from Elaine to me. "You know how I feel about that." Her look of disdain says everything.

"Red, please. What you need is to go find yourself a good man too," Elaine says in that motherly way she has. "Your friend Pinkie Pie got herself wise. Now you two need to as well."

I grin at her calling Mia 'Pinkie Pie' because while Mia's hair goes through a rainbow of colors, she does tend to dye it pink more than anything else. With her calling Char 'Red', I wonder if she calls me 'Brownie' in her head to keep with the hair color theme, but it doesn't seem the time to ask as Charlotte's gearing up for her soapbox speech about not needing a man to complete her life.

"'Bye, Felicia," Charlotte finally says, wrapping up her latest story about the guy she kicked out for telling her to make him a sandwich.

I mean, he actually said that to her, unironically. Charlotte said he even scratched his balls as he said it, but I suspect she's embellishing there. But she's smiling a little as Elaine leaves. "That woman's a trip and a half."

"Don't I know it," I reply as I cut a big spoonful of chocolate yumminess and chew slowly. "Remember, I'm the one who works with her damn near every day of the week. But she gets a pass when she serves me big pieces of pie like this."

"Mmmhmm," Charlotte agrees before putting her spoon down. "Now, tell me about this man? Catch me up?"

"Just a cute guy who came in the past two nights," I demur, trying not to gush too much.

I give Char a rundown on Gabe because it's fun to think about him and gossip with my friend since I usually have zero to contribute to social life chats.

"Oh, and he's got that thing where when he smiles, only one side goes up and then the rest of his mouth catches up in slow motion. Like you can see the smile race across his lips. Makes me want to chase it. With my thumb or maybe my tongue." I can hear the wistfulness in my voice.

"True sign of a player," Charlotte says even as she gives the same sort of lopsided smirk. "What about life outside the diner? Classes okay?"

"I suppose," I reply, remembering that I have a test coming up. A test I know I'm not ready for.

"You sure?" Charlotte asks, piercing through my veil of toughness pretty quickly. When you've known each other as long as we have, that's not too hard, and I'm sure she can see the weariness I wear like a cape most days. "If it's not school, what is it?"

"Well, Russell's starting to harass me." I start telling her about his threats and visits to my house demanding payments.

I've always tried to minimize my financial difficulties with my friends, not hide them, exactly, but I don't go around whining about how tight my bottom line really is. But they can read the silent little signs like they're neon lights. I know they'd help me if I'd let them, but I don't want their charity. I want to handle things on my own.

But this thing with Russell is becoming something else altogether. Not just a bill, but a real danger, so I've tried to talk about him the least.

So when I'm finished, I'm shocked at how long I've been blabbing and how much I shared.

"Anyway, he's a huge pain in the ass. And if you get a call from the county jail, answer it and bring me some bail money because I've probably maced him for lurking around my fence and mouthing vulgar shit."

Charlotte's pissed. "That son of a . . . I should kick him in the balls so hard they come out his nose."

"I'm not sure that's possible, Char." But her vehemence makes me smile a little despite the ugly situation.

"I don't care!" Charlotte hisses. "I'm worried about you, babe. I mean, he threatened you!"

"He's woofin', that's all."

"Uh-huh. Still, if it were me in your position, I'd forget the mace and get a gun. You never know what's out there, and that guy is a piece of shit, Izz."

I freeze, the last bite of pie suspended on my spoon, shaking a little. "A gun?" I say in shock.

I mean, I've never even held a gun and would definitely be the dipshit who accidentally shoots themselves in the foot if I ever wrapped my hands around one.

"Babe, you live alone. In not the best part of town. And you've got a dope fiend hitting you up for cash. I'm not saying you need to be Rambitch and lug an Uzi around, but something small? Enough that if someone does force things, you can defend yourself. That's a good idea."

She makes good points, but there's one kink in her line of thinking. "Yeah . . . and how'd I buy one when I'm barely getting by?" The words slip out before I realize how they sound.

Char reaches for her purse, but I stick my hand out. I've got a hard policy, no pity pennies from my friends. "Char, no!"

"Fuck that. Listen, I've got a coworker, Brady. His brother runs a gun club just outside of town. Brady always said that if I gave his brother this card, he'd hook me up with a good deal. Lessons, a starter gun, everything. Just give him a call and see what it costs. Maybe it's not that bad?"

"Yeah, well, thanks, but I don't need a gun."

Char still holds out the card, and finally, I take it, tucking it in my pocket. "You know this is ridiculous. Guns are just . . . I don't know."

"Listen, honey, in most instances I'd be right there with you. I'd be more inclined to shoot some asshole's swinging dick off with it than use it to defend myself," Charlotte jokes.

At least I hope she's joking. "But really, your situation is different . . . oh, hell, no!" she says, smacking the table.

"What?" I ask, and Char rolls her eyes, sighing heavily like she's disappointed in me.

"I make one dick joke, and your eyes went all spacey on me. You were thinking of Beefy McSmiles again, weren't you?" she points a manicured finger at me accusingly.

Caught red-handed, I look down, a little embarrassed. "His name's Gabe, not Beefy McSmiles. Although that has a nice ring to it," I tease, and then quietly fake a porn-star breathiness. "Ohh, Beefy!"

"Gabe, Beefy, Tyler Durden, what does it matter?" Charlotte sputters, shaking her head. "Come on, we took the pledge together. Don't tell me you're backing out?"

She holds up three fingers, her thumb holding her ring finger down, and her face solemn like she's taking an oath.

"No, but really, Char, a pledge to become celibate married lesbians if perfect men don't sweep us off our feet by thirty?" I ask, remembering the promise we'd made each other in a drunken night of commiseration a few years ago. "Not saying you're not my main girl, but you really want to marry me and totally give up on men?"

"It's not like I'm into you that way," Charlotte reminds me. "But you're a good cook, you make me laugh, and best of all, we'd never fight over the toilet seat in the middle of the night. Actually, the best part is I can trust you, and that's worth sleeping in separate bedrooms the whole time."

"I'm also an utter slob," I argue, though that's not at all true. More seriously, I say, "You know I've got your back no matter what, Char, but isn't life more hopeful than that?"

"So says the girl who has zero social life, much less a sex life, lives in a shack, and needs to learn how to handle a gun."

I growl in frustration, arguing back the only thing in her list I can refute. "I do not live in a shack! It's not that bad!"

"Hey, I'm not hating. At least it's *your* shack," Char reminds me. "I rent my place so I don't have room to talk. But I'm serious. I don't want to hear about you on the news with your body parts scattered all over Roseboro because I am not adopting a mommy-less Vash. She's cute and all, but I'm a dog person."

"Hey, Izzy, last charge!" Elaine calls, and I raise a hand to acknowledge her.

"Listen, I need to help with the drunk rush before closing time and start cleanup. It's good to see you though. Thanks for coming in, Char." I do appreciate her stopping by because between all the other things on my plate, a girls' night out isn't likely to happen anytime soon.

She gets up and drops a five on the table, even though we both know Elaine's not going to charge for the pie.

"Seriously, babe, think about it. The gun, that is. And about Mr. Beefcake, check him out before you get too hung up. Remember, Mr. Hitachi will never *ever* let you down."

"We'd never work. I don't speak Japanese," I joke, and Charlotte laughs. We hug, and I squeeze her tightly. "I promise, I'll be okay, hon."

"Okay, I'll check in soon."

Elaine and I handle the last batch of customers that come in as we finish the prep work for the morning crew. After we lock the door and run the numbers at the end of the night, I look at my totals for the shift. Maybe it was easier back in the day when most tips were cash, but now with so many people paying by card, I have to wait until the end of the night to see my final tally . . . and it's pretty damn pathetic.

"Fuckin' Pork Chop Guy didn't even round up to the nearest

dollar," Elaine complains as she looks at the printout on the register receipt. She sees my downcast face and pats my shoulder. "It'll be okay, hon. Payday's on Friday, at least."

I force a smile, rubbing the back of my neck. "Let's just get cleaned up."

Elaine nods, and I see her slip an extra twenty from her own tip pile into mine as we clean, but I'm too defeated to say anything. There go my damn morals.

"You know, hon, why not talk to your friend's fiancé?" Elaine asks as we get ready to leave. "Seriously, the man can buy half of Roseboro, and you'd pay him back, I know it. Hell, I'd hate to see you go, but maybe he could even set you up with something that pays better."

She looks through the dark windows to the night outside, and I wonder if she ever dreamed of getting out of here when she was younger. Her lips purse, and I amend my thought, wondering if perhaps she still dreams of it.

"I . . . I'd prefer not to, that's all," I admit. "Guess my pride's still pretty mixed up in all this. I want to stand on my own two feet."

"Yeah well, sometimes, we have to accept a little help, even when we don't want to, to get to where we're going. I'm sure that Goldstone boy would help. You could pay him back, and when you get to solid ground, you return the favor and help some other stubborn girl who could clearly benefit from a bit of a boost."

She looks at me hopefully, like she wants me to hear the genius of her idea.

I nod and mount my scooter. "Maybe," I say, but it's a lie.

CHAPTER 6

GABRIEL

"You have seven days. Or else I will be upset."

Blackwell's words replay in my mind, weighing upon my shoulders like a ton of bricks as I dissect them repeatedly. There's not much to the two sentences, a deadline and a threat. But it's the threat's ambiguous nature that turns over and over in my head.

What is he willing to do?

How far will he go?

I pause to take a breath and look up. In front of me is a nearly sheer rock wall.

While I've always been a good athlete, nothing quite gets my blood pumping and my endorphins going like nature. It's the one thing that helps me clear my thoughts and center myself.

Which is what brought me to this spot, about twenty minutes to the west of Roseboro, in the middle of a national forest.

"You know you don't have to do this," I tell myself as I wipe my hands on my shirt. It's the truth. I passed the sign for the hiking path to get to the climbing entry point I'm at now.

Yeah, I could take the easy way to the top . . . but this'll help.

I approach the wall, one last visual of the line I've chosen up the face of the cliff. And then I reverse my way down until my eyes land directly in front of me and take the first grip, lifting myself off the ground and adjusting my feet.

Free climbing is like no other form of climbing. There's no rope, so I can't take the same risks that someone who's tied in would. At the same time, I can't go too slow, because with each passing second, my ankles and forearms are being tested. One release, one slip, could be instant death.

But it's exhilarating, and as the fire starts up my calves, I can feel my head clear. It's like I split in two, half of me focusing on staying alive this very second by picking out the next handhold, the next place to put my foot, while the other half of me chews over my problem, unfettered and free to jump from idea to strategy to potential consequences without logic or rationality to get in the way.

Isabella Turner . . . my *assignment*.

Blackwell's paying me a shitload of money to make it happen, but the information he promised is far more valuable. That information is the whole reason I'm in the life I'm in.

Still, that doesn't change the fact that she's someone who doesn't deserve the fate chosen for her. If anything, she deserves to get a hand up in life.

An image of her proudly serving customers, head held high as she works herself to the bone, flashes through my head. Followed by one of studying hard in the library to better herself, and then standing her ground against an evil shit stain of a man who's obviously trying to take advantage of her.

If anyone deserves a lucky break, it's Isabella Turner.

But luck has nothing to do with this. And I'm definitely not a lucky charm, more like a tragic curse.

My left foot slips slightly, and I dig in with my right hand, pulling myself up a bit higher before my foot can find purchase again. I'm halfway up the rock face, but from here the going seems easier. There's a relatively large crack in the rock that looks wide enough for me to get both a hand and a foot inside, and it runs nearly all the way to the top of the cliff itself.

I pause, shaking out my hands and feet by alternating rest holds, and cruise the rest of the way up, reaching the top with a good amount of sweat built up but more excitement than anything else. It's been awhile since I've had the chance to really freeclimb, and I've missed it.

You learn about yourself on the rockface with nothing to catch you, no safety nets and no do-overs. You learn about who you really are when you have to look death in the eye and know that it's chasing you and the only things holding it back are your own will and skills.

It's a sad commentary on modern society that someone can go their entire life without ever learning whether they're a coward or not. I forget who said that, but it's true. And while I might not be a good man, at least I know I'm not a coward.

Going to the edge of the outcropping, I look down, seeing that the fifty-foot drop is definitely worse at this angle than from the bottom. There are all sorts of jagged-looking rocks and outcroppings that would kill anyone unfortunate enough to slip off this cliff face.

But I didn't fall. Not this time. I made it to the top, cheated Death once more in the poker game I'm not sure he knows we're playing.

I shake my head and take a deep breath, banishing the idea and looking around. The walking path continues off to my right, and I decide to follow it, stunned a moment later when the trail curves around the mountain and I'm treated to a view of the valley.

It's beautiful, rugged and untouched, pure forest that reminds me that no matter my struggles, my pain, or my promises . . . the world doesn't really care. It's not sad. It's almost liberating.

I can see, though, where I can make a difference. Because the forest thins out, a power line here, a fire road there, a stream that diverts and slows, forming a lazy river, and slowly, Mother Nature gives way to man, and Roseboro emerges to dominate the middle distance, a small idyllic city that looks postcard-worthy from this vantage point.

Of course it's not idyllic. Even from up here, I can see some of the older areas of town, and my eyes are drawn to where I think I can pick out Isabella's neighborhood, close to the railroad tracks that run north and south through town.

Every town's got that wrong side of the tracks. Even ones without railroads.

Still, the scene stretched out below me is iconic, beautiful, and as I sit down on a rock to watch, I marvel at the twin towers that dwarf the city.

Closer to me, there's the Blackwell Building, dark and foreboding, looking like a spear that's been shoved into the ground, piercing and penetrating the city, plundering. Ironically, it's the older of the two buildings, and the city actually grew from it.

The other, Goldstone Tower, rising up and reaching for the clouds above, shorter than its older cousin but somehow more inspiring with its golden-hued glass. It's the yearning of the city for a better future, unafraid to shoot for the stars, secure in the knowledge that it's only through the risk of failure that great successes are built.

"You're getting sentimental again," I chastise myself, turning away and looking at the pool behind me. The water's not totally still, the waterfall and the outflowing stream guarantee that, but it's peaceful in its perpetual motion, tranquility in the churning bubbles.

I reach down and gather up a handful of pebbles, tossing them in one by one to watch the ripples flutter over the surface, and my past sneaks up on me, reminding me of another pool.

"Jeremy!"

My little brother, Jeremy, stops and turns back to me, a grin splitting his face. We're close in age, so close that my uncle calls us 'Irish twins', which confused the hell out of me when I was younger. We're not Irish at all, from what I know of our family.

"Come on, Gabby. It's just the Union."

I sigh, tossing a rock across the small pond that we've been sitting next to for the past hour, watching it skip across the flat green water, the white stone so bright in contrast that it makes me stop, watching it bounce five times before dropping beneath the surface with a soupy plop.

Eleven months apart . . . we're actually somehow in the same grade in school, but I swear Jeremy's nothing like me. Like today. Mom and Dad told us to stay close to the house, and the pond technically qualifies since I can squint and still see the house from here.

But the Union? Where all the high school kids hang out and play basketball? Of all the places in town our parents don't want us to go, that's the one they've both named specifically.

And of course, Jeremy wants to go there. He's been working on his layup recently and wants to put himself to the test, even if we don't start junior high until August.

"Come on, Gabby!"

"Jeremy, stop calling me Gabby!"

A breeze blows across the valley, and tears threaten as I think about my brother. He was always the adventurous one, the one willing to break the rules.

That first time we snuck off to the Union, he was six inches shorter than everyone else there, but he already had big brass ones. Even though he got elbowed right in the eye at one point, he still kept going for that damn layup and wore that purple bruise like a trophy for his gutsiness.

"Why'd you never slow down?" I whisper, shaking my head. "And you somehow kept getting me to go along with it, too."

Go along with it. Isn't that what I'm supposed to be doing now?

Just go along with the plan, or pick from any of the half-dozen that I've formed in my head already, and kill her?

Yeah, it'll suck, and I'm going to feel like shit . . . but I felt like shit for three days after Jeremy got into a fight with Mickey Ulrich and his buddies and the two of us got stomped out royally.

I still never regretted jumping in to save Jeremy's ass, even if it was six on two.

I never regretted sticking with him.

Until the one time that I didn't.

"Jeremy, come on!" I growl, looking up from my keyboard. "I get it, you wanna show off for Jenae, but newsflash . . . she's not feeling ya, brother. And I've gotta get this damn history report done by tomorrow!"

Jeremy scowls at the dig about the girl he's tailing after, his stringy cotton tank top already hanging off his toned shoulders, showing off a body that's changed a lot over the past year. I guess I got the jump on him there. I've got two inches on him and I'm already having to shave, but Jeremy . . . with his looks and personality, he's going to be getting girls long before I do.

"Blah, blah, blah, Pilgrims, maize, We the People, and sum it the fuck up!" Jeremy jokes. "You really want to tell me that you'd rather do a history report than play ball with the girls watching?"

"Yes, I do."

"Tiffany Robinson's going to be there."

My fingers falter for a moment, and I think of Tiffany. I swear she's looked at me from across the room in math class, and while I can't be sure she's interested, it's gotta be a good sign. I mean, we run in different social circles, but stranger things have happened, right?

He's got me, and judging by the slick grin on his face, he damn well knows it. "Not yet," I growl, looking down. "Just . . . gimme a half hour to finish up, and I'll go."

"Sorry, bro, but Jenae's got work later," Jeremy says. "Listen, I'll head

down now, and you can join me when you can. I mean, even if Tiffany has already left by then, it'll still be fun, right?"

He's right. It'd be fine if it's just the guys playing, but he's even more right that it'd be better if Tiff were there.

Jeremy's words help fuel a furious bout of rapid-fire typing, and twenty minutes later, I feel like I can take a break. All that's left is the bibliography and figuring out what I'm going to say when I have to do the presentation on it in class later this week. But I can bullshit my way through that with the paper as a foundation.

I hurry and get changed, yanking on an old Angels T-shirt and some shorts before pulling a ballcap on. I think I'll see if Tiffany will hold it for me while I play, and if I'm lucky, she'll wear it herself. It'd be a good look, that girl in my hat.

I jog down to the Union, praying she's still there. I'm almost courtside when I hear something that I swear sounds like a typewriter, or fire-crackers, and then the screams start.

"Jeremy?" I ask, my heart stopping in my chest as someone else screams his name. "Jeremy!"

"I promised you I'd find out who did it," I whisper, watching the ripples in the pool but talking to my brother's ghost in the wind. I feel the responsibility of the vow I made to my brother's grave to get vengeance for his death.

It wasn't grief talking then. It was fury, it was righteous justice that no other family need go through this.

"And Blackwell says he can point me in the right direction. But it's complicated, Jer."

In my pocket, my phone buzzes, and I'm surprised I get a cell signal up here. Pulling it out, I see I've got a text from a blocked number. Still, I know who it is.

I'm waiting for your word it's done. There's a difference between patience and stalling.

I don't react, my emotions going cold as I put my phone away and stand up.

I knew this assignment wouldn't be easy, knew I'd have to get my hands dirty. But it'll be worth it to fulfill the promise I made.

At all costs, at any expense. Even if it's my own soul. Even if it's her life.

CHAPTER 7

ISABELLA

*W*ednesday comes and goes, and as I wipe down the counter, I sigh. It's nearly nine o'clock now, and still no Beefcake.

For days now, I've been daydreaming about him. While that's admittedly more than a little creepy, a ridiculous infatuation with a man I've shared a total of five minutes of conversation with, I can't stop looking up every time the bell over the diner door dings. And I can't help feeling a stab of disappointment each time it's not him.

Maybe Char's right. I don't need Gabe . . . I need Hitachi.

"Izzy, you have a minute?" Martha asks from the door to the back, waving me toward her. I glance around the diner and see we're pretty quiet. We're in between the dinner rush and the late-night surge. The other waitress on duty, Shelley, can handle things by herself for a few, but still, I glance at the door one more time before heading back.

"What's up, Martha?" I ask when we get to her office. "Everything okay?"

Martha always does paperwork on Wednesday nights, which usually means she's locked in her office for the bulk of the evening. Hopefully, whatever she needs won't keep me here long because I need to get back on the floor after having to scrape my bank account down to six dollars and thirty-two cents to get together enough cash to keep Russell off my ass, I need every extra quarter.

"Not quite," Martha says, picking a receipt up off the table with a perplexed look on her face. "You got a complaint over the weekend."

"What?" I ask, surprised. "Who?"

Martha hands me the receipt, and I glance at the time and date. Sunday night, near closing . . .

"Oh. That guy."

"What do you mean?" Martha asks as I look at the note he wrote on the back of the receipt. *Weitress is crap. Zombie the hole time. POS servus.*

It's not the bad spelling that hurts. It's the big fat double zeros in the tip space on the receipt, not even rounding up to the nearest dollar. Not even a line through the space . . . a big set of double zeroes.

"This guy came in last week too," I explain to Martha, handing the receipt back. "He bitched about the pork chops, sent them back, and scammed for a burger. When he came in this time, he sat down already bitchy. I did my best, but I don't think he'll be happy, no matter what."

"He's a regular?" Martha asks, and I shrug. "What's he look like? Somebody I'd know?"

"He's a delivery driver," I reply, sighing. "He comes in occasionally. I guess you could call him a regular. Anyway, if you want backup on his attitude, ask Elaine and Henry."

"No, your word's good with me. Next time, feel free to give him a little sass or have Elaine take care of him. We don't need troublemakers like that around, so if we can run him off nicely, all the better. Otherwise, I'll pull out the big guns," Martha says.

I appreciate that she has my back and that she'd be willing to kick the guy out for being an asshat, because she is definitely the big gun that takes no crap and tells you what's what with blunt efficiency and a solid lack of fucks about what you think.

"There is one other thing, though. I need you to cover another shift."

"Another?" I ask, torn. Right now, I've got twenty-one dollars to my name, including the few dollars I have in the bank. I do some fast figuring and think I can make it last, but a couple more bucks would make it easier.

But I'm also struggling to stay awake in class, and I know my grades are starting to suffer because of it.

You're still passing classes though.

"What do you need?"

It's the sound of the hamster wheel turning.

Martha looks at me carefully for a moment, then turns to the calendar on the wall. "Hiring a new server for the front's been tough. I wanted to see if you'd like to pull a double this Saturday, and next month, I might need you to do Wednesdays."

"Martha, that's potentially like an extra twenty-five hours next month, and a double on Saturday?" I ask, torn between joy and frustration. On one hand, it's money I desperately need. On the other hand, Vash is going to forget what I look like, and I'm going to have a feral cat by Christmas at this rate.

Martha blinks. "Shelley can't do it because of the kids, but I can ask Elaine if you want me to?"

Way to guilt trip me, I think. Elaine is fierce and feisty, but I know the years of being on her feet caught up to her long ago. An extra shift each week would kill her. "Okay, you know I'll try my best."

Martha starts scribbling my name on the color-coded calendar, and all the orange 'Izzy' entries make me a little dizzy.

"Thank you. Listen, I can't do much on the pay stub side of

things, but I'll talk with Henry. Maybe we can at least help you on the tip side of things. Uncle Sam doesn't need to know about an extra twenty bucks cash you get as a shift incentive."

"Thanks," I reply, knowing that over the next four Wednesdays, I certainly won't be pulling in eighty bucks in cash tips. Still, Martha's trying and I appreciate that, especially considering how she's always had my back with my changing school schedule and lets me study at the counter when we're not busy. "I should go help Shelley."

I head back out, reminding myself that I was the one who came to her saying I needed extra hours recently. She's just giving me what I wanted. But the enormity of my schedule is killing me, slowly but surely.

As I hit the diner floor, I look around, hope that Gabe has arrived blooming in the desert of my heart. But the room's empty other than Shelley, who is marrying ketchup bottles in a booth by the window.

Stupid heart. Gabe's no Prince Charming, sweeping in to save me from the stress of my crazy life. Not even as a momentary distraction.

I grab a bottle of sanitizer and a rag, making my way to the table in the corner furthest away from the door. Ducking my head down, I get to work. Not once do I look at the door or even out to the parking lot for headlights. It feels like a hollow victory.

"I think Char's right," my other best friend, Mia Karakova, soon to be Mia Goldstone, says. We're not at The Gravy Train for once, but at a coffee shop near campus, mainly because she's buying and it's got free Wi-Fi.

"Are you nuts?" I reply before rolling my eyes. "This isn't a new bra she wants me to buy. It's a friggin' gun."

"Obviously, but that doesn't change the fact that Charlotte's right," Mia repeats, sipping her latte. "Russell's bad news, Izzy."

"I'm not disagreeing with that. He's an idiot, and as soon as he gets his next hit, he'll forget all about me," I repeat, even as I wish I hadn't told Charlotte about my problem with Russell at all.

I know she means well, but I don't need to hear about it from two sides at once, especially since that lets me know without a doubt that my besties have been talking about me. I know they worry, but their comparing notes on me brings back too many crappy childhood memories.

Plus, Charlotte's not even having coffee with us today so I can give her shit about selling me out. I stick to my usual party line, hoping it shuts down this attack as well as it usually does.

"Seriously, next week, I'll be fine."

"You've been pitching that same line for a long time now," Mia says, disappointed in me. "Next week, you'll be fine. Next paycheck, you'll be fine . . . same thing ever since your aunt passed away. You're more stubborn than even Papa, and he's worse than a damn mule."

"Then you know not to argue with me," I reply, hoping to sidetrack the conversation to safer ground. "How is he doing, anyway?"

"Gushy. He can't wait for the wedding," Mia admits. "It's sort of cute. But stop deflecting. You want to be stubborn, I'm going to be blunt."

Before I know it, Mia's reached into her pocket and pulled out a piece of paper. She plops it on the table in front of me. It unfolds on its own, and I feel a stab in my gut as I see the number of zeros on the check Mia's giving me.

"Mia, come on, this is bullshit! You know I can't accept this!"

"I'm not *giving* it to you," Mia says simply. "It's a loan. Izzy, we've been friends since we were munching on Lunchables together. I've subjected you to hundreds of hours of anime and video games, and meanwhile, you keep refusing help from the friends who love you, choosing to work yourself to the bone instead. Do you think Char and I don't know how tough things get for you?"

I startle, wondering exactly what they know because I thought I'd done a decent enough job hiding the rougher aspects of my life. Sure, they know I'm busy and strapped for cash, but definitely not that there are days I only eat my employee meal and that I've uselessly searched my couch for coins to keep the lights on.

But my pride still won't let me take the check. "I appreciate it, I do. But I can't." I try to shove the check back her way, but the paper sticks to my fingers. Well, okay, it doesn't stick so much as my thumb and pointer finger won't let go of it.

"Look, I know I've let you push off help, but that was when we were all struggling to some degree. Things are different now. I've got enough money to help you, and I promise my bank account won't feel it."

"Feelin' your privileges now?" It's a tacky and vicious thing to say, and I'm not jealous of Mia's fairy tale. She deserves it, worked for it with the beast she calls her man, but I can't help the shock of pain that goes through my gut at her ability to write a check like this and not give it a second's thought.

Mia stares at me with enough venom that I blush in embarrassment, looking down in shame. "Sorry, Mia. I know you didn't mean it like that. And I'm glad you're doing so well. You're my hashtag-goals, you know that. Degree, a job you love, and a guy you adore."

"It's okay," Mia says gently, thawing a little. "Listen, babe, I get it. I remember the way kids used to bully you. I remember those busted ass hand-me-downs you wore through high school. I know why you didn't go to prom, and I know why you still rode a bike to school after everyone else had their licenses. And as if that wasn't enough, fate bitchslapped you again when your aunt died. You've struggled for so long, I think it's just your normal. But this thing with Russell is different. And I've got the means to help."

"I feel more comfortable working for it, though," I reply with finality. "Mia, I love you. You're my number one girl—"

"Your future wife's gonna hate hearing that," Mia teases, knowing about the drunken pact Charlotte and I made. I smile a little at the joke.

"But I have to refuse this. It's too damn much! And I've heard too many stories about friendships getting ruined over dollar amounts a lot less than this. I won't risk *us* on *that*," I say, pointing at the check.

Before Mia can reply, I pick up her check and tear it in half, then in half again two more times before dropping the pieces in the glass of ice water that came with my Americano. Mia sadly watches the paper soak through and sink into the glass, then looks up at me.

"I was going to drink that," she deadpans.

"Didn't you just say you've got stupid money? I'm sure you can afford another glass of free ice water," I joke, grinning. "You mad?"

"I can't be mad at you for long," Mia says, leaning back. "But I want you to promise that if Russell amps up his stupidity, you'll reconsider. You can't pay anyone back if you're dead because some junkie got grabby hands for your cash or your other assets."

It's probably the reason she and I are best friends, because as I look her over, you wouldn't know she's getting married to one of the richest guys on the West Coast. She's still the same Mia she was a few months ago, with a green streak and red tips in her hair, a T-shirt for some Korean boy band, and ripped jeans.

If there's any difference in her lately, it's that she's got a little bit of a happy glow to her . . . probably from all the bedroom gymnastics she's getting up to, because I know she's not pregnant. Her Papa would have a heart attack if his princess so much as hinted at a pregnancy out of wedlock.

We drink our coffees, and as she finishes her latte, Mia smacks her lips. "By the way, I heard you un-godmothered me."

"Well, Vash doesn't quite fit the penthouse lifestyle. I promise you, give her a week, and she'd end up in Thomas's office or something, leaving a hairball on his desk blotter."

"Yeah, well, she's still my fur baby," Mia says before pivoting in that sudden, not-quite-sneaky but disconcerting way she has. "Which is why you need to learn to defend yourself."

Most people would say she's being mean, sucker punching . . . but I know her. I know the way she thinks, and there's a connection in her mind that most people just aren't seeing. And this is definitely another seed Charlotte planted.

"Why?"

"To defend my fur baby!" she exclaims, and then she smirks. "Oh, and you too."

"Ah," I reply, lifting my cup for a refill. "What are you saying, I should get some pepper spray?"

"Pepper spray isn't a good idea. Vashy could get into it and lick the tip or something," Mia says, assured in her correctness. "Can you imagine that poor cat with her tongue hanging out, numb and burning from what she just licked?"

"Probably what Thomas looks like most evenings," I reply, laughing.

She grins, then grows serious. "Seriously, Char told me she mentioned you should learn how to handle a gun. It might not be a bad idea. Hopefully, you'd never have to use it, but just in case. Papa taught me how to handle one. If I were in your situation, I'd at least consider it."

"But I have Vash to protect me," I reply weakly, knowing I'm fighting a losing battle with my besties. "She's a trained scratcher."

She glares at me, compelling me to take this issue seriously.

"Fine," I say, crumbling. "I'll look into it." But I know I'm not going to, still resisting even as I half-promise nothing.

"And you'll take this," Mia says, holding out a folded-over pile of bills. "No arguments, and if you say no, I'm giving it to Charlotte's arms dealer buddy anyway. Take it and make sure you get a quality piece and learn how to use it."

I grumble but take the wad of cash. I still don't want a gun, but this seems like the lesser of two evils considering the big check she tried to give me. I realize she played me like a damn pro, knowing she'd win either way. I'd take the big loan or the money for the gun, but I can't turn them both down.

And I am scared, in denial and full of wishful thoughts that Russell will OD before the next payment is due but fearful about the dangers his presence brings my life. I think about going home late after my Saturday double, the street dark and quiet, no one around but me and Russell hiding around the side of my house.

Or worse, in my house. He's threatened that before too.

"Okay, but I'm giving you a receipt and change on this."

CHAPTER 8

ISABELLA

*I*t's Friday, and by a miracle of scheduling and Shelley's generosity since she knows I have a double tomorrow, I have the full afternoon off.

Taking advantage of it, I drive over to Roseboro Arms, which sounds a lot more like a high-end apartment complex than a gun shop to me.

Whatever. Maybe the name gets the upper echelon of gun buyers who are nothing like me. I get off my scooter and head inside, opening the door cautiously, like I'm going to be greeted with a 'yee-haw' and a hail of shotgun pellets. *I've really got to get my fear of guns under control.*

I'm not quite sure what I expected, but what I find is a quiet, neat little store that looks more like a jewelry shop than anything else with glass cases surrounding the space.

The deep burgundy office-style carpet looks freshly cleaned, and in a surreal twist that must be fate laughing ironically at me, the sound system is quietly playing *Do You Really Wanna Hurt Me?*

"Hi, can I help you?" the man behind the main counter asks, looking up from the magazine he's flipping through.

"Uhm, hi. My friend, Charlotte, recommended I come down here, says she works with a guy named Brady?"

"Brady? That's my little brother," the man says, smiling. "The name's Saul. What're you looking for?"

"Home . . . uh, personal defense?" I reply. "Something I can carry in a purse."

"Well, first thing I'll tell you is that you need to get your permit to carry concealed," Saul says, "but it's pretty straightforward. I'll help you with the forms. Now, let's see what we can do for you."

It's almost dizzying, listening to the man talk about calibers, actions, trigger weights, and more. I give him respect, though, because he's not 'girlifying' it for me. He's giving me the information straight without any of the condescending attitude I expected.

Still, I feel like an idiot. "I'm really not sure—"

"Maybe I can help?"

Even though I've forced myself not to think about him, and my schedule has helped fill in the void, keeping my mind preoccupied, the voice is like cool water on a hot day, instantly quenching my thirst but making me want more at the same time.

I turn, seeing that half-smile on Gabe's face as he looks at me with those piercing eyes. Instantly, butterflies take flight in my belly and my thighs clench together.

With every drop of blood rushing elsewhere, my mouth opens before my brain can filter my thoughts. "You didn't come in Wednesday like you promised. And what're you doing here?"

"Yeah, sorry about that. I had some last-minute business come up, and I got held up out of town longer than I anticipated. I apologize," Gabe says, stepping a little closer. He's just inside my personal space bubble, but instead of feeling like it's an invasion, I want him even closer.

I want to be mad, and maybe I am . . . at myself for getting tied up in a guy I don't have time for and that doesn't have time for me, judging by his trip out of town. But maybe that makes us even? So I let him off the hook a little.

"Well, I didn't give you my phone number, so I can't blame you for not telling me," I murmur, smiling a little. "So what about the other question? What're you doing here?"

"Just shopping. Shooting's a hobby." He shrugs like it's no big deal that he pulls the trigger on a powerful machine that spits out life-ending projectiles. For all my nervousness about guns, the idea of Gabe directing and controlling all that power is sexy.

I can feel the heat on my cheeks and try to cover my dirty thoughts. "Hobby, huh? I guess you know something about guns?"

Gabe chuckles, nodding. "A little. I enjoy target shooting in my spare time. Boring sport to some people, punching very expensive holes in paper . . . but I like it. Thought I'd get some practice in during some down time. What about you? Come here often?" he lets the words ooze off his tongue flirtatiously, but it's with a big wallop of humor laced through.

"Personal defense," Saul injects into our conversation, his own smile not dimming at all. "I was just about to recommend the Glock 43."

"No," Gabe says, his smile never fading but his voice gaining an authoritative edge. "Let's try the Springfield XDM."

Saul nods, always the happy help. "That's a fine choice too," he says to Gabe before turning to me. "Now we just need to make sure you know how to handle it."

I look to Gabe, but he lifts his chin toward Saul. "Let him do the full beginner tutorial. I'll shop around and leave you to learn so you're not distracted." He must see the disappointment mixed with fire in my eyes because he leans close, whispering by my ear, "I'm not going anywhere. I'll check on you in a few. Go get 'em, tiger."

~

THINGS ARE A LOT LESS FUN THIRTY MINUTES LATER AS I HIT THE button on the little paper target thing and it rolls in close to me, showing me where I've hit.

"More like where I've missed," I grumble, looking at the three holes in the paper. Ten shots, and I only hit the paper three times? Three friggin' times in ten shots?

I could throw the bullets down the range and hit more often than that.

It's the kick. I know what Saul showed me in the lesson he gave me, but between pulling the trigger and the way the gun seems to jump in my hand, I just feel out of control with each shot.

And the tighter I hold the gun, struggling to control it, the harder it is.

Suddenly, I feel a warm, hard body close to me, and before I can react a strong arm wraps around me, holding my wrists. Then my borrowed earmuffs are pulled down, the cacophony of echoes in the room hitting me full force.

"You're doing it all wrong," a gravelly voice says in my ear as I feel Gabe's body nearly envelop me.

"Well, it's my first time," I say, coating the words with innocence, but my smirk makes it obvious I know exactly what I'm doing. With the flirting, at least, but definitely not with the gun.

Gabe inhales sharply, and his voice is even deeper, his chest rumbling against my back. "Let's start from the beginning. Show me your stance."

He steps back and I miss his warmth. Still, I assume the grip on the pistol the way Saul showed me, and Gabe watches. I can feel his eyes on my body, looking over my shoulders and back, then drifting down my hips and legs before starting back up. It feels clinical, though I hope he likes what he sees.

"Not too bad for a first-timer." His tease is playful, making me smile, and then he lightly asks, "So, what made today the day you purchase a gun? Anything in particular spark this?"

His eyes quickly trace up and down again, though this time there's nothing professional about it at all.

I lower my pistol, setting it on the bench before clipping in a new target. "My friends encouraged me, for the most part. They're concerned about my living alone."

My eyes widen as I realize I just told a strange man . . . a very sexy strange man, that I live alone. *I'm quite literally the too-stupid-to-live girl in every cautionary tale*, I think to myself.

Well, at least he knows I've got a gun. But then again, unless he's the broad side of a barn, he's got little to worry about from me.

"Probably a smart decision in that case," he says pragmatically. "As long as you know how to use it. You know, I think a woman who can handle a gun is . . . sexy."

The way he says it turns up the heat in the firing range by about twenty degrees, and I glance over my shoulder to see him looking directly at me with a dimple-framed smile. "Okay, now what?"

"Reload, and I'll show you," Gabe says, picking up my empty magazine and quickly slipping ten fresh rounds into it. "Oh, and earmuffs. Always shoot safely."

My mind must be twisted, because I swear I can see his eyes twinkle when he says it, but I put my earmuffs back on and send the target to the end of the indoor range. I reload the gun, and Gabe watches, coming around me again and resting his hands on my wrists, his body pressed lightly against mine.

The wanton slut in me begs permission to rub my ass back against his dick, but I refrain, appreciating that he's not using this as an excuse to grind on me like most guys would. Gabe is a gentleman, *something I'm not used to*, I think wryly.

He pulls one earmuff away an inch, his voice muffled against my ear. "Relax your grip. I can feel it in your forearms," he says, and I will my muscles to release.

"There you go. Now, just focus on the front sight. The target's not moving. It's not going anywhere, and when you're ready, squeeze slowly . . ."

He lets go of the earmuff, and I take aim down the barrel of the gun the way Saul showed me, aligning my sights and the target. I take a slow breath and squeeze slowly.

The pistol pops in my hand, and as soon as it does, I can see the paper jerk and a little white hole appear in the black part of the target, the high scoring rings that I've never hit before. Gabe looks and smiles.

"Nice shot. Now, try again."

I'm no Annie Oakley, but this time, I hit the paper nine out of ten times, and best of all, five shots in the middle. I can't help but smile, and Gabe throws his hand up for a high-five, which I return carefully, keeping the gun aimed down range.

"Improvement?"

"Much better," I agree, my shoulders still tingling from where I felt his chest pressed against my back. "Uhm . . . mind showing me how you do it?"

"Sure," Gabe says after a moment. "Can I use your piece?"

I nod, hooking up another target and sending it out while Gabe reloads again.

I step back, expecting the slow, methodical, two to three seconds between shots that I did, but instead, Gabe's an explosion of shots, ten rounds before I can barely take two breaths, his brown eyes going from warm to icy as he jabs the button and reels the target back in.

The paper, which has a few pieces of tape on it from where I've patched holes, suddenly has ten brand-new punctures in the paper, and all of them damn near bullseyes.

"Whoa," I whisper, looking at him with newfound amazement. "Forget buying the gun, I should just bring you home." I slap my hand over my mouth, my eyes going wide.

Oh, my God, did I just say that? I didn't mean it like *that*. Okay, maybe a little, but I wouldn't have said it so boldly if my ovaries weren't exploding like the target paper bits did. Gabe's right, someone who can handle a gun is damn sexy.

Gabe's smile tells me he heard exactly what I said, and what I meant, and those butterflies once again start fluttering like a hurricane in my stomach.

"If you'd like," Gabe answers my accidental proposition but without pressure. "I'm just glad I can help."

"Hopefully, I won't need this, but the strung-out guy down the street has been coming on a little too strong lately."

Shit, I just keep blurting things out that I shouldn't be.

Gabe's jaw clenches. "A neighbor?"

"Kind of. Technically, he owns the land my house is on, a land lease. And he keeps coming by to collect aggressively. He's bad news in general," I explain with a lift of my shoulder. "What're you gonna do?"

"You think he's dangerous?" he asks carefully. His eyes go icy as I tell him how much Russell scared me that morning outside my house, and I can see his hands curling and uncurling. "I'm sorry that happened to you."

"Yeah, well . . . I guess it scared me enough that when Mia and Char said I should come down here, I did," I admit, stepping a little closer. "I mean, there's nothing wrong with learning to defend yourself, right?"

Gabe's eyes are serious as he closes the distance, and if he were to reach out right now, he could wrap me in his arms again. But he just stands there, hands at his side.

"There's nothing wrong with being strong enough to take charge of your own fate," he says, his expression darkening, and I wonder what trick of fate he's trying to control.

Gabe blinks, the iciness melting a little as he reaches up, his hand curling around the nape of my neck as he moves in close enough to kiss me.

But instead, he says softly, "You don't have to give me yours, but I'm going to write down my number. If he gives you any problems, you call me, okay?"

I nod but minimize the situation. "I'm sure everything will be fine. This is just a precaution," I tell Gabe, not wanting to bother him, though secretly, I think that's exactly what I want. After all, he's getting me very bothered. And hot. Hot and bothered, that's me.

Gabe smiles a little, warmth and iciness mixing somehow as he looks at me. It's like he's being warm and intimate with me but could still hand out pain to anyone who's a threat to me. It's the sexiest look I've ever seen on a man's face.

"I insist. Now, let's practice some more."

We try again, and as we keep going, I can't help but get more and more turned on. It's intimidating, the power in my hands, and as I try to shoot, my mind keeps flashing to the brief moments of Gabe popping ten rounds in that circle the size of a grapefruit faster than I could believe.

It was terrifying, but also sexy, watching him in total and utter control of the instrument of death in my hands.

"Remember, relax," Gabe says softly, coming behind me again. He puts his hands on my shoulders and presses them down gently. I hadn't even realized they'd crept up toward my ears. "You're thinking about the results and not the process of getting there. And that's making you tense, throwing you off."

His voice is almost hypnotic, and as his hands start to knead my neck and shoulders, I feel hormones flood my body. I'm turned into Silly Putty under his thumbs, and in my mind, I wonder if anyone's ever made me feel such a twin mix of sensations at the same time.

Scared and attracted, turned on and relaxed, worried and comfortable . . . Gabe's got all of them swirling in my chest, and I feel like there's not enough oxygen in the room.

"There," Gabe says in my ear. "Now, just line up the sights. Remember, you're just shooting a piece of paper . . . and go."

Ten shots, and I feel like a machine.

Breathe.

Aim.

Squeeze.

Breathe.

Aim.

Squeeze.

Ten times the cycle repeats, and when the paper comes in, there are ten holes in the black rings. "Very nice. Very, very nice," Gabe praises.

"Thank you," I reply, grabbing the target.

He takes his turn, hitting all bullseyes again, but I never even look at the target, instead focusing on him. Feet spread wide, hips square, jaw clenched, and eyes narrowed. It's like an action hero popped off the Hollywood screen, especially when he takes the last shot and turns to me with a boyish grin.

He sets the gun down and glances at the clock on the wall. "Listen, I have to go, but maybe we could get together and do this again? Or dinner? Not at the diner, to be clear."

He blinks a little faster, the smallest sign of nerves at asking me out, which I guess is understandable since I shot him down last time. I'm not making that mistake again.

I dig in my bag for a pen and grab my successful target sheet, thinking it might be nice to save as a souvenir of my first shots, but instead scribbling my number on the corner and giving the paper to Gabe.

"Here, take this. You really helped me a lot, and I think this shows that." I smile warmly.

He takes the paper, looking both at the number and the scatter of holes, then back to me. "Thanks. I'll call you soon."

He starts to leave but turns back, and the butterflies in my belly flutter, thinking he's coming back for a kiss. But instead, he tosses me one of his signature panty-melting half-smiles.

"Bye, Bella."

I bite my lip at the name. I liked it when he wrote it, but hearing him say it is even more of a wow. I wave and then he's gone.

Saul steps back into my lane behind me, asking politely, "Ready for me to show you how to break it down for cleaning and safe storage?"

I nod, but the excitement of a moment before is gone with Gabe's exit.

CHAPTER 9

GABRIEL

*T*he morning is downright cold, a quick reminder that here in the Pacific Northwest, autumn comes a lot faster than it does where I was born.

I don't say where I live, because for the past ten years I can't say that I've had a home.

I tend to stick around the corridor from San Fran to Seattle when I'm not on a contract, in the hopes I'll find out something about what happened to Jeremy. But even here, I don't have a home, or even a home base. Just hotels, short-term-lease apartments, and sometimes an AirBnB.

I adjust my hooded sweatshirt as I watch Isabella's house. It's not so cold that my fingers are numb or that the windows fog up.

No, the only thing obscuring my vision has been myself. And that has to stop.

Yesterday, I'd been following her, hoping she might do something 'wrong' on her day off, something that would explain why I've been hired. I'd sat in the gun range parking lot for almost ten minutes, arguing with myself about going inside.

Would she think it was too big of a coincidence and bolt like a rabbit? Or would she be happy to see me?

Ultimately, I'd given in to the curiosity, telling myself that it was possible she'd found out who I am and was getting protection against me. That's something I'd need to know in my line of work, so I'd gone inside, knowing it was more excuse and less truth but happy to justify it to myself anyway.

And I saw her blossom, the confidence she gained as she quickly learned how to shoot turning me on just as much as the warmth of her body pressed against mine.

She was the sexiest thing I've ever had in my arms. From the lean strength of her shoulders to the way her legs spread as she assumed the shooter's stance, and the biggest turn-on was her willingness to stand up for herself against that sleazebag, Carraby. She's a powerhouse, that Isabella Turner.

My brain was torn in half, one side admiring her as a budding marksman and strong person, the other side wanting to pull down the jeans she was wearing, tap her feet a few inches further apart, and fuck her as hard as I could while she bent over the shooting bench.

She makes me want to see if I'm up to the challenge of being worthy of her. I know I'm not, my soul is obviously sullied well beyond what a princess like her deserves, but I want the test anyway.

Even after leaving, I had to go back to my motel room and beat off twice just to give myself enough control to get through the rest of the night.

Which is why I have to get this done quickly. In the gun range, I could feel my self-control slipping, this close to abandoning my mission just to have her at my mercy in another way.

I wanted to bury my nose in the thick flowing locks of her hair, to nibble at her ear and reach around, tugging on her nipples until she creamed all over my cock.

I can't have that happening.

My phone buzzes, and I see it's a message from Blackwell.

Five.

The countdown pisses me off. He knows how I work, and the added pressure from him makes me question this whole contract all the more. But I can't back out.

I'm close, I text back, wishing I could be certain this course of action is warranted. But am I too close to Isabella already? Too blinded to see the ugly truth?

Sure, I've used my good looks and personality to get close to targets before. Isabella is different, though. She's threatening that line where it becomes more than just my attraction to her body.

Watching her at work, it's painful to see her swallow her pride and do whatever is needed to keep trudging along. I've snuck into her classes, lurking in the shadows in back of the lecture hall, smiling to myself as she gets every answer correct.

It was even more painful yesterday, observing as she emerged from her self-imposed shell, blossoming as she gained confidence with her shooting.

I took pleasure in every smile, every twinkle in her eyes, the times I made her laugh. More than her body, that's what I thought of as I stroked myself last night. Not her ass or her tits or any of that.

I fantasized about her laugh.

I fantasized about being the man who could help her wake up from the hell she's living in.

I fantasized about being the one to rescue her, to whoosh her away somewhere safe and spoil her rotten with attention and love.

And that's dangerous. It's more addictive than any drug her landlord might be on.

With Isabella, I feel pulled in equal and opposite directions at once, and the more I wait, the more I'm ripped in half.

Isabella's door opens, and she comes out, pulling her backpack over her shoulders. She doesn't have a heavy load of books today, so she must have gotten some studying done last night. I hope she got some sleep too, poor thing.

Shit. I'm doing it again. Too much, too close. Back that bus up, Gabriel.

She stops, reaching into her pocket and pulling out her phone. She dials, and I'm shocked when my phone starts to ring next to me. I look and see . . . it's *her*.

I slouch down, making sure I'm not able to be seen, and pray nobody in the neighborhood honks their horn. "Hello?"

"Hi . . . Gabe? It's Izzy Turner."

"Bella," I reply automatically, before I can even think about it.

She makes a small, happy noise, and I curse myself inside. I let myself call her that the night I left her a note . . . now I'm using it all the time with her. I've had to remind myself to not even *think* of her that way, but it hasn't sunk in yet.

If anything, it's made the nickname dig itself deeper into my psyche.

"Yeah, it's me. Listen, I know this is stupid, but you mentioned getting dinner and I'm slammed with late shifts for the next six nights in a row, but I'd like to see you."

She hums nervously, and I wonder if she's ever called a guy before. Does she just wait for them to come to her, like woodland creatures seeking out Snow White?

Or is she too busy scraping by to even think about guys?

The thought of her with another guy makes my teeth click together, but she must not hear because she rambles quickly.

"I was wondering if maybe you'd like to stop by the diner? I promise you, Henry's a great cook on more than just the Country Special."

"I'd like that," I reply, twisting inside as I know I'm both lying and *not* lying.

There's half of me that would like nothing more than to share some food and good conversation with her.

The other half . . . wants to run.

Only the tiniest fraction of a percent of me wants to actually kill her, even if I desperately need the information Blackwell has. And I hate that dark, monstrous part of me.

"Great!" she says chirpily, twisting the knife in my gut a little more. I'm actually making her *happy*. "Well, I've got a break at about nine, or if you want to wait until closing time, come by around ten forty-five."

"Sounds good. I'll try to be there at nine for your break and then hang out until you get off, if that's okay?"

Bella giggles, and I swear she sounds happier than ever. "Okay. See you then. Bye."

She hangs up, and I curse myself as moments later, I hear the buzzing noise from her scooter pulling away.

I watch her go and then grab my lockpicks. I walk up to her house, intent on doing what I should have done before approaching her.

I'm going to have to come up with something to tell Blackwell, and fast.

I need an excuse, one way or the other. Something that'll let me do this as I promised I would, or something that breaks my codes and will let me refuse the contract under the already stated terms.

My employers know my rule against innocents, and I'm very thorough in explaining the exit clauses for me and the hiring party. As depraved as it may be, this is a business transaction and I treat it as such.

Blackwell's no different, but at the same time, he's the employer I've least wanted to piss off. Not only is his reach wide, but his offered reward is the Holy Grail I've been searching for. How, then, do I deal with this?

The lock on her back door's a piece of crap, six seconds to pop, and I open the door onto one of the saddest things I've ever seen.

I knew the row of mill houses was in a sad state of disrepair, but from the outside, it seemed like Bella's was one of the better ones. But from my kitchen vantage point, I can see it's a fucking miracle this thing is still standing.

The hardwood floor carries the ghosts of seventy or more years of use. The once-warm stain is worn nearly white where generations of people have walked paths.

The walls are faded, old wallpaper that's so thin I can almost see the plaster and lathe behind it. Whatever color and design it was when it was hung has turned into a washed-out pale brown, with blobs that probably used to be flowers.

The furniture is vintage '70s, a tweed couch with wooden arms and a stained Formica two-seater dinette table.

Everything I see is the same. Old, patched, barely above homeless levels.

But I can see the effort she puts into her home. The spotless countertops, the sheet carefully tucked around the couch cushions to make it less scratchy, and the scent of lemons in the air. It's not much, but she cares for it.

Hate her? How could I hate her? How can I declare her evil?

It makes me want to cry.

Her life's a bad joke, a broken-down house even worse than I expected, a job that works her to the point of exhaustion, and dreams she will likely never reach at the pace she's going. But still, she doesn't give up.

I look around and start to get even more pissed at Russell. How could anyone want to hit up anyone for money for this place?

I'd be doing her a favor if I just burned this whole place down.

I continue exploring, going into what has to be Bella's bedroom.

She doesn't have a bed frame, just a mattress on the floor, but her blankets are spread out neatly and the single pillow is centered and standing up against the wall where a headboard would be. A series of photographs stuck to the mirror with yellowed tape catches my eye.

The mirror is huge but obviously cracked through the middle, or else it would most likely have been pawned or sold long ago to keep the bills paid.

It doesn't take me long to identify Bella in the photographs. Her hair and eyes are still the same stunning rich dark wood color they are now, and I idly wonder how many hearts she broke in school. Quite a few, I suspect.

The oldest photos are of her in much better environs, an upper-middle-class looking house if my estimation is right, Bella between a man and a woman, with a boy in the background. The woman's obviously her mother, she's got the same cheeks and lean bone structure, but the man's got Bella's hair.

"Her father," I whisper in wonder. I touch the picture of the boy, who's got freckles and is smiling widely. "And brother."

Underneath the photo is a slightly newer one, this time Bella in elementary school with a woman who's not just lean but positively gaunt.

It was taken in this house, although things looked a lot better twenty years ago than they do today. The woman is Bella's aunt, her mother's sister, if my research was correct. The woman looks worn out and exhausted by life, though judging by Bella's age, the picture was taken a whole decade before she died.

I swallow and look down to see a cheap jewelry box, probably empty, but something inspires me to lift the lid. There's a tiny little ballerina inside, but it doesn't turn, either because it hasn't been wound in a long time or, more likely, the mechanism's broken.

More interesting, though, is the small folded piece of newspaper, slightly yellowed with age but carefully preserved, nonetheless. Feeling like the world's most depraved thief, I pinch it between two fingers, fishing it out and unfolding it carefully.

Local Family Killed in Tragic Plane Crash

The story's short and rather sad, telling the story of Oliver Turner, his wife, Sarah, and their only son, Roy. Oliver, a successful businessman, was also an avid private aviator and had decided to take his wife and son on a fun little jaunt over San Juan Island to catch the orca that you could see off the coast there.

Unfortunately for them . . . they never returned. Their daughter, young five-year-old Isabella Turner, was the only surviving member of the Turner family because she'd been left behind with a babysitter, according to my intel.

The story finishes with Bella being mentioned almost as a foot-note, just a line saying she would live with her aunt.

I carefully fold the paper back up, tears once again threatening me. She's already been through so much, and I feel like a cold-blooded bastard for even accepting this contract. But how could I have known?

Her life hasn't just been a tragedy. It's been a comedy, not the ha-ha kind but the sad, gut-wrenching, sob-inducing kind, where the universe laughs at you while it smacks you around again.

I know the feeling, but I suspect I've barely scratched the level of shit that Bella's had to endure.

I put the newspaper clipping back, leaving her room to check out the rest of the house. There's one other bedroom, and when I open the door, I'm floored by what I see.

It's . . . a painting.

On the wall itself.

The soul poured into what I see makes my stomach clench with emotion. A painting of an airplane soaring over the ocean, the sun gleaming off the silver wings . . . and an island.

There's so much sadness in each brush stroke, the painting done in what looks like poster paint, or maybe house paint. It doesn't really matter. It's the emotions wrapped into every inch of the painting that makes it stunning.

The second pillow that belongs on her bed is sitting in the middle of the room, like she sits in here with the painting a lot. That strikes me as important, the way she takes a few moments for herself in the midst of her busy life. To grieve, to remember, to wish for a different life?

Not really knowing why, I reach out to the painting, wanting to touch the memorial that Bella's painted to her family, but before I can, a yowl from the depths of hell itself rips through the room, and a screaming ball of blackness leaps from the closet next to the painting.

"Holy fuck!" I growl as pain flares through my right hand before I can hurl whatever the fuck it is across the room. Once it lands with a soft thud, I can see it's a cat, green eyes nearly glowing in the middle of a black face, a V-shaped white mark scrunching up as it hisses at me.

My wrist throbs, and I look to see that the cat scratched me pretty badly. "You're lucky, kitty. My reflexes are usually deadlier than that, but I wouldn't hurt you."

The cat meows back at me, like it's telling me that I'm the lucky one, and I back out carefully, leaving out the same door I came in through before heading to my truck.

I have to figure out what the hell I'm going to do about this mess because I've made up my mind and I know it. There's zero chance that I can go through with this contract.

Bella doesn't deserve the ending that's been chosen for her.

And that'd be that, except for Blackwell.

He's already losing patience with my timeline. While I'm known as patient and methodical, we're stretching into the ridiculous levels here.

For an unprotected civilian with no idea of the blind justice they're in store for, a reasonable timeline would've been a week at most. I'm running on three between research, first contact, to today.

I've killed men like Blackwell, protected by security, aware of threats, and risk averse in less time than I've taken on Isabella Turner.

And Blackwell's not a man known for loyalty *or* patience. If I delay too long, he'll circumvent me, probably adding an addendum to include me with whomever he hires for the new contract.

But as I drive, I keep thinking of that painting.

That's why she's sacrificing so much . . . why she's killing herself to keep that broken-down house.

And if it means that much to her, I want to help her keep it too. And more importantly, keep her safe and alive.

CHAPTER 10

BLACKWELL

I sip my tequila, mentally bemoaning the fact that people are so predictable. It's a plus for me, really, allowing me to see the chessboard of life and plan accordingly. But sometimes, a bit of a twist would be nice.

I smirk to myself, reaching over to the bar in the back of my limo to grab a lime wedge. I squeeze it into the clear alcohol and shake it around, mixing the sour into the expensive alcohol. "A twist indeed," I say to the empty backseat.

The divider between the driver and me lowers. "Excuse me, sir. We seem to have picked up a tail. Would you like for me to lose them or continue on to your meeting?"

I glance over my shoulder, only seeing the bright round lights of the cars around us on the streets of Roseboro.

Streets that I own, control, and paved. When I came to Roseboro, it was a nothing town, in a depression from lack of employment and in the midst of a mass-exodus of families. Through my skill and nurturing, I've returned life to this city.

I'm the reason housing prices in this town have risen every year for twenty years and why the town's high school has grown from a podunk afterthought to one of the biggest and best schools in the entire state.

The reason this town exists is *me*.

And the city is forgetting that. They mock me, with terms like 'Black to Yellow' to describe the workers who leave me to go work for Golden Boy.

Even worse are those who leave to become successful on their own, using the things they learned from me to compete against my company. As if they don't owe me some loyalty for the changes I've brought to Roseboro and to their piddly lives.

I purse my lips as the tequila burns my tongue and gums, holding it in my mouth until it becomes a light numbness before swallowing the sip, having drawn out every molecule of flavoring from the potion. The burn and subtle vanilla and oak flavors help me delay my anger. To focus.

And I have much to focus on.

I finally answer the driver, "Drive around for a bit. I'll be a little late for my meeting, but it's an acceptable delay."

He nods silently, the divider quietly returning to its place a moment later.

I know you're following me, Gabriel Jackson. The question is why?

I'd hired him because he's the best in the business, able to adapt and deliver under a variety of circumstances. Silent or bold, messy or clean, the appearance of an accident or message-sending publicity . . . whatever your needs, he can meet them, and according to reputation, has done so with unequivocal success. I'd known his methods are precise, something I can appreciate, but it seems he's getting cold feet.

It can only be because of *her*.

This delay has become untenable, his questions as to my motivation less amusing and more disrespectful, and I'm reaching the end of my patience. Especially as he seems to be more interested in my behaviors than those of his contracted prey.

That's why I have already hired a private investigator to follow Mr. Jackson. Not a competing hitman, at least not yet. But rather a man skilled at being invisible. I like the idea of keeping my pawns compartmentalized, only holding a portion of the bigger picture I readily see.

His reports show that Gabriel's contact with Isabella is perhaps more intimate than I'd predicted, though he did say that Gabriel investigated her home today, so maybe he's not entirely been led astray by her feminine wiles.

Considering that she used tears and a false story to implicate my previous associate, I'm not willing to put anything past the seemingly innocuous Isabella Turner.

"You should hurry, Mr. Jackson," I whisper to the dark night, taking another sip of tequila. "My patience is running thin."

CHAPTER 11

ISABELLA

*N*ine o'clock comes and goes, and though I try to delay my dinner break, I finally sit down in Martha's office to slam a sandwich and fries.

Usually, I sit on the floor or stand at the counter, but with Gabe not being here like he said, I don't want to look pathetic. And I know I'd be watching the door like a hawk, because that's what I did from eight thirty to nine fifteen.

I remind myself that he said he'd 'try' to be here at nine and then hang out until I got off, and that's not exactly the same thing as a sure date. Any number of things could've come up between this morning and tonight.

With a final swallow, I set my dishes in the back sink, straighten my apron, and wash my hands. I slick a quick layer of tinted lip balm on and pinch my cheeks, trying to perk myself up from the disappointment of another dinner alone.

All business, all the time. That's me, and I don't know why I thought for a minute that I maybe could have something else, something lighter and livelier and just for me. I know better. That's not my life.

But Mia used to be all about number-crunching and she had an amazing thing happen to her, so maybe there's hope for the rest of us, my romantic heart murmurs.

Torn between fantasy and reality, I hit the floor again, thanking Elaine for covering my tables.

It's nearly nine thirty when the doorbell tinkles and my heart leaps in my chest. I can feel the difference in the room when Gabe walks in, a smile on his face. "Hey."

"Hey." *Some stellar conversationalist skills I've got*, I think. "Glad you could make it," I greet him, genuinely smiling for the first time all shift, but then I intentionally add, "I already had my break, couldn't wait any longer or Elaine wouldn't be able to cover for me."

He winces, rubbing at his hair. "Sorry. I didn't think it'd be this late, but I got hung up with work and knew you couldn't check your phone much while you're on shift. I'm glad you didn't wait. You need to eat when you can. I was hoping I could make it up to you by hanging out until you get off? Maybe we can do something then?"

His face is open, and it appears he's being sincere, both of which go a long way in my book. Also, he gets brownie points for knowing I can't be on my phone and that I needed to chow down when I could. *He said he'd 'try' to be here at nine*, that same voice hisses in my ear.

I think for a moment, letting him stew a little bit but knowing I've already made up my mind. He's exciting and different, a bright spot in my doldrum life, something just for me. And I'm not going to deprive myself of his yumminess, however it comes, however often he stops by, or however long he stays.

Maybe that makes me easy, but I think it makes me human.

So I smile as I push my hair behind my ear and point to a stool at the counter. "Sounds like a plan. How was your day?" I let all my previous doubts and insecurities go, happy to just be here with him in this moment.

Take life as it comes, Izzy.

"Not bad. Looking much better now," he says, sliding into a seat at the counter.

He tosses that half-smile that leaves me forgetting that my feet hurt after a long day of running around. Hell, that smile makes me forget how to breathe. And judging by the way it morphs into a cocky smirk, he damn well knows it.

"How was yours?"

"Good, one morning class, then helped my bestie do some house moving before my shift tonight," I reply.

Seeing Mia and Charlotte today for a little while had been great, especially since it was a milestone moment for us. One of our trio is moving up the adulthood ladder by moving in with her man.

Mia had gleefully shown us around her new penthouse home while simultaneously directing the movers, liberally sprinkling 'our house', 'our bedroom', and 'our plans' into the whole tour.

It'd been pretty adorable, actually, but make no mistake, when we got to her precious gaming setup, it was all 'my', 'mine', and 'don't touch' in her occasionally-present Russian accent, even to Thomas, who'd wandered in to say hello.

He'd ignored her semi-joking selfishness like it was their norm, which it probably is, and just wrapped her in his arms and nibbled on her neck, distracting her from telling us *all* about the new TERA game update. He'd winked at Charlotte and me, mouthing *you're welcome*.

I'd been thrilled for her, and even as I stand here on uncertain ground, I'm still happy she's getting her happily ever after. She deserves it.

I bring Gabe a menu, and as he reaches for it, I notice a bandage on his wrist. It's a big one, and I wince. "Ooh! What'd you do, try to get yourself killed?"

Gabe looks at the bandage and chuckles. "Just a scratch. The bandage makes it look a lot worse than it actually is."

I devil him a bit, pretending to poke at the wound. "After your crack shot gun skills, I'd have thought you'd be damn-near invincible. Guess you're human after all, huh?"

He sets the menu down, his bandaged hand going to his lap, and I see something pass through his eyes, but it's gone too fast for me to recognize and label it.

A customer calls for me, and I hold up a finger to excuse myself from Gabe. I head over, taking their order.

As I do, I think back to my conversations with the girls today.

Mia is understandably on the side of love, lovemaking, and generally spreading glittery happiness everywhere. It's a good look on her.

Surprisingly, Charlotte is virtually the polar opposite right now, her sourness coming from the last guy she dated and really liked, who'd ended up as a married father of five.

She'd dropped him faster than he could say, "My wife knows and doesn't care!" So she's reasonably on the side of caution and distrust. Realistically, Char's more likely correct even though Mia spouted off statistics about marriage rates, divorce rates, and some other numerical info I couldn't possibly keep straight.

Mostly, I keep hearing Char's voice, telling me to be wary, slow my roll, and run a background check on Gabe. It's not like I think he's *the one*, but I probably should be careful.

Keep it flirty and just have fun.

"It really has been too long," I mutter under my breath, mentally arguing with Mia and Charlotte. To my surprise, Gabe chuckles. I look up, not even realizing that I had drifted back closer to him.

"What's been too long?" he asks, and I can sense the heat to his question.

Even if I'd been talking about too long since I'd had a nap, which

I wasn't, I'm thinking about sex now. And to be fair, I was thinking about how long it's been since I've had a partner-accompanied orgasm. B.O.B. has been my sole date for months.

"Oh, nothing," I deflect. "Sorry. My friends are living rent-free in my brain."

"You should charge them. Might help things," Gabe teases lightly, making me laugh and thankfully not pressing for an answer to his previous question. "What are they saying?"

"Well, first, you have to know that one is literally in the midst of her happily ever after and one just got blindsided. So it's all filtered through those lenses." I point to my right shoulder, and say, "Mia here is jumping up and down, clapping and telling me to go out with you, or stay in with you, but to see where this goes."

His eyebrows climb his forehead and his eyes darken, but there's a sparkle of joy in them. "And the other?"

I look to my left shoulder, intoning, "Charlotte is telling me to be polite but recognize that I don't know you, and realistically, you don't give off the vibe of someone staying in town long-term. And she reminds me that I'm not a one-night-stand kind of girl."

I barely hold back offering 'but I could try to be' because for Gabe, I might 'hit that' even with no promises.

There's just something about him that calls to me, body and mind, and I know if I don't at least try, I'll always wonder and probably regret it.

His mouth opens and shuts like a fish, and I'm pretty sure I just dumped way too much information on his shoulders.

The door dings before Gabe can gather his thoughts enough to ask me which way I'm leaning, and I look up as heartburn walks in the door.

Well, not exactly heartburn, but the same delivery driver, along with two other customers behind him.

We're usually not this slammed this late at night, but they just keep coming today.

Seeing my conundrum, Gabe waves me off. "Go take care of business. I'll be here when you get a minute. And I'm staying until you get off tonight."

My thighs clench together with hopeful wishes that he means that in more than one way.

Shut up, Charlotte, I can be a one-and-done if I want to be.

Within ten minutes, The Gravy Train's in chaos and Elaine and I are in the weeds. Besides seating the three new tables, two other tables want to add extra orders, and it's so bad that Henry himself has to bring the plates to the counter because we're doing our best to keep the main floor caught up.

"Here you go, ma'am," Henry says, setting a plate down. "Sorry about the wait, seems we've got a packed house all of a sudden. Food's worth it, though." He's trying to be charming and kind, but the woman's having none of his apologies.

I glance over from where I'm writing down Delivery Driver's order, thankfully simple tonight with a double cheeseburger and fries, when the woman replies. "It's kind of hard to mess up a ham and swiss melt."

Henry shrugs and heads back to the grill, but I can see the vein throbbing in his temple and know he's getting stressed out, which isn't good for his ulcer and therefore, isn't good for any of us.

I clip the driver's order to Henry's spinner and scan the floor. Table seven needs refills, which I make quickly and deliver with a smile, promising their onion rings are coming right up. Table twelve is making a waving check mark in the air, so I flip through the slips in my apron and drop it off.

Thankfully, they offer cash and don't need change.

"My burger's fucking ready. You gonna get it or should I do it my damn self?" I hear from behind me. I glance up, and though

Henry never hit the bell, Delivery Driver's burger and fries plate is sitting on the warming shelf.

My lips spread in the plastic not-smile everyone who's ever worked customer service has and tell the man, "I'll grab that now." But I don't hurry. He doesn't deserve for me to raise my heartrate one extra beat in hustle for his sorry ass.

"Shitty fuckin' food and shitty fuckin' servers. Lazy bitch."

My teeth are grinding as I move behind the counter to grab the plate, slow as dripping molasses as I check and double-check for accuracy.

Quality assurance at its fucking finest by Ms. Isabella Turner. You'll get your burger when I'm damn good and ready to deliver it.

Suddenly, I hear a commotion behind me as hands slap on a table and a voice growls out, "Apologize."

I turn, my jaw dropping as I see Gabe on his feet, his back to me as he stares at Delivery Driver. "What the fuck?" Driver asks, his face going a little white as he looks up at Gabe. "Seriously, man?"

"The people here are working their asses off and doing the best they can. Doesn't matter how much you hate your life, it doesn't give you the right to spread that anger onto these folks."

"Who the fuck are you to tell me—"

"I'm the guy saying you need to find another late-night hangout if this is how you're going to behave," Gabe says, reaching down and 'helping' Delivery Driver out of his seat. "Get out and go learn some damn manners."

For a moment, I'm worried Delivery Driver's going to throw a punch. But I'm rooted in place, something freezing me as I watch him stare into Gabe's eyes. The coldness is back, the same coldness I saw at the shooting range.

Right now, Gabe could hurt this man and not even blink an eye. Tension fills the air as Driver's hand clenches but then relaxes, and he takes a step back, knowing he can't win against Gabe or a roomful of people all sneering at him.

Henry's out of the kitchen again, and behind him is Martha, who's watching from the pass-through to the kitchen with the phone in her hand. My guess is she's already half-dialed 9-1-1 because while she's intimidating as hell, this is beyond even her skills.

"Fuck this. I don't need this place anyway."

Gabe doesn't move as Delivery Driver backs up, stopping at the door. "Hey, cook boy. You should fire that bitch."

He points a thumb my way, making it clear who he means. But then he locks his gaze back on Gabe, anger fraying his control even when his brain knows it's a losing battle. He puffs up, head tilting wildly as he adds to the charges against me.

"Letting people like this asshole get all up in people's faces. Fuck this place."

He storms out, and everyone in the place holds their breath for a second longer. I'm surprised when Martha starts applauding softly. I wasn't sure she'd take too kindly to Gabe taking it upon himself to kick a customer out.

A couple of other customers, including a few regulars, join in, and heat flushes my face as Gabe turns around and gives me a look that has my stomach flip-flopping.

Never has a man looked at me with such possessiveness, care, and more than a little desire. I'm about point-two seconds from running and launching myself at him, ready to ride him like a cowgirl. Luckily, or maybe it's unluckily, Martha gets in the way of my straight beeline to Take-Me Town.

"Thank you," Martha tells Gabe as she comes out, an unfamiliar smile on her face. "Saved me the trouble. I was about to do the same damn thing." We all know that's not the least bit true. Even if she'd wanted to, I don't think Martha, as intimidating as she is, has anything on the fear factor Gabe can inspire. "Though I'd appreciate it if you'd let me do the kicking out next time."

Gabe nods, and Martha hums, satisfied.

Martha turns to me. "Looks like you've got an extra burger and fries. Why don't you give that to your friend as a thank you? Then help us get caught up and get outta here. You've earned it, and Elaine and I can handle this place. We did for years before you came along, honey."

I start to argue out of habit, the running totals of bills versus tips sizing up in my mind. But tonight, I can't seem to care. Martha is right. I've earned this.

A night off to be young, dumb, and broke, as the song says. I've never had that, always too serious, too weighed down with responsibilities, too stuck in could've-beens from my past. So tonight, I'm shrugging all that off. And telling the mini-Charlotte on my shoulder to shut up and let me be a little wanton tonight if I want to be.

I look to Elaine, who nods, eyes darting to Gabe and then the door, telling me to take that man and go.

"Thanks." I shove the cheeseburger plate in front of Gabe, who's sat back down at the counter, promising, "I'll be quick."

He picks up a fry, taking a big bite and talking around it. "I'm here until you're ready to go. Whenever that is." And then he winks at me, like a legitimate, actual wink. That's something I thought guys only did as a cheesy pickup move, but on Gabe, it looks sexy. Like he knows tonight's something special for me.

Heat creeps up my neck, and I know my face is probably a few shades of bright pink as I get to work.

It seems like everyone in the diner is in on the 'Get Izzy Out of Here' plan because every table is beyond easy, asking for refills and a check or saying they haven't had Martha as a waitress in so long, they'd like to request her. I sneak glances at Gabe, who's shoving the burger and fries down his throat like he wants to be done as fast as possible.

Me too, man. Me fucking too.

Fifteen minutes later, I've helped clear out the main floor and Martha's standing in front of me with a to-go box. "Take this and get out. I'll see you tomorrow."

I take the box, handing it to Gabe to hold while I run to the back. I'm definitely hustling now, elbows damn-near pumping to get to my purse as fast as I can. I take a quick minute to yank a brush through my hair, slick on ChapStick, and pop a mint.

I can't do much about the fry grease-smelling shirt, so I spritz a little body spray on top of it, hoping French fry-lavender is a pleasing combo.

When I come back out, I can feel everyone's eyes on me, but mine meet Gabe's and never waver. I watch as the light sparks in the darkness there, see the slight crinkles at the corners as his smile blooms in slow motion. "Ready?"

"Yep." I mean it to sound cool and casual, but it comes out breathy and dreamy.

His smile turns to a cocky smirk, knowing that he's causing me to lose it. But it's mutual. For all his chill control, I can feel the swirling tension coming off him in waves. And fuck, do I want to swim in that ocean, get pulled under by his riptide, even if it sets me adrift in his wake after he's gone.

He holds out a hand, and I slip mine into it, interweaving our fingers. As we walk out, I almost feel like it's a movie, the diner customers watching out the window as we make our way across the lot.

We stop next to a red SUV and Gabe opens the door for me. I start to climb in and then freeze. "Where are we going?"

"First, we're going right here. Martha told me there's cherry pie and ice cream in this box, so we need to eat it now or the ice cream will melt and ruin the pie. We probably could've eaten it inside, but I was afraid if I didn't get you out of there, we'd never leave."

I laugh, knowing he's right. "And then?"

He moves in close, not touching his body to mine, but so close that I can feel the electricity flowing between us. I tilt my chin up, inviting him, damn-near begging him to kiss me, wanting to taste him and see if he's dark and bitter like coffee or sweet and bright like candy. Maybe a mix of the two?

But he doesn't kiss me, instead using his free hand to cup my jaw. "And then we'll see where we want to go from there."

He's giving me an out. A gentlemanly thing to do, a way to slow the pace to whatever I'm comfortable with. But tonight, I don't want slow and nice. I want . . . Gabe.

"Cherry pie with cream it is," I say, teasingly channeling my inner Jessica Rabbit sultriness.

He laughs, and I'm not sure that's a good thing, but I go with it and laugh back as he helps me into the SUV. He walks around to the driver side, getting in and setting the to-go box on the console between us.

He opens the plastic-wrapped spoon, looking at me only half apologetically. "Martha said you were running short on plasticware, only gave me the one."

Ooh, that sneaky fox. I know there's a whole box of plastic spoons, forks, knives, even sporks in the store room. But in this case, I'm not arguing as Gabe scoops up a mouthful of delectable dessert and offers it to me.

I let him feed me and smile as he alternates, feeding himself from the same spoon too. "It's good, right? Martha's family recipe."

He moans appreciatively, and the sound makes me imagine what he'd sound like slipping into me.

His thoughts don't seem to be as dirty as mine because he asks, "Tell me about you? Who is Isabella Turner?"

The way he looks at me warms me in a different way. Mia and Char know my story, and after working here so long, Elaine does too, but not everyone listens. He seems actually interested, though, not like he's making polite conversation and expecting a textbook 'normal childhood' story.

"Well, let's see. I wasn't born here in Roseboro," I start, looking down. "My family and I lived up near Tacoma, my parents and my big brother. I . . . I lost them when I was only five."

"I'm sorry," Gabe says quietly, but not in that uselessly superficial way. Instead, he looks like he genuinely feels bad for me. "What happened?"

"A plane crash," I whisper. "Uhm, Dad was a businessman. I guess a lot of businessmen have a side hobby, but instead of golf or art or anything like that, he was into airplanes. I only remember little bits, but his home office was filled with models, and he had this Cessna. He'd take us up, fly us over Puget Sound, but I didn't go up often. I was little and Mom was nervous about me touching something I shouldn't. So Dad would let me sit in his lap when the plane was grounded, letting me pretend to fly as he promised that one day, he'd teach me. They left me at home with a sitter that day. Freak accident that couldn't have been prevented. Dad . . ."

I choke a bit and clear my throat to cover it. "He did everything right, did all he could. It just wasn't enough."

I wipe a tear from beneath my eye and look down. "Sorry, that's probably more than you wanted to hear."

I know better than to get too deep into the tragedy of my childhood. Most people don't truly care or they think I should be over it by now. It's always safer to gloss over it and move along, but something about Gabe made me feel safe enough to share. That instinct proves accurate when he doesn't flinch away but instead asks for more.

"I'm sorry, Bella," Gabe says again. "What happened afterward?"

"Well, I was sent to live with my aunt, my mom's sister. She was the only person left in my family who could care for a young kid. She lived here in Roseboro, so I moved here to stay with her. My grandparents were older, but they helped as much as they could. They passed a few years later, and then it was just me and Reggie."

I sigh, looking down as I twist the napkin in my hands. "Reggie was kind. She had a lot of love in her, but not much else. She was my mother's older sister, the wild child of the family. She'd *mostly* settled down by the time I came around, and taking care of me left her with no time for crazy escapades. But she didn't have a diploma or any real skills to speak of, and her body was decades older than it should've been from the years of abuse. So she couldn't work much, and when she did, we . . . well, things were like that old Wu Tang track. Rough and tough like leather. But she loved me, and I loved her. She was all I had."

"Was?" Gabe says quietly. "When did she pass?"

"Three weeks after I graduated high school," I recall. "Pancreatic cancer. Fast and lethal. The hospital bills sucked up all we had, ironically taking the small inheritance I had left from my parents because we'd been too busy working, didn't have time to get it transferred out of Reggie's name. The hospital didn't care that it was really my money, not hers, saying that since she was techni- cally on the account, they were taking their money first. It was all of it."

I can't help but huff a humorless laugh at the memory of the scared eighteen-year-old kid I'd been, begging a guy in a suit to leave me with something as he shrugged his shoulders like there was nothing he could do.

"And that guy I was telling you about?"

"Ah, that guy," Gabe says, his voice dropping to a fierce rumble. "How's he fit in?"

"Reggie bought the house a long time ago and had paid it off with my parents' money to give me a secure place to grow up. But it sits on land that's owned by someone else, originally

Russell's parents. Their family bought it back when it was mill housing for the factory workers, I think. They wouldn't sell Reggie the land, but they didn't charge her much for the lease. After she died, they told me they'd do the same thing for me, which was a huge relief. They were decent people, knew that house was all I had left of my family."

I growl, my mood shifting, "But when they died, Russell took over and things went to hell in a handbasket. Russell's the creepy neighbor."

Gabe looks at me sharply, his voice low and protective. "Any more trouble?"

I shake my head, trying to be reassuring. "No. The gun is put away safely, but I can get to it if he gets squirrelly. I really think he's more talk and bluster than action, though." I silently pray that saying the words will make it truer because the reality is, I don't believe Rusty is harmless and mouthy. I think he's getting more and more dangerous as each passing day draws him deeper into addiction.

I can tell Gabe doesn't quite believe me, but he lets it go, surmising with a bit of awe, "But you keep going. You've never given up."

"No . . . I guess I haven't," I admit. "Reggie always taught me that education was the way out, said dropping out was her biggest regret. So I worked my ass off in high school to get good grades while helping with the household bills, and I'm still working my butt off, paying my way through college, semester by semester. It's taking forever, but I'm going to get there." This time, I don't need the universe to hear the truth of the words. I'm going to make it happen myself, no matter what.

"I admire that," Gabe says honestly. "You've fought for everything you have, and when you have what you want in life, you can look back and say you earned every bit of it. Not too many people can honestly say that."

I chuckle, and Gabe tilts his head at the odd response to his compliment. "What?"

"You should meet my friend, Mia. She's got this saying." I adopt her fake Russian accent. "*Don't ask for it, Tovarich. Earn it. Do that, and you'll be rewarded.*"

Gabe's brows shoot together, the question in his chocolate eyes before his mouth forms the word. "*Tovarich*? Mia's . . . Russian?"

I lightly tap his arm, careful not to spill the melted mess of ice cream in the to-go box between us. "Very good. She'd be proud. We tease her that she's pseudo-Russian. Her Papa most definitely is, but Mia was born in the US. Her history is important to her, though, and she has all these 'Russian' sayings and can put on an accent that'd make you think she grew up in Central Moscow. She's a hoot, a rainbow-haired, number-crunching geek who just moved in with her uptight, suit-and-tie-type man."

Gabe hums, smiling a little as he deadpans, "Sounds like a match made in heaven." He finishes with, "Wise words, though."

"So what about—" I ask, but before I can ask about his life story, the light in the parking lot changes. I look over to the front of the diner and see the glowing red 'Open' sign has gone dark. Inside, I can see Elaine, Henry, and Martha peering out the door, smiles on their faces as they very obviously talk about the fancy Range Rover in the lot and its two occupants. "Oh, God, they probably think we're fucking right here in the diner lot," I mumble, burying my face in my palms.

Gabe's laugh is a big burst from his belly, filling the cabin of the Rover. "You make a habit of that? Or have a lot of problems with lot lizards?"

I turn my head, glaring at him. "Of course not. The Gravy Train is a classy joint." I say it with a straight face but can't hold it, and suddenly, I'm laughing too.

"Maybe we'd better get on out of here?" Gabe asks. "Before they call the cops on questionable activities in their parking lot?"

He's still asking, kind and sweet, about our progress even as I sense the need churning in him. But he's got it on lockdown, controlling the wildness I want him to unleash.

"Definitely," I say before my fear changes my mind. I'm not scared of Gabe, not at all, but maybe of doing something crazy just because I want to.

It's not the responsible and future-minded Izzy I've always been. But a bit of untamed joy in the present moment sounds like something I've always needed and pushed aside. Maybe it's not the right time to indulge, with Russell threatening me, school finals looming, and next semester's fees due any day. But maybe it's the conglomeration of those things that makes this the perfect time to let loose for once.

I deserve this. I've earned this.

Gabe starts the SUV, the headlights turning on automatically and the instrument panel glow lighting his face. I can see his relief that I agreed, his desire burning my skin where his gaze touches me. It's a lot to take in, and I inhale, turning toward the window for a moment to let the butterflies in my belly settle.

I see that Elaine's smile is huge now, a knowing look in her eyes, and then she waves goodbye with a nod, like she's proud of me for doing something just for me for once.

I wave back, and as Gabe pulls out of the lot and into the light midnight traffic, I sink into the seat, letting the luxurious leather wrap around me. I've never done anything like this before.

"So, where are we going, anyway?" I ask as Gabe gives me a dazzling smile, his dimples bookending his white teeth.

"It's a secret," Gabe says with a lift of his brow. "A gem of a place I discovered."

CHAPTER 12

GABRIEL

*I*sabella sits quietly in the passenger seat as I drive, the twin headlights of my 'real' vehicle stabbing the night. I enjoy this Range Rover a lot more than the nondescript throw-away truck I've been using as a work truck, if only for the ride.

It's interesting to see Isabella tense, then relax as I accelerate out of Roseboro. I suspect she's been riding that scooter for so long that she's forgotten what sixty miles an hour feels like as the lights of the city pass us in a blur.

Or maybe her intermittent stiffness is because of me. I have to remember that while I know everything about her, both from her lips and from her file, I'm a virtually unknown entity to her. I'm sure that's weighing on her as much as the speed with which we're racing out of town.

We get to the parking area closest to the secluded spot I found, and I come around, opening the door for her. I help her step down, warning, "Careful, it's a bit of a drop." The words resonate in my head like warning bells, but I refocus on here and now, on Bella.

Looking in the back of my Rover, I grab a military surplus parka out of the back, nothing fancy but something I keep for bad weather . . . although the camo print has proven useful once or twice for surveillance.

Bella smiles as I shake it out flamboyantly, unzipping it and slipping it over her shoulders. "Nice."

"Thanks," I reply, zipping the coat up the front of her, watching as her curves disappear beneath the coat. The oversized parka almost swallows her. She looks . . . adorable, and it makes my heart twist in my chest. "I got it for rainstorms. You know how they can sometimes spring up and catch you unaware."

"Not just weather. Life does that too," Bella says, adjusting the cuffs and zipper, and truer words have never been spoken. She certainly caught me unaware, is still surprising me at every turn. "So, where are we going?"

"It's not far. We'll take the easy route," I say, reaching out and taking her hand.

She pulls me back, her voice sassing in the dimness, "I don't need the easy route."

This woman, challenging me when she doesn't even need to, scared to let something be comfortable because she's so used to fighting for every scrap and morsel she gets, and accustomed to life being hard for no sensible reason.

I shrug like that doesn't gut me and ask straight-faced, "Suit yourself. I guess that means you're an experienced nighttime free-climber then?"

Her eyes shoot wide open as her jaw drops. "A night what? Climbing what?" I can see her backpedaling literally as she takes a step closer to the SUV like she's going to hop back inside.

"The spot I want to show you, it's accessible two ways. One, by the short, easy hiking path I planned. Or two, by climbing up the rock face from the valley below. Your call, just let me know if I should grab my gear. I have two sets. I follow the Boy Scout motto of 'Be prepared.' " I wait patiently, curious how she's going to back out of this because she obviously has no desire to rock climb, especially by the light of the midnight moon.

After the span of two slow breaths, I let her off the hook and offer an easy grin. "Hike sounds best to me. Never know what creepy crawlies might be on the rock face at night."

She shudders, obviously not liking the idea of nocturnal insects or other animals. "Fine. If you'd rather hike, we can do that."

I laugh loudly that she's still not admitting that she can't do the climb but is instead sticking with using me as her out. She glares at me, shooting daggers, but then cracks up too. Our laughter echoes through the trees, disturbing some night fliers, judging by the sound of flapping wings.

Bella steps a bit closer to me and I whisper in her ear, "No worries. I'll protect you from the bugs."

I let my thumb trace a circle on her hand, feeling the soft satin of her skin. She nods and finally, we're off.

Using a flashlight from my gear pack, we walk up the hill, listening to the sound of the waterfall get closer and closer. When we emerge around a bend in the trail, I stop, looking over the scene. We're both silent, taking it all in.

"It's beautiful."

Bella's hand comes to her chest, and I can understand. The moon's broken through the clouds that have been peppering the sky all night, and now it's in its full glory, huge and silver as it shines down on the forest below. The whole scene looks ethereally frosted, not frozen but like it was crafted out of ebony and velvet, dusted with diamonds, and lit from within by the slowly pulsing heart of the forest itself.

"Gabe, this is amazing," Bella whispers, her voice choking. She walks to the edge, gasping again. "I can see most of Roseboro from here!"

I come up behind her, placing my hands on her waist. Even

through the parka, I can feel the flare of her hip, the nip in at her midriff.

Part of me wants to pull her from the edge, hold her closer and grind on her until our bodies demand more.

I'm ashamed to say there's a tiny part, fractionally small, that hisses I could do it here, shove her over the edge into the black valley, fast and painless, and that the camo jacket I gave her out of kindness would likely hide her body until I could get safely out of town. That tiny bit even argues that it'd lead to too many questions because several people saw me leave with her tonight, and that'd make me suspect number one in her disappearance.

But even with the automatic response slithering through my psyche, I know it's not happening. I've already made up my mind. I blink slowly, staring into the stars above us.

Sorry, Jer, I can't. Not her.

There's no response, but I'd like to think he understands. There's got to be a way. A different way.

"This place is magical," Bella says, breaking into my dark thoughts as she leans back against me, pulling my arms around her. "How'd you find it? Did you really rock climb up here?"

I swallow, inhaling the scent of her hair and holding her more tightly, betraying my contracted word but honoring my loyalty to myself in a way I haven't in a long time. "I did. It's not as crazy as it sounds." I'm hedging. It's absolutely as insane as it seems, but that's why I love it. "Honestly? I've always been an outdoors kind of guy. This place kind of reminds me of when I was a kid."

"I'd like that story," Bella says, rubbing my arm to keep me warm since she's bundled in the one coat, but I think it's also because she's tracing the muscles in my forearm. *Arm porn girl*, I think with a cocky grin she can't see. I flex a bit, squeezing her jacket and popping the muscles for her. Though her eyes stay locked on the amazing view, I feel her legs move like she's trying to subtly rub her thighs together for relief, and heat blooms in my balls.

"Or do you bring all of your conquests into the woods like a wild man?" I can hear what she's truly asking disguised in the joking question. This sweet woman, who never takes care of herself but is choosing to spend her precious time with me tonight, wants to know if this is as special to me as it is to her.

"You're the first," I reply, and I feel Bella's chuckle before I hear it, her back bouncing against my chest. "What?"

"I seriously doubt I'm your first anything, Gabe."

I lean down and bury my nose in her hair before nuzzling her ear. "Point taken. I mean the first here. I just found it a few days ago, and I wanted to share it with you."

What the fuck am I doing?

It's one thing to fail a contract, to go back on my word and refuse it mid-agreement by not killing her. It's quite another to bring my work into my personal life. But unwittingly, that's exactly what I've done. Isabella Turner hasn't been a job for a while now. She's been something else entirely. I'm not sure what it is, exactly, but I want to know everything about her, protect her at all costs, even from herself, and somehow make her every dream come true.

Nothing big or major or hard about any of that, I think sarcastically. *Should be able to get that checked off the to-do list in no time.*

But self-recriminations aside, it's the truth of what I want. And I don't have the first fucking clue about what to do about it, especially when the safest thing for me to do is to bail, to hit the highway and just run pell-mell back to a life where every day is the same, a cold existence where my primary focus is tracking down my brother's killer.

Bella looks over her shoulder, smiling wryly. "Does that mean I'm *special*?" Disbelief drips from her tone, like it's the cheesiest of distasteful pickup lines. Like off-brand Velveeta in word form.

One look in her eyes, and I feel my resolve crumble. I'm not going to kill her like I was hired to do, *and* I'm not going to walk away like I should do.

Instead, I answer honestly, from my heart and my gut. "Bella, you're far more special than you realize, more than I dreamed."

I can tell she doesn't believe me. "You . . . you confuse me."

I turn her around, wrapping my arms around her waist again and pulling her tight to me, where she gulps when she feels the rising thickness of my cock against her belly. "Is that so?"

"You're not the first to hit on me at the diner. But usually, they wanted just one thing. You . . . you're different."

I touch my forehead to hers. "You have no idea."

She sighs, and I feel the heated breath whisper across my mouth. I lick my lips, trying to taste her.

Her voice is a hoarse whisper, softly rasping in my ear. "You're right. I barely know anything about you, but I feel like this is right. Tell me about you, Gabe."

It's my own question thrown back at me, but whereas she opened up the Pandora's box of her life story, I can't. Even if I wanted to, which surprisingly, I do, I can't tell her. It's too ugly, too monstrous, and she'd never understand.

So I do the only thing I can. I give her my truth with a kiss, molding my mouth over hers as I truly taste her for the first time and hope it's enough to answer her reasonable request for more from me.

She responds immediately, moving her lips with mine and allowing me access to dip my tongue into her on a breathy sigh.

I run my fingers into her hair, tilting her head the way I want and diving in for more, wanting all of her, wanting to give her all of me in this kiss.

Jeremy would want this for me. Blackwell can fuck himself. I'll get the information he's holding over my head another way. Or maybe not at all?

The thought of losing myself in Bella is somehow soft and hazy, a misty dream I hadn't fully considered. But when she mewls under me, pulling a groan from my own chest, I let the fantasy of retribution go in favor of the reality right here in my arms.

I'm a monster, but on her lips, I taste absolution.

Forcing my eyes open, I step her backward toward a nearby rock. But instead of pinning her to it, I turn us and lie back on the cold, rough hardness myself, pulling her against me and letting her have some semblance of power. I don't want to overwhelm her, and I'm barely hanging on to the edge of my control with a white-knuckled grip. Her hands come to my chest, finding the sweatshirt and pulling me in for another kiss.

I slip my hands under the thick parka, cursing it for not letting me feel her nipples pressed to my chest. Instead, I find the belt loops of her jeans and move her hips against me, making her slide along the ridge of my cock to let her know what she's doing to me.

"Fuck, Bella."

She bites her lip, white teeth denting the puffy pink fullness and driving me wild. I shift her, spreading her legs around my right thigh and pressing her core to the thick muscle there. Her hips shudder involuntarily at the sensation, and Bella's eyelashes flutter as her eyes roll back.

I can't give her everything, can't take all that I want from her. But I can give her this. A night she deserves, a night to remember. "Ride me, Bella. Use me to get yourself off."

Her eyes snap to mine, timid hesitancy covering desire. She doesn't move at first, so I guide her, feeling her heat even through our jeans. But soon, her instincts take over and she starts to roll against my thigh.

"Oh, fuck, Gabe . . . but—"

"Do it, Bella," I growl in her ear as I reach around and grab her ass, squeezing the firm cheeks and adding to the feelings shooting through her. "Come on me."

Bella resists for a few seconds, but then the feeling of her clit rubbing against my thigh and my teeth tugging on her ear over-whelm her resistance, and the sound that comes from her is the sexiest thing I've ever heard in my life. *"Fuuuck . . ."*

I kiss her neck, feeling the flutter of her heartbeat and letting her have control of what she needs. It's torture, guilt and desire pulsing through me with every beat of my heart. My cock aches. She's so sexy that I can barely contain myself, but the fact that just minutes ago, that dark voice was encouraging me to kill her makes me want to punish myself, deny myself the pleasure I know she could bring me.

Instead, this is for her, and I take my joy from every sound Bella makes as she dissolves in my arms, lost to an ecstasy she so rarely gets in her rough life.

As her hips speed up and her body starts to tremble harder, I encourage her. "That's it. Rub that pussy on me." She moans, and I want to swallow the sound. I keep going, judging that she likes the dirty words pouring from my mouth. "You need this, Bella. Fuck, I need this. I can feel how hot you are, probably messy with your delicious honey. You gonna let me feel you come, then let me lick you clean?"

She loses the rhythm, and I take over, pulling and pushing her back and forth as I flex beneath her. Her hands dig into my shoulders, and then gloriously, her head falls back and she cries her orgasm to the night sky. It's a symphony of sex, and I love every stunning note, instantly wanting an encore.

"Oh, my God," Bella rasps when it's over, and I let her down slowly, the moonlight illuminating her rapturous face. "That was . . ." She searches for words before she meets my gaze, clear-eyed and powerful, demanding, "More."

That I can do.

And while it's faint comfort for the pretenses this began under, I'm going to assuage my guilt by devoting myself to giving Bella as much pleasure as she can handle for as long as she wants me.

And I'm going to protect her—from Blackwell, from me, and from herself.

CHAPTER 13

GABRIEL

*I*t feels strange and exhilarating to pull up in front of Bella's house *with* her and not to scope out her routine. Bella's almost drunk on desire as I pull her into my arms again, kissing her deeply as she fumbles with the gate latch, giggling as we make our way up the walkway.

I cup her breast over top of her shirt before we even make it inside. The parka's gone, banished again to the back of my Range Rover, and I feel her nipple pebble under my fingers as I tug, making her moan.

"I fucking need to be inside you," I growl against her neck.

"Let's get inside so I don't give Old Mrs. Petrie a heart attack," she says, glancing over her shoulder to the house across the street. And then she drops her voice low and slow, "And so I can have something softer for my knees."

The naughtiness in her voice draws me with her like she put a leash on my desire and I'm at the mercy of her whims. She unlocks her door and enters, not even reaching for the light switch. I wonder if she's trying to hide the reality of her home from me, like it's something she can ignore if she doesn't turn the light on. But truthfully, all I see is her, even in the dark.

Besides, you already know what her house looks like, fucking creeper.

Instead, we walk through the darkness, her fingers wrapped in mine as she pulls me down the hall to her room. The blinds are open, the streetlight shining in, and we're greeted by the same cat who slashed me this morning.

It yowls when it sees me, leaping to its feet, back arched and green eyes glowing with malice. It apparently hasn't forgotten my intrusion into its domain this morning, but Bella just laughs.

"Vash, relax, honey! He's our guest!"

Shooing Vash out of the bedroom, she closes the door quickly, turning and grinning sheepishly at me. "Sorry . . . she's usually a sweet kitty. I don't know what got into her."

"Jealousy?" I ask, lifting an eyebrow. "Pheromones?"

Bella laughs, while inwardly, I remind myself to make peace with that damn cat ASAP. "I guess there are some things you can't charm, huh?"

"I'll work my magic on Vash later. Right now, I'm only thinking about charming you," I reply as I look into Bella's eyes. Even in the dim light, I can tell that she wants this, whatever it is between us.

She made a comment that she's not a one-night-stand girl, and that doesn't surprise me, but she's not asking for more than that right now. I think she probably expects me to be gone in the morning, if not before. But she doesn't realize this is the first step toward something bigger, deeper than just tonight.

She may not realize it yet, but I do.

I don't have it all planned out in my usual way, but I'll figure it out. Just not right now, not when I can feel her body stretching toward mine. And especially not when she reminds me of her earlier demand, "More."

Reaching down, I pull my sweatshirt and T-shirt off, letting Bella see me naked from the waist up. My breath hitches at the contact of her hands on my chest, her palms lightly rubbing through the faint dusting of hair.

"So many tattoos? I want to lick them all," she confesses, or maybe it's a promise.

My cock throbs at the thought of her pink tongue dragging over my skin, and I palm myself, trying to get some relief.

"Lie down," she whispers, pushing me back toward the mattress on the floor. I nod and step back, toeing my boots off as I sit down and she stands above me, her own eyes gleaming in the light.

She strips quickly and efficiently, but the sight of her naked form clad in nothing but dim street light will stay in my memory banks forever. The cool air makes her nipples harden as soon as she has her bra off, and her bare pussy beckons to me. She pulls the clip from her hair, and the dark waves tumble over her shoulders beautifully.

"Fucking gorgeous, Bella."

She smiles, looking pleased at the compliment, and then she kneels down on the mattress beside me, my hand finding her goosebumped skin. "Not yet . . . it's my turn."

She seems utterly confident as I let her lead and explore, her hand making its way to feel my cock through my jeans. I'm already painfully aroused for her before she even touches me, and I groan as she brings me to an impossibly steely hardness in an instant, my balls already drawing up and threatening to spill like an out of control teenager.

"You like that?" she purrs, kissing me as her soft hand slowly massages my cock, warmth divided by just a thin layer of denim.

Pressing her body against mine, her hand naughtily plays with my belt, teasing and tormenting me. Finally, she turns, presenting her pussy to me as she kisses down my stomach, tracing the ridges of my abs and a few of my tattoos with her tongue. She opens my jeans, humming happily as my cock tents my boxers.

I run my hand down her back, caressing her ass as she fishes my cock out. I lift my hips, helping her shove my jeans and boxers off, and then we're bare together, every contact point electricity-filled.

She licks the tip of my cock, making my eyes roll up in my head, and I grip her ass a little harder. It's been more than a little while for me. I've been so fanatical about my quest for revenge that I haven't had time for a woman in my life. I suspect it's been a while for Bella too, so we both have lost time to make up for tonight.

She rains butterfly kisses over the head of my cock, and I fight the urge to shove into the wet heat of her mouth. To keep a restraint on myself, I focus on Bella's pleasure instead of my own.

I bring my fingers lower, between her legs to stroke the soft lips of her pussy, teasing before slipping a fingertip in between. Bella gasps, her lips flaring to cover the entire head of my cock, suckling as I stroke up and down, gathering her wetness on my fingertips before bringing it up to her clit, rubbing her button with featherlight strokes.

"Mmpfh!" Bella moans around my cock, her hips jerking as I find the stroke and pace that she likes best. Her knees spread some more, and in the orange light I find myself enchanted by the gleam of her pussy opening for me as she bucks into my fingers. It's sexy as fuck in its obscenity, a woman taking the pleasure that she wants from me while her mouth and tongue please me back.

I rub my thumb between her lips as I play with her clit, getting it slick and ready before pushing it inside her, where her tight muscles immediately clutch me, almost sucking me in. She's so tight, a slick vise on my thumb as I pump it in and out, guided by the sounds Bella's making. Being inside her mouth and her pussy at the same time short-circuits my brain, and I can't hold back anymore, can't let her be solely in control. I lift my hips, slipping my cock deeper into her mouth, right on the edge of entering her throat.

She pulls back, using her spit and my pre-cum to fist my shaft.

"Oh, God, Gabe . . . more," Bella rasps, pushing her pussy back into me as she pumps my cock. "Stretch me so I can take you, and then fuck me."

Growling, I pull my hand back before replacing my thumb with both of my fingers, thrusting them deep inside her and making Bella moan in pleasure. She bends forward, swallowing as much of my cock as she can while I pump in and out of her, fucking her with my hand as her juices run down my palm and onto the cut on my wrist. Distantly, I realize I lost the bandage somewhere along the way, but I can't care right now.

The slight sting centers me, though, allowing me to focus just on Bella and not on the feeling of her velvety-soft lips wrapped around my shaft or the feeling of her tongue exploring the ridge around the head of my cock. She slurps on me happily as precum oozes out for her to feast on, her pussy gushing around my fingers.

"In my pocket, my wallet," I tell her, not able to wait any longer, and I think she gets my meaning.

I feel her move, reaching for my jeans on the floor. She moans on me when she finds my condom, unwrapping it before pulling off, gasping, "I fucking love Boy Scouts."

"Be prepared, they taught us," I tease breathlessly, adding a third finger to her pussy. "How's that feel?"

"Fucking amazing . . . maybe big enough to not have this kill me." She whimpers as she rolls the condom down my cock. It's tight, but the constricting rim of the condom helps hold back my orgasm as Bella gets me ready before pulling off my fingers and turning around to straddle me, rubbing the head of my cock between her dripping folds. "Are you ready?" I ask her.

I reach up, taking her waist in my hands and helping her as she lowers herself onto my cock, both of us moaning in a sexual harmony as her body wraps itself around my pulsing shaft. She's so warm, her honey-coated walls taking me in and holding me in a perfect embrace. Bella's chest hitches, her breasts shaking as she trembles, wanting more but needing to stop when I'm about halfway inside her.

"Take your time, Princess. I won't hurt you."

The words have so many layers of meaning, more than she could possibly know, and are as much a promise as I can give her right now.

She rides me slowly, my cock sliding deeper and deeper inside her with every rise and fall of her hips until I feel her hips press against mine, and she throws her head back in triumph.

"It feels like you're splitting me in half, but I can't stop," she grunts as her hips take over. I encourage her, reaching up to stroke a stiff nipple, watching as her body bounces up and down on me.

It's the sexiest thing I've ever seen, this beautiful woman getting all the pleasure she can just from me. For once in her life, she's demanding and wanting something selfishly, and I want to give her everything I can, reward her for all the hard times she's gone through, and insure that every day from here on out is better by my side.

I reach around, cupping her ass and helping her. "I have you, Bella . . . I have you," I murmur, more to myself than her, making sure this is reality and not some dream I'll wake up from. I thrust up into her as she comes down, meeting her body with my own as I marvel in the sight of her on top of me.

She's a princess, a queen, and I vow in this moment that I will do what I can to be her knight in tarnished armor.

Bella's hips plunge up and down on my cock, both of us rising together until she pitches forward, kissing me deeply. Her pussy clenches around my cock, and she moans her orgasm into my mouth, gifting me with her release.

It pushes me over the edge, and I hold her tight, thrusting two more times until I explode, filling the condom with hot cum. My body shakes as we fall apart together, her lips grounding me as I hold her safe. And that feels like exactly what I want . . . for her to give me the foundation I haven't had since Jeremy died, and in return, I'll make sure she's happy and secure. In this moment and every other.

We lie together, the sweat cooling on our bodies until she shivers, and I wiggle around to pull at the blankets. I arrange them over us until we're wrapped up like a twin burrito, not perfect but still warm. I grab her single pillow and tuck it underneath my head, pulling her to nestle against my chest with my arm wrapped around her shoulders. "Comfy?"

"Mmm-hmm," she says sleepily. Moments later, she's snoring softly, her body exhausted by all that she's done today. I hold her carefully, close enough to feel her body without waking her while my mind works overtime.

I wasn't kidding about being a Boy Scout, and in my line of work, preparation is key to successful contracts. But I'm unprepared for my current situation and I need to rectify that. I think over what I know.

Blackwell said he wanted Bella killed to send a message to someone else, so she's not the player here but merely a pawn. Perhaps there's a way I can leverage that, offer an alternative path to his endgame?

But from what I know of Blackwell, and that's a significant amount of intel because I don't take contracts lightly, he is not the type to allow an outsider to have input into his chosen strategy. I'm merely a tool for him to use, a resource for a skillset he doesn't wish to employ himself.

So he's not going to let this go, of that I'm reasonably certain. I can put him off for another couple of days, but with the degree of suspicion and impatience he's already fostering, I wouldn't put it past him to line up another hit. And include me in the target roster.

I consider reversing the game. I'm a skilled hitman. Perhaps I should flip the script and take out the threat to Bella . . . Blackwell himself. That'd solve the problem, but it'd be beyond difficult. He's aware of my presence, so the element of surprise is nonexistent. And he's well-protected with enough security that it'd be nearly impossible to get close to him unless I called for a meeting, and doing that would make for a messy exit.

The answer that makes the most sense is to run. Take her with me and leave Roseboro forever. We could do it, start fresh somewhere no one has ever heard of Blackwell. But even as I dream of laying Bella on a sandy beach somewhere exotic where it's just the two of us, I know she won't go. Not even if I tell her the truth, which I need to do regardless. But I know her. If she thinks Blackwell is using her for some reason, my girl is going to put her face to the storm and rage back to protect whoever Blackwell is trying to get at.

Which puts me back at square one. My mind continues to turn, but slowly, the warmth of Bella's body seeps into me, and I drift off. No answers, but all I need is in my arms.

Early in the morning hours, I wake and watch her sleeping. My fitful slumber contrasts with her peaceful exhaustion, and I marvel at the rest of the truly innocent. It's something I can never again have but something I want to protect now. Tracing her back and teasing her to wakefulness, I slip into her once again. It feels like . . . heaven.

CHAPTER 14

ISABELLA

I feel the soft touch of something on my neck and ear, making me giggle lightly as it nudges me from sleep. Something warm and hairy rubs against my cheek, and I wiggle, wondering how Gabe got so fuzzy overnight.

"Really? I've got morning breath," I say, turning my head away, but a smile takes over my face.

Meow.

My eyes flutter open to see Vash curled up next to me, her head tilted to the side quizzically like she's asking me just what I mean. Stretching, I reach over and realize I'm in bed alone, at least human-wise.

For a moment, I think maybe I dreamed the whole thing, conjured it up out of my desire to do something crazy, be irresponsible for once, and to feel Gabe's body against my own. But as fast as I think I made the whole thing up, my body lets me know that last night was real. Very real, and very large.

I stretch out my muscles, loving the way they feel used in different way. This isn't the typical sore-feet and tired calves I wake up to, but rather a whole-body feeling of Jell-O.

Meow!

"Vash . . . off!" I grumble, nudging her away. Instead of scrambling, Vash tosses her head and jumps down, confident that she's woken her human up properly and that we're about to get on with the day.

Dammit.

Disappointment floods me as I realize Gabe really has left, and I panic a little, worrying at how stupid I've been.

"Hit it and quit it," I whisper.

I told myself I was going to go with it and have fun, and I did. I don't regret that, but I can't help but have a twinge of something sharp in my belly. More than disappointment, maybe disenchantment? I guess I hoped Gabe was different.

A flash of white on the floor next to my panties catches my attention, and I sit up, realizing that all my clothes are neatly folded, and my bag, which I left in Gabe's SUV, is sitting next to the pile. The white is a piece of cardstock, one I'm familiar with since it's the same cardboard that The Gravy Train uses for their take-home container tops.

This one's been folded in half, though, tented, and has a large *Bella* written on it. Reaching out, I open it.

Princess,

I'm sorry I didn't wake you, but you looked so peaceful and I know you need sleep with your busy schedule. I had to go to work, but trust me, there is nothing I would've rather done than to hold you all morning.

I know I promised you a ride to the diner to get your scooter, and I'm sorry I couldn't do that before I leave. But I left you a little something on the kitchen counter to make up for it and make your day a bit easier.

I'll see you tonight, nine o'clock sharp, but I'll be thinking about you all day.

It's signed with a scratchy capital G that I trace with my fingertip. Okay, so he left, but he didn't bail on me. That's a good sign, right?

Touched, curious, and desperately needing to pee, I get out of bed and slip into the bathroom, where I take care of biz quickly before walking into the kitchen. I am floored by what I find.

It's a bag . . . a *big* bag, and while the red and yellow 'M' on the side might not be my favorite restaurant in town, the smell of pancakes, syrup, sausage, and cheese inside has my mouth already watering. I haven't had a real breakfast in too long, and I can't believe he'd do this for me.

More surprising is what I find inside the thoughtfully folded shut bag. In addition to three sandwiches, there's a small carton of milk with *Vash* written on it. It's so sweet of him to think of her, especially considering she wasn't particularly welcoming last night. It's then I see the cup of coffee, bottle of orange juice . . . and a Range Rover key fob. Shocked, I look up through the front window, and it's still there, candy-apple red and gleaming in the morning light.

I press the key against my chest, everything feeling like I'm being broken apart again. It's such a kind gesture, the type of thing I'm not used to people offering. And if I'm honest, the sort of charitable generosity I'd refuse if Mia or Charlotte tried to foist it on me. But from Gabe, it feels different. Like he's taking care of me because he wants to, not because he thinks I'm failing at doing it myself. That's probably fodder for a therapist, or at least a wine-fueled girls' night in, but right now, I'm not examining it too much.

Take life as it comes, Izzy. And enjoy.

My body hums happily in soreness from last night, my eyes itchy with tears that I don't want to let fall, and my stomach grumbles for the smorgasbord of food before me. This could be the start of an awesome day.

Meow.

I look down to see Vashy rubbing against my legs piteously, and I'm sure she's hungry. Grabbing the milk, I open it and pour a saucer for her. I'll get her food out before I leave.

"Okay, Vashy . . . ten minutes' vacation before we get back to the grind, okay?"

Vash meows again, looking at the bag, and I chuckle.

No wonder Gabe included three sandwiches.

～

"UH-OH. CHAR, I THINK WE HAVE A PROBLEM."

My two besties lean against each other, whispering and giggling loud enough for me to hear them as I walk into the cafeteria at Goldstone Inc.

Mia had begged for us to do our weekly lunch on her home turf this time instead of our usual Gravy Train break. She said something about a big project and data this, trends that, and at that point, I'd just agreed to get her to stop talking analytical statistics. I swear, half the reason I went into graphic design was so that I never had to delve as deep into numbers as Mia does. But she loves it, thankfully. Better her than me, I suppose.

"What?" I ask, checking my shirt for stains and that the fly of my black skinny jeans hasn't slipped down. *There's nothing out of place*, I think as I slip my dark hair behind my ear. So why are they still smirking at me? "What?" I repeat.

Mia breaks first, drawling out, "Hey, cowgirl, been riding that pony long?"

I finally get the joke they're telling on my behalf and shove at Mia, a sporting laugh popping free even though I try to hold it back. Mia devolves into giggles and even Char looks damn amused at the tease. "I'm not walking funny," I argue good-naturedly, then pause a minute before asking more seriously, "Am I?"

Char rolls her eyes, turning her nose up. "I am not talking about sex when I'm not getting any. You two can take your hot dicks and keep them to yourselves." She sounds half serious, half joking, and Mia's eyes catch mine.

Before we can communicate via eyebrows, though, Mia smiles widely. "You said 'hot dicks'. I'm thinking you're trying to speak it into existence, girl." She nods sagely, and Char huffs, striding off toward the line of people waiting to get lunch.

We follow, silently agreeing to change the subject because Char seems more than a little touchy. I wonder if she had another bad date? But when we get in line, she's perked up, talking to the lady who just brought out a big tray of rolls.

"You have a Hobart mixer that handles the dough with no problem? I splurged and got a KitchenAid a few months ago, but I would give my left arm to play with a commercial setup."

I have no idea what Charlotte's talking about, and I realize that maybe I haven't been the best of friends with her the way I should be. I'm ashamed to admit that I've been a bit caught up in my own mess to push her to share, especially when she's tight-lipped. But I try to draw her out now. "You turning Chef Ramsey on us? I'm up for any taste tests you want to schedule."

She grins a bit, telling the roll lady thanks before answering me, "I've been playing with some recipes and learning a lot. I really love baking. Cakes, pies, cookies, rolls, breads. All of it. It's a bit magical, adding all these basic ingredients in precise measurements, mixing it properly, all *just* so. But then you bake it, and instead of some boring result, it's beautiful melt-in-your-mouth goodness."

Mia grabs one of the yeasty, golden rolls and plops it on Charlotte's plate, then does the same to mine and her own. "I'll take some melty, yummy goodies too. Hey! You should do that as a job. It's not like you're happy at Blackwell's, so why not? Ditch your job and chase the yellow *biscuit* road to a bakery gig. Or open your own!" Mia claps like she's solved the biggest problem in the world, which honestly, if it were a math problem, she could likely do.

But Charlotte dips her chin, uncertain. "I don't know. It's more of a hobby right now, my sanity saver. Maybe one day." She sounds wistful and dreamy, but a little lost too. I know she struggles with her current job and the overall pall that is the culture at Blackwell's. Bland, dark, heavy with stressful responsibilities, and definitely not worth the amount of work she puts into her role as receptionist and screener.

But I get why she's doing it. If anyone would, it'd be me. It's not like I dreamed of being a waitress one day, but I'm doing what I need to so that the future is a bit brighter. Char's doing the same.

We sit down and each take several bites of our food. It's not as good as Henry's, but I'm mostly happy just to eat a full meal at one sitting, including, wait for it . . . a salad. An actual salad loaded with fresh, crunchy veggies. I could inhale it. But I savor each bite, thinking I should suggest to Henry that we include a salad option on the menu at the diner. It'd likely sell, and if it didn't, I could take the almost-stale lettuce and carrots home with me. Win-win.

Charlotte returns us to the previous conversation, even though she's the one who said she didn't want to talk about it. "Okay, so give us the Beefy McSmiles update. Just hold back on telling us about the magnificence of his hot dick, 'kay?"

Mia grins, pointing with a carrot stick. "You said 'hot dick' again. Preach it, girl, drop to your knees and send that message to the universe."

I save Mia from Charlotte's friendly backhand smack by answering, "He stayed over last night."

Both their eyes jump to me, locking me in place. I want to tell them everything, but at the same time, I want to hold it all tight to my chest. The memory is like a trembling soap bubble, perfect and swirling but so fragile that even a whisper could pop it, letting the magic fly out. So I stick to the bareboned basics.

"He came to the diner, and then we went for a drive, ended up at my place for the night. He left this morning before I got up but left me his car because he'd promised me a ride to the diner today to get my scooter. He's supposed to come by tonight too." I can feel the stretch of my smile, lips spreading ear to ear as the butterflies slam around in my stomach like it's a heavy metal mosh pit.

"Whoa. One taste and he gave you his car?" Char teases despite her protestations that she's not going to listen to commentary about sexual things. "Izzy, I didn't know you had such a world-class cootch!" She laughs at her own outrageousness.

"Charlotte, please have some manners!" Mia admonishes. "We don't use vulgar terms like that. I prefer to think of it as a perfectly provocative punanny. Much more alliterative."

"Only if she used her punanny," Charlotte volleys back. "What if it was literally a booty call?"

"Hmm, good point. We need more data." They look back to me as they wrap up their comedy routine.

"Enough. You two are crazy. It was *not* a literal booty call," I hiss, trying not to laugh because I don't want to encourage them. I guess I never thought about the weird things we talk about because it was always about Mia or Charlotte, not my nonexistent sex life. But when the spotlight is shining on me, hot and bright, I kind of want to hide like a prudish nun, even though there is nothing puritanical about what I did last night.

Mia slurps from her Coke, her eyes twinkling. "Don't knock it 'till you've tried it." She sets her drink down, asking carefully, "So you're seeing him again tonight?"

"Yes, Mama Mia. He's coming by, and no, I don't know what the plan is. We'll take it as it comes, I guess." It's a reminder to myself more than anything. No expectations, no strings, just enjoy it while I can.

Mia looks to Char, but she holds her hands up, palms facing us. "Nope, I'm out on this little parental lecture. You don't want to know what I think."

I look from one to the other, almost too afraid to ask. "What?"

Mia inhales, still pulling words together as she starts. "Look, when you came in, it wasn't your swaggered walk that sold out what you've been up to. It was the smile on your face. I haven't seen that kind of smile on your face in forever. Like you're actually happy, like the world isn't a giant river of shit you have to slog through." I interrupt, making a disgusted 'ew' face that Char echoes.

Mia ignores us, pointing a blue-tipped nail my way. "You like this guy, a lot. And I love that you are putting yourself out there, and more importantly, putting yourself higher on the priority list. Just be careful, that's all."

Unexpectedly, I feel a sting in my eyes at my friend summing up so disgustingly and eloquently what I'm feeling. Happy, for the first time in a long time. "What if he hurts me?"

Char jumps in. "So what if he does? Just because it hurts, doesn't mean you quit. *Hello*." She gestures at herself, and I wonder again what her latest dating disaster was, wishing she'd talk with us about it. "Of the three of us, you're probably the most well-equipped with handling some painful shit. Lord knows, you've been through the wringer. So who cares if this is a short-term thing or he disappears back to Albuquerque or wherever? You're having fun *now*. He makes you feel special *now*. You deserve that. And that's worth the heartache you might have at the end."

But the look on her face says that's not necessarily true. I can see the pinch around her eyes, the hurt it causes her to say these things. "Are you okay, honey? You can tell us, you know. Whatever the bastard did, we're on your side. Team Charlotte, all the way."

She smiles, though her eyes shine. "It's fine. Just got a little blindsided, but it's a temporary situation. I'm not heartbroken, more just . . . ugh!" She growls instead of labeling whatever it is she's feeling, and my heart hurts for her.

She shakes herself, flinging off the emotions that have overtaken our lunch and sitting up straight. "Okay, immediate subject change. Mia, you're up."

Mia grimaces, not meeting my eyes, and the mood shifts uncomfortably. I see her swallow and know something's wrong. "What's up, Mia? Thomas kick you out already? You can stay with me, you know?" It's meant to be light, because if I know anything, it's that Thomas Goldstone is one hundred percent head over heels for my girl, Mia.

She smiles, not laughing. "Okay, so I did a *thing*. A thing you're going to be mad about, but I swear it was with the best of intentions. Remember that, 'kay?"

My brow furrows. "What did you do?"

I glance to Charlotte, looking for some insight, but she shakes her head. "Nope, all her. But for the record, I agree that she was right. Just putting that out there, up front."

Mia licks her lips and continues. "So, after we talked before, I told Thomas about how Russell was jerking you around, scaring and threatening you."

My jaw drops, genuinely hurt. "That was private." Shame blooms, hot and acidic as it burns its way through my veins.

She nods, rushing onward before I can get too upset. "I know, but listen. So, I told him what was going on and that Russell had been a prick before but had really amped up his bully routine the last few months. So Thomas looked into it."

I glare at her, feeling betrayed but also wanting to know what Thomas found.

"Remember a few months ago when Russell went radio silent for a little while?" I nod, remembering how wonderful that month had been, but it'd been the calm before the storm, because he'd come back with a vengeance, demanding more than ever. "He was in jail for thirty days, ended up with some major legal fees and interest on some drugs he'd bought on credit. That's why he went so hardcore. He truly needs the money to make good on his own shit. And he's using you to do it."

I'm silent, processing everything she said. It makes sense, but Russell's reasons don't change the fact that I still legally owe him.

"Crappy story, but that doesn't change the reality. He's got the legal right to charge me, and I'm going to pay, no matter how hard I have to work, because one day, I'll be caught up." I'm taking Mia's suggestion to heart, speaking it to the universe and hoping fate will help me make it come true.

She rubs at her cuticle with her thumb, showing her nerves, and I realize there's more. "What? Just spill it."

"I paid him," she mumbles under her breath, and I'm sure I misheard her, but then she repeats herself, a bit louder, a bit stronger. "I paid him. The back balance is paid in full, and I set up an account to release the monthly payments on a schedule so he can't hassle you anymore." Her expression is stony, daring me to fight this.

My first reaction is absolute, utter relief. A huge weight off my shoulders, a fear in my belly dissolving, and hope blooming in my heart. Then I realize . . . "I can't let you do that. I can't accept that kind of help, Mia. I appreciate it more than you know, but it's too much." I shake my head vigorously, like that'll make it not true.

She shrugs, like what I just said has no weight at all. "You can't undo it. Thomas helped me set it up so it's all trackable, no cash payments he can say he never got. Russell already took the back payment, so that's a wash. You could stop the monthly payments if you want to, but I'm begging you to let it go."

She reaches across the table, grabbing my hand. "Let me help you this way. I don't want the money back, but if you feel like you need to call it a loan, then wait 'till after you graduate and get settled in a job you love. Then worry about it. I can't sleep another night wondering if that asshole's gone off the rails and hurt you, because he's going to, Izzy. He's losing it, and you're going to be the collateral damage."

Char lays her hand on top of mine and Mia's, the stack of the Three Musketeers ready to tackle the world.

"She's right, Izzy. I know you don't want to hear it, but you need some breathing room, and getting Russell off your ass does that." Her voice is quiet but fierce, brooking no argument. "You're a grown ass woman, and you do a great job handling your own shit, but some problems you shouldn't have to bear on your own, especially when you have awesome friends who are happy to have your back."

I sulk a bit, wishing it hadn't come to this. My head shaking, I try not to be pissed at their ganging up on me, even if it's for a good cause. "I've been scratching and clawing for so long, fighting every step of the way. I won't give up on myself now." They both try to speak, jaws dropping open, but I cut them off. "This is my problem, and I'm going to take care of it."

Charlotte shakes her head, muttering, "Stubborn pain in the ass."

Mia takes the more direct approach, growling, "Your problem, my ass. We may not be blood, but we're sisters." She calms by the slightest margin, pleading, "I can't continue sitting up at night, worrying about you. Do you know that we check in with each other, call The Gravy Train sometimes, all just to make sure nothing has happened to you?"

Charlotte adds to the guilt trip, whispering, "We appreciate that you got a gun, got some training on shooting, but that was before we knew just how desperate Russell is. He's giving me the creeps, honey, and I have a bad feeling about this whole thing. Do what you need to so that you make peace with Mia's help, but take the money."

I look at them both, but they're dead serious. They mean business. And I guess I'd been so lost in my own struggles that I hadn't considered that they might be this worried about me. Hell, at this point, Mia might track Russell down herself and get some of her Russian dad's friends to make a visit. They're teddy bears, but they definitely don't look it.

Letting out a huge sigh, my shoulders sag in defeat. At the end of the day, I know they're doing this because they love me. But my God, they're killing me with this level of kindness.

"Fine," I relent. "But I'm paying you back as soon as I can."

Mia can't even manage to be gracious about winning what I'm betting she thought was a sure loss. She sticks her tongue out at me before saying, "Sure thing. Your first payment is due the next night off you get, two complete hours jamming in a dungeon."

If anyone else said that to me, I'd probably punch them, but Mia's hardcore gaming addiction means there's at least part of her that's always yearning for hours spent in front of a screen with a controller in her hands. It's not my favorite pastime, but Mia is my bestie, so I've played more than my fair share of her favorite game, TERA.

"Deal, but I am paying you back for real."

Maybe they don't understand, but I have to do this. I can't just take the money. Crossing that line once makes it easier to do it again and again. Before you know it, you're saddled with so many emotional weights on your soul, you just give up.

I can't give up.

I won't give up.

"I gotta go, guys," I say, standing up. "But we're good. And really, thank you. I mean it, I really appreciate it."

Mia and Charlotte stand up too, wrapping me in a hug. I stand still for a moment, and then I give in and hug them back. Tears burn my eyes, and I choke out, "Thanks, guys."

"We love you, you know that, right?" Mia says, holding me at arm's length and obviously concerned she's pushed me too far but willing to do it anyway for my own good.

I nod, knowing she's also right. I might not have any blood family . . . but I've still got two sisters. "I know. I love you too."

Getting in the fancy SUV, knowing that this huge axe hanging over my head is gone, feels foreign, like this life isn't my own. But it is. With good friends and a nice guy, maybe I'm finally turning a corner and going to make some progress.

Maybe, after taking part-time classes for so long that I have teacher's aides younger than me, I can finally graduate. Then I will repay Mia.

"Think of it like a . . . private student loan," I tell myself, and though it's a piss-poor balm on my soul, it does help a little bit as I drive home to get ready for work.

I head inside, making sure to lock Gabe's Range Rover. Vash greets me with yowls for food, as always, and I pour her a bit, relieved to know I might be able to afford her next bag more easily.

The knock on the door makes my heart jolt, hope that Gabe stopped by instantly springing to mind. I rush to the door while trying to not get tangled up with Vash, who insists on winding herself around my legs.

"Vash! You trying to kill me, girl?" I ask, taking a huge step to avoid her tail. I'm still looking down at her loud meow as I open the door. "Hey, Ga—"

"What the fuck is going on? You got some bigshot sugar daddy now?" Russell barks, a distasteful sneer on his face.

"Fuck you, Rusty," I growl, moving to slam the door. But he shoves a dirty, cheap workboot-covered foot in the way, blocking me from shutting the door.

"We're not done," he says, an evil grin splitting his ugly face as he slams his palm to the door.

In a twisted way, I'm just thankful he didn't slap me that hard. That's what I've been reduced to, grateful to not be attacked. I wish I had my gun, even though I fought against getting it in the first place. Right now, I wish it was in my hand because I truly fear that Russell is going to push his way into my house. And then it'll just be the two of us.

And I realize that I'm in bigger trouble than I'd ever imagined.

CHAPTER 15

GABRIEL

"*Jeremy!*"

I run around the corner, where chaos reigns supreme. Out of the corner of my eye, I see a black car peeling out of the parking lot, but I'm focused on Jeremy, who's lying on his side.

People are screaming, some running, others frozen in place as they pale in terror.

And somehow, there's a group gathered around him . . . doing nothing. My brother's lying on the ground, and they're not even helping him up.

"Out of the fucking way!" I roar, shoving people aside. Someone grabs my arm, and before I know it, I turn and punch them just so I can break free. It's the next day before someone tells me it was Tiffany Washington whose nose I broke.

Jeremy's bleeding all over the blacktop. There's so much blood that I'm not sure how my little brother held so much inside him. I gather him into my lap, letting his head rest on my leg as I look down at him. "Jeremy . . . don't you fucking die on me!"

"It doesn't hurt, Bro," he whispers, blood trickling out of the corner of his mouth. "But—"

"No," I beg, pressing my hand over the hole in his stomach to stop him

x

143

from leaking all over the place. But the pool of blood under him keeps getting bigger, and it's bubbling up around my fingers. "Jeremy—"

"I love you, Ga—" he says, but before he can complete my name, his body breaks into convulsions. I hold him close, praying it stops, but when he stiffens and a blood-stained breath hits my face, I know.

"Jeremy . . . I promise I'll find who did this."

I wake up in the afternoon dimness, the sun coming through the curtains in sanguine ripples, the dream that haunts my sleep coating my face in sweat. I wipe it away, reminded of how I had to clean Jeremy's blood off my body. He'd soaked everything, and later I found out that both bullets had gone all the way through, one of them clipping his spinal cord, which is why he didn't feel any pain.

Small comfort.

I shudder, sitting up in the cheap motel bed and burying my face in my hands, letting the pain wash over me for as long as it needs to. It's the only way I can face the rest of the day clear-headed.

I remember everything.

I remember watching the ambulance show up, the way they made a big show of trying to help Jeremy at first until they knew it was just that. I remember the look the two paramedics exchanged when they thought I wasn't looking.

I remember the funeral, the way everyone stared at me, the way my parents both seemed to have the light in their eyes just wink out as Jeremy's coffin was lowered into the ground.

I remember everything.

Since that moment, my brother's head cradled in my lap, his last breaths ghosting over my cheek as I pleaded with the Grim Reaper to take me instead, I have never let anyone or anything get in the way of my single-minded pursuit of Jeremy's killer.

I couldn't find out who'd done the shooting the 'proper' way, though I'd tried. The local police proved unable to find the culprit, and the local DA quietly dropped the matter since he was running for re-election and didn't want newspaper headlines about an unsolved murder of a dead teenager messing up his campaign.

So after a while, I turned my back on my friends, my family, my life, and immersed myself in the dark, dirty world that had spawned Jeremy's death.

Along the way, I've gotten plenty of dirt and blood on my soul. It started small, little steps that I thought would get me closer to some kind of answers. But along the way, I got lost. Even with my ethics, my own moral code and rules, the list of my sins is long. More than once, I've wondered if I've become just as evil as the monster I've been searching for.

But I hadn't questioned my life until her. I'd taken this job thinking it was going to be one like so many others, except I would finally get what I'd been searching for . . . the truth. Or at least some real intel that would send me in the right direction.

I wasn't expecting my princess, or this warm buzz in my chest every time I think of her. I pray the feelings I have for Bella aren't just my guilt catching up to me, latching on to an opportunity to feel 'clean' again. Whether she does that to me or not, and she does, she deserves better than to be used just so I don't feel so bad.

I climb out of bed and head to the shower. The hot water pulses on my neck and shoulders, cascading through my hair as I wash, trying to think.

"What should I do, Jeremy?" I ask the steamy bathroom air, trying to get some clarity. "How do I get out of this and do right by her?"

How should I know? You're the one who's spent years learning how to be a killer. You've picked up a few other skills in that time too.

Even in my head, my brother's biting sarcasm resonates, making me feel close to him.

I quickly wash and step out of the shower, drying off before checking my shave in the mirror. A day's growth . . . no need for my razor today. Instead, I head back into the motel room and open up my travel bag, grabbing jeans, a black T-shirt, and a red zip-up hoodie to get dressed. Leaving the motel room, I get into my 'work' truck and drive, trying to think about how I can protect Bella.

It's the million-dollar question that's been tearing me up since I snuck out of Bella's bed this morning with no more ideas than I'd had when I fell asleep with her in my arms.

It's a ticking time bomb situation and I have to make a move.

I pull over into the parking lot of a convenience store on the north side of town. There isn't much else around, and it's ancient enough that there are probably no cameras on the side of the building where I park.

Using the privacy, I pop open the console next to me and take out my burner phone. I dial a number from memory, knowing it'll be missed but that my recipient will get the voicemail and respond accordingly.

"You've reached Larry's Plumbing. I'm out of the office. Leave a message."

"Hi, I've got a problem with my toilet. The ball float won't do its job. If you can replace it ASAP, I'd appreciate it," I say, using the necessary code words. "A rush job, if you're available."

I hang up, knowing I just tacked a hefty fee onto what I'm asking, but there isn't much I can do about it. I need help now.

It doesn't even take two minutes before my phone rings. I pick it up. "Hello?"

"You called about a toilet?" the voice on the other end asks. I've never met Larry the Librarian, but there are few in the under-world who don't know that slightly nasally voice. I do wonder just how he's able to pull off a front of being a plumber, but for all I know, that's just his damn cellphone line. *"A rush job?"*

"Yes, Larry, I did," I reply. I hear the grunt on the other end. He knows me and recognizes my voice. "I need a supplement."

"Just a moment," Larry says, and a moment later, I hear an electronic beep in my ear. *"Go ahead. The line's scrambled."*

"I need everything you can give me on a man named Blackwell."

He whistles, long and low. *"I can't help you with that."*

"Excuse me?" I ask, surprised. Never in the years that I've been using Larry as my primary information broker has he refused a request.

"No. As in, if you want to stay topside and not six feet under in an unmarked hole in the forest, you'll drop any inquiry into that man. There are people you should not look into. He's one of them."

"That a threat?"

"Just advice. From one professional to another. Goodbye, Gabriel."

Before I can say anything else, Larry hangs up. I try the number back, but I don't even get the voicemail, instead getting a computer voice that tells me the number I dialed is no longer available.

Shit.

Not even a moment later, my other phone buzzes, and I see it's a text message.

I want an update.

Speak of the fucking devil.

"Fine, you want an update?" I ask, starting up my truck and pulling out of the convenience store parking lot. "I'll give you one," I say to myself.

CHAPTER 16

BLACKWELL

*T*he office is cloaked in shadow as I sit behind my desk, waiting and plotting. I tap my hand on the desk, quickly shadow fingering my way through Ravel's *Piano Concerto For the Left Hand* to slow my rising blood pressure.

My father, decades ago, had forced a much younger and more malleable version of me to learn the piano as a means of structuring my thoughts. At the time, I'd hated the hours at the ivories, had pleaded to stop practicing, and the dismissive response my father gave had been the beginning of the end of any positive feelings I had about him.

Coupled with the look of disappointment in his eyes when I didn't perform to his satisfaction, on the piano and in my young life, it'd been enough to eventually make me hate the man. Enough that when he died, I got drunk . . . to happily celebrate his passing.

But still, the lessons stuck, and I often find myself absentmindedly pressing out the broad strokes of notes along a nonexistent keyboard.

The clock chimes eight, and my temper rises a notch. Previously, my guest had arrived early, but now, he is precisely on time. A telling change. While not disrespectful per se, it shows the variance in his feelings about this job, perhaps about me. It's a power move that shows his hand, whether he realizes it or not.

The door to my office opens, without a knock, and Gabriel Jackson comes in, unescorted this time. While that could be seen as a sign of danger, I know that my personal security detail frisked the man when he stepped off the elevator and they'd be in here at the press of a button if I needed them. Still, I won't be careless, considering how Gabriel's reputation precedes him.

"Mr. Blackwell."

My hand stops before the second movement of the piano piece, and I stand up, ignoring Gabriel's greeting to walk over to my wet bar. This is also a power move, one of many I employ regularly, allowing me to stand over my guest and to control the beginning of the conversation more readily. The show of good manners also makes people underestimate the degree of cruelty I am capable of.

I pick up a decanter of tequila, not yet looking at Gabriel. Over my shoulder, I toss, "You're late. In many senses of the word."

"Your security man was extra thorough," Gabriel says as I turn around, adjusting his tie as though my guard had left him disheveled. "I haven't been that violated since my last trip through airport security."

"When someone is as dangerous as your reputation says, it's in my best interests to be . . . cautious," I reply, pouring myself a glass and intentionally not offering one to him. "Have a seat."

Gabriel sits, and I lean against the bar to study him for a moment. Typically, I find that a silent, pregnant pause on my part leads others to shift and fidget nervously, especially when they are well aware they have not met my expectations.

But not him.

Gabriel sits still and patient, but ready, a light tension coiled through his muscles. Unable to wait any longer, I let him have the appearance of the upper hand by initiating. "So—"

"There have been developments," Gabriel says evenly, looking unfrazzled as I sip my tequila. "The job has required more finesse than I expected."

"How so? It should be a rather easy one for someone like you." It's a compliment and an accusation in one. "She's unprotected, unskilled, and slinging slop in a rundown diner. Unless your reputation of handling high-value targets is overinflated, this should've been the fastest contract you've ever completed."

I'm tired of excuses, but at the same time intrigued. I have hired gangsters before, usually as muscle to intimidate someone, but Gabriel Jackson is unique. His demeanor demands further study and a little bit of vigilance.

Gabriel nods, folding his fingers together. "Of course not. But she has very powerful friends."

"Which is why I hired you in the first place," I hiss, setting the tumbler of tequila down on the surface of the bar, realizing a beat too late that my outburst exposes my reasoning for being interested in a podunk diner waitress.

"Tell me why you hired *me*, not a thug, for this contract," Gabriel says lightly.

I scoff, dismissing the request. "I'm not here to stroke your ego."

He shakes his head but continues. "Of course not, but perhaps the answer to your concern is contained in the information you already have." He inclines his head, waiting patiently.

"You are thorough, careful, able to meet specific needs of unique jobs. Your reputation as a cold-blooded killer appeals to a certain type. In particular, it works well for power plays." Hmm, perhaps he is correct. The reasons I hired him and not a Craigslist-advertised hitman are rather apparent. "But the results are not holding to your hype," I finish icily.

"Rest assured, I've earned my reputation," Gabriel replies, still looking unruffled. "If you have any questions on my effectiveness, feel free to ask my former employers. They're all men and women who would stand equal to you in their respective fields."

I've been around a long time. I know a veiled threat when I hear one. And while I'm not normally a man to take threats lying down, I say nothing. The situation has become a bit of a chess match. Luckily for me, I don't play by the rules and am quite comfortable stacking the game in my favor.

However, while I have done many things that normal people would consider evil, Gabriel Jackson is the type of man that one keeps at arm's length when possible.

Besides, he's right. I know Gabriel's former employers, and what he says is the truth.

"Then what are the developments that are staying your hand?" I ask.

"As you're aware, I don't create collateral damage. And I will maintain that professional standard."

"You didn't answer the question. What is staying your hand?"

"Her friends," Gabriel challenges. "You said the job was to send a message to someone in her circle. I suspect you did not predict they would anticipate this sort of reaction from you, and she has been given extra protection." He gives me a hard look, daring me to contradict him. It's on the tip of my tongue to tell him that I know more about Thomas Goldstone that he ever will, but I bite that tidbit back, not wanting to further divulge my obsessive nature with an underling.

He continues at my silence. "Each time I've observed her at the diner, she has had three customers consistently with her. Their presence seemed beyond commitment to the subpar food, so I did some looking. I have yet to identify two of them . . . but one I know. She's a private bodyguard, used to work Secret Service a few years ago."

A small amount of pleasure blossoms that perhaps Gabriel has noticed the PI that I hired to follow him. I'm impressed to some degree. But he doesn't know who the man is or what he's been sent to do. Another play in my favor.

Though my PI hasn't mentioned anyone else in play, but perhaps his vision has been so laser-focused on Gabriel, his intended target, that he didn't parcel out other potential hazards to my plan.

"And this stops you how? You've already said you're not doing the job at the diner."

"I've seen this same woman drive by Isabella's house. It gives me *pause*," Gabriel says, drawing the word out. "Mr. Blackwell, understand this. I'm a professional, not a suicide bomber. I'm a man who has a particular set of skills and rules. If you wanted something done at any cost, you wouldn't have come to me."

"So are you telling me that you cannot complete your task?" I ask, wondering how badly this man is trying to fuck me. I wouldn't be surprised if he turned the whole situation around on me, considering my experience with men in his dark line of work, but he surprises me with his answer.

"Hardly . . . just that we should be careful," Gabriel replies. "It's for your protection as much as it is for mine. I just need time. Mr. Blackwell, I do play a rather effective seducer." His cold demeanor warms in a blink, a charming smile and boy next door joviality replacing his threatening aura.

"So I hear," I say tauntingly. It is a calculated comment, meant to make him feel pinned under a microscope and show that while he may think he has the upper hand in our conversation, he is woefully unprepared compared to a man like me.

His good-natured act disappears, icy frost in his dark eyes as they lock on me.

"Rest assured that I do what I need to so that the job is completed as agreed upon. I have already made initial contact." The words are correct, but they fight their way out, as if he'd do anything to not say them.

Interesting.

The question of whether Gabriel is becoming closer to Isabella as a means to an end or as something else still looms. I consider the options, and her seduction and humiliating end has a certain irony and justice to it that I can appreciate. Fine . . . maybe it will be worth it to see if Gabriel Jackson is actually going to do his job.

I sip my tequila, thinking. To know that Isabella Turner went to her grave degraded and heartbroken . . . that would be a sweet taste of revenge indeed. "Fine. But I want proof. And quickly."

Gabriel nods and gets up. "You can be assured you will get your proof. As soon as her bodyguards relax, I'll make my move."

Gabriel walks to the door, but before he can open it, I call out again. "Mr. Jackson, do not make me lose faith in you. I am not the sort of man you should double-cross."

Gabriel turns, his hand moving so quickly that I can hardly see it before a stainless steel throwing knife embeds itself in the middle of the wet bar, not more than three inches from my hand. "The same could be said about me. You need better security, but *currently*, I'm no threat to you. Goodnight, Mr. Blackwell."

Gabriel leaves, softly closing the door behind him, and for the first time in years, fear makes my hand shake as I set my tumbler down. I pry the throwing knife out of the wood, grunting with effort as the knife's embedded deeply in the antique oak.

The low lights in my office reflect off the muted silvery surface, and in it I can see a warped, wavy reflection of my face. It makes me look like a monster, and after a moment, I set the knife down, pondering the meeting.

First lesson. Gabriel Jackson is not a man to be trifled with. Young, yes. But foolish? Doubtful.

Still, the threats, the lack of fear Gabriel showed . . . they irk me. I'm a man used to having others quake at the very mention of my name. Even those of a caliber to afford hiring Gabriel would not normally go against me.

And yet, Gabriel hurled a knife in my office like it was nothing. Like *I* am nothing.

I need to know, is that the reaction of a man truly without fear, or an act born from fear, the violently desperate reaction of a cornered animal?

The tequila has warmed my stomach, but another warmth spreads through my body . . . the warm fire of anger.

The little shit, daring to threaten me.

Going over to my desk, I sit, my fingers mindlessly tapping out Ravel again as I consider my options.

"Fine . . . I'll give you some more rope," I finally say, opening my desk to search for a very specific phone. One I only use in very specific circumstances. "But only enough for you to hang yourself with if you betray me."

Dialing quickly, I wait as the line rings, bounced through at least two redialing services based off the changes in tone.

I detest using such devices, but in this case, it is as secure as it can be. Finally, after a long period of near-black silence, the line is picked up.

"Yes?"

"Jericho? This is Blackwell."

"It has been awhile. What can I do for you?" the voice says, giving me shivers. And that is why I am using it. If Gabriel Jackson can frighten me, then logically, hiring someone even more deadly, though not quite as *quiet* and certainly not as *ethical*, is the best option.

"I'd like to discuss a potential job offer."

There is silence on the other end of the line, and I wait patiently while Jericho considers his words. "I can be at SeaTac in two days."

"Excellent. I'll meet you there personally. Send me your arrival time."

The line hangs up, and I turn off the phone before putting it away.

My PI will continue to follow Gabriel, perhaps get a read on whether he is being sly or has fallen under Miss Turner's charm. And in two days' time, Jericho will take over this mission if it has not been completed successfully.

That piece of business taken care of, I stand up, reaching into my desk drawer for the small pistol that I keep, just in case.

I have a security guard to chastise.

CHAPTER 17

GABRIEL

I pull my truck over to the side of the street, mindlessly pulling off a near-perfect parallel parking job about a mile from the Blackwell building. Taking a few breaths, I go over exactly what Blackwell said, looking for tells, gaps, and information.

The back and forth nature of conversation is sometimes the worst enemy to a well-laid plan, sharing more than intended. Conversing with Blackwell had been more chess match and power posturing than usual, though.

Everything had been going mostly according to plan, and I'd even gotten a bit of insight about his motivation for wanting the hit on Bella. My bluff about security because of her big-wig friends had been just that, a bluff based on the research I'd done and the connections I'd made myself about what in Bella's life could put her at such risk. But Blackwell had all but said that he is using Bella to get at Thomas Goldstone. It seems like an obvious slip of the tongue, which makes me question the accidental nature of it.

But all in all, it'd gone pretty well, I'd even managed to put off his urgency at completing the job, until I'd mentioned using seduction as an effective tool.

So I hear, he'd said.

And the game had changed, pivoted on a dime.

In three words, he let me know that he was holding more cards than I'd prepared for.

I'd had to play along, telling Blackwell, the one man I don't want to look too closely at my relationship with Isabella, that I'd already begun a seduction course of action. Of course, the best cover is as close to reality as possible, so in making Blackwell believe I am seeing Isabella in order to complete his mission, perhaps I can distract him from my true intentions.

But that is only a temporary solution.

It's a tangled web of deception, and Blackwell is powerful enough that trying to outmaneuver him is a difficult and delicate undertaking.

I grin at the memory of throwing the blade near his hand. That had been delicate, but not difficult at all, and a show of danger is something Blackwell will respect.

I glance at the digital clock, glowing in the dim light of the truck cab. Eight thirty, just enough time to see Bella for dinner.

Quickly, I pull back into traffic and drive my truck to the motel. I change back into my casual clothes, running my hands through my hair to muss it a bit. Grabbing an Uber, I make my way to the diner.

But this time, as I walk inside, I glance around a bit more carefully. It's part of my nature, especially in my line of work, to be exceedingly careful. But despite Blackwell throwing out a hint about surveillance, I don't see anyone or anything suspicious.

Inside, I simply watch Bella for a moment before she realizes I'm here. She floats around the room as if she's dancing, her tennis-shoe-clad feet barely touching the floor as she does her best to provide good service to her customers. Warmth fills my heart, seeing her work so hard but never complaining, watching as people's blank faces transform into smiles from a conversation with her and the glow she is suffused with shining so beautifully from her very being.

And when she looks my way, her smile broadens. Amazingly, I did that. The man whom most people fear, whom they never want to see darken their doorstep, can bring happiness to this woman. This princess who deserves the best but only gets me.

"Hi, Bella," I say, laying a light kiss to her cheek. She blushes, pink heat beneath my lips for a split second before she pulls away.

"Hey," she says chirpily. "Kinda swamped, but have a seat anywhere and I'll grab you a menu."

I shake my head. "Just order something you'd recommend for me. I'll wait until you get your dinner break and we can eat together?"

She bites her lip, nodding like that sounds excellent. But before she can truly answer, a polite voice calls out, "Miss?" and almost with a click of her heels, Bella is back to work.

I sit down to watch her some more, but part of me is scanning the rest of the diner customers and the parking lot, wondering and thinking about Blackwell's words once again.

At some point, Martha walks up to talk to Henry, and we meet eyes through the kitchen window. She wags a finger, telling me to wait a minute, as if I'm going anywhere. After finishing her conversation with Henry, she comes over, sitting down in the booth across from me.

"I wanted to say thank you again for saving our girl the other night. And by 'our girl', I mean the Gravy Train's. Izzy is one of us, and while your protective instinct is rather chivalrous, and I like that, I'm a bit of a Momma Bear. I'm sure you understand."

I flash her my charming, boy-next-door grin, not for seduction but to charm her, nevertheless. "Of course. I understand and appreciate that you and the rest of the Gravy Train family have taken such good care of Bella. She's not an easy person to take care of, bound and determined to do it all on her own. I admire that about her, but no one is a solitary force. We all need a little support now and then."

Her lips press together, but the edges tilt up so I take that as a good sign. "Not to sound too old-school, but what are your intentions here?" Before I can answer, she adds, "And a short-term fling is a reasonable answer if it's the truth. I just want to know what Izzy's getting herself into so that we're ready to give her that support you talked about when it's needed."

I can't help but find Bella in the room, my eyes drawn to her as much as my heart is. My words are to her, though Martha hears them loud and clear. "I wasn't looking for her, at least not like this. But I found her, or maybe she found me? Either way, the result's the same, I guess."

I shrug, looking back to Martha. "I don't have a lot to offer, no sweet promises of whisking her away to an easy life, or even answers to your questions. Because the truth is . . . I don't know. All I know is that I like her a lot and I want to spend time with her, share the load she carries as much as she'll let me, and make her smile. I don't know if that's enough, but it's all I have."

Martha's eyes look a little glassy, which surprises me. I figured she would be a tough old bird, hardened by life and bitter about love, considering the sarcastic banter she shares with Henry. She swallows, dabbing at her eye. "That'll do, Gabe." She gets up, and I feel like the firing squad is inexplicably letting me go. But she pauses and lays a hand on my forearm. "For now."

I smirk, thinking that perhaps her biting nature is a bit of show and a bit of warning. Carefully, I ask, "Martha? Can I ask you for a favor?"

Her brow raises, but she nods. "Kinda felt like I just gave you one by letting you see Izzy, but shoot."

"I'd like to take Bella on a date. A real one, not just parking lot pie, though the pie was delicious. Is there any chance you could find coverage tomorrow so she could have the night off?"

Martha smiles big and bright at that. "Hell, yes. I can work some magic and make that happen. If, and only if, you'll work some magic and take her someplace nice."

"Deal," I say happily.

"Just one thing," Martha cautions, "you've got to tell her. Good luck getting her to forgo a night of tips for something as self-serving as a date. If you can get her to do that, you'll know she thinks you're really something special."

Martha's words ring in my head as I tell Bella the hopefully good news over the Belgian waffles she ordered for us.

"So, you just asked my boss if I could have the night off? Bit of an overstep, don't ya think?" she challenges. I can see the worry in her forehead, the lines popping out as she furrows her brow. I think she's doing math in her head. X hours times Y amount per hour plus Z in average tips equals . . . a very expensive date.

"It was. In my defense, I simply asked if it was possible from Martha's perspective. If you don't want to, we won't do it. On the other hand, if you do want to go out with me, on a real date where we get dressed up, I pick you up and tell you how nice you look, and we go out for a quiet dinner, just the two of us, then you're free and clear at work." I give her the full-wattage smile, hoping the hard sell was enough.

She laughs, loud and open-mouthed. "Ooh, you're playing dirty. I like it. All right, you got yourself a date." She leans back in the booth, looking toward the kitchen, and yells out, "Well-played, Martha. Guess I'll be needing tomorrow night off."

Martha answers with a wink. "Have fun, you two. Don't do anything I wouldn't do . . . back when I was twenty-five!"

Bella turns back to me, snickering. "That leaves pretty much everything open. Martha once got arrested for protesting by streaking across the football field during the last two minutes of a homecoming game."

I laugh, but fight imagining it in my head. "Ah, the perils of being young and stupid."

Bella shakes her head, eyes wide in horror. "Uhm, this was about five years ago. She was protesting the boys getting away with all sorts of shit under the guise of 'boys will be boys.' She stood right up in front of the judge and said, 'Well, women will be women then too, I suppose.' She didn't even get community service."

"Let's maybe aim to not get arrested at least, though you could streak through the privacy of your own home and I'd chase you straight to the bedroom."

Bella touches the tip of her nose, winking. "I'll remember that."

Her dinner break is nearly over all too soon. She shoves a last bite of waffle into her mouth and wipes her lips with a napkin. "I'd better get back to it. You gonna hang around again tonight?"

I can hear the heat in her tone, the want so blatant and sexy. But I can also see the faint smudges under her eyes. She puts on a great act, a good front, but my girl is tired and needs some sleep.

Plus, I should try to figure out how Blackwell is getting his information before I spend the night again. For Bella's sake and my own.

"Tonight, I want you to go home right after you get off work, take a hot bath, drink a glass of wine, and think about our date tomorrow. I know it's customary for the guy to pick the place, but I'm not all that familiar with Roseboro and I want this to be exactly what you want it to be, so can you choose a restaurant. Anywhere, anything, your wish is my command, Princess."

She sighs out a happy breath, like the mere idea of that sounds blissfully amazing.

"I'll pick you up tomorrow night at seven thirty." I get up, and though we're in the middle of the diner, I can't help but wrap my hand around the back of her neck, weaving my fingers into her hair. I lean down, kissing her softly, memorizing her taste and getting my fill to last the next twenty-four hours.

She's dazed for a moment, and like a proud peacock, my ego inflates that somehow I can kiss her stupid because I'm feeling a bit buzzed on her myself.

She clears her throat and pats her apron. "Oh, let me get your keys for you. Thanks for the sweet ride today, by the way. And the breakfast goodies. I think Vash was swayed by your milk offering."

"That was the intent. To win her over—and the human she lives with."

CHAPTER 18

ISABELLA

*I*t's creeping up on midnight when I finally pull my scooter in the gate at home. I do a look-around to make sure Russell isn't lurking around, but it seems clear. Until I get to my doorstep.

There's a brown grocery bag propped against the door. My first thought is a bomb because I watch too much news on the evening shift at the diner. Then my more reasonable brain considers that a bomb is highly unlikely. I mean, aren't those supposed to come in boxes or something?

Still, I kick it with my toe while holding my face as far away from any explosive contents the bag may hold.

It crinkles.

Curious, I look inside. And my heart stops. Literally, jerks to a stop at the overwhelming kindness.

I pick up the bag, unlocking the door and hurrying inside. After locking the door behind me, I spread out Gabe's sweet gift on the kitchen table. There's an industrial-size bag of lavender Epsom salts, two masks, one for my hair and one for my face, a candle, a bag of chocolates, and a chilled bottle of wine.

It's late, and I should fall into bed. But with all this bounty, I can't help but want to self-indulge. Just this once.

So I splurge, doing as Gabe asked and taking a pampering hot bath before bed. It's luxurious, decadent, and just what I needed. And as I slide into my cotton sheets with moisturized skin, dreams of tomorrow pop into my head like bubbly possibilities.

I could get used to this.

I SHOULD COUNT MY LUCKY STARS THAT I ACTUALLY DO HAVE SOME nice clothes. Once upon a time, I used to spend hours thrifting to find deals on clothes that were cute and affordable. After Reggie died and things became much more desperate, clothing had been the least of my concerns, but tonight, I'm glad to have kept some of the nicer things I got on clearance at the Roseboro Thrift.

"Vash, what do you think? Black?"

I hold up the black dress with a long, diagonally-cut skirt, but Vash lifts her chin, clearly unimpressed.

"Okay . . . green? I could add a scarf, maybe?"

Meow.

"Critic. Okay, what about the red one?"

She tosses her head, not amused and stalking off toward the kitchen in that way only Vash can. "Fine . . . I'll do it my damn self!" I call after her swishing tail. "It's my first official date in I don't know how long. I'm not going to trust the opinion of a creature that hacks up hairballs anyway!"

I do end up deciding on the red piece, mainly because I've got the best heels to go with it. They were a gift from Mia, of all people, from way back in her crazy single college days when she wanted a wing girl to go out clubbing with, and as I pull on the black open-toed strappy heels, I twirl, sending her another round of thanks.

"God, they feel good," I murmur as I turn this way and that, wishing I had a full-length mirror to see how my legs look. Yeah, I'm just in my best lingerie and heels, so I probably look more like a stripper than anything else . . . but I feel sexy as fuck doing it. "Been too long since I felt like this."

Getting into the dress is a lot easier than it looks. There's no zipper but instead a swath of stretchy fabric that I sort of wiggle and shimmy into until it hits my hips and then tumbles to my knees.

Pulling my hair back, I imagine myself, and finally can't resist going to the bathroom and doing my best to see what I can in the tiny mirror above my sink. I can't see much, but what I can see—

"Vash!"

Meow?

"Gonna need you on 9-1-1 duty when Gabe gets here, babe. Because he might just have a heart attack once I get my makeup done."

I start on my eyes. I have dark eyes, so going too smoky on the eyeshadow and liner just makes me look like a raccoon, but I do want to look sultry and sexy. Thankfully, this red dress gives me just what I need, and a swipe of black eyeliner tilted up at the end brightens me up a little bit.

My lips I go deep red, lush and shiny, wanting to draw Gabe's attention to everything I'm saying all night. If he's thinking about what else my lips could be doing . . . well, that's a bonus as well.

I know I've for damn sure been thinking about what his lips could do to me.

Finally, I'm done, and I do my best with my hair, pulling the chocolate curls over one shoulder to trail down over my breast.

God, I feel beautiful.

There's a knock at my door, and I hurry out, doing my best to run in heels. "Who is it?" I ask. I assume it's Gabe, but after Russell's boot-meets-door performance, I'm not chancing it.

"It's me, Princess," a muffled voice says through the door, and I can't help but giggle as I unlock it for him.

"Gabe, I'm hardly a—" I start before all the words in my head dry up.

He's amazing, in a dark black suit that highlights his dark hair and bright brown eyes, his smile dazzling in the dim light of my porch. Forget the date. We're already wearing too many clothes.

Gabe looks me up and down. "You look stunning."

"Uhm, thanks," I stammer, not so smoothly, my heart hammering in my chest as he looks at me with undisguised attraction and appreciation. I've never, in my entire life, felt more desired that I do right now. "You look . . . wow."

"Thank you," Gabe says, half bowing, but I saw his pleased smirk. "So . . . shall we?"

I step back, waving him in. "Do you want to come in? I need to grab my purse."

Gabe doesn't move though. Well, he doesn't come inside. But he leans against the side of the door frame. "If I come in there, we're not leaving. Not with you looking like that, and not with what I see in your eyes right now. And I really want to take you out, treat you right, and show you off in that red dress. Grab your purse, Princess."

His voice is deep and rumbly, nearly a growl of restraint that turns me on, makes me think his coming inside to rip this dress off me is date enough.

But my heart overrules my pussy.

I want to be wined and dined, romanced and wooed. And as frivolous as that sounds, it's the truth. So I leave Gabe at the door, picking up my purse. It doesn't match, but it's the smallest I have and mostly black.

The candy red of his SUV nearly matches my dress, a happy coincidence, but in some small way, it makes me feel like I belong here as Gabe opens the passenger door to help me in like a gentleman. He climbs into the driver seat and begins backing out, asking me, "Did you decide where we're going?"

"I have," I reply but keep some surprises to myself. "Just turn where I tell you to."

It doesn't take long to get to our destination, a slightly worn-down Chinese restaurant in an older part of town. Gabe says nothing as we pull up in front of Golden Dragon, but he escorts me inside, holding out an elbow for me to take and then pulling out my chair for me as we sit down at one of the tables. Coming around, he sits in his own chair, the old green vinyl looking out of place considering the glitz and glam of our clothing.

"I guess you'd like to know why here?"

"I'm curious," Gabe admits, glancing around but quickly re-centering on me. "But I trust your instincts. One, you know Roseboro better than I do. And two, you work in the food service industry, so I'm sure you know where all the good spots in town are, both five-star and hole-in-the-wall."

He's right, but I can appreciate that he trusts me because I know Golden Dragon isn't exactly impressive-looking. "Good point," I reply, wondering just how good my chopstick skills are after so long. "Although it's not just the food quality that brings us here."

Gabe hums, guessing my meaning. "History?"

I sigh, the memories already rolling as I look around the restaurant. "This was one of the few places that I could go with my aunt. Great food that won't break the bank."

Gabe checks the menu, his eyes scanning quickly up and down the four columns. "I'm betting you had the spicy chicken combo platter?"

The eight-dollar special . . . my throat catches as I remember the nights we'd come here. "Good guess. We used to share it. It's nothing fancy, but it was always special when we came. I've had at least a dozen holiday meals here."

"Then let's celebrate it in the way it's meant to be," Gabe says. "Your aunt did what she could, and she did it with love. Whether it's a five-star spread or a single Hostess cupcake . . . it's the company that makes it special."

I blink, looking at Gabe in amazement. The tears are gone, and what's replaced them is a new feeling, honest pride. "How . . . how do you do that? How do you always know what to say? To make me smile. To make me not ashamed."

"Why should you be ashamed?" Gabe asks, looking confused. "From everything you've told me, you're one of the strongest people I've ever met. You should be proud of what you've accomplished and of what you are still trying to do."

"I've spent so much time zombieing my way through life," I reply, trying to explain. I take a deep breath and hold it before letting it out. "And there are still times when I think I'm never going to be free of it. I'll always be 'that poor girl', either because of losing my parents or because of how Reggie and I struggled. But I don't want to live that way forever. I want to live again, to be bright and free. To feel like I did when you and I were in that clearing on the mountain."

"You can do just that," Gabe replies.

I duck my head, not able to meet his eyes for this part despite his assertion that I shouldn't be ashamed. "It's safer, easier to stay asleep at the wheel, to drudge through and follow the plan I set ages ago, with hopes that it'll all be better one far-off, distant day in the future. To live big, to be able to actually see the top of the mountain . . . to do that now, I need a reason," I admit.

It's a big request of him, even though I'm being fairly vague in order to hedge my bets. "If I'm going to wake up, take that risk, I need a reason."

Gabe reaches across the table, taking my hand. "I hear you, and I will happily help you up every step of the mountain. But I want to be clear on something. *You* are reason enough. You deserve to wake up and *own* every second of your life, enjoy them now, not just later when you feel like you've earned it. You've already earned it, Bella. But I would be thrilled to enjoy it along with you."

His answer is somehow even more perfect, though I definitely notice he's not making any undying professions of love, but it's far too soon for that. "I'd like that," I say, his words filling gaps in my spirit I didn't know were there because I've been too busy filling the hole in my belly with the bank account leaking money like a sieve. "It might take a while, though."

"I know."

With a start, I remember my manners. "Thank you for the goodies last night. They were unexpected and wonderful. I definitely enjoyed every second of that bath."

His grin goes lascivious, and his eyes dart downward to where I know I'm giving him a tantalizing glimpse of cleavage. "God, I'm picturing you naked in the tub, bubbles piled up over your nipples and curled tendrils escaping a bun to fall down to your neck, where I could nibble and taste the lavender. Tell me all about it."

There's a hint of cockiness to the order, not bossy but bold, and I'm more than happy to meet it with my own sassiness.

"Well, I got home and thought the bag was a bomb, or maybe a dog-shit surprise, but it was so much better, of course." He laughs at my crazy ideas, urging me to continue with a squeeze of my hand. "It was wonderful. I filled the tub with water all the way to the top, as hot as I could get it, and soaked in the Epsom salts until I was a prune. And like some girl on tv, I ate chocolates and drank wine while I sat there, boiling like one of Henry's potatoes."

"I think my fantasy was of the sexier variety, but I'm so glad you enjoyed them."

The waitress comes by, and I order two of the spicy chicken

combo platters. "Ooh, big spender," Gabe teases. "Can we get some of the almond cookies for dessert?"

"If you behave," I tease. "Speaking of, I did the 'tell me about yourself' spiel, complete with tears and trotting out my trauma. You have yet to do yours, so tell me about yourself, Gabe."

I know I sound a bit stiff, like this is a job interview, but if so, he's already got the position. Any and all of them he wants.

"I'm not sure where to start," he says, and I can read the tension around his eyes.

"Just start at the beginning, like 'once upon a time, a beautiful baby boy was born.' Or stick to the basics, like do you have parents? Siblings? Where are you from? What do you do?"

He nods, dropping his chin before answering, "Yes, I have parents, no springing forth, fully grown, from a plant pod. I had a brother, but he died." He swallows. "Not a story I want to relive right now. Sorry."

I bite my lip, sad to see his pain and feel his loss so sharply. "No worries. But I'm here if you change your mind and need someone to talk to."

One side of his mouth lifts in that half-smile he has when he's not sure. It makes him look like a sweet troublemaker.

"As for what I do, I guess you'd say I'm a consultant."

"A consultant? Well, that just clears up everything," I joke, his answer clear as mud. "What do you consult?"

"I'm a systems troubleshooter," Gabe explains, though he again somehow clears nothing up. "Companies or people call me, and I come in and consult with them on solutions. Sometimes the problem's easy, sometimes it's hard. But it's fun."

"And you . . . I mean, where are you based out of?" I ask, and Gabe shrugs. "What's that mean?"

"It means I have enough work that I usually live out of motel rooms. If I were hard-pressed, I'd say I'm a Red Roof guy. I mean,

I did three months in Calgary once, nearly six months in New York, but then I've done jobs as quick as two or three days and I'm on the road again. When I don't have work, I'll sometimes use the gap time to relax, take a vacation or something, but other than a PO Box for the IRS, I don't really have a place."

"I can't decide if that sounds lonely or adventurous," I say honestly. "Having never been anywhere, the thought of constant travel is appealing, but not having a home base seems so nomadic. I'm literally fighting to keep the only roots I have, even when it'd be so much easier to let them go."

His face falls, and he shakes his head. "You have the home you shared with your aunt to hold those memories, so you clutch to it, understandably. When my brother died, my family basically fell apart, and the memories I hold of home, history, family, they're all in my mind, in my heart. So anywhere I go, they're with me. He's with me."

He's quiet for a moment, and I can tell he's tortured by the ghosts haunting him right now. Curiosity has me wanting to ask a million more questions, but I can respect that he might not be in a place to share right now, so I redirect the conversation to lighter topics in the hope of lifting his spirits once again.

"So in your vast experience of traveling the world, can you use chopsticks? Because I'm seriously doubting my skills."

His lips curl in slow-motion. "I can absolutely use chopsticks. I have all sorts of skills that'd surprise you."

Something in his tone sounds like he truly believes that, which makes me all the more tingly to see him use each and every one of those skills.

CHAPTER 19

GABRIEL

*W*hile I stop at one beer, Bella enjoys herself, which is just what I want. She deserves to relax, have some fun. There's going to be too much bad shit coming, and maybe this fun night will help her through those times.

"You wanna know my personal record of how many shifts I've worked in a row?" she asks as she sips at her third Mai Tai. "Too many!" she laughs, but then her eyes narrow in thought. "Actually, I think twenty is my record. Can you imagine? Twenty days in a row, no time off at all, serving those big ass blue plate specials?"

"I bet you put some muscles on during that stretch."

"Yeah, right." She snorts but then says proudly, "That was a long stretch, but I made my tuition payment in cash one week before the semester started."

"I have to ask, why stay there?" I ask as I sip at my green tea. "You work too many hours for too little pay. I'm sure you could find something better, even if it was only temporary."

"Maybe I could, but I like it there. I love the people, and Martha works with me. That reminds me of a funny story, actually. Well, it's funny now, looking back, but it definitely wasn't at the time," she says, not slurring her words but definitely getting giggly.

"What happened?"

"It was right after my aunt passed, and I'd been fired from my retail job because I took off two weeks to grieve and plan a funeral. I had no idea what I was going to do for money or even food. I'd applied at a ton of places but just wasn't getting any bites."

Her eyes have gone hazy, her mind faraway in the past, so to bring her back, I tease lightly, "You're right, this story sounds hilarious."

It works as she rolls her eyes, a small smile curling her lips. "Anyway," she draws out sassily, "I was at The Gravy Train and ordered a sausage biscuit breakfast, thought I had the five bucks on me. When I went to pay and looked in my wallet, what I thought was a five was a grocery list. I was dead-broke, literally with just a few cents to rub together, and my bank account was on zero. I was so embarrassed."

"What'd they do?"

"They called the cops!"

My eyes go wide, thinking of sweet and protective Martha and her beleaguered husband calling the police on a poor, broken-down young woman. "No way."

"Hell, yes, they did!" Bella laughs. "But while we were waiting, Henry started lecturing me on looking for handouts and being sneaky about stealing from good people. Somewhere in the middle of his Disappointed Dad routine, he threatened to call my parents, wagging finger and all."

She mimes a stern face, pointed finger rant, then her face softens. "I told him I didn't have any. That stopped him short and he got real quiet. His lecture turned into more questions, and I was too raw to hide anything about Reggie or my situation. By the time the cops got there, he said it was a misunderstanding and gave the cops a coffee each to go. I apologized for the mistake, promising that I'd pay him back as soon as I could, but he put me to work washing dishes that day. He sent me home with a to-go box . . . and ten bucks tucked inside the lid. Within a month, I was waiting tables. So they've always been good to me. They're like family to me, and in a way, I feel like I owe them. They saved me when things were really dark and have had my back with schoolwork and schedules, cheering me on through every final and project."

I nod, thinking about the mental debts we place on ourselves. "I'm glad you have them and they have you. It sounds like a match made in heaven."

Bella inhales, confiding, "I like to think Reggie sent them to me, knowing I'd need someone. Martha and Henry are the closest thing I have to parents now."

Her words pierce the air, and she looks down, clearing her throat. I reach across and take her hand. "It's always good to have folks you can turn to. I wish I still did."

"Your . . . your family's gone too?" Bella asks.

"My parents are alive, out there somewhere." I glance to the window, like my mom or dad might unexpectedly be standing there, but of course, they're not. "But when my brother died, our family did too. We didn't know how to love each other through it, and our grief took us further and further apart. I left as soon as I could, and my parents divorced shortly after that, both of them moving to the other side of the country to get away from the memories. I think seeing each other just reminded us of who was missing. Of the family we'd never have again. We kinda silently agreed to just let it all go to not hurt each other anymore."

"I'm sorry," she says simply. I'm glad she doesn't give me shit for not seeking my parents out, especially considering her past.

It's a complex thing, a parent-child relationship, and though it should have a foundation of love and be sprinkled through with happy memories and hopes for the future, sometimes, that's just not possible.

"The last time I saw my mother, she accidentally called me Jeremy and we both froze," I admit, a story I've never shared with anyone else. "I know she didn't mean anything by it, certainly didn't wish it'd been me and not him, but it was a dagger into both our hearts. I think *not* seeing me, with my similar appearance and my future he'll never have, makes it easier to shove it all down and live on superficially without dwelling. At least that's what I tell myself when I think about reaching out to them and need to talk myself out of it."

Bella reaches out and places her hand on top of mine. "Thank you."

We finish our meal, sharing mostly happier stories and learning about each other. I have to be careful to not divulge too much, which is surprisingly hard. I'm accustomed to lies and half-truths, diversions and distractions. But I find myself wanting to tell Bella everything, ugly truth and all, but that's a danger neither of us can afford. So I stick to lighter times and she seems to follow suit.

By the time we finish, my belly hurts as much from the laughter as the overabundance of spicy glazed chicken and rice, and Bella's cheeks are stained a soft pink.

As we walk out, Bella's good humor and a bit of the alcohol sillies amps up. "I just had a *date*." She does a cute wiggly-ass dance move that makes me think dirty thoughts about smacking that round globe before she teeters a little.

"Whoops!"

"*Had?* It's not over yet, Princess," I correct her, steadying her. "I didn't know you were a lightweight with the Mai Tais."

"I'm not a lightweight!" she protests, eventually standing steadily on her own. "I just haven't had a real drink in like . . . months. But mostly, this is just me being . . . happy." She smiles, looking clear-eyed, and I realize it's true. She's not tipsy, or at least not too tipsy.

"Are you sure I shouldn't take you home, give you a polite kiss on the cheek at the door, and go back to my motel room?" I ask, smirking but serious. "I wouldn't want to take advantage."

Bella blanches and slaps my chest. "If you even think of doing that, I'm going to be so pissed at you I'll sic Vash on you!"

"Ooh, not that! She's a demon beast," I deadpan. "Guess I'd better plan to stay a while, then?" It's not until I say the words that I realize how much I truly want to stay with Bella, not just tonight, but for a lot longer.

A tiny whisper in my head says *forever*, but I quiet it with reminders that I'm not the type of man a woman like Bella needs. Scarred, monstrous, feared, with blood-covered hands and a sin-soaked soul is not the way to reach the mountaintop she wants.

I turn the radio on low as we drive back to Bella's house. She's changed the station, and while The Weeknd isn't my normal cup of tea, the intense sexual beat of *Call Out My Name* supercharges the atmosphere inside my Range Rover. I look over at Bella, who's smiling, biting her lip as she tugs at the hem of her dress, sliding it up her knee and making it hard to tell myself that she's not mine, not for me, because fuck, do I want her, and she wants me in return.

"Gabe?"

"Yes?" I ask, but I see that she's prompting me, my eyes darting back and forth from the road and her creamy thighs.

I clear my throat, reaching over and putting my hand over hers just before she can reach her panties. "If you don't stop, I'm either getting in an accident or pulling over and taking you in the back of this vehicle."

Bella chuckles and takes my hand, placing it very high on her left thigh. "I'm so tempted, but I'll be good and wait." I give us both a taste, a promise of what the night holds by drawing a small circle on her satin skin with my thumb.

When we get back to her place, Vash is waiting for us, yowling in protest when the door opens. "Oh, hush, you spoiled brat!" Bella tells her, feigning a scolding, but the love is apparent. "Go catch a mouse or something!"

I reach down to pet her, hoping the milk offering will have made her friendlier toward me, but she hunches her back and eyes me warily. No hisses at least, so maybe I'm making progress.

Before I can get Vash to come to me, Bella shuts the door and pulls me to her. Cat forgotten, I press Bella against the wall, kissing her deeply as I lift her leg, running my hand up her thigh and under the hem of her dress. Her skin's electric, and as I reach higher, cupping her ass, she moans into my mouth.

"Knew I loved these heels," she purrs as I massage her cheek, pressing her ass back into my hand. "Just the right height."

I growl in her ear, my desire taking over. Last time, I held back, letting her have what she needed . . . but while I've opened up to her tonight, I haven't told her everything.

And that everything is more than she can even guess. It's what drives me, telling me that if I'm going to make this woman mine, then I'm going to make her *mine*.

It's the only way we'll survive.

"Bathroom," she purrs, pushing my jacket off my shoulders to fall to the floor.

I pull her to me, kissing her hard as we stumble toward the bathroom, a trail of clothing in our wake. I'm dimly aware in the little corner of my mind that never turns off that the door to her 'painting room' is shut.

All questions about why are driven from my mind as we enter the bathroom, the tile cool on my bare feet. I step back, watching Isabella strip the rest of the way for me.

The shower head angles over an old-fashioned clawfoot tub, surrounded with a clear plastic curtain that she pushes out of the way. I watch Isabella reach over and turn on the water, and I can't help but give her ass a good smack, making her gasp.

She leans over a little more, and her legs part invitingly, giving me a view of her pussy. "Stay there."

I kneel and bury my tongue in her from behind, my hands pulling her to me. I'm rewarded with a deep moan as I bathe her pussy with a wide, flat tongue, feasting on her essence.

"Yes, Gabe, yes!" she cries softly as I slip inside her. She's sweet and spicy, and I lick furiously, thirsty for her sweet slickness, desperate to drink her down.

Isabella pushes back into my face, her knees quaking when I find her clit with my thumb as my tongue thrusts inside her. Her head drops, a deep moan of pleasure tearing through her as her knees unlock. If it wasn't for her hands supporting her on the high side of the tub, she'd collapse, but I don't let up, wanting to wrench every bit of pleasure from her that I can.

"That's it, Princess . . . give me your come," I growl against her puffy, sopping-wet lips. The sounds coming from my mouth are deep, primal as I suck and lick, my tongue snaking as deep as I can inside while I consume her.

I'm addicted. I'm never giving her up. She's mine.

Isabella's body shakes as she finds the deep release I've been driving her toward, whimpering as her orgasm shakes her, and I pull back, holding her as she trembles. "You're mine," I whisper in her ear, letting my possessive thoughts take weight in the words. "You're mine, and I'm going to show you what that means."

She nods, her legs still spaghetti as we get into the shower. The warm spray feels amazing on my back as I hold Bella close, my cock rock-hard and pressed against her back.

I let her recover, picking up the bar of soap and washing her body, my fingers tracing the curves of her stomach and hips before massaging her breasts.

Her nipples pebble tightly under my slippery fingers, and she turns her head, looking at me with lust-filled eyes. "You . . . I need you, Gabe."

"You have me," I reply, kissing her lips softly at first. Isabella turns around and wraps her arms around my neck as the warm water cascades over us, our bodies slipping together as we kiss again, need building quickly between us. I lift her leg, holding under her knee until her foot finds the rim of the tub as I push her back, pinning her against the tile wall.

"Tell me what you want," I command, looking in her eyes. "Tell me who you belong to."

"You . . . I want you to fuck me with that big cock," she rasps.

My lips smash against hers the second she gets it out, kissing her hard. My hips drive forward, and I'm rewarded with her cry into my mouth as my cock splits her open, swallowed by her tight pussy until I'm deep inside her. Her arms tighten around my neck, holding me still as she adjusts, and I grind against her, letting her feel me until she relaxes, and I feel her nod slightly against my neck.

"Please."

Her voice is soft, barely audible over the rush of the shower spray, but it's all I need as I pull back and start pumping my hips hard, my cock thrusting in and out of her as Bella holds onto me. The slightly curved bottom of the tub and the angle of our bodies mean I can't go full out, but somehow, that makes each stroke even more enticing.

Her pussy squeezes me as our bodies press against each other, her nipples dragging over my chest as I pump in and out of her, our bodies moving not frantically, but with a harmony that grows within the confines of the shower.

"Give it to me, Gabe," Bella grunts in between my strokes, her eyes looking deep into mine. A little hope flares inside me that there are layers to what she's saying, and my cock swells, emotions adding to the pleasure pulsing through me with every slide of my cock in and out of her body.

"You're mine," I growl again, looking in her eyes and hoping she can understand that my two words mean a lot more than just my cock stretching her and setting her nerves on fire. She moans, and my hips speed up a little faster, my toes gripping the porcelain as best I can as the two of us come together, our bodies shaking as we approach the precipice.

Her pussy's a vice around my shaft as the head of my cock rubs over the spots that she loves best, her stomach clenching as I pound her, deep and powerful. Bella tightens, her breath hitching as she's driven to the very edge, and I kiss her hard again, swallowing her cries and biting her lip as I slam into her.

Once again, she shatters, her legs giving out, and she's held up by just my arms and my cock, buried deep inside her perfect pussy. Her convulsions shake through her body and my cock, triggering my own climax. Lost in the waves of pleasure, I growl into her mouth, pulling out at the last possible second to cover her ass with my cream as my fingers dig into her hips, holding her still.

We stay there, frozen in our climax until the water starts to cool down, and I pull back, shutting it off. "Guess we ran out of hot water."

Bella chuckles and nods, getting out. "Take me to bed."

I WAKE AS CLOSE TO PARADISE AS I'VE EVER BEEN. BELLA IS NESTLED in my arms, her soft warmth pressed against me and her lips parted as she snores lightly, squirming every once in a while in her sleep.

She's like this adorable combination of cuddler and gymnast that woke me up more than once as we slept. She'd turn, move, and nearly flip over me at times, all while totally asleep.

Her most recent position has her sleeping with her knees tucked up underneath her, her head turned toward me and her hair half lying over her eye. I run my hand over her back, and she hums, smiling in her sleep.

I don't wake her up, even though the touch of her thigh against my cock is certainly waking *it* up this morning, but I let her rest.

Instead, I watch her, my hand tracing soothing circles on her back until she smiles. "I can feel you looking at me."

"Didn't know I had such a weighty gaze," I murmur, kissing her forehead. "How're you this morning?"

Bella stretches out, turning toward me and half opening her eyes. "I'm pretty sure I'm going to be walking funny again."

"Are you saying I should be gentler?" I ask, making her laugh softly and snuggle against me, but I can feel her shaking her head, almost as if she's embarrassed. "No?"

"I want it every way I can get it," she promises me bravely, nuzzling under my chin. "But before anything else, I need two things . . . brushed teeth and a potty break."

I pull her into my arms, kissing her gently. "Deal."

Bella goes to take care of her bathroom needs while I do my best to make peace with the cat, giving her a bit of canned tuna in her bowl. Vash warily looks me up and down, then struts by like the actual owner of the house she is before starting to eat.

"Yeah, I see you, Vash. I get that you're the boss. Maybe we can call a truce?" She doesn't answer, but her tail waves lazily left to right, so I take it as a sign that she's considering my offer.

I go back to the bedroom and pull on my pants before running my hands through my hair to tame the crazy mess I'm rocking. I'm barely half-dressed when Bella comes into the bedroom, her face freshly washed and looking as pristine and beautiful as an angel. "Bathroom's yours."

"Thanks," I reply, going in and washing my face. Using my finger, I do a quick little rub over my teeth, hoping it's enough to kill the morning breath, and while I do, I hear someone knock on the front door.

I'm instantly on alert, realizing how quickly I relaxed into being here with her and how readily I forgot about the dangers lurking.

As Bella comes down the hallway, I poke my head out of the bathroom. "Hey, let me—"

"I got it," Bella assures me, tugging a long T-shirt over her head and down to brush her thighs. She goes to the door, opening it before I can say anything else.

Fuck.

"Good morning, Izzy. I've come to collect."

I hear the sniveling voice, half bullying and half whining, and my fists clench as I realize who's at the door. Carraby.

"Go away, Russell," Bella says in a tired voice. "We're done, remember? I'm paid up and on a payment schedule. I don't need anymore of your bullshit."

"Bullshit? We'll see how much bullshit it is when I kick you out on the street."

"You're not kicking me anywhere, legally or otherwise." I'm proud of how steady her voice is, so I pause, giving her a chance to handle this herself if she wants to. I'll give her backup if she needs it, but Carraby should be glad that I don't teach him a lesson the hard way.

"You'd best watch your tone. You're paid up, but there ain't nothing keeping me from taking what I really want."

Even from here, I can hear the slimy threat. Money . . . and more.

I won't tolerate any more.

I grab the hand towel, wrapping it around my right hand as I hear Bella say, "You mean like human morals and ethics?"

I take the three steps down the hall to find Bella staring at Russell, her face etched with fury. She's got one hand on the door and one on the frame, acting as a roadblock to keep him from entering, but he's taking advantage of her unwillingness to move back and grant him access by moving in closer and closer.

"You need to leave," I say coldly. I'm measuring the distance from me to Bella, me to Carraby, and Carraby to Bella, already formulating how I'm going to protect her while quickly disabling him. It won't take that much . . . it's just how much I can get Bella to move out of the way.

Carraby looks at me, taking in my shirtless upper body and zipped but unbuttoned pants, his eyebrows lifting. I can see him trying to look more intimidating, and I already know this is going to end badly. He's too out of control, too stuck in a rut of habitual bullying that he doesn't recognize when he's challenging someone better than him. Of course, that's part of my special skill set. I'm an intimidating guy when I need to be, but it's like a switch I can flip on and off.

"Oh, tough guy, huh? Fuck off. This ain't none of your business."

I move closer, slowly and methodically cutting the distance between me and the front door until I lay my hand on Bella's shoulder. I ease her back from the threshold, taking her place. As soon as I do, I pull the door open wide, not wanting it to impede my actions if I have to make a move.

"*She* is my business. You heard her. You're paid up. Leave, and don't come back. I'll be handling any future *discussions* you might need to have."

It's a huge overstep on my part, considering this isn't something I've talked about with Bella, but I need to protect her from assholes like Carraby who will take advantage the instant my guard is down. He needs to learn now not to mess with what's mine, and on a larger scale, that he can't do whatever he wants without consequences.

There's always a bigger fish in the pond, a sneakier fox in the henhouse, and a crueler hunter in the forest.

Carraby looks like he's about to argue more, but instead, he takes one step forward. I let him, even step back as if I'm retreating. It's a ruse, but I'm the only one who knows it.

Quick as a flash, he takes another step, leering wolfishly, and Bella cries out, "No!"

But it's just what I want. As Carraby gets fully in the front door, he unleashes with a short-armed haymaker that barely avoids hitting the doorframe. I let the punch land on my chin, dodging just enough to let him connect but not hurt me.

And now the tables have turned.

He's both come in, effectively trespassing without permission, and assaulted me first. Every legality is on my side. More importantly, though, he's off balance, and I can do any of a half-dozen things to him that would range from inflicting pain to inflicting death, and he can't stop me.

But I can't overplay my hand with Bella here to witness this. So I temper my brutality and grab his shoulders, throwing a single powerful knee to his gut, delighting in the whoosh of air that leaves him as he doubles over.

Not letting him gain any distance, I turn him, wrapping my arm around his neck and holding him in a loose chokehold, darkly growling in his ear as I shove him toward the door. "Leave. Do not come back. Ever. Do not speak to Bella ever again. This is the only warning you'll get, Carraby. Nod if you understand."

His head moves slightly inside my arm, and I take that as agreement, though I know he's only giving in right now because I have the upper hand. This isn't over.

But any further actions will take place away from Bella.

I shove him out the door, and as soon as the pressure is off his neck, he begins blustering, red-faced and yelling nonsense, "Messed with the wrong . . . gonna regret . . . fucking bitch."

I want to follow him, take him to a deserted place in the woods and teach him a real lesson in fear and intimidation. But instead, I use every ounce of willpower I possess and close the door, turning to face Bella.

Hoping she isn't disgusted by me, by my actions and overstepping comments, I await her judgement. It comes as she breaks down and launches herself at me, hugging my neck and wrapping her legs around me. "Oh, my God, what the fuck? I can't believe—"

Her seeming appreciation is broken by a loud 'bong' sound outside. It's the sound of a boot hitting metal, likely Russell's foot connecting with my Range Rover. But that doesn't matter now, not with Bella in my arms, safe and sound. And not flinching away from me after seeing the violence in the one place she considers a sanctuary.

"He's gone. You're okay, I've got you," I say, rubbing her back.

"Thank you," she breathes against my neck, and though I don't say it, I think the same thing back, thankful she didn't kick me out too.

CHAPTER 20

*A*fter a dramatic and crazy morning, the spell I've been in, the fantasy Gabe wove around us, shatters. It feels awkward and there's something niggling in the back of my mind that I can't stop prying at.

But I can't figure out what it is.

Gabe drops me off at the Gravy Train for my shift with a kiss and a soft question of whether I'm sure I'm okay. I reassure him that I am, even though I'm not sure myself.

"I'm sorry about Carraby. I didn't mean for that to happen, but I'm glad you're safe. I won't let him hurt you, okay?" He pushes a lock of hair behind my ear, eyes imploring me to believe him. "I'll see you tonight for your nine o'clock dinner break?"

There's something in Gabe's voice that piques the little concern working itself around in my brain, an uncertainty he doesn't usually have. He's not arrogant, but he's always come off as confident.

But maybe this morning bothered him too?

I nod and get out, shutting the door behind me with a deep breath. Fuck. I can't believe Russell attacked Gabe and Gabe had to fight him off.

The scene replays in my head—Russell's leering threats and attack, and Gabe's immediate and powerful response.

As the mental movie of this morning replays again in my head while he pulls out, I see a different side to Gabe. A side I didn't know he had. He threw that knee with the skill and ease of someone who's done it before.

Suddenly, it clicks.

Carraby.

That's the thing that's bugged me this whole time. When I shared my problems, I told Gabe about Russell and his threats, but his last name? I can't remember ever telling him Russell's full name. But Carraby rolled off his tongue like . . . he already knew.

But how? Why?

And what does that even mean?

Memories of Charlotte's words ring in my ear. *You should run a background check, girl. Wish I had, would've saved me a lot of heartache if I'd known who he really was.*

Shit. Is Charlotte right? Only one way to find out.

I run inside and head straight to the back, hollering, "Martha!"

"What?" she exclaims, coming out of her office quickly, her eyes wide and questioning.

"I need your keys. It's an emergency. Please," I say, holding my hand out and bouncing on my toes.

She digs in her purse, grabbing them and handing them over to me. "Are you okay? What's wrong?"

I shake my head, hoping I'm not too late. "I'll explain later, I promise. Cover for me today, please!" I take the keys from her, running out to her silver Toyota. I have just enough time to fire it up before Gabe's bright red SUV pulls through the intersection just down the street, turning left.

I do my best to follow, glad that Martha's car is small and nondescript. More than once, I 'hide' behind other vehicles, wondering what I'm doing as I follow him.

Last night, everything had seemed to be going amazingly well. I'd begun believing that maybe Mia was right and that love, or at least the first tingles of it, can strike when you least expect it. Certainly, I'd felt like this thing between Gabe and me had grown well beyond a one-night stand considering all we'd shared, the stories we'd told, and the multiple times I'd seen his dimpled smile in response to a story I told, even when they were more tragically funny than outright humorous.

And I'd learned a lot about him as we chatted, flirted, and slurped down those delicious noodles. He told me about his job, or well . . . some about it. He told me about the things he likes and dislikes, and while we didn't get too deep into his family history, he never shirked a single question I had for him.

But this morning, when he looked at Russell, there was something in his face that scared me. I felt like I was looking at a totally different person, someone with the same face and body as Gabe but a totally different soul.

I don't know how I ended up following him. It just seems like the thing to do in the moment. Questions and concerns overlap each other in my mind with my sudden mistrust of Gabe, making me a little crazy.

Am I being irrational? Have I just gone a little cuckoo?

I know it's a bit much, but even so, I don't stop. I don't turn around.

Gabe pulls off the road and into the parking lot at a strip mall, and I follow, watching as he goes into . . . a Walmart?

That seems anti-climatic. I don't know what I was expecting, but my gut is still telling me something is up. And since I'm not really one to get weird vibes, I'm listening to this one, no matter how nonsensical it may be.

So I sit in Martha's car, waiting.

When Gabe comes out, he's got two bags and calmly beelines for his SUV. As he turns, I can see that one bag looks like it's got some snacks in it, while in the other, I can see the clear outline of a rubber mallet.

Gabe gets in his Range Rover, and I have a moment of clarity. Do I stop this madness or keep following? I glance up to the rearview mirror, seeing my eyes bright with worry.

"What am I doing?" I ask my reflection. Relationships are built on trust, but relationships are also built on honesty, and my gut tells me I'm missing something important here. I just don't know.

But when I see the candy-apple red SUV pull out, I know I'm doing this. No matter how weird, how stupid, how embarrassed I'm going to be later when it ends up that I'm overreacting to nothing, I need to know.

I keep sight of him, following as he makes his way to one of the motels in what could be called the industrial section of Roseboro. Not that Roseboro has a huge industrial zone, but there is that chunk of town that's sort of older businesses, I guess.

I park across the street, watching carefully as Gabe goes into a motel room. I'm just about to give up, thankful that nobody caught me going stalker psycho and thinking about how I'm going to explain my behavior to Martha, when the room door opens and Gabe walks out.

But he looks different than he did when he went in. I guess that's understandable. He was still wearing his dress shirt and suit pants from last night before, but looking at him in black jeans, a dark grey hoodie, and work boots . . . I don't know.

There's something off.

It's not like there's anything all that different about what he's wearing from what I've seen before. Almost every time we've been together, he's worn jeans and a T-shirt or something. Last night's fancier dress was definitely the outlier for us both.

But it's in the way he walks as he crosses the parking lot that has me confused.

He looks like he has a purpose. A mission.

And there's no hint of his boyish smile or charming personality. He looks robotic, mechanical.

I'm even more confused when he passes his Range Rover and goes to the end of the lot, getting into a silvery gray Ford truck.

"Wait . . . haven't I seen that truck before?" I murmur as I scooch down in my seat so he doesn't see me. I swear I have, but it's so common a style and color that maybe I'm just mixing it up with another vehicle? I mean, it looks just like Russ—

No.

No *fucking* way.

That time Russell came by, it was right around the time I met Gabe, if I remember right . . . there was another truck just down the block. At first I'd thought it was Russell coming back to bug me again.

But what if it'd been Gabe? Is that possible? Surely not.

Or maybe?

What does that mean, though? Maybe he was just in my neighborhood or knows Russell some other way? That might make sense I guess.

But something tells me that's not the case. Or at least there's a chance there's something else going on. And that's what's making me chew my lip.

I wait until Gabe pulls out of the lot, and then going by my gut, I take a shortcut toward my house. It means hopping on a dirt backroad for a mile, which does a number on Martha's suspension. But it can't be helped, I keep telling myself as my head bounces off the roof of her Toyota. I come up on the back of my neighborhood and park along the curb by the main road in, watching.

The car is dead silent as I pray that I'm wrong.

He could be going anywhere, might need a mallet for any number of things. Maybe Gabe is contracted to fix a problem at a warehouse and is on his way there now? And the truck, maybe he just has a work vehicle and a personal one? That's not unusual.

Even as I try to talk myself into believing that, my tears threaten to spill.

And then the gray Ford truck drives by.

Fuck. Fuck. Fuck.

What do I do? Do I keep following him or call the police? And tell them what? That my kinda-sorta boyfriend whom I've known for all of two weeks is acting sketchy as fuck and I think he's up to something beyond being overly protective of me?

They'd laugh me out of the precinct.

So I follow, still wishing none of this was happening, wondering how it's come to this.

He doesn't stop at my house and instead heads further down the street, turning two blocks up. There's only one house this far out in the neighborhood that Gabe would be interested in, and my stomach drops.

Russell's.

So he is going to pay Russell a visit.

My inner voice whispers, *you already knew that.*

It's true. I knew this was going to end with Gabe beating Russell up. Russell deserves it for sure, but I can't help but feel this is too much. I guess I was hoping the knee to the gut Gabe delivered this morning would be enough to warn Russell off?

I abandon the car, breaking into a jog and ducking through Mrs. Reddington's back yard to cut some more distance off my trek. It's not far, and I'm only part of the way there when I see Gabe's truck, Gabe behind the wheel, parked on the side of the road and waiting.

"What the hell are you doing?" I whisper to myself, kneeling behind an overgrown bush near Russell's house, watching. I know I should approach Gabe, stop whatever he has in mind. On some level, it was my whole purpose of following, but something stops me. I need to see what's going on. I need the truth of whatever this is. Of whatever he is.

My phone buzzes in my pocket, and I see that it's The Gravy Train. I ignore it, I'll make sure to call Martha immediately after. After *what*, I don't know. But I shut it off and keep watching.

It's surreal. I swear Gabe's watching for Russell, while meanwhile, I'm watching Gabe. A little tickle goes up my neck, and I wonder . . . is someone watching me?

No, I'm just paranoid and weirded out by what's going on. But still, I look behind me, scanning the street and bushes.

Suddenly, Gabe's door opens and he gets out of his truck. He approaches Russell's door, but there's something odd about his gait. Like his arms aren't swinging naturally but are stiff at his sides instead. He moves out of my view, but I hear loud knocks, three forceful bangs that reverberate through the still, cool air.

I hear the door open and chance peeking around the corner, staying low to the ground and looking between the branches of the bush. I have a decent view, can see Russell in faded smiley-face boxers, his face bleary and maybe even a little high. He looks at Gabe, who's lifted his hood up, with confusion.

"Who the fuck are you?"

Instead of answering, Gabe grabs Russell by his greasy hair and hurls him backward into his house. I'm so shocked I can barely believe what's happening, and a second later, Gabe's inside as well, gently closing the door to the house behind him.

It's the quiet click that shocks me the most. It's too calm, too premeditated.

Fuck. I shouldn't have sat there and watched.

"Gabe, what are you doing?" I ask, feeling like I'm yelling, but an almost inaudible whisper comes out as I move, leaving the camouflage of the bush in favor of pressing my face to a window.

There's barely a crack in the yellowed curtains, but it's enough to peek into the living room. I can hear Gabe's voice but can't see either of them, just the back of the dingy couch and the wall on the far side of the room.

"You . . . threatened her with breaking and entering, sexual assault . . . you harassed her with propositions of sex," Gabe growls, his voice low but so threatening that I shiver even though I'm outside. "You fucking deserve this."

"Dude . . . what the . . . what are you talking ab—OOOWWW!" Russell replies, his voice rising in a scream at the end. There's a wet thudding sound, and I realize what it is. A rubber mallet smashing down on Russell.

No. No way. Admittedly, I had suspicions that something was off, but not this. I didn't dream it would be . . . this. I guess I'd thought the worst-case scenario would be that he threatened him with it, but this is so much worse.

Gabe, my heart cries as it shatters.

There are no other houses nearby. Russell's property is at the dead end of the street and only the mailman comes down here. Besides, I know nobody gives enough of a damn about Russell to check out what's going on, even if they did hear him scream.

"That was your shoulder," Gabe says conversationally before a slapping sound splits the air and Russell starts sobbing. There's the sound of bodies moving, and suddenly, Russell's in a chair next to the window, his movement having shaken the curtain enough that I can see a little more.

Gabe's . . . not Gabriel. At least, not the charming, deliciously naughty man I've known and dreamed about for the past few nights.

This man's . . . ice. His dark eyes are emotionless, his face tense but totally neutral.

He really is like a Terminator. My God, this whole time, he's been this way. Charlotte was right. He has been hiding something.

"Please . . . please, man, whatever you want, I'll—" Russell pleads, but Gabe swings the mallet again, and even though it's rubber, the sound of it smacking into Russell's thigh cuts his words off into another scream.

"Shut up. I've spent days looking into you, Russell Carraby. How you've pissed away your family's fortune. How you take advantage of the few tenants you've got left. You're a waste of oxygen."

There's another *thwack*, and I recoil, realizing I have to do something. "Gabe, no! Stop!"

I stand from my hidey hole, running for the front door. I turn the knob, and it sticks for a split moment, making me think it's locked, but then it gives way to reveal Gabe with his gloved hand around Russell's throat, who's an utter mess. A spray of blood is already splattered on Gabe's face, and the mallet is lifted for what has to be a final blow.

Russell's out, unconscious with his head lolling and only held up by Gabe's grip. Gabe's eyes are deadly, focused and cold.

"No, don't!" I plead as he looks at me in utter shock.

Then Gabe blinks, and while it's not my Gabe, the Gabe I'm used to . . . he's human, at least. I can see the pain flashing hot and sharp in his eyes as his brow furrows.

"Bella? You shouldn't have seen this," he says, letting go of Russell's throat and stepping back as the body drops to the floor. "Fuck, I wish you wouldn't have seen me like this."

CHAPTER 21

GABRIEL

I can feel his worthless body slump under my hand as I hit him in the chest with the mallet.

I bought the rubber mallet because I knew I wanted to hurt him but didn't want to actually kill him. Handy factoid, the rubber disburses the power of the strike, causing pain but significantly less damage than a normal hammer or bullet would.

I'd already done research on Russell Carraby, even before this morning. As soon as I knew he could be a threat to Bella, I looked into him and then watched and learned.

He wakes up at eleven, still half-drunk, and has a nasty habit of pissing in his own bushes on his way back inside from collecting the mail. He spends his days smoking and playing video games. He mostly only comes out to buy more drugs, steal shit from any store he's not banned from, or to bother the decent people unlucky enough to live on the land he owns.

I'd known he was bad news, but Bella was handling it, and honestly, I didn't want to answer the questions she'd have if I physically jumped in to save her from him. But this morning, everything changed, getting far worse than even I could have anticipated. I hadn't had a choice.

The one knee had been the smallest taste of what I'd wanted to do, and I'd known I was going back for him without Bella there to witness it. Even if it damns me, I'll save her. I'll punish him.

It's what I do.

And anything I dish out, up to and including death, would be warranted and well-deserved by a piece of shit like Carraby.

I'd swear I took the same precautions before approaching his house that I do with every entry I make, but obviously, I was at least partially distracted. Because now I've got Bella, standing in the doorway gawking at me, while I'm over a man whom I just beat unconscious.

And she's looking at me like I'm some sort of monster.

The truth hurts.

"You shouldn't have seen this, Bella," I say, stepping back from Russell and lowering the mallet. "I wish you wouldn't have seen me like this."

"Gabe . . . please, don't kill him," Bella says, her hands coming up in a prayer-like pose at her chin. Oh, my sweet princess, if you only knew how much better your life would be if you'd let me take care of this asshole.

But I didn't come here to kill him, and looking in her eyes, I wouldn't be able to go through with it even if I had.

I sigh, lowering the mallet. "I won't kill him, hadn't planned on it. But he . . ." I shake my head, knowing I can't beat around the bush with this any longer. "Please, I'll explain everything. At your house. I'll tell you everything."

"Why?" Bella asks, her eyes widening as panicked fear pierces her shock. "Oh, God, you're going to kill me." She takes a step back, and I force myself to stay still though every impulse makes me want to chase her and pull her back to me, make her see that I'm doing this for her, that I'll do anything for her.

She looks at Carraby, still unconscious but wheezily breathing through a broken nose. "No . . . no, I'm trying to save your life," I tell her, holding my hand out placatingly. Something in my tone must get through to her because her eyes flash back to me. "I swear, Bella, I'll protect you . . . but you have to understand that you're in danger."

Bella looks at me for a second, then points. "My house."

"Bella—"

"No, Gabe . . . I need a minute to process."

MOMENTS LATER, I'M PARKED IN FRONT OF BELLA'S HOUSE. THE front door is open and I can see her sitting on the couch. She's waiting for me. I tried to give her a minute like she asked for, even using Carraby's kitchen to clean up as best I could. But I know she'll probably still see the blood spatter marking me, even though it's gone.

I take a deep breath and get out of the truck, walking up slowly. She watches my approach warily, letting me come in and close the door. I sit down across from her, noting the phone and the gun on the makeshift table between us.

I wonder if she's already called the police. Or her friends, Mia and Thomas. That'd be most fitting since they're the ones who got her into this situation by asking her to interfere in Blackwell's plans. Even if it'd been unwittingly and had seemed like she was only playing a minor part in catching a corporate saboteur at Goldstone.

"Explain." Her tone is fury mixed with fear.

I count it a miracle that she's even here, honestly. And maybe just as much one that I'm here too. This is the point where I should cut my losses and run. But I can't leave her unprotected, because while I'm a scary man, Blackwell will just send someone with less scruples than I have if I leave.

How did I get so emotional about this? And how did my

emotions make me so sloppy?

"First, please understand, I'm still the guy who's talked to you, who's taken you out, who's made love to you . . . but I'm more than that too," I admit, watching as she stands to pace back and forth. "It's complicated."

"That's one way to put it!" she says, raising her voice. "I want the truth! All of it. Because the man I saw today isn't the same man I've been falling for!"

The words hang in the air, both of us stopping, and they sting as much as they fill me with wild hope.

She's falling for me? What have I done to deserve that, when I was sent to destroy her?

But maybe it's not too late to be who I was before revenge took root in my heart.

I need to unburden all those hidden lies to find out if it's possible.

"Bella . . . I'm falling for you too," I admit, looking down at my clasped hands, and I realize I'm literally begging her to believe me. "Russell Carraby is a bad guy, more so than you even realize. He's escalating, both in his drug habit and in his threats. I couldn't let that go." I look back up, imploring her. "What if I hadn't been here this morning? He very easily could've pushed his way in here and done . . ." I shudder at the thought of what that vile man would do to my sweet princess.

She finishes my sentence, "He could've done exactly what you did to him. Assault me, hurt me, kill me. But he didn't. You did. And neither of you had the right, him to do that to me nor you to do that to him."

"I know, but it's what I do, who I am. I'm sorry to say that, but it's the truth." I've never been ashamed of what I do before, having trusted in my rules and research enough to know that sometimes, working around the law to punish the truly despicable is the only way. But Bella's eyes light up like she's seeing me for the first time and isn't liking what she sees. At all.

"So you're judge, jury, and executioner all rolled into one?" She means it as an expression, not the actual truth, but I can see that she's starting to get it, realization dawning that my attack on Russell isn't a one-off situation but rather a single repetition of a recurring behavior.

Trying to calm her, I promise, "From the moment we first talked, I knew I couldn't do what I was hired to do." Baby steps to the truth. She deserves it all.

"Which is?" she asks, but I can see she doesn't really want to know.

I clear my throat. No other way to get around it. "I was hired by Blackwell to kill you."

Shocked, Bella stops pacing and shrieks, "You what?"

"From what I have gathered, you were instrumental in foiling some plan of his to discredit a business rival, Thomas Goldstone," I explain, charging on before things spiral any further out of control. "Blackwell's a vengeful son of a bitch, and he wanted to send a message. That's where I came in. But I have a code of ethics, my own moral guidelines, and he damn well knows it. It's why I looked deeper than his initial report. It'd said you were conniving, a key player in this business deal going sour. He knew I wouldn't kill an innocent person."

Bella pales, her hand going to her mouth. "Is Mia in danger? Or Thomas?"

My girl, always thinking of others before herself. Giving to a fault, even when she's the one to suffer for it. "No. At the moment, Blackwell feels certain that they're too high-profile, and eliminating them would create questions that could lead back to him. It's why he aimed for you. Your death would hurt them, but you're an easier target."

Her breath hitches at the description.

"I don't know the specifics, but I did take the job. I did my normal routine, observing you, learning your schedule, where you lived, worked, everything about you. Something felt off. None of what Blackwell said made any sense once I got to know you from afar. I needed to investigate further, to see if I was missing something. So, I approached you."

"And everything from there was just a fucking lie?" Bella asks, her voice rising to a yell. "Was everything just some . . . some way to make it easier to kill me?" She sounds incredulous, like this isn't possibly her life, but it is. And she's in very real danger. I have to make her understand.

"No!" I rasp, standing to face her so she hears me clearly. "Every moment I shared with you just made it harder. Bella, with every time we've talked, from the first moment I touched your hand, I felt split in half. When we went up to the overlook, I knew I could never do it. You're too good, too pure . . . you are what this world needs. Not Blackwell, with his jealousy and his hate. The world needs you. And so I've been delaying, making excuses, putting Blackwell off, trying desperately to figure out a way out of this."

"Why not just walk away?" Bella asks. "Why not go to the cops?"

"Because they're in his pocket," I reply with a dark laugh. "The man's got influence that stretches far and wide." I glance out the front window, remembering Blackwell's words and the suspicion that he has information superhighways feeding all sorts of intel right back to his ear. Particularly ones about Bella and my lack of follow-through on this assignment.

"And walking away isn't an option. At first, it was because he has information I need. Jeremy was killed in a drive by, and I've searched for a decade to find his killers. I've damn near sold my soul just to find out who did that to my sweet brother and Blackwell knows. He claims to know who killed Jeremy. He knew I'd do just about anything to get a lead and preyed on that. It's why I took the job in the first place. But I've given up on that. All that matters is you. But if I don't complete my contract, he'll just hire someone else to do the job . . . and probably add me as target number two."

For the first time, Bella shivers, realizing the danger she's in. "I just wanted to help Mia."

I nod. "I know. You're a good friend, a good person, and I'm trying my damnedest to be a good protector for you."

"Protector?" she scoffs, her eyes going hazy, and I suspect she's picturing the monstrous version of me she saw looming over an unconscious Russell. "Is that what a protector is?"

"I'm not a good man. I was angry at Russell, and even if I didn't go there to kill him, I can't promise what would've happened if you hadn't shown up. I know what I'm capable of, and it's not pretty. The only thing that gives me hope is that you've seen something in me that might be redeemable. I don't know."

"And why shouldn't I call the cops on you? You've been hired to kill me. You've been stalking me. Maybe I should have you arrested since you're the immediate threat."

It hurts, but I hold out my wrists as if she could cuff me right now. "If you wish, I won't stop you. But Bella, I promise that I will give my life to protect you. Yes, I'm falling for you . . . but I'm not foolish enough to think that I deserve your love after knowing what you know about me. But please . . . give me a chance to save your life."

"How?" she whispers. I can see the weight of the conversation taking its toll, the heaviness of what could have happened pressing on her chest as she visibly shrinks before me.

I shake my head, wiping at my cheek and realizing there's wetness there, horror at what I've done to this poor woman. "I haven't totally figured that out yet. One does not simply walk into the Blackwell Building and start recreating the lobby scene from *The Matrix*. Not if they expect to actually get Blackwell."

Bella opens her mouth to say something, then closes it, turning around and starting to pace again. "This is insane. I'm sitting here discussing killing people with a hitman who I want to be my boyfriend, and he's just put my sorta-landlord in the hospital."

"Do you still want me to be your boyfriend?" I ask, glomming onto the one piece of hope in her summary.

But she ignores the question, still lost in her own rehash. "Why not go to Thomas?" Bella asks. In her voice, I hear encouraging tones. She's in shock, but she's at least accepting what I'm saying without dismissing it outright. Belief might still be a little way off, but for now, she's at least listening and taking it in, offering solutions. "You know, the enemy of my enemy is my friend. And Thomas is a friend of friend already."

I consider it, even though it's one of a myriad of possible ideas I've already gone through. "It may come to that. Power for power, but right now, I think it would be like throwing kerosene on a bonfire, and Mia and Thomas would be the ones to pay the price if they jump into the fray. As scary as it is to consider, right now, Blackwell is focused on you, and they are safe."

It's a shitty move to make, because I know she'll do anything to keep her friends safe, even at the expense of herself. But it's the only way I can see getting her to agree with the only idea I've come up with, delay until I can find an angle on Blackwell. I throw the hook, baiting her.

"But I have another idea. Honestly, it's the only way out that I can see right now."

She looks at me through her lashes, not knowing how innocent and scared she looks. It draws out every protective instinct I have. "What?"

"We're out of time. We need to get you out of town, where I can keep you safe until I figure out how to keep Blackwell off you."

"I'm not running!" Bella says, and in her voice and face I see the determination, the spirit that has me falling for her. She's not going to retreat. She's going to take on the world on her own terms, and there's not a damn thing anyone can do about it.

"Bella, I'll do everything I can to protect you. I'll get you back here to your home, to your friends. But we need to get out of town if I have any chance of implementing any sort of plan."

"How can I just leave with you? I have so many unanswered questions. This is crazy."

I walk closer to her, slowly and steadily, giving her time to flee, but she doesn't move. Not even as I push her hair behind her ears and hold her face up, forcing her eyes to mine. "I'll answer any question you want . . . when we're on the road. I can see you want to push me out that door and go to your friends, the ones who have had your back your whole life. I get it, I do. But they don't have the skills I do. And I say that knowing it makes me even scarier in your eyes. You shouldn't trust me . . . but I need you to. Because more than anything else in this world, I don't want you to end up dead."

Bella blinks at the verbal shot, and then her eyes focus, questioning me. But I can't say the words she wants to hear. Not like this, not when it'll seem like a ploy. So I give her another truth. "You deserve all the best things the world has to offer, but the world deserves the very best of Isabella Turner too. Let me make sure that happens. Please."

CHAPTER 22

ISABELLA

I don't remember agreeing, exactly, but I must have because Gabe is suddenly shuffling around my house to pack my bag. I can't help, frozen and still trying to make sense of the information dump and paradigm shift I was just subjected to. It doesn't work. I'm still so lost.

It feels like no matter which way I turn, there's a threat looming, scary men using me as a pawn, taunting me into running and nipping at my heels to direct my destination the way they want. It's enough to make me want to say fuck it all and run on my own, just ditch my life and start over someplace fresh.

But I can't do that. I have people here whom I love and who love me and a future I've worked hard to secure and am so close to achieving. I won't give it up because some asshole in his fancy tower deems me a beneficial loss.

Gabe stops in front of me, my backpack slung on like he's ready to roll. He puts his hands on my shoulders and looks at me. "Say it, Bella. I'm not kidnapping you, but I want you to come with me. If you can't, we'll find another way. I just don't know what that is."

This is the moment of truth. My decision time.

I don't know Gabe, I realize. I thought I did, and even now, what he shared feels real. But what if it was a ploy? I search his eyes, holding my breath and hoping for some sort of sign.

He takes it as an answer, dropping the backpack to the floor. Running his fingers through his hair, he paces. "Fuck. Okay, we'll stay if that's what you want, but I gotta figure out . . ." His voice fades as he mumbles to himself, eyes going wild before he focuses sharply. It sounds like he's running through scenarios and options for staying here and keeping me safe.

It's what I need. Some small piece of reassurance that he will do what I want, even in a situation that is largely beyond anything I've ever considered, and even if it's not what he thinks is best. I guess I thought he'd shove me out the door regardless, kidnapping me, as he said. But that he is willing to follow my lead somehow gives me peace that what I've been feeling is true and what he feels about me is real.

I bend down to pick up my own bag. "I need to stop by the diner, give Martha her car back, and ask her to watch Vash."

His eyes jump to me, my agreement instantly stopping his play-by-play of possible outcomes and strategies.

He doesn't ask if I'm sure, taking me at my word and moving toward the door. But he stops, one hand on the frame. "We need to assume we're being watched. I chose your school bag so it'll look like you're just heading out for a usual day. But if we look suspicious or angry, basically anything other than the happy couple, it'll rouse concerns."

"What do you want me to do?" I ask, hearing that he's leading up to something.

"We're going to walk outside, kiss goodbye like everything's fine, and get in our vehicles. I'll follow you to the diner, and you need to tell them that this is a vacation or something—like I'm whisking you away, so act happy. And then we'll leave town in my truck."

I take a big breath, realizing just how crazy this sounds. "That's a lot. Martha will know something's up. And don't you need to go by the motel?" I mean it to be more of a sting than it really is, a show that I know something, at least. But it doesn't land, and he brushes the question off.

"I'll get what I need on the road. I do it all the time. Sell Martha on this. Please, Bella."

The kiss outside is awkward, but Gabe pulls me to him and cups my jaw in his powerful hand. If anyone's watching, it probably looks like a sweet, sultry kiss. And for sure, Mrs. Petrie across the street is watching, but if Gabe is right, who else is?

The drive to The Gravy Train gives me time to think, but even without Gabe's influence, I can feel in my gut that this is the right thing to do. If Blackwell's after me, and I do believe Gabe that he is, this is the best way to be safe.

A single butterfly flutters around in my belly at the thought of being away from my tough life, alone with Gabe and all his terror and his sexiness. And even the fear and questions surrounding this situation aren't enough to contain the slight buzz. It makes me feel a bit pitiful to be excited about something dire, but it's a different sort of fear than not making the rent or having Russell bark and bitch at me.

Russell. Even thinking his name draws up the image of his body slumping to the floor. Is he okay, I wonder, or did Gabe finish the job after I left? A shudder racks through me, but I realize shamefully that even if he did kill Russell after I left, I don't care. God, I'm awful. But Russell has made my life a living hell, scared the piss out of me so many times I've lost count, and is an absolute terrifying waste of a human life. His death would be mourned by none and quietly celebrated by many.

So I don't call the police or an ambulance, even now that I could. Maybe I should do something, but I can live with the guilt of non-action more than I can live with the consequences of Russell taking vengeance for this on me.

The parking lot at The Gravy Train is full, a blessing because it means Martha won't have time to focus on me the way she would if there was no one calling for a refill.

Inside, I wave and smile, feigning that everything's fine the way Gabe said to. "Thanks, Martha. Sorry for the drama earlier, but uhm . . ." I bite my lip, nervous about this part. "I have a huge favor to ask."

Her eyes narrow, but then she lifts her brows, inviting me to ask away.

"Gabe wants to take me away for the weekend, a last-minute getaway." I freeze. "I mean, vacation. A last-minute vacation. Is there any way you could get Shelly or Elaine to cover for me and feed Vash for me?"

"I can do that, but only if you tell me what had you running out of here like your tail was on fire earlier." She crosses her arms, looking every bit the stern mom-figure she's been for me.

I stammer, not sure what to say, and Gabe slips an arm around my shoulders. I hadn't even realized he was behind me. "I'm afraid that's my fault. I was trying to surprise her and might have accidentally let the cat out of the bag, so to speak. She freaked a bit."

Martha smiles like she completely understands that I would do something like that. She reaches for my hands, looking so charmed she might as well be blessing our union. God, if only she knew the truth, she'd be stringing Gabe up by his toenails and she'd use Henry's good knives to destroy the evidence of killing him for being mixed up in this.

"Go, honey. Treat yourself for once. You do so much here. Let us do for you this time." She pulls me in for a hug, and while it feels good to have her love envelop me, I feel bad for lying to her. She turns to Gabe, patting him on the cheek. "You must be something special if she's ditching us for a weekend away with you."

There's a warning in her tone, and I wonder what they talked about the night I saw them talking while Gabe waited for my dinner break.

Outside, Gabe opens the door to his truck, helping me in. I see him scan the lot without moving his head as he walks around to the driver side, just his eyes moving. "I think we're clear. Not sure if that's a bad sign or we're just fucking lucky. But we'll be careful on the way out of town to make sure we're not being followed."

We're quiet on the way out of town, but slowly, conversation starts as my fear fades. It's not that I'm no longer afraid, but merely that my body has burned out all the adrenalin and I'm feeling flat and tired now.

"Tell me how it got to this point," I say.

Gabe scratches at his lip with his thumb, glancing into the rearview mirror for the tenth time. "Like I said, you helped Thomas catch a corporate saboteur whom Blackwell planted. He felt like you were an easier target—"

"Not me, you," I interrupt. "Oh, wait. I just realized something. I don't think Mia and Thomas know Blackwell had anything to do with that whole mess. They thought it was just a single man's vendetta. Well, I guess it is, but they don't realize the man is Blackwell. I need to call them."

I look around for my phone, and Gabe shakes his head. "I left it behind. It's traceable, Bella. You can call Mia from a burner phone if you need to, but I think we need to wait until we figure out the game plan before we get them involved. Can you give me a little bit of time?"

I sigh, turning to look out the window. It feels wrong to not tell my bestie this, but as long as she's safe with Thomas, I can wait a day or two. I still double-check myself again, but as crazy as this all sounds, it also makes sense and feels like the truth. Gabe's truth about why he's here and hanging out with me, so I have to take the leap of faith and not call Mia immediately, no matter how much I want to.

Gabe clenches his jaw, gritting his teeth like he's the one hurting. "After Jeremy died, I fell apart. It was slow at times, so incremental I didn't even notice, and then I'd take a leap, lashing out at the world."

My head snaps his way. "Tell me," I demand again. And this time, he knows what I mean.

"It started with me asking questions, simple enough but hard, nevertheless. All too quickly, things got violent as I demanded answers from people who ultimately had none to give. But I developed a reputation for a rather in-demand skillset. In a way, I put aside my own mission for other people's, but doing this ugly work let me hide in the shadows, seeking information in a way I couldn't as a regular guy." His eyes leave the road, quickly glancing over to judge my reaction.

"I've tried to maintain my own sense of justice, of right and wrong, by carefully choosing the contracts I accept and doing my own due diligence. That's why I realized that you were an innocent, because I looked into you and couldn't find a single evil thing about you. But I found plenty about Blackwell because I always research my employer as well. It's good to know who you're getting into bed with."

I scoff. "I agree."

But I'm not talking about business arrangements and he knows it.

He reaches over slowly, placing a hand on my knee and squeezing. "You know me. Everything between us was real, is real. There was just another layer you didn't know about then, but now you do."

I want to fall into him, desperate to believe but unwilling to plunge carelessly. "But it's the very foundation we were building on, and now I find out that it's faulty."

He swallows thickly and clears his throat. "Then we'll start fresh and rebuild."

CHAPTER 23

ISABELLA

"*B*ella?"

I look over, where Gabe's sitting behind the wheel of the truck, a worried look on his face. We've stopped for gas, and I guess I haven't said anything in awhile. "Sorry . . . I was just thinking."

"Ah," Gabe replies, starting the truck up and pulling back out. "You just looked . . . I'm not sure."

I nod, turning to him. "How'd you get that nickname? The Fallen Angel?" He's been telling me about his life in bits and bites as we drive, more about his work and 'fall from grace', as he calls it, and about who he'd been once upon a time, before his soul had been stained with his dark actions.

Gabe turns back onto the highway, leading us toward the ocean. "I think mostly because of my name. One of my first contracted jobs was with an Italian guy who was very into the Church. With my looks, it sort of stuck."

I can't help it—it makes me chuckle. "Your looks, huh?"

Gabe looks over, tentatively smirking. "You want to know the only thing worse than someone who's obsessed with their looks? A good-looking person who's full of false humility. It's ironic, really, because I'm the least angelic man, with the ugliest soul. Jeremy was the saint, not me. Don't get me wrong, he was a ladies' man, but he died too young and innocent."

"Tell me about him," I ask as we come around a turn. We're in the mountains, on one of those roads that really should be expanded from the two-lane overgrown logging roads they used to be, with sunlight barely drifting between the trees behind us. "What was he like?"

"Funny," Gabe says immediately, grinning. "That kid . . . I was the older brother, though not even by a full year. But our whole lives, he was the one who was devil-may-care, and I spent . . . shit, if I have any gray hair at all, it's because I spent so much time worrying about that kid."

"What did he do?" I ask, grinning a little. It's helpful and reminds me of the human side of Gabe that still makes my heart flutter in my chest.

"What didn't he do? Have you seen the 'hold my beer' meme? That was him, though non-alcoholic, mostly," he says with a wink. "If he saw someone jump their bike over something, he would be outside the next day, busting his ass and trying it. This one time, just because he saw it on YouTube, he did the flying dive . . . fucking still amazed he survived that one."

"What's the flying dive?" I ask, my imagination trying to picture it, and each picture is crazier than the next.

"He'd seen some college guy do a leap off his roof into a swimming pool, elbow dropping this inflatable zebra or some damn thing. We didn't have a pool at home, but our town's youth center had one. So the next time we're there, Jeremy goes, 'Gabe, keep the deep end clear.' Then he gets out of the pool and goes inside, nonchalant as fuck. I'm wise enough to Jeremy's bullshit by this point. I know I can't stop him, so I just made sure no little kids were in the deep end. Suddenly, the big sliding window to the second-floor game room opens, and five seconds later, Jeremy comes flying out, stretched out like fucking Superman or something. Scared the shit out of me. It was at least a six-foot gap of concrete he had to clear."

"He made it?" I ask, and Gabe nods.

"Biggest, ugliest belly flop ever, but yeah, he was fine. After we got kicked out, we walked home. His chest and stomach were pink and bruised for days. I've never seen anyone with black and blue nipples before him."

He shakes his head, laughing at the memory and making me laugh at the mental image he painted of Jeremy. "Did you two look alike?"

"Jeremy took after our mother more. He had these big green eyes. He could sweet-talk anyone. Like the community center? He somehow got us allowed back in within a week, and by the end of the summer, he'd even kissed Wendy Partridge, the head lifeguard who was pretty much every teenage boy's dream for two summers. I was too serious, too involved in studying and being the outlier to really make the same strides he did."

I squint, trying to imagine Gabe as anything but a handsome charmer. It's damn hard, even knowing what I know about him. "What do you mean, outlier?"

"I guess I was kind of a loner. I mean, I wasn't bullied or anything. You don't bully a guy my size, though I was a bit lankier back then. I just did my own thing. It was me and Jeremy, two peas in a pod, even if he did go out a bit more."

I can feel in his words that he cared a lot for his brother. "You loved him."

Gabe clears his throat. "He was a pain in the ass, but yes, I did. After he was killed and I started down . . . down the path that I've gone in life, I guess I started emulating some of his traits. The first time I had to stand up to a guy with a gun, that wasn't me slickly talking my way out of that shit. That was Jeremy talking through me."

The mountains suddenly stop, and I'm stunned at the sight

before me. The highway comes almost to the beach itself, and in front of me, the wild, untamed Pacific roars and rages, crashing against the rocky coastline in gigantic sprays of foam.

Just off shore, maybe less than a quarter-mile, are a couple of rocks that are too big to be properly called rocks but too small to be called islands. One of them, the largest, is almost perfectly domed, ringed with trees and standing in the middle of the sea in front of me.

"This is . . . wow. I didn't expect a safe house out here."

"Well, it's not an actual safe house, but we'll be protected here. It's a rental property, remote and isolated. Just the two of us." His voice goes husky, and I know that there's no way I'll be able to resist him if there's no one around to buffer the heat he so easily stirs up in me.

The rational side of me revolts against the idea, wanting to start over like he said and build slowly and carefully, maybe even wait until the danger passes and I can see if he disappears like fog in the sunshine. But there's another side of me saying that if I'm going out, I'm doing it on my own terms and sexually satisfied.

I'm honestly not sure which side I want to win.

Instead of deciding now, I question him. "If it's a rental, that means there's a record. That's dangerous, right? Blackwell could track us right to the front door."

He looks over, a pleased smile developing, and then his dimples pop. "Good girl. I like the way you're thinking."

Warmth heats my belly and my cheeks, and he continues. "I used an alias to book the rental, so it's not traceable to me at all."

We keep driving, and when we turn off the coastal highway, I can still see the big domed rock. But what takes all of my attention is on the gate in front of us. Large and imposing black iron, but pretty and ornate. Gabe stops at the box and rolls his window down to tap a few numbers on the keypad. It slides open, and Gabe drives a few feet to the other side before stopping.

He gets out, waiting as the gate slides back closed, and then goes over to the mechanical box. He opens it, doing something I can't see, and then gets back in the truck.

"Turned off the gate mechanism and took out the fuse so it can't be turned back on without it. Now the gate won't work electronically, and it's too heavy to manually side open. We're secure against vehicles because the fence goes around the whole property."

It strikes me that he specified 'secure against vehicles' because that means we're not secure against someone scaling the fence. Because that's an actual risk. Again, I'm struck with how crazy my life has become.

The blooming anxious fear is stopped abruptly as we come through a row of trees to a clearing and the house comes into view.

It's stunningly beautiful, turn of the century styling but updated to be modern. Gabe makes quick work of the front door, and we walk into a foyer with two-story ceilings. A plush rug softens my footsteps as I gawk, spinning in place.

I can't think of the last time I was in a room that was like this. Or maybe never? The walls are elegant, decorated in a slightly Victorian floral wallpaper, and as I look out the big window in front of us, I'm struck by how beautiful the view is. The ocean stretches as far as I can see to the horizon, and the beach beckons.

I realize Gabe is watching me take in the house. "This is what you deserve, Bella. Beautiful things, luxury at your fingertips, and more."

I look away from the view to meet his eyes and shake my head. "This is amazing, but I don't deserve it more than any other person does. All I want is to be safe, to be able to go home to my friends, who are safe, and for everyone to be happy. That's enough."

His smile is sad. "Let me do a run-through. Will you wait here?"

I nod and he disappears. I hear him opening and closing doors and several beeps as he messes with the alarm system. I move to the window, and staring outside, it feels like we're the only two people left in the world.

Moments later, he's back and follows my sightline outside. "I need to check outside too. Do you want to walk with me? We can walk on the beach?" he beckons, the hope that it'll entice me in the gravel of his voice.

I follow his lead out the back door and down the wooden steps to the sand. The beach isn't sugar sand, and while it's beautiful, I can't really see anyone using it for sunbathing. The sand's too coarse, the breeze coming off the ocean and hitting the mountain just a little too brisk. Even in summer, it'd be too cold for a bikini for all but the most hardcore of bathers, and the waves are so wild that every breath of air is tinged with the flavor of salt as the cool mist kisses my skin.

We walk, the sand crunching under our shoes as I listen to the roar of the water, trying to let go of the terror that sneaks up on me and then fades away just as unexpectedly. It's not that anything in particular eases me. It's just not sustainable to live in constant fear, looking over my shoulder. I'm not built that way, jaded and scared of the world. But I get the feeling Gabe is.

We've spent so much time in the past eight hours talking. The thought of his own personal tragedies makes me shiver, and I tug on the sleeves of my sweatshirt to disguise the reason.

I reach over, taking Gabe's hand. His brows lift in pleased surprise, and though his brown eyes stayed locked on me, I turn to look out at the ocean. "I miss my family too. Seems we're both alone."

"You're not alone, Bella. Your family might not be blood, but they're the ones you've chosen and who've chosen you back."

I notice he doesn't make the same correction about himself. Perhaps he truly is alone. The thought makes me sad.

"I try to remember my family, but it was so long ago and I was so little. I'm glad you had your brother for so long, that you were so close. For a long time, I wanted that, would wish that I'd had another year, a month, a week, even a day. To have more memories, but what little I have are faded with time." I look down, digging the toe of my tennis shoe into the sand., "Sometimes, I can't even remember what my mother looked like or what her voice sounded like. I've tried so often."

It's a painful confession, one I don't share lightly or to just anyone.

"The trick is to think of context," Gabe says. "Don't just think of her face or voice. Think of something you did together. Think of a time you had fun together and picture the whole scene. That'll make it come to you."

I close my eyes, and after a moment, it comes to me. "My fourth birthday. She made orange cupcakes with Fruity Pebble sprinkles, just like I asked for. They were so sweet even half of one gave me a stomachache, but I loved them all the same. I can hear her asking me if they were what I dreamed they'd be. I remember her smile when I jumped up and down, yelling yes over and over," I say with a teary smile.

I turn to Gabe, hugging him. "Thank you."

"Always, Bella. I learned that from using the same trick to remember Jeremy."

I shiver, hugging him tighter. When I let go, he takes my hand and we resume walking. "I need to finish the perimeter check. You okay to walk with me?"

I nod, but as we leave the empty beach with sightlines for miles to move into the treed area around the house, I can feel the change in Gabe. He drops my hand, his eyes scanning carefully and occasionally checking the fence line.

I follow along, useless to help, and the one time I try to speak, he gently hushes me with a finger to my lips. He whispers, "Shh, I'm listening for anything in the woods." So I bite my tongue and trudge behind him.

The sun is low in the sky when we get back to the house, the long day taking its toll physically and the emotional roller coaster crashing over me mentally.

Gabe helps me settle on the couch and then moves to start a fire. When he's satisfied that it's going well, he sits beside me and wraps an arm around my shoulders. Too exhausted to be upset any longer, I melt into him.

This should feel wrong. I should be scared of him.

But after everything, both before this morning and after, some-how, this feels right. I feel safe in his arms. Maybe that's stupid of me, but that ship has long since sailed, right about the time I climbed into his truck. Actually, maybe before that, when I let him into my house to explain.

Charlotte whispers in my ear again, *background check*.

But I am where I am, and I don't know that I'd change it even if I could. So I sink deeper and let myself be enveloped by him, even if there's a price to pay.

Even if it's my life.

CHAPTER 24

GABRIEL

*T*he room glows in a soft firelight, the flames dancing in Isabella's eyes. We haven't said anything for the past ten minutes, just exchanging slow kisses.

They were tentative at first, like she's not sure if this is really what she wants.

So I'm letting her lead for now, knowing that I'm responsible for a lot of our current situation and that Bella is a woman who likes to be in control of her own destiny. This time, I'll let her decide where this goes, even if it's her to one bed and me to another.

But words aren't needed any longer when she reaches up and pulls off her shirt, shrugging it off and freeing her breasts from the simple bra she wears underneath.

Each apple-sized handful sways back and forth as she traces her stomach with her fingertips before lying back on the couch.

"Show me," I whisper, and Bella bites her lip, her hands cupping her breasts before she teases her nipples, pulling on them until her tits are nearly pyramided up from her body and making her gasp in pain and pleasure before she lets them go.

While she kneads her right breast, I run my hand down her body, caressing her soft skin. She writhes, her belly sucking in as I move to the waist of her jeans. She nods, giving me silent permission, and I slip the button free and unzip them, pushing them over her hips. She lifts, helping me get them off, her panties coming off at the same time.

And then she's bare before me.

Beautiful, trusting, good. Too good for me, but I can't stop myself from worshipping her body, tasting her kind heart.

I spread her knees, one to the back of the couch and the other at the edge of the couch, but Bella sets her foot on the floor to open more for me. I can see the gleam on her sweet sex, already puffy and slick with need.

I take her hand, kissing her fingertips and then directing her to her core. "Touch your pussy. Finger fuck yourself for me, Bella," I command, pulling my shirt off as she traces her slit before rubbing her clit with feather-light strokes. She moans, her eyes never leaving me as she slides two fingers deep inside herself, pumping them in and out slowly.

My cock's rock hard, watching her lips cling to her fingers and knowing that soon, my cock will be lodged deep inside her and feeling the same sucking kiss.

"I . . . I can't help it," she mewls, her hips lifting to meet her fingers as she speeds up a little. "Gabe, I need you. Take me. Fuck me, please."

Her words make me speed up, and I stand to strip off my jeans, my cock aching to be inside her. Bella sobs in want as I pause, and she pulls her fingers out, wrapping them around my shaft. She strokes me, coating me in her honey and driving me wild, but I keep a tight grip on my control.

She needs me, needs this, but I can't go too hard on her. Not right now. She doesn't know it, but she needs some tenderness right now, with her heart and with her body.

That I'm even getting the chance to be with her this way is a gift, one I won't waste or cheapen. Already trembling on the edge of no return, I pull my hips back. "Bella, I'm too close. Need to be inside you."

Her breath hitches as I hover over her, holding myself up so I don't put my weight on her. She reaches between us, guiding me to her entrance, holding me still.

"Do you feel that, Princess? That's you and me. No lies, only truth, only us. No matter what," I promise, taking her free hand and entwining our fingers. Bella nods, releasing my shaft, and I press deep inside her, filling her with all I have.

She whimpers, stretched even after her fingers have been plunging inside her. Her fingers tighten in mine, but she doesn't protest, trusting me completely.

I press into her, our bodies grinding together, and I can feel her clit rub against the base of my cock. Her pussy gushes over my shaft, and I pull back, pausing before stroking deeply again, leaning down to kiss her as I push her into the couch cushions.

I pump slowly, relishing every clench of her body around me as I drive into her, pinning her underneath me. I can see the look in her eyes, pleasure and pain and worry and trust swirling in her mind, released in every gasp.

"That's it, Bella," I rasp, speeding up until our hips start slapping together. "Come hard on my cock. I'm here for you."

I pound her, speeding up, but my arms give out, needing to feel her body pressed to mine. I lie over her, hip to hip, chest to chest, my arms wrapping around her. She responds by wrapping her arms and legs around me too.

I bury my nose in the crook of her neck, inhaling her lavender scent as I listen to her moans and mewls in my ear. She gets louder, crying out, and I lift slightly to look at her. Her cheeks are flushed, her eyes widening more and more.

"Right there, Gabe. *Fuck*."

I pull back and drive hard, hitting a spot deep inside her that lights her on fire, until she shatters with a wail, writhing underneath me. I ride her through it, letting her pussy's contractions push me higher and higher.

I tremble, pulling back and thrusting once more before I go over as well. I pull out as I come hard, my cock spewing over her pussy and belly as I mark her, painting her satin flesh with my seed.

BELLA SLEEPS LIKE THE DEAD, BARELY MOVING A MUSCLE SAVE FOR her parted lips occasionally pursing as she snores softly. Like a creeper, I watch her sleep, unable to relax myself. Even with a nightly check of the perimeter and the alarm, I feel like there's too much at risk, too great a danger to let my guard down.

It's barely dawn when I finally get out of bed, figuring I should go ahead and start the coffee for the day. I am sipping my second cup, looking out over the water, when I hear Bella padding around.

I feel her enter the room, her warmth reaching me even from the doorway. Or maybe it's just that she makes me warm inside, thawing a heart I thought had been irreparable and a soul almost certainly irredeemable.

"I made coffee," I tell her, taking a drink.

"Don't move," she whispers.

Instantly, I'm on alert, turning to look out the window but seeing nothing other than the rising sun in the sky. "What's wrong? What do you see?"

She laughs lightly. "You. Stay, just like that."

She runs off, and I hear her shuffling around before she reappears with her laptop. I only let her bring it because I knew she couldn't get Wi-Fi without my help, and it would help her calm down. "I want to draw you. The light is magnificent."

She sits across from me, telling me how to pose and basically putting me back how I was when she walked into the room. She works quietly, looking back and forth from me to the screen.

"What are you doing, exactly? Is this going to be Picasso-esque and I'll have to smile politely and act like I get the deeper meaning of abstract art? Or are you more a realist and I'm suddenly going to be paranoid about the size of my nose?"

Her smile is soft, but her hand never stops moving. "I'm more of a realist if those are the only two choices, which they aren't. But I've played with all sorts of styles. I love it all—paints, canvasses, pencils, charcoal, and of course, digital. And each medium lends itself to a different feel."

"Is that why you're going to school for graphic design? To be an artist?" I ask, wanting to know everything about her. Not just the dry facts on paper, but the meaning behind her choices, her thought processes as she decided her future.

Her shrug is one-sided so as not to disturb her drawing. "It's a way for me to do what I love and make money. Right now, it's mostly typography-type things. Like I designed the logo, did the menus and boards for The Gravy Train. That was a labor of love, but I also want to do other things. Book covers, maybe, or even video game design? Mia is a major gamer and always begs me to play. The play itself isn't my favorite, but I love seeing how the graphics change and the artist creates the different scenes. It's just like a painting, but digital. I'm not sure yet. I just love art and want to be able to create for a living."

The passion with which she speaks is inspiring, making me wish I had something as pure and beautiful that I believed in. Once upon a time, I hoped that, even in the ugly things I did, I could find some balance. Dark for light, evil for good, make wrong things right.

But I can see the truth now. Bella has shown me that.

And I know that I'll never return to my previous life. I can't. It means I may never get the answers I need about Jeremy's death, and while I'm not sure I can let that go without the retribution I promised, I can feel down to the last shredded tatters of my soul that I cannot kill in cold blood again.

Well, except for Blackwell. But killing him wouldn't be in cold blood. My heart would be pumping fast and hard to have a chance to take him out, my blood heated with fury for the opportunity to insure Bella's safety once and for all.

Bella taps the screen of her laptop a few times in quick succession, breaking my heavy thoughts. "What do you think?" she asks, turning the computer around.

It's me. But not.

She's captured a side of me I don't think exists. Or if it does, it's only in her mind. Is this how she sees me?

It's a profile picture, the sun improbably shining brightly behind me, giving a halo effect. But my expression is dark, my jaw clenched. There's a tightness to my eyes, a sad beauty highlighted by the single solitary tear trailing down my cheek.

I am every bit a Fallen Angel.

But when I look at her, seeing the hope that I like her painting lighting her eyes, I think maybe I could be redeemed. If anyone can save me, it's her. And if anyone can save her, it's me. It's a match made in heaven. Or hell, depending on the outcome.

CHAPTER 25

GABRIEL

*T*he last twenty-four hours have been sheer madness. Bella and I have cussed and discussed every which way to get her out of this mess. The best idea we've come up with is ridiculous, something that only works in movies.

But considering this whole scenario is pretty cinematic, with the evil hitman who falls for his innocent target and a malevolent villain in a tower overlooking the little people of Roseboro, a good fake death seems apropos.

Oddly enough, my dark background is our best secret weapon. I've seen too much death, know what it looks like, smells like, feels like in those moments, and while staging that with Bella as the victim turns my stomach, it's the only way.

If Blackwell will believe she's dead, and we can hide her away, then it'll give us time to figure out something long-term. That's the point where we're going to need Thomas to step in and use his power in this chess game. A pawn simply can't win it, but Bella can be the strategic move to get the ball rolling.

I finish blending the most disgusting shake I've ever made, pure powdered sugar dissolved in water with a dash of cocoa and an entire bottle of red food coloring. I wasn't sure the internet was right, but even my eye would be fooled by the murky, dark red liquid. Hopefully, when combined with a camera filter, Blackwell will be too.

I pour the mixture into a sport bottle and add it to the bag of supplies. "You ready?" I call out.

Bella appears at the kitchen doorway a moment later, looking nervous. "Yeah, I'm ready. Guess that means this recipe was a solid counterfeit?"

I hold up the blender, tilting it so she can see. Her face scrunches in disgust, and she turns her head away. "Oh, my God, that's so gross. It looks so real!"

Evilly, I stick my tongue out and catch a drip running down the side. She screeches and I can't help but laugh. "Totally edible too," I tease.

She shakes her head, walking away. "Only if you're a vampire!"

We gear up, and with a steadying breath, we set out with a prayer that this plan works.

Thirty minutes later, we reach the summit of a cliff I found on a perimeter check yesterday. It's even more remote than the house, with a view that would warrant it being called a 'lookout point.' Most importantly, the mountaintop gives way to a stair-step of cliff edges off the main ridge.

Taking our time, we get everything set up. Well, mostly, I do while Bella tries to breathe and calm down. There's no need to rush. We need this to look believable, so the beginning has to seem as though I've seduced her completely and we're on a romantic walk through the woods where she suspects nothing.

Right now, though, she looks like there's an invisible firing squad aiming for her. Which, while somewhat true, will not sell our story.

"Relax. You can do this, Bella. We can do this," I say soothingly as I come over, stroking her cheek. "It's going to work."

We've spent hours creating this visual chain of effects, from selfies at the trailhead before we set off on the hike, to the quick video of her ass walking in front of me while I catcalled, telling her to 'swing that ass for me.' Her sweetly shy look over her shoulder had been real, and I want to save it just for me, but it's a puzzle piece in the bigger picture here.

I add a couple of shots of the horizon and the forest below, even taking a 360-degree panoramic that ends with Bella and me together, big smiles on our faces. A few more shots of the happy couple and then it's time to get to the real work of today.

"Are you ready?" I ask, and she bites her lip but nods.

I count down, "Three . . . two . . . one," and hit the record button. "What do you think? Beautiful, isn't it?"

She nods, her voice quavering, but it works for the setup. "It is, but fuck, this is high. I'm scared of heights, Gabe. You know that."

Her voice has just a bit of hysteria to it. I know it's because she's truly getting scared about the intensity of what we're about to do, but it effectively sells the fear of heights she doesn't have.

"Don't worry, I've got you. Come on."

I move toward the edge of the cliff, walking past Bella and showing a view of the forest below us, careful not to show the cliff face with its juts of rock that create platforms below the level we're standing on.

I extend my hand, pulling her to my side and angling the camera toward us. I kiss her, soft and slow, taking my time to help calm her.

"Absolutely breathtaking," I say, bringing the camera close to her again. This close, all you can see is her face, and I can see the wonder and the tremble in her cheek. I want to reassure her, but her reactions look real and are exactly what we need, so I hold myself back.

"You're not filming the view," she scolds me lightly. "Look at the birds flying out of that tree," she says, looking past me.

"Nope," I say, popping the *P*.

"Why are you filming me, Gabe? It's kinda weird." She blushes like she likes it, even as she protests.

"What do you mean?"

Bella cuts her eyes to me, smiling nervously. "I feel like I'm in one of those 'found footage' horror movies. Some monster's going to swoop out of the forest and snatch me or something."

I lick my lips hungrily, ready to get this over with, but don't lower the camera. "Sorry, but the monster's already here."

"Wha—" Bella says, but before she can finish, I grab her by the throat, shoving her down onto her knees. "Gabe, what the—"

I slap her, but it's pulled, and Bella doesn't roll with it, making me stop the video. "Shit . . . Bella, are you okay?"

Bella gets up, nodding. "I'm fine, but . . . that was terrible."

"Okay, let's try again."

"Wait," Bella says, taking my hand.

"This is supposed to be real. Slap me," Bella says simply. "You're barely hitting me, and I'm supposed to go down like you knocked the shit out of me."

I clench my teeth, wondering if I've got the strength to do it.

We start from the top and make it to the strike again, and this time, I don't hold back. Feeling horrible, I growl at her, "Stupid bitch."

Bella falls to the dirt, hard, and blinking in utter shock as she looks up at me. "What?"

The fear is palpable now. The tears trickling down her cheeks are real.

"You thought a guy like me would be with a loser like you? So pathetic. You're just a pawn in someone else's game. Useful, until you're not." The hateful vitriol pours off my tongue, the opposite of everything I believe, but I force the words through gritted teeth, hoping it reads as spite.

"Gabe, why?" she whimpers, and I almost stop, but I soldier on.

It's for a good reason. It's the only way to keep her safe a little longer.

"Gabe . . . please, I—" She's crawling away from me, her hands and knees getting scraped up and snot beginning to run down her face from her continued cries.

I pull my pistol, aiming at her chest. "Don't move," I order her, and she freezes in place.

Stepping closer, I meet her eyes. They're wide and wild as she shakes her head, pleading with her hands outstretched as if she can stop me. "No, oh, God, please . . . no, Gabe."

The shot rings out, a loud crack in the quiet woods, and Bella collapses to the dirt.

I drop the camera face down, cutting the video. Rushing off to the side, I grab the bottle of fake blood and turn back to Bella, who's trying to get up and shaking her head. "Don't move. Stay just like you are so it looks right."

She lowers back to the ground, hissing, "Fuck, that was loud."

I squirt the red viscous mixture on her chest, as if it's leaking from a small but deadly heart hit. "Hurry, we've got to get the timing right."

We talked through the plan from every angle, and one flaw we saw was the camera cut, but there was no other way. We don't have a thousand dollars of Hollywood special effects, and I wouldn't know how to work those anyway. So in order to keep the time stamps lined up, we have to get the video restarted quickly.

My heart hammers in my chest as I see the 'blood' on her.

How close was I to damning myself? How could I have ever considered doing for real what I'm pretending to have done to Bella?

How have I done this for as long as I have? How many souls stain my hands. I know the number, of course, but it's not one I'm proud of. Bile rises in my throat.

I need to atone. It's as good a word as any to get me moving.

Bella smears more of the blood through her hair before lying down in a puddle of it.

Stepping back, the cold side of me takes over, saying it looks good enough to fool anyone but a pro. All bloodied and bruised from the repeated slaps, Bella feigns unconsciousness, her eyes open wide in shock and her breath held for as long as she can.

I take several still shots, showing the damage. I let her get a breath in and then I restart the camera for the next video snippet, showing my booted feet as I roll her to the edge of the cliff using my toes to keep her moving.

At the edge, I bend down, facing the camera myself. "Job complete," I say to the glass circle, all cocky arrogance and ugly indifference to the loss of a human life.

I push her over with a shove of my hand, and she silently tumbles from sight. She'd been nervous that she'd scream, but she holds it in, along with any natural instincts to flail. The result is that it looks like she's already dead and just being dumped into the ravine.

"Bye, Isabella Turner," I say with a wave.

I cut the video again, my heart frozen in my chest as I look over the edge and pray that she hit the rocky platform below us just right.

She's there, but she's still. Too still. Was the drop too far? Did she knock herself out somehow?

"Bella?" I cry out, dropping to my knees to try to descend to her.

She opens one eye slowly. "We clear?" she whispers.

Relief washes through me, and I nod. "Clear."

She opens both eyes then, laying out wide on the rock as if she's sunbathing. "Good, help me get up there. It's a good thing I'm not really scared of heights, but this is really high up."

I toss her a rope, helping pull her back to the top as I coach her about where to place her feet for holds to make the climb up easier. As soon as she has both feet on the ground, I pull her away from the edge and into my arms. "Oh, my God, Bella. I'm so sorry," I say, cupping her face and turning it this way and that to verify for myself that she's okay.

"Hey . . . you look worse than I feel, Gabe. It was just acting. I know you were just doing what you needed to. Are you okay?"

I clear my throat, ashamed. "Yeah. Just some dark thoughts about the kind of man I've become. How do you feel?"

"I'm good. Messy, but good. Let's get this done and then we'll talk."

The image of a blood-splattered Bella, blood actually dripping between her teeth and over her lips, shocks me, and I stumble back, dropping the phone before plopping on the ground. Cradling my head in my hands, elbows on my bent knees, I break.

My mind's overwhelmed, images of the past several years flooding back to pummel me.

"No . . . no," I moan weakly as I see their faces, remember the names. The bodies, the destruction, the ruin I've brought to people.

It's all coming back to haunt me.

I remember the first person I killed, a drug dealer named Guillermo 'Big Willy' Lopez. He'd died with a look of surprise on his face, like he couldn't believe that his time on Earth was over.

I remember the second, Hunter Earle . . . and the third, and fourth . . .

I remember them all, and my self-control breaks. Horror sweeps over me, and I shudder and sob as I'm wracked, unable to control myself.

What have I become? What . . . what have I done?

I feel a hand on my neck and I jolt. "I . . . God, Bella, I'm evil," I force out, hiccupping as my body rebels again. "Everything I've done . . . no matter how bad those people were, it wasn't worth it."

"Come on," Bella says, holding out a hand. "Let's go to the stream we passed. I can wash this shit out of my hair and change out of these clothes, and we can talk."

I nod, numb as Bella helps me up. The stream is only about a hundred feet from where we staged all this, and while it's not huge, it's enough for Bella to dunk her hair and face before changing her shirt.

I sit numbly on a nearby rock as Bella cleans up, and when she comes back, she says nothing, just waiting until I'm ready to speak.

"When I slapped you, and I looked down, I was horrified," I tell her. "Because I remembered the different ways I'd considered taking you out when I first accepted the job and didn't know you yet. And when you sat up, eyes glassy and looking into my soul . . ."

I shiver, hugging myself, and Bella comes around behind me, wrapping her arms around my shoulders. "I'm okay, Gabe."

"But they're not," I protest. "There is no coming back from what I've done. I curse everything I touch with death." I can feel them all around me, like ghosts of my past, whispers of answers I never got and a brother I let down in the worst way.

"You can't change the past. It's come and gone. But what you can do is live your best life for them. For Jeremy, for all the bad people you killed, for me. For yourself." Her voice is quiet but powerful, speaking to the jagged, broken edges in my soul.

"I don't know if I can. I don't deserve to," I whisper. With a swallow, I force myself to look at her and confess. "I don't deserve you. I'm so sorry, Bella. So fucking sorry."

She hugs me again, cooing at me. "It's okay, we're gonna be okay. We're going to get through this, and then you know what you're going to do?"

I shake my head.

"You're going to be the best Gabriel Jackson you can be. Don't dishonor them by forgetting them . . . but don't let their ghosts stop you from living the life you are meant to have. Don't let the past stop you or make you afraid."

She jostles me a bit, like she's going to rattle the pep talk into my brain. It works a little bit, but mostly, it's just this amazing woman loving me. She should be running from me, getting help from just about anyone but me, but against all odds, she chose to trust me to help her. And I won't let her down.

I take her hand, pulling her around to sit in my lap. "Fuck, you are so beautiful."

Her brow crinkles cutely, "What? Uh, I need a shower. That fake blood mostly came off, but still . . . ew."

I look at her. Bare-faced, hair a mess, running for her life, and trusting a monster, she's never been more stunning, inside or out. And she's mine.

I set the truth free, hoping she'll believe it. "Beautiful. And mine, Bella."

Her lips part in surprise, and I dive in, taking her mouth and promising her that I'll fix everything as I explore her with my tongue. I nuzzle into her neck, leaving a line of biting kisses. She tastes sweet and sharp from the fake blood, but underneath, it's her.

My Bella.

Her breathy agreement is a balm to my monstrous heart, giving me hope. "Yours."

CHAPTER 26

ISABELLA

I can't believe what just came out of my mouth, but as soon as I say it, I know I'm right. Forget the scene, forget the dirt and the sweat and the fake blood. Forget all of that.

Gabe needs this.

I need this.

I kiss him hard, taking away any chance he has to protest, and he pulls me on top of him as he lies back on the rock, his hands grabbing my ass and squeezing me through my jeans as our bodies press together.

Like that first time in the woods, there are just too many damn clothes in the way. But as he kneads my ass, his thigh pressing between my knees and up against the zipper of my jeans, I moan into his mouth.

But I want more than a grinding orgasm this time. I want all of him.

I realize that's truer than it should be. I had fallen for him, but when I saw him attack Russell, my heart had shriveled up and retreated in confused fear. And though it's only been a short time, my heart has opened back up to him as we've talked and bared our souls—the good, bad, and ugly. Though his is certainly tipping more toward the bad and ugly than mine.

But I understand what he was doing and who he is. He is going to such lengths to help me and keep me safe, including the whole thing with Russell. Gabe really does mean that he'll do anything for me. Truly . . . anything.

The weight of that settles me down, emotionally grounding me in him and this moment.

I slide down his body until I reach his waist. He watches, his eyes dark with hunger as I unzip his pants and free his thick cock.

I run my tongue up the underside of his throbbing shaft, and he moans, grabbing a handful of my hair to guide me back where he wants me.

"That's it, Bella . . . fuck, your mouth feels so good on me," he moans, his words disappearing as I inhale him. I can't get enough. The taste, the velvety steel texture, the way he stretches my jaw as I take more and more of him inside me . . . the power I feel.

Here I am with this sexy, powerful, deadly man at my mercy. He's not perfect, that's for sure. No, he's every bit the dangerous hunter, but he's mine. Poor Izzy Turner, the girl everyone made fun of and pitied, who never had a single thing go her way and struggled just to eke by. But that's not who I am with Gabe, and maybe he doesn't have to be the Fallen Angel with me. We can just be Gabe and Bella, ourselves.

I suck him, hollowing my cheeks and bobbing up and down over every inch of his manhood, devoting myself to him. Even as I pleasure him, I can feel the heat building between my own legs.

I look up to him through my lashes, and he thrusts deep into my throat before pulling me off. "Hey, I wasn't done," I protest.

But he pulls at my shirt, signaling me to take it off. I step back, making quick work of the tee and my bra. My nipples tighten in the fresh air, standing at attention and begging for Gabe's tongue, hands.

I glance down to my jeans to work the button and shimmy them off, kicking my shoes off in a mess I'll straighten out later. When I look back up, Gabe is stroking himself as he watches me strip. If I'd realized, I would've done it more gracefully or sexily, but judging by the red, angry color of the head of his cock, he liked my fast stripping just fine.

"Hands and knees, Princess," he commands. It's the first time he's called me that since our painful conversation in my living room, and it feels symbolic that we're back on course, on the same team. Even if the team is Hell's Angels. If that's what it takes to be with him, I'll gladly trade a bit of my soul, darken my spirit to match his intensity.

Dropping to my hands and knees in the soft pine needles, I toss my hair over my shoulder so I can see his approach. Gabe's eyes are on me at first, but as he lowers to his knees behind me, his gaze sinks to my ass and I can see his hand twitch. I arch my back, inviting him, and moan when he slaps my ass, loving it.

"Say it again," he begs, sliding my panties to the side. My wet lips clench as the cool air hits them, and Gabe spreads me open with his thumbs. "Whose are you?"

"Yours."

In a heartbeat, all my breath leaves me in a whoosh as Gabe shoves his thick cock deep inside me in one smooth stroke.

He's huge, and each time we're together it's like being split open, but the initial pain electrifies my body. I feel alive while he pounds me, hammering my pussy as my fingers claw at the rich, moist earth underneath me and I'm pushing back into him, crying out with every slap of his balls on my clit.

I don't need the roughness . . . but I love it and trust him to not go too far. He takes me, completely and fully, and when I clench around him, crying out my orgasm, he grinds deep inside me, letting me ride it out before he starts again.

I can feel each plunging stroke, the throb of his cock and the pulse of his heart as his fingers dig into my waist. He smacks my ass again, and I yelp, loving it and throwing my hair back.

"Gabe . . . please!"

I need him. He needs me.

I am his. He is mine.

Both flawed and scarred, damaged beyond repair, but somehow perfectly matched.

Gabe swells and thrusts hard as he cries out, warmth filling me as he finds his ecstasy. He groans my name, triggering my own shattering. I spasm around him, my eyes rolling up in my head and the shakes coming over me again as I keep him inside me until it passes. I feel Gabe gather me in his arms, holding me close and safe off the forest floor.

"Fuck, Princess." His voice is ragged. "I feel like I'm damning you to hell with me."

I cup his face. "I feel like I'm pulling you out of hell to be with me."

$\sim$

THE WALK BACK TO THE HOUSE FEELS DIFFERENT. OUR PLAN IS already in action, and it makes me nervous. I trust Gabe, but even he says this is a risky gamble and the stakes are high. Our lives.

I'd hoped our return would feel more triumphant, like we're taking life by the horns. Instead, I feel like I've grabbed on to the tail of a bull and am just holding on for dear life as I slingshot around.

Gabe kisses my forehead, more sweet than sultry. "Go rinse off and we'll head back. You're sure Mia won't mind our dropping in?"

I give a small smile, laughing softly. "Mia won't mind us stopping in with a moment's notice, but she's gonna flip when I tell her what's going on. But she'll get on board. Probably have a statistical analysis of every angle in five-point-three minutes and a half-dozen suggestions on ways we can proceed from here. It's who she is."

He nods, letting me go clean up while he packs up the house and removes any trace we were ever here.

Alone, I pick up the burner phone Gabe told me to use for the call. It rings and goes to voicemail the first time I call, which I'd expected. Mia isn't the type to answer to random phone numbers. So I hang up and dial again immediately, and she picks up.

"What? I ain't buying whatever you're selling," she says in her fake Russian accent.

"Mia? It's Izzy," I say, and the floodgates of her fury open.

"Where the actual fuck have you been, girl? I called Martha to check on you because I haven't heard anything in a couple of days and she tells me that you went on vacation. Vacation?!" she says incredulously. "Do you even know what that word means? And with some guy we haven't even met, much less vetted? Charlotte is having a fucking cow about this. And not the cute black-and-white dairy ones, but like a big ass, horned monster of a cow. W. T. F. Iz!" She says the actual letters, like double-u, tee, eff, and then finally takes a breath so I can get a word in edgewise.

"I know, I'm sorry. But I've got reasons. Can I come by in a bit? We need to talk."

I hear her inhale, and I'm sure she's got her hand on her chest in worry. "What's wrong? What did he do? I'll fucking kill this Gabe character, string him up by his ball sack, slice and dice him open, and make him choke on his own stomach contents."

"Whoa, no. That is rather . . . descriptive and disgusting. He's fine. He's helping me, actually. But I need to talk to you. And Thomas," I say solemnly.

"Tommy?" she asks leerily.

"I know you have a lot of questions," I interrupt quickly before she can go off on another question-filled rant. "I have even more than you do, probably, but we'll figure it all out soon. We'll be there soon, so be home, okay?"

"Got it," she says, but I can hear the worry in her voice.

CHAPTER 27

GABRIEL

I keep an eye on the traffic behind us the whole way to Roseboro, looking for anything that could resemble a tail. I take an indirect, circuitous route to be sure, and only then do I pull into the Goldstone building's garage, parking close to the express elevator that will take us directly to the penthouse he and Mia share.

When the elevator doors open, Mia and Thomas are standing there waiting for us. Mia and Bella instantly launch themselves at each other, screeches and wails of 'missed you' and 'what the hell' surrounding them as they hug it out like they haven't seen each other in a lifetime instead of only days.

For Bella, I suspect it does feel like a different lifetime. Before, her life was tough, but simple and safe and predictable. Now, it's none of those things.

While the girls have their reunion, Thomas and I eye each other. I know who he is, mostly because everyone knows of the wunderkind who climbed the ranks fast and makes a huge difference in Roseboro. I have the slightest advantage there, because while I know him, he has no idea who or what I am.

But one look in his eyes tells me that's about to change.

It's an odd feeling to intentionally expose myself after so many years of hiding behind masks, ensuring that no one knew the true me. Everyone only seen the part of me I wanted them to, whether it's the ice-cold hunter or the congenial boy next door, both equally a part I merely play and the truth somewhere in the middle.

Scarily, part of me even wonders if the masks have become my reality, so pervasive, that I don't know the difference any longer. Or worse, that this monster I've created is all that I am now.

But for Bella, I'll do whatever I have to. Even if that means exposing my vulnerabilities to the people she trusts.

Because unfortunately, this is a battle being waged on a grand scale. I can handle the smaller moves and strategies, like keeping Bella by my side, safe and sound. But the true threat, Blackwell, can only be handled by working with Goldstone.

I hold my hand out, a peace offering I wouldn't usually give. "Gabriel Jackson. Thank you for seeing us."

Thomas shakes my hand, and in his handshake I get another measure of the man. He's strong and confident enough that he doesn't have to show it off with a crushing grip. "We'd do anything for Izzy. She simply has to ask."

I like him already. He's smooth and direct, warning me and lovingly reminding Bella that she has people, if she'll just open up.

"I'm afraid that's why we're here. Can we sit? The information we need to share is rather involved and upsetting."

"Tell me about this vacation—" Thomas touches Mia's shoulder, breaking her interrogation of Bella. "What? Oh, yeah, we can sit down instead of doing this in the foyer, but we're talking about this, Iz."

We follow Thomas into the living room, but Mia is continuing to monologue the whole way. "Disappears without a call for a whole weekend. Must be some dick to get her to take off work."

But when we sit, Mia really looks at Bella's face and reads that this is bigger than an impromptu vacation, and the scolding jocularity disappears from her voice. "Okay, spill it. What's going on?"

Bella looks to me, so I begin.

"Like I said, my name is Gabriel Jackson, Gabe. But people call me something else too . . . The Fallen Angel."

Thomas's eyes narrow, and I can see his inner alarm bells going off. Somehow, I've actually overestimated and underestimated him at the same time. My research since finding out Blackwell's true motivation showed Thomas to be relatively clean, but you don't get to his level of influence without being aware of the murky waters business often entails.

I'd wondered if my professional name would even mean anything to him, but it seems it does. Smart man, but given what I know of him, he's a good man too and has achieved his success the 'right' way.

He's also incredibly brave, because I can see that he's willing to fight me, if need be, to protect his woman and Bella too, going so far as pushing Mia behind him in preparation. The man's got big brass ones, I'll give him that.

"Izzy."

He reaches a hand toward Bella, and I growl. But before things can turn overly ugly, Bella reaches over to me and entwines her arm through mine, taking my hand rather than Thomas'.

"Thomas, I know exactly who he is and what he is."

Mia peeks from behind Thomas, confusion in her voice. "Okay, for those of us not in the know, can someone tell me why some cheesy nickname—no offense there, Gabe—is making my man go all uber-protective caveman?"

I chance taking my eyes off Thomas, the most significant threat in the room, to look at Mia. "I'm a hitman." She gasps, but I keep the shots going, getting it all out at once. "I was sent to kill Bella but fell for her instead. I was hired by Blackwell."

Thomas drops back to the couch in shock, but he recovers faster than one would expect and his eyes flare back to life, looking from Bella to me to our locked hands. "Start at the beginning and tell me what the fuck you're doing here. All of it."

What follows for the next hour is an uncomfortable and awkward exposé on all my sins and faults. It's painful but necessary as I tell Thomas what Blackwell said about using Bella to hurt him and Mia, revealing the depths and the backstabbing connivery that Blackwell's willing to go to in his quest for power.

Mia moves to hug Bella several times as we both share the story of the last few weeks, stopping at the point of us running away.

Thomas is understandably furious that someone is watching him from the wings, pulling strings and strategizing threats, both with the corporate saboteur and with Bella. "I had no idea. Fuck, why does he even give a shit about me? That makes no sense. We're both doing well in Roseboro. Hell, I thought we were doing well for Roseboro. Sure, we weren't friends, but . . . is he insane?"

"I've noticed that most of my employers are either psychopaths or sociopaths," I reply, finally smiling grimly. "In Blackwell's case, he's a little bit of both, I suspect. Definitely a narcissist."

While Thomas mulls that over, Mia looks to Bella, gesturing to me with a toss of her head, making her purple hair swing. "You sure about this, about him?"

My breath hitches sharply. It's a moment of truth for us, because while I am confident in her answer, there's still that uncertainty, a lack of understanding of why she would choose someone like me when she deserves so much better. "I'm sure. We're . . . together."

Bella looks to me, her eyes shining brightly, and though we still haven't said the words, I can see them in the depths there. I hope she can see the truth in mine too.

I expect there to be arguments, at least a few protests that she's throwing away her life with a criminal. Or even that this is a ploy at Blackwell's behest. Something to pull Bella and I apart. It's what I've come to expect in the world, harsh coldness and indifference.

Instead, Thomas and Mia quickly go into analysis and planning mode, and inside my chest, I feel a warmth build. Is this what trust and friendship feel like? I don't know, but maybe I'm getting more out of this than just a girl and a cat.

"Okay, so we understand why you came to us. We can provide security and more resources—" Mia says, but Bella jumps in.

"We already have a plan. Well, part of one, so Blackwell will think I'm dead. It'll give us some time, we think."

Mia's brows raise so far on her forehead, I think they might disappear into her hairline. "Seriously? Your grand plan is to fake your death?"

She mumbles something in Russian I don't understand, but the eyeroll and palm-to-forehead smack are pretty clear.

Bella nods, clearly used to these sorts of theatrics. "We already filmed it, and Gabe sent the videos and pictures to Blackwell as we came back into town. Gabe has a meeting with him tomorrow."

"Show me," Thomas demands.

I reach into my pocket and pull out my fresh burner phone. I'd already sent the files to Blackwell and to this new phone before yanking the battery and SIM card on the original so that Blackwell couldn't track us on it.

Thomas and Mia watch the videos and look at the pictures, horror dawning on their faces. "Oh, my God, that's awful, Izzy. I can't . . ." she says, looking away for the part where I roll Bella over the cliff's edge. Her face's gone slightly pale green, and I can sympathize with her. Watching it on replay had my own gorge rising. Somehow, the small-screen on the cell makes it look even more realistic, even more horrifying.

Bella gets up and hugs Mia, knowing her friend needs reassurance. "It's okay, I'm okay."

But Mia won't be calmed. She shakes her head, burying her face in her hands. "We got you into this. Fuck, I'm so sorry, Iz. I had no idea."

Bella pulls her back in, not letting go. "You couldn't have known. None of us knew what was going on behind the scenes, and I won't let you beat yourself up for it. I'll sick Vash on you if I have to."

Mia huffs a laugh and hugs Bella back. "Nirvash loves me more than you, and we both know it. Martha said she's fine, by the way."

Thomas and I lock eyes again, letting the girls have their moment of normalcy because we both know it's about to end. When I nod, he clears his throat, his voice deep and resonating as he sits forward, his elbows on his knees.

"Okay, so let's get to work on a plan because it sounds like we need to know our next move when Gabe meets with Blackwell tomorrow."

I appreciate that he doesn't try to stop me on this, thinking that he's going to take over now. There are several things in play, and I know Thomas will have to keep Mia and his business at the top of his mind. But my mind is focused on one thing and one thing only.

My princess.

"Here's what I know," I start as I outline the skeleton of a plan I've come up with. Soon, we're bouncing ideas back and forth, each of us contributing and focused on one goal.

Stopping Blackwell.

The only unknown is what ends we'll have to go to.

CHAPTER 28

BLACKWELL

*W*agner plays over my office's sound system, and I sit back, enjoying the view of Roseboro after dark. Other than the lights from my sound system and the soft red glow above the door that beckons as if it's the only exit strategy, the only light in the room is the dim glow of the lights filtering up from the city below, which is just how I like it.

I watch the white and red lights on the street below, people skittering this way and that as if their actions have any meaning. Perhaps in some small way, they do. A parent coming home to a child, a doctor going to work, things of that nature. But even then, it is a moment of time, a minor importance in the big scheme of life.

I focus my gaze closer, seeing my own reflection in the glass, and note my austere appearance, the power that surrounds me like a cloud of dominance. I stand taller, broader, luxuriating in my supremacy, my image making the same moves in return.

A legacy. That is something important. Something I will leave, even as I sit here in my tower, overlooking the pawns I move like a master.

Letting my eyes look further out, I cringe inwardly, anger burning deep in my stomach as I see the lights still visible in

Goldstone's abomination, glowing brightly like some happy little celebration of the young upstart's arrogance.

I'm coming for you, Golden Boy.

I pick up the tablet in my lap and once again look over the photos I received today, my lips twitching as they try to lift into a smile. But smiles aren't warranted yet. I have too many doubts about their authenticity and the man who sent them to me.

Besides, this is merely step one, intended to be an uncomfortable thorn in Goldstone's side to make him focus elsewhere while I move on to step two. A diversionary tactic.

If this proves authentic, I wonder if Goldstone knows yet. Probably not, but I can still imagine the moment his data-hungry strumpet discovers that her best friend in the world is gone, the screams and tears she'll let loose. I imagine Thomas comforting her, weakly focusing on her loss instead of keeping his eye on the prize.

His company.

When he's distracted, I'll move in and take back what is mine. My rightful place as the leader of this town. More than merely a king, but a creator, the one who designed everything from the infrastructure to the governmental minions who are in place because of my financial support.

I swipe to the next picture. The images are realistic, and on the surface are beautiful proof of her death, and I feel dark excitement bloom in my chest. I zoom in on a blood spatter on Miss Turner's cheek, noting the already purple tint from Gabriel's blow.

I'll admit that I have had serious doubts that the well-regarded Fallen Angel was going to come through this time. He'd seemed rather caught in Isabella Turner's web, but perhaps he's a better actor than I'd given him credit for.

If he's authentic.

I watch the video again, enjoying the moment when Isabella realizes the monster she's let in, see the confusion and fear dawning in her eyes.

And for just a moment, I do smile, letting myself celebrate a small victory and feeling excitement for what's to come.

My office phone rings, and I turn around, picking up the private line. "Yes?"

"Sir . . . it's Jericho."

Just the man I was looking to hear from, for he holds the verdict on Gabriel's actions. I lean back in my chair, setting the tablet aside. "What news do you have for me, Mr. Jericho?"

"Your concerns were correct. Jackson has been lying to you."

My hand grips the phone tighter. So much for small victories. But I don't let Jericho hear my disappointment or anger. "I see. And you are certain about this?"

"Yes, sir."

"Fine. Come to my office as soon as you're in town."

"Of course, sir. I'll have options for you when I arrive."

Jericho hangs up the line, and I pick the tablet back up to glance at the pictures again. Too good to be true, a false reproduction of the horror movie result I wished for.

I should've trusted my gut all along.

That a woman of so little importance is costing me this much in time, effort, and finances is ridiculous. I'm regretting not hiring a two-bit thug at this point, one that would've been completely expendable after the job was done. But my penchant for elegance in my revenge was too strong, and now I'm paying the price and past ready to move on to the aftermath of Isabella Turner's death.

But a good strategist knows to keep forces in reserve, to build plans upon plans, with contingencies for every possible outcome. So Gabriel's betrayal is not a crippling blow, but a new opportunity for bigger, bolder moves.

My lips twist wryly as I consider various ideas, from simple to complex, before deciding on a course of action.

He and Miss Turner will be the new assignment. It shall serve them right for their deception, and serve me well for my plans for Goldstone.

The fresh thought of his name makes my blood boil in my veins. Even without knowing it, he's thwarting my plays. How can one man be so lucky?

I may not have Lady Luck on my side, but I have something far more beneficial, unfettered cruelty. And I'm all too willing to acquaint Goldstone with what a true leader of this city can do when he puts his mind, will, and pocketbook to work.

I squeeze the tablet in my hand tightly and then unleash my anger, the device flying through the air and hitting the glass.

I look over, seeing the lights of the city as a starburst effect through the shatter. They add highlight and shadow to my refracted image, giving me a monstrously hideous appearance.

"You have no idea what's coming for you, Golden Boy. But I do. I have so many plans for us."

CHAPTER 29

GABRIEL

The park's quiet, and across the pond I can see a couple of basketball courts that are currently empty. It's a weekday, a school day, and it's still way too early for almost anyone to be up for a pickup game.

I approach the bench where Blackwell sits, taking a deep breath to calm myself and do a final scan of the park for gunmen.

Get it done. Buy yourself time to figure out what you're going to do with this snake, I tell myself when I'm satisfied it's safe.

Setting my concern aside, I finish my approach, mentally verifying that my gun is tucked away in easy reach, in the false pocket of my light jacket. The jacket is more for concealment than the weather. The early morning sun is shining brightly enough that I don't feel the cold yet.

Blackwell, as always, is well-dressed, this time in a dark suit. I'd feel honored, except I know enough about Blackwell to guess that he never dresses down. I'd bet the man wears three-piece pajamas to bed, with a matching robe for every set.

"Right on time, Mr. Jackson."

It sounds more observational than complimentary or conversational, so I don't respond. I sit down on the bench beside him, angling myself to have an advantage. Though I'm well aware that if this doesn't go off successfully, I'm a dead man anyway, here or in some unsuspecting alley later.

"You know," Blackwell says as he pulls out his phone, turning it over in his hands. I wonder if he's recording what we're saying or if someone's listening in through it. "You've really not done what I hired you to do."

I can hear the threat in his voice, but I knew there would be some strong-arming with him. I have to deal with his skepticism now before it gets out of hand. "You asked me to eliminate Isabella Turner and I did. You have proof."

"I hired you to kill her to send a message to my enemies, to take their hearts from them," Blackwell growls, raising a fisted hand like he's holding an actual beating heart. "I wanted more than pictures."

"If you want to take your enemy's heart, what better way to do it than to actually capture it first before you crush them?" I ask coldly, letting a bit of that side of me out, even though it's now devoted to protecting Bella. "Now he can spend days, weeks, and months being eaten up with doubt and worry. It's more effective than cancer."

"Hmm . . . I have yet to know a cancer that had the side benefits you indulged in."

"It was an effective tactic to get her alone and trusting me," I explain calmly. "She had a difficult life. She trusted very few people. Even before this, she had been betrayed and disappointed by most people she'd met. Getting her to leave her protective detail behind for the day was damn-near impossible, but I did it. And I'm sure that when she didn't return as scheduled, the guards sounded the alarm. And if you think she wasn't terrified, you need to rewatch those videos. Hell, send them to Karakova if you want to really torture Goldstone."

The words turn my stomach, talking about my Bella that way, but I have to add just a touch of sociopathy in order to make this

256

convincing. Blackwell has to actually think I don't give a damn one way or another about what happened, that it's just a job.

It helps, but Blackwell hums anyway.

"Photos and videos are scant proof. I want the body."

"Good fucking luck," I growl, looking over at him. "That cliff was an hour's hike into the woods, and I dumped her into a ravine. I sure as hell wasn't hauling a human body out of there over my shoulder, and I dumped it there for a reason. It's already been twenty-four hours. By now, the body's most likely in some wolf or bear's belly. Besides, the lack of a body is what will destroy Mia, and therefore, Goldstone. A body, a funeral, and a casket lowering into the ground at a place you can go talk to a tombstone give closure of a sort."

It's the painful truth. Visiting Jeremy's grave is a pitiful substitute for him, but it has helped me over the years.

"Without a body, they'll only have questions and get none of that peace. Ever," I continue. "And like I said, when the questions have eaten up so much . . . that is when you do what you want."

It's a bluff, one I'd prepared for. Still, it's a reach, and as Blackwell stares at me, I remember why I'm doing something so dangerous. I remember what I have to live for.

It's going to be the force of my personality and my balls that'll get us through this, hopefully getting us enough time until I can ensure Bella's safety.

"You should know I'm not a man who accepts excuses," Blackwell rumbles after a moment. "If I want a body, I get a body. I should withhold payment."

"Keep your money," I reply with a shrug. "We both know that's not why I took this contract. But if you want to walk out of this park alive, I expect you to keep your end of the bargain and give me the information. And if you think your security men can stop me before I pull the trigger on the pistol I have in my pocket . . . well, try me."

"Is your dead brother really worth that much to you?"

I nod, looking into Blackwell's eyes. It's the first time I've really seen him clearly, not hidden in the murky shadows of his office but in the exposing light of day, and I don't see any humanity in those dead orbs.

Then again, people probably say the same thing about me, or at least they did before Bella brought me back to life. I worry he can see that in my eyes too and deflect.

"You damn well know that's what I've been after."

I'll hand it to Blackwell, he doesn't flinch, though I doubt too many people dare to speak to him that gruffly. Calmly, he reaches inside his jacket, but I'm on edge and move towards my gun.

He smirks and holds up a staying hand. Slowly, he withdraws a small envelope, like the kind you'd put a greeting card in.

He holds it out, and I take it, feeling the data card inside shift around. "This had better not be encrypted."

"It's not." Blackwell rises and puts on a fedora that once again casts his eyes in shadow. "I'm afraid I have a meeting to attend. Don't move from this bench until I've cleared the park, Mr. Jackson. I have eyes on you. Standoff, yes?"

I chuckle, shaking my head. "A standoff only works when both parties give a damn about actually walking away. Remember that, Mr. Blackwell, if you considered welching on your data."

Blackwell purses his lips, and I can't tell if it's in amusement or anger. "I don't think we'll be meeting again, Mr. Jackson. At least not in this life. Perhaps in hell?"

I give him an evil grin, like it's a date I'm looking forward to. "I'm sure you'll be waiting with a proper barbecue and torture rack all ready for me on the outermost ring. Face it, they wouldn't let you into hell anyway."

"Oh?"

"They'd worry you'd take over." I chuckle like it's a joke, though there's more truth than I'd like in the words about the power-hungry nature of his soul.

He tips his hat to me and walks away. After a few moments, I stand up, heading in the opposite direction. I don't know if Blackwell really has eyes on me. The whole idea that you can feel when someone's watching you is just stereotypical horror movie acting, but I'm careful nevertheless. I definitely can't go back to Goldstone's, not now that I truly might have a tail.

So I head to the motel, alone. I hope it was enough, that Blackwell will move on to bigger fish, namely Thomas, who's preparing for him. But that'll only happen if Blackwell bought my bullshit and there's no way to know if he did yet.

What's not bullshit is the data card in my pocket and the feeling inside me, hoping against hope that I'll be able to have my cake and eat it too for once in my life.

CHAPTER 30

ISABELLA

"*S*o, how'd you sleep?"

I yawn, stretching as I pad my way into the 'living room' of Mia's penthouse, rubbing the sleep out of my eyes. "Hard," I admit, smiling as I see Mia looking cute in black pants and a T-shirt from a band she sent me the link to. She calls it 'recommended listening'. I call it 'have an opinion by the next time I see her or she'll shove earbuds in my ears.' Tomato, tomahto. "Cute shirt. And yes, I listened. Starlight was okay, but I liked the older stuff better. And who names their band Babymetal anyway?"

Mia grins, giving a light golf-style clap. "Well done. There's hope for you yet. We'll see if Charlotte does as well on her musical pop quiz too." She's half-joking but mostly telling the truth. I can already foresee an in-depth musical analysis in my future.

For now, she's distracted by bigger fish though. "Gabe's already gone?"

I nod. Letting him go had been hard, knowing that he was walking into a potentially deadly situation. But he'd taken every precaution, leaving extra-early to decrease the chances he'd been seen at Goldstone Tower, carefully tailoring his windbreaker to conceal his gun, and even letting me check everything too, carefully following the steps Saul at the range showed me in an attempt to ease my worries.

It'd worked for a minute, but as soon as he'd left, I'd curled up in bed, terror gripping my stomach in its icy fist. I basically chewed my lip off and picked at my cuticles with nerves, wishing I had a phone to at least check in with him by text message if nothing else.

But the anxiety had worn me out, especially given the stress of the last few days, and somewhere along the way, I'd fallen asleep. It's almost lunch now, and still no word from Gabe. I knew he wouldn't be able to call for a bit in an attempt to make sure everything is clear before we make contact again, but that doesn't assuage my worries.

"When is Charlotte coming over?" I ask Mia, eager for any sort of distraction.

"She should be here any minute. She's bringing a bag to stay too, so we can keep the whole gang safe together. I gave her the bare bones of what's happening but kept it pretty generic since we were on the phone. And I told her to look frantic, scared, and basically freaked the fuck out as she left work, rushed home, and came over. She's no actress, but I think she can fake the tears she'd cry if something had actually happened to you."

I nod, glad we'd gone over including Char, and we'd put together something for her last night in our strategy plan. With Gabe telling Blackwell I had a protective detail, the guards would realize I'm missing in action pretty quickly and report to Thomas. So my girls should be losing their shit and circling the wagons.

And now, my part of the plan is basically to stay in hiding. It's a pretty vital part of the whole scenario, since I'm supposed to be dead and all.

The elevator dings, and Mia shoots me a look. I hop into the pantry, closing the door, just in case. But a second later, the elevator opens and Charlotte comes barreling in. "Someone had better tell me what is going on immediately."

I come out and am swept up in Charlotte's arms for a hug. "Fuck, girl. We always worry about you, but Mia said you're in some real trouble. Not that Russell isn't real, or your school stuff isn't important, but this is like next-level. You okay?"

I smile as much as I can, hugging her back. "Yeah, for now. Though this is all way above my paygrade. I'm having to trust Gabe and Thomas to figure some shit out and set all this right. And you know how much I *love* to depend on other people to handle my life."

The sarcasm stings, but it's the truth. I do wish I could just stomp my way into the Blackwell building, tell him to fuck off in an epic mic drop, and go on with my life.

But it's not that easy, and I have to admit that someone else is probably better equipped to address this strategically. In the meantime, while I stay hidden, I need distraction. I need my besties.

Mia and Char glance at each other and then take action. "Lunch and rom-com movie, stat. We've got you, girl." And then like whirling dervishes, Charlotte pulls plates and glasses from the cabinets and Mia disappears to the media room to get the movie set up.

Char opens the fridge, and I happen to catch a glimpse of the inside. It's stocked full, and I do mean full, of what looks to be the entirety of a grocery store. "Damn, I wish my fridge looked like that! Is that a whole container of raspberries?"

I must sound more desperate than the awe I was aiming for because Charlotte turns around, a frown on her face. "Izzy."

But I cut her off with a hand extended, shaking my head. "Nope. I'm fine."

She presses her lips into a thin line, holding back the argument she wants to make, settling for grabbing the berries and setting the whole bowl in front of me. "Eat."

I don't argue, popping one of the bright fruits into my mouth and moaning at the explosion of sour sweetness on my tongue.

Mia chooses that moment to walk back into the kitchen, grinning. "I'll have what she's having if it'll make me sound like that."

I laugh around a mouthful. "Ha-ha, Sally, but we're not watching you fake an orgasm over lunch."

The movie reference makes them both smile, reassuring them in a small way that I'm okay.

"Apparently, we're listening to you moan and groan, so what's the difference?" Mia teases back. "Speaking of moaning and groaning, I want every dirty detail of your weekend away. And don't you dare tell me that you two holed up in a safe house and didn't get any action."

I shake my head, protesting. "We were scared for my life, on the run. Sex was the last thing on our minds while we tried to figure out a way out of this mess."

My girls look at one another, using each other as a barometer, then simultaneously reach behind their backs and toss invisible flags into the air, Mia whistling loudly. "Calling bullshit on that. Flag on the conversation."

I laugh and give in. "Fine, there was action. But those dirty details are all mine."

Charlotte gives me a friendly pop on the shoulder, making a mock-angry face. "Spoil sport! I'm living vicariously through you."

I rub my shoulder, even though she didn't hurt me. It's just part of the game, and I'm willing to immerse myself in it for a bit to keep myself sane. "Well, I'm just trying to see tomorrow, so you'll have to find your own dick for entertaining stories."

She smirks, weaving her head back and forth. "Fine, no dick tales from you and definitely none from me, then what about the rest of all this? Are you sure about Gabe, about hiding out, about Blackwell not coming after you? What about Russell?"

"I changed my mind, let's talk about the awesome sex," I reply, my forced levity dissolving as I find myself torn between my friends' attempts at cheering me up and the worry about where Gabe is and whether he's safe.

But I realize that right now, I need a deeper conversation than how much meat my man's packing between his legs.

"Actually, I don't know what's up with Russell. He definitely saw Gabe and me together, and Gabe definitely put him in the hospital based on the beating he gave him, so that could come back to haunt us. But I feel like Russell is small potatoes compared to everything else."

"After Gabe told us what happened with Russell, I did a little research online using the town's arrest records, and more importantly, the Roseboro rumor mill," Mia shares, sitting down on a stool. "So word is, Russell doesn't remember getting a beatdown. He woke up, or I guess regained consciousness is more accurate, and got himself to the hospital. Right now, he's claiming he doesn't remember who, but everyone thinks he pissed off the wrong rock slinger."

"Wait, so Gabe's totally in the clear there?" I ask, shocked. Did Russell get hit in the head, or was he really that scared by what happened? No cops, no pissed off Russell? "That's awesome, better than we'd hoped."

"We?" Charlotte says, busting me and returning our focus to the topic she wants most. Gabe.

"Yeah, we," I say, blushing just a little bit. "We might've gotten a weird start—actually, we're still mid-weirdness—but we've got something. He's something . . . special."

Mia coughs, not subtle at all as she says, "Tell her everything."

And for the second time in just over twelve hours, I'm running through everything that's happened in the last few weeks, from both my perspective and Gabe's point of view. It's harder not having Gabe to fill in the parts that he did last night, when he gave me an out in the difficult areas, but I power through it, knowing I need to toughen up and be strong if I'm going to get through this. And that means facing my best friends and admitting that I'm falling for Gabe.

As I wrap it up, Char looks like she's about to be sick. "How in the world am I supposed to go to work in that building, work for that monster, when he put out a hit on my best friend?"

I give her a hug, patting her on the back. "With a smile, that's how. We don't know what Thomas and Gabe are finding out or what we're going to do yet, so in the meantime, you're going to play along. Act like I'm missing, be worried, but try to carry on, and if it gets to the point that you have to pretend I'm gone, we'll put in a plan to cover that. Start with taking a few days off, like you're poking around and worried, also known as laying low and staying safe. Because if he targeted me, he could target you."

She nods, though she looks uncertain. I understand. She doesn't really recognize just how much danger she's in. Until I saw Gabe and Rusty, I didn't understand either.

After a long moment, Charlotte says, "Okay, movie time. Let's do this because I don't think my brain can take any more. I need a fluffy comedy with a guaranteed happily ever after. And then, I'm making us cupcakes. I'm trying a new recipe and I need testers."

"Deal," I say, and Mia echoes my sentiment a half-beat later.

I love these girls. My best friends, who would support me through just about anything, up to and including fake deaths and conspiracies, apparently.

CHAPTER 31

GABRIEL

I pull my hoodie over my head, even though the night makes it unneeded. But the more generic I can be, the better, and disappearing into the darkness is a definite benefit.

Coming around the corner of the narrow road, I approach the building in front of me, an old industrial-looking place with a sign out front that says Roseboro Textile Services. The drive here had taken me almost an hour, not because of the distance but because of how careful I'd been to lose anyone who might be following. At this point, I have full faith that Blackwell has a tail on me, and while I haven't identified who it is, I'm going to be careful.

I'm a dangerous guy, but I'm far from the only shark in the water.

That's why we're having this meeting here, a place unrelated to either of us and therefore untraceable.

Checking the door, there's a worn title painted on the metal . . . shift supervisor. This is the place.

I don't knock, but out of habit, I stand back and to the side as I swing the door open, making sure I don't stand in the area most people are likely to aim. But no gunshot or threat comes, just a deep voice from the dimly-lit interior.

"Come on in. We're clear."

I step into the room, plain and bare save for a dented government surplus metal desk and a couple of beat-down chairs. Thomas sits in one, gesturing to the other. Closing the office door behind me, I cross the small space and sit.

There's a bit of a silent tension coursing between us for a moment, neither of us used to working with others, at least not like this, when everything we care about is on the line. Finally, he starts. "How'd the meeting with Blackwell go?"

It's the icebreaker we need to get this ball rolling. No accusations, no bullshit. Just focus on the job at hand. "Okay," I say, humming as I think back. "He seemed to buy Bella's death, but he wanted to see the body, not just pictures and video. I told him to go get the damn body himself if he wanted it so bad. He believed it enough to give me the information that was my main payment, so that's something."

I shrug, but my brows knit together.

"What?" Thomas asks.

"It was too easy," I admit, leaning back in the chair as I try to recall all the details of the incident. "Blackwell is slick and smart, and he took me at my word that it was done. Too easy, which means he probably knows something's up."

"Maybe, but those pictures and video were pretty fucking believable. Maybe he wants to believe it enough to not look too closely. Especially since Izzy's not really his objective. I am." I can hear the pinch of pain in his voice. "Fuck, I never should've gotten her mixed up in this."

I toss him a small grin. "Don't know that you would've had much of a choice. I don't know Mia, but if Bella thought for one second that she could help you, she'd do it. No matter the cost."

He nods, seeing the wisdom of my words. "That's true. But look how that's ended up. What do we do now?"

There's a tone to his voice that immediately increases my respect for him. Since our first meeting last night, I've wondered how he, the law-abiding businessman, would react to me, the law-breaking hitman.

Mia, I had no worries. Once she saw that Bella had chosen me, she's been all about the data, about using her skills to protect her family.

But Thomas . . . well, I couldn't know for sure he wasn't just putting on a front for his woman until this moment. He looks at me not as someone who's looking to be told what to do, shirking his responsibility in favor of my voice of experience with the seedier side of business. But also not with disdain or disgust, trying to take over as the mover and shaker he typically is.

Instead, he's looking and talking to me like a teammate, knowing that we both have skills the other can use and that by operating as a single unit with a single objective, we can find success.

Just in this case, success means safety, not profit.

"First, what would you do if Bella *were* actually missing?" I ask him. "That's your next step. Go to the media? Private investigators? Police? Obviously, I'd prefer not to utilize that option, but it could be unavoidable. But what would your instincts be if something really did happen? A big, public spectacle on TV asking for help, or a quiet, behind-the-scenes investigation?"

Thomas thinks, then says without a trace of arrogance, "Depends on the situation. If I thought it was her prick of a landlord, I'd be down there myself with the cops. Something like this, though . . . I'm a man of means, with a reputation and image to uphold. I wouldn't involve the police or the media, not at first. I'd be expecting a ransom note, to be honest. I'd definitely hire a PI."

I nod, agreeing. "Then do that, someone local so Blackwell knows about it quickly to validate that you believe Bella is missing. You and Mia should take him to Bella's house, maybe even to The Gravy Train so it looks like he's investigating Bella's life. But do your best not to freak Martha out, okay? She cares about Bella and I don't want to torture her needlessly."

"And Blackwell?"

We're treading into murky areas, and I measure Thomas honestly. "Do you really want to know the dark plans of evil men?"

Thomas nods. "Firstly, I don't think you're evil."

"I'm not good," I retort. "Maybe just a different kind of evil?"

"Perhaps, but that's an argument for another time," Thomas says. "Second, I'm not the kind of man who sends others to do my dirty work just to keep my hands clean. If we need to do dark acts, then I want to know and want to be a part of it if I can. This is my family involved. I won't sit in the background."

My respect for him increases ten-fold. "Fine. My gut tells me to kill the bastard, though it'd be difficult with the degree of security he keeps. It could also be messy, considering he has to be expecting something." I can see the tightness around Thomas's eyes. "But I'm guessing that's not really your style."

Thomas sighs, looking around the room. "You ever known someone who does the right things for the wrong reasons?" He doesn't wait for me to answer, continuing on with his point. "I feel like that's Blackwell. He has done some amazing things for Roseboro, and for a long time, I looked up to him as a business leader. But where most people would feel good about helping the library get new books, or a Little League team getting uniforms, he sees it as a way to gain notoriety. He gets off on galas in his honor, statues in his likeness, and brass plates with his name on them."

I tilt my head, curious. "Sounds like you know him rather well?"

But Thomas shakes his head, "Barely had more than small talk with the man in all the years we've traveled in the same circles. But you can just sense it from some people, you know?"

"I've gotten pretty good at reading people."

Thomas nods. "Regardless of this situation with Izzy, we need to eliminate this threat. Blackwell lives off the power, the legend he's created in his own mind. I think that's where I can hurt him the most. Take away his influence, make him powerless and inconsequential. Becoming obsolete and forgettable, that's his fear."

It's a good plan, though more of a subtle long game than my style typically calls for.

"You might be right, but here's what I know. There are people who do wrong just for wrong's sake, for the hell of it because it's fun for them in some sick, twisted way. And they're unpredictable, you can't put them in a box or make plans for what you think they'll do because they'll surprise you at every turn. They don't think like you and me. Blackwell's a man who is not going to go quietly into the long night, he's capable of outright evil beyond what either of us would consider. Are you prepared for that? Because what you're describing is a war of attrition."

I pause, letting that sink in. "He's been playing that strategy too, but the game just changed when you became aware of it. And the longer you let this play out, the more dangerous he becomes. If you back him into a corner, step by step, he'll reach a threshold where he acts out in unexpected ways. The slow dance you're both doing will go nuclear. You already didn't see his moves with the sabotage and me, so I'm afraid you don't know him as well as you think you do."

Thomas' eyes tighten, and his fist clenches on the desk. But I don't let up, adding the cherry on top of the bad news. "If you're wrong in this approach, Bella pays the price."

He fires back. "And Mia, and me, and Roseboro. I can respect that Bella is your concern, but as important as she is, this is bigger than her. You waited to come to us with this, knowing you could make moves to set up a better solution. I'm asking you to do the same for me. Let me figure some shit out, see what I can do and how I can situate us to handle Blackwell once and for all."

It's against my nature. Teamwork, delays, slick corporate business deals. I don't want to do any of it, would rather just slash and burn Blackwell to the ground and stomp on the ashes of his life.

And that's exactly why I agree with Thomas's request. I want to step out of the darkness of my grief, my solitary life, my anger at the world that I take out on my victims. They're not innocent, not by any stretch of the imagination, but this is the first step to living in the light with Bella, of creating a life instead of destroying them. My one shot at happiness, and I'm going to take it.

"Okay, but you need to move fast. Because I suspect Blackwell isn't done with you, and you're playing catch-up for plans he's already set in motion."

Thomas dips his chin once and starts to get up, but I hold out a staying hand.

"Wait, I have two things before we call this meeting to a close." It's the smallest of jokes, that a guy like me has some sort of fancy business meeting with a guy like him, but Thomas's lips tilt upward. "A favor and a question."

"Shoot," he says, then grimaces. "Uh, not literally."

I give him the same bare smile. "Blackwell gave me a data card with info about my brother's killers. Do you think Mia would look at it for me? While he said it's not encrypted, I can't be sure he didn't do some other kind of skullfuckery to it, and computers aren't my thing, but Bella says Mia's next-level genius with them."

He holds his palm out, and reluctantly, I place the envelope in his hand. I want to know everything there is to know about Jeremy's death, but handing over the intel to someone I don't know, don't fully trust is about as crazy a move as I've made since beginning this journey for answers. But it's a necessity.

He slips the envelope into his jacket pocket, the reverse of what Blackwell had done, and the symbolism isn't lost on me. These two men, for all their similarities with business and brains, couldn't be more different at their core. And that thought alone gives me the smallest peace at letting Thomas have the data card.

"And your question?" he asks.

I look around the room and then back to Thomas, who looks out of place in the old, worn out factory. "Why'd you want to meet here? A broke down factory doesn't seem like your style."

He smirks, tapping his temple. "This factory is actually closed, it's been shut down for the past six months and I'm considering buying the building and turning into a new youth center." He looks out towards the mostly dark factory floor, continuing softly. "There's a group of young men, a boy's home, that I help out at not far from here, though they don't know that it's Thomas Gold-stone that is behind it. I don't want attention and accolades like Blackwell. I like to keep some parts of my life private, like my good deeds and my woman. You understand that, right?"

"I do," I say, nodding. "Keep Bella safe for me, please. She's all I have, and I sure as shit don't deserve her, but I need her. She has my heart," I confess.

If I hadn't seen how hard Thomas is hung up on Mia, I don't think I could've told him that. But I saw their love and I want that for Bella and me too.

He leans forward, confiding, "Pretty sure you have hers too, man. She's like a sister to Mia. I'll keep her safe and out of sight while this plays out."

He stands, offering a handshake, and then we step out onto the factory floor. It's not large enough for a basketball court, but it could be other things. "What're your plans for this, anyway?"

"A lot of the boys at the home, they think they've got no chance in life. They don't need a head start, they need to get to the starting line of the race. And while Roseboro High's fine, it still needs improvement. I was thinking here, they could learn all those skills that high school doesn't teach. Coding, basic electric-ity, wood shop . . . all that cool shit that they don't teach kids in high school anymore."

"A trade school?" I ask, and Thomas shakes his head.

"No . . . or at least, not just that. The kids are going to help build it. Like, one of my first projects for them . . . they're going to build their own gym, right here for this part of the floor," he says. "Come on, I've gotta get this data to Mia."

He looks around the space, his eyes soft in the dim light as if he can already see the youth center in his mind. And then he comes back to the present time, shitstorm brewing and all.

We walk out into the darkness, and before I peel off, I give him a nod. He nods back and climbs into his own truck, driving off into the night. As his taillights fade, I think about what he said.

Good deeds. Doing the right things for the right reasons.

My trust in Thomas grows.

CHAPTER 32

BLACKWELL

*T*he air has a chill in it as I wait on the roof of my building, looking out toward Golden Boy's abomination of a headquarters and analyzing every nuanced detail. It's what I always do, regardless of whether a strategy is going to plan or not. Only through constant awareness can I make micro-adjustments as needed. Because people are not static, stationary, and predictable one hundred percent of the time, no matter how much I wish it were so.

And it is in their actions and reactions that I find the most interest.

Goldstone has hired a private investigator, is paying an exorbitant amount of money to track down his little fleshpot's friend. So it appears that he does not know where Isabella is and is getting worried. It's the barest hint of a reward for what I've already gone through to see this particular plan to fruition.

But Jericho assures me the pictures are frauds, and that Miss Turner is alive, not rotting in some forest as Jackson vouched. At this point, I believe Jericho over the photos, considering the lack of a body.

So the question becomes . . . if she's not dead, where is she?

Jackson's resources are vast, both personally and in his connections, so he could have stashed her away nearly anywhere, but I suspect he'd keep her close.

That damned woman, drawing men in like flies to a spider.

"Give me a stable firing platform up here and I can have that entire penthouse reduced to ash in thirty seconds," Jericho calls from behind me. That he knows where I am looking is concerning in itself, since I have not told him anything of my issues with Thomas Goldstone, merely giving him the needed orders for Gabriel Jackson and Isabella Turner. I do not like others having information beyond what I choose, especially when it is about me.

But a man of his particular skill set is not to be wasted, so I delve into his expertise. "An interesting proposition, and one I've considered," I answer, sipping my tequila. "I once thought about what it would take to bring a sniper up here."

"A very difficult shot with a rifle," Jericho confirms, squinting and staring into the distance as he analyzes the conditions. "The wind is favorable though. Still . . . a missile would be much better. Larger payload and certain to defeat any sort of bullet-proofing he might have on his windows."

"And very visible," I counter. "Even in this town, I can't silence every security camera, every idiot with an iPhone. There would be too many questions I couldn't silence if someone used my roof for destruction . . . even if it would carry with it a certain pleasure."

"Questions . . . is that why you haven't given me a green light?" Jericho asks. "Concern over visibility?"

It's a subtle probe of my intentions, and maybe of my steel. If so, Jericho will find that I stand while others fall. "I have other plans for your target . . ." My lips spread in an evil smile, and I correct myself. "Forgive me, I mean targets."

"Targets?" Jericho asks, lifting an eyebrow. While his outer shell barely reacts otherwise, I know the truth. He's a true sadist, a man who lusts for cold cruelty.

"I want Gabriel Jackson dead. Betrayal and dishonesty are simply something I will not tolerate. But the saying 'two birds with one stone' seems rather apropos. Use the girl to lure him, then kill her in any manner you wish. Dealer's choice," I offer, knowing that by gifting him with free reign, he will shine in his monstrous form of creativity. "However you do it, she will serve her purpose."

I don't explain the impact her pain will cause. I have no need to justify myself to a man like Jericho. And he doesn't need any explanation. His sadistic nature means he will do my bidding in this job happily, though a dangling carrot couldn't hurt. "If you can do it inside two days, I'll give you a bonus that will make it worth your while. Let you relax on a beach somewhere warm for as long as you wish."

"Are there visibility concerns for Jackson and Turner?" he asks. I appreciate his attention to detail, consideration for my specific wishes.

I frown, shaking my head. "Only to the people I want to know of their demise."

"Two days," he agrees. "Consider it done."

As he slips back out the door, I swallow the last of my tequila and look across the entirety of Roseboro to the gold building glimmering in the moonlight once again. Perhaps it's a fortuitous sign, but the moonlight's not pale but ruddy, almost bloody against the tower's surface. It makes me smile.

"Soon, Golden Boy."

CHAPTER 33

ISABELLA

J'm trying my damnedest to focus on a school project, moving the text in the layout I'm designing one click to the left and then back, one click to the right. I can't decide which is better. Or maybe I just need a different font?

"Ugh," I tell the empty room, leaning back in my chair and stretching.

If you'd told me a few weeks ago that I could get several days off work to relax, sleep, and do school work, I would've said it sounded like a dream. Add in a stocked refrigerator, endless hot water, a tub that qualifies as half jacuzzi, half swimming pool, and a mattress made by NASA, and I should be feeling like a damn queen.

But the reality of being in hiding is that I'm going stir-crazy. No phone, no internet, and most of all, no Gabe.

Coming to the Goldstone tower would be a sure sign that something's up, so he's stayed away. And even with his burner phone, I understand the security risks. Someone might listen in and catch that I'm alive and well, chilling on the twenty-sixth floor in the penthouse apartment like some spoiled brat.

I wish. I don't feel spoiled. I'm worried.

I get it, we discussed it all. Gabe laid out his concerns, and I put in my own two cents as well, and I agreed to go along with it. But that doesn't mean I like it.

The elevator dings, and I stand, instantly on alert. It's late in the day, but Mia and Thomas should still be downstairs in their offices, working.

Mia had stayed home with me at first, but when Thomas came back from his nighttime meeting with Gabe, the idea of putting her to work analyzing Blackwell was the right move. I feel safer with her jamming on her supercomputers downstairs and finding a solution to this than being with me, trying to figure out which anime she was going to distract me with next.

I don't say anything, quietly peeking down the hall.

"Iz? Honey, where are you?" Mia calls out. There's an odd tightness to her voice.

I come down the hall, hands wringing and not sure I want to hear this. "What's wrong? Is it Gabe?"

She gathers me in her arms, not answering, but she's pale. Tears burn my eyes because whatever she's about to say, I already know it's bad.

"Come sit down, Izzy." She directs me to the couch and sits beside me, holding my hands.

"Just tell me, Mia. Is Gabe dead?" I force out.

She shakes her head. "No, he's fine. Well, I haven't talked to him, but as far as I know, he's fine. But I got a call from the private investigator Thomas hired. He's watching all sorts of alerts and . . ." she swallows, her eyes dropping before they lift back up to mine. "It's your house, Izzy. It's on fire."

"What?" I screech in shock.

It's like a punch in the chest, and I sag into the couch, all the wind taken out of me.

It's nowhere near as bad as Gabe being hurt or worse, but that house is a symbol of my whole life. It's me and Reggie singing carols around a paper cutout of a Christmas tree, it's patching up the backdoor screen again because the squirrels keep coming in to eat breakfast with us, though we both secretly fed them, and talking through the walls at night.

And it's my painting, in Reggie's old bedroom, my memorial to a family I was never able to properly say goodbye to.

It's all I have left. And I've worked so damn hard to keep it.

I stand up, clearing my throat before the tears start. "I have to go."

Mia grabs my hand, yanking me back to the couch. "The hell, you are. The fire trucks are already there, and the firefighters are doing what they can. But this is a ploy, and you damn well know it. It's too convenient. So you're going to sit your ass on the couch and stay here." She's all business, and on some level, I'm glad she's thinking clearly because I'm definitely not.

"Dammit, Mia, my . . . my . . ." I stammer, tears coming to my eyes as I think of what's being destroyed. My painting. Mom, Dad . . . my memorial to a family I was never able to say goodbye to properly.

Vash chooses that moment to wander through the living room, meowing for food. I pick her up, hugging her as tight as her little kitty body will allow me. "Oh, my God, Vash. What are we going to do?"

"You're going to take care of Vash, take care of yourself," Mia says softly, her voice full of love. "That's what matters. I know you don't have much, and what's in that house is so important to you, but they're just things. The real memories, the important things, are right here." She touches my head and then my heart.

"But—"

"Izzy, Izzy. I love you, babe," Mia says, stroking my hair. "I'm sorry, I really am."

I sniffle, and while Mia's hug helps, it's not the arms I want around me right now. "Where's the phone?" I choke out as I set Vash down. "I need to call Gabe."

"Sure, honey," Mia says, grabbing the phone from the side table of the sofa. "Here you are."

It doesn't take long to call Gabe, and he picks up quickly, already knowing the reason for my call. "I just heard."

"Gabe, that was my house!" I cry, but the shocked sadness is beginning to be tinged with anger. It settles me somehow, like a dash of cold water in my face helping me focus. "If this is that asshole—"

"It could be," Gabe says. "But we don't know yet. It might have been something in the house, or it could've even been Carraby," he says, but I can hear that he doesn't believe that for a second.

He sighs. "I think this is most likely a tactic to draw you out, which signals that he doesn't believe the story I fed him. That means you need to stay where you are. The stakes just got a lot higher."

I cringe inside but understand why he's saying that. It's the same thing Mia's saying, and I need to listen to their advice right now while my emotions are pushing me to act irrationally.

"Is there any way you can come over? I know it's dangerous, and it's stupid of me to ask, but I need you. Gabe?"

He's silent for a moment, thinking ,and then finally agrees. "It'll take me a little bit to make sure I can get there cleanly, but I'll be there soon."

We hang up, and I tell Mia, "He's coming."

She nods and just sits with me. We must talk, but I'm not really processing anything and couldn't repeat what she says or what I reply.

I don't know how long it's been when the elevator dings again and Gabe comes in, taking Mia's place next to me on the couch and wrapping his arms around me.

I bury my nose in his neck, inhaling his scent to ground myself. I hear Mia excuse herself, saying she's going back downstairs and to call if we need anything. In seconds, we're alone.

Gabe twines a lock of my hair around his finger, whispering in my ear, "I'm so sorry, Princess. Is there anything I can do?"

I shake my head, but feeling him here with me after days apart does soothe some frayed bits inside me. I look up through my lashes. "Can you make me forget all of this? Blackwell, the fake death, and my house. I need to . . . not think about any of it."

His eyes search mine questioningly, his voice soft. "Are you sure?"

"Sorry, it's stupid," I reply, sagging. "I just feel like I'm losing everything."

He tilts my chin back up, looking deep into my eyes. "Bella, you're not losing everything. You have me, and I have you. We'll figure out the rest, deal with Blackwell, and rebuild your house if we have to."

I lick my lips, drawing strength from his steady gaze. "Why? Why are you doing all this for me?"

It's something I've been wondering in the back of my mind all along. Gabe is beautiful, brilliant, and smooth. Why would he want a woman with nothing but dreams?

Gabe's smile is the slow one I like best, starting on the left and moving across his lips until his dimples pop out. "Don't you know? It's because I love you, Bella. I love you with everything I am, everything I have."

Somehow, in the middle of this mess, he knows just what to say to bring everything into focus. "I love you, too."

His slight intake of breath is audible, like he's surprised by my admission, but I suspect we've both known the truth for a while and were just too scared to speak the words, hoping the actions would be enough to communicate the depth of what we're feeling.

But even with the words hanging in the air between us now, I need the action, both to revel in our shared truth and to distract myself from the building storm coming for us.

Our mouths meet, tasting our declarations, though I don't know if he moved to me or I moved to him. I feel him pick me up, his rough hands on my ass as I wrap my arms and legs around him. "Which way?"

"Down the hall, second door on the right," I tell him, licking and sucking on his neck.

In moments, I'm spread on the guest bed, soft cotton beneath me. "I promise you, Bella, I'll do whatever it takes to keep you safe and by my side."

I put my arms around his neck, just holding him and seeing the love I feel reflected in Gabe's eyes.

Every time I'm with him is a new exploration, a way for us to discover not just our bodies but our souls and our hearts. Nothing is truer than this moment, and instead of tearing into each other with rabid passion, clothes flying like a clearance sale in a Marshall's, we lie on the bed, looking into each other's eyes as we run our hands up and down each other's body, memorizing every inch.

"I'm nervous," I admit, feeling goosebumps form on my arms. "It's the first time I've ever said those words to someone who wasn't family. Mia and Char being family, of course."

"Me too," he admits, taking my hand and placing it over his heart. "But I know every beat, every thought, everything I am . . . it's for you."

Gabe cups my face, and I lean in, kissing him softly at first before our kiss deepens, our tongues entwining and our lips caressing each other as we slip and squirm out of our clothes. Finally, I help him slide his jeans off, and our skin presses together, his heat coursing through my veins.

"Lie back . . . let me," he whispers, urging me onto my back and kissing his way down my body. I arch my back, pushing my nipples toward him, but instead, he traces my stomach with the tip of his tongue, dipping into the shallow well of my belly button before kissing lower. He pulls away to kiss up the inside of my thighs before he soulfully kisses my wet pussy.

He doesn't tease me, instead just kissing my lips tenderly, letting his tongue explore my soft flesh. He's driving me crazy, physically and emotionally, with how sweet he's being. But this is what I need right now, and he knows it.

My hips lift, pressing into his mouth as I grind my pussy against his lips and teeth. "Oh, God, Gabe . . . that's amazing . . . oh, God, yes, yes, yes!" I say before my voice leaves me, devolving into a stream of breathy yesses that blend together as I buck against his tongue.

My thighs clamp around his head as I come, and I can feel my body gushing for him. Gabe drinks me down like I'm a fine wine, which only makes me come harder.

He kisses his way up my body to look in my eyes before taking my mouth in a deep kiss to let me taste myself on his tongue. It's a heady combination of the two of us. As we kiss, he thrusts into me slowly, filling me with his thick cock. We move as one, our hips coming together in waves.

My nipples rub against his chest, pearling up, and he dips down to suck on one. But with a groan, he pops off and lays over me, pressing me into the bed with his weight. I feel cocooned in him, surrounded and impaled by everything he is. And I take it, grateful that he is letting me into his heart the way I'm letting him into mine.

The new angle hits a spot deep inside me, and I cry out, "Oh, God, Gabe. Right there."

"Come for me, Princess," he says, and I reach for it, so close to the edge and so desperate to fly. "Come with me."

And that does it. I want to come with him always, both in bed and anywhere life takes us. The thought of our being together forever, however long that may be, considering the threat we're under, is sharply glorious.

Gripping his shoulders as he thrusts deeper and deeper into me, we find our moment of eternity, Gabe crying out his own release as I spasm and clench around him, milking his cum from his balls.

I don't realize I'm crying until Gabe wipes the tears away with his thumb. "Hey, you okay?" His brows knit together in concern.

I bite my lip, nodding. "Yeah, it's just a lot. But with you by my side, I think I can handle anything."

He smiles, dimples popping for me again. "There's nowhere else I'd rather be. I love you, Bella."

I wish I could say his words make the world waiting to destroy me disappear, washing it away with the power of his love. But that doesn't happen. Instead, his vow makes me feel like no matter what is coming down the pipe, I can handle it with him. Hopefully, he feels the same way about my promise.

"I love you, Gabe. Now and forever."

CHAPTER 34

GABRIEL

The darkness is nearly perfect, with a full, cloudy sky that seems like a blessing, a sign that maybe this stupid move isn't *entirely* reckless. But I wouldn't have been able to say no to Bella regardless.

Wait. Actually, I had said no multiple times, but she'd worn me down, and finally, I'd given in with some rules. And that's how I find myself with a supposed-to-be-dead Bella sitting in the passenger seat of Thomas's work truck as we pull up to her house.

Well, what's left of it.

It's not as much of a burned-out husk as I'd feared, though. From the left side of the front yard, it even looks fine. Or at least as fine as it always was. But from the right, you can see the black char and destruction. The back corner, where the kitchen and living room sat, is basically gone, a black void into the heart of the house yawning open.

I look over at Bella to see how she's taking this, expecting her to be on the verge of falling apart. But the reality seems to have either put her into shock, or she's moving into an anger stage, because she looks fiercely determined in the dim glow of the dashboard lights.

As I park, she moves her hand toward the handle. "No, we talked about this. Stay here until I clear everything."

She nods, sighing and revealing a crack in her brave façade. "I know. I just need to get in there and see what's left."

I rub her thigh comfortingly, making sure the switch on the dome light's off to keep the car's interior dark as I open the door. I don't want to make it easy for anyone to see that it's Bella. The whole point of using Thomas's truck and both of us dressing in solid black with hoodies is so that anyone who happens to see us will assume we're Thomas and Mia coming to check on the house.

I do a scan of the surrounding area, noting all the hiding spots even though I've done this multiple times before while I watched Bella. Then, I was looking for places I could hide. Now, I'm looking for possible threats.

Seeing nothing amiss, I open my door and get out, keeping my head on a swivel. Holding the button on the door handle, I close my door quietly before coming around, carefully walking to avoid stepping on any tree branches or anything else that might make noise. Bella maneuvers herself behind the wheel, poised to crank the engine and run like hell if she has to, and inside, I'm proud of her. She remembers the plan and is ready to jump into action if need be.

As I make the short walk toward the house, I keep my hands in my hoodie pocket, my right one gripping my pistol, ready for action. It seems strangely normal but at the same time silly to go up the two steps to the front door, considering there are gaping holes in the walls and the door itself has been kicked out. But the door frame's still there, so that's where I go.

Glancing back, Bella seems okay, or at least the truck is dark and quiet, so I proceed into the house. It's an odd discord to go inside and be able to see the stars because of the huge holes in the roof. The one good thing? The place is still standing. It's a miracle the fire department had anything except cinders to hose down, as old and dried as this place was.

Once I'm inside, I take my gun out, not worrying as much about visibility behind the few still-standing walls. I check each room, both my footing on the weakened structure and for anything or anyone threatening.

Back out front, I open the door for Bella. "How bad is it?" she asks.

"Not good. There's a lot of damage you can't see from the street, and the whole house has water damage."

She nods grimly, seemingly prepping herself for the horror she knows she's about to see.

Inside, she's silent as she looks around. I keep expecting the tears to start back up, but she must be cried out because her expression stays stoic. Her borrowed black boot kicks out at the ashy remains piled up in what's left of the living room floor. A pile of silvery grey dust puffs into the air at our feet and then falls to the cinderblock-framed ground we can see below since there's no subfloor in this area anymore.

"Watch your step," I warn, pulling her back. "I checked, but I can't be sure it'll hold."

She backs up and moves towards the hall and I follow. I see her take a deep breath, her shoulders rising and falling before she steps through to the guest bedroom. Even in the dim light, I can see her painting is ruined, the sheetrock saturated with water.

"I know it was just a painting," she says, looking at the mess in front of her. "But it meant a lot to me. I painted that right after Reggie died, and it got me through those dark days when I'd lost everyone, everything. It was my therapy, a sign that there could still be beauty in the world, even if I had to make it myself."

She moves to the wall, reaching out a hand to touch the color-smeared and crumbling sheetrock.

"I'm sorry, Bella," I say softly, putting my free hand on her shoulder. "Do you want to see if there's anything salvageable?"

She nods, kissing her fingertips and laying them over the spot where her family used to sit in their plane, memorialized and remembered.

In her bedroom, she squats down in front of the closet, blindly digging deep into the pile of things that have survived the fire. She pulls out a small metal case, about the size of a lunch box, and a sad smile lifts her lips.

"What's that?"

"A memory box Reggie gave me when I first came here," she says, reverently tracing the outside of the box. She opens it and her eyes shine with the tears I've been expecting as she looks heavenward. "Thank you."

She picks up a few pieces of folded paper and some small squares that look to be photographs. Unable to see them in the dark, she lays them back into the beloved box and closes it with a soft snick. "Okay, this is all I need."

I look at her, this woman who has survived her whole life with barely anything but hard times. And when life conspires to take even more from her, she doesn't crumble, burnt and destroyed by the flames. No, she rises like a phoenix. She has only what she packed in her backpack and this metal box to her name, but it's all she needs.

She is gloriously grateful and humble, knowing what's truly important isn't a house or clothes but memories and people.

"You ready?" I ask, giving her one last chance because I don't know when we'll be able to come back here with the dangers lurking around every corner.

She sighs but shakes her head and I step in front of her to lead us out.

I look down the hall before we exit the bedroom, carefully stepping our way back to what remains of the living room. Everything seems clear, but as I come around the corner, a sharp blow hits me in the jaw, sending me stumbling and taking me by surprise.

I don't get surprised. Ever.

My instincts take over, and even though it's damn near pitch black, I blindly turn to fight my attacker. I see a shape, and I focus on that, calling out to Bella, "Run. Go."

I hear the scuffle of her feet and pray she's doing as I said as I launch myself at the attacker. She needs to get out of here, leave me, and get to safety.

In the dark, there's no space or time for throwing blows. Instead we wrestle, slamming each other against the weakened structure of the house. I'd try and use my gun against him, but he's just as skilled as I am, using knees and elbows to blast me rapid-fire style, though I'm giving as good as he is. But I don't have even half a second to reach into my pocket for the pistol, and firing into the dark is a dangerous option since I'm afraid I might hit Bella accidentally.

So I stick to keeping close enough to sense him, laying body shots when I can and blocking his hits as best I'm able. A moment later, I take a sudden knee to the balls, doubling me over in blinding pain.

As I bend over, I reach out to grab the backs of my attacker's legs, taking him down and we scramble across the floor, which creaks eerily beneath the onslaught.

I already know this can't be Carraby, there's no way that pussy could give me this much fight even if he had a nightstick to help him.

So if it's not him, coming to take advantage of Bella's unexpected open-door policy, it's somebody much, much worse. It's something much worse.

"You fucked up, Angel," a disembodied voice says from beneath me. The attacker might be on his back, but I don't have a solid upper hand against him. He's countering my every move, his jiu-jitsu so good I get the sense he's playing with me. Like he knows my next move before I do.

And the fact that he called me by my professional name sends chills down my spine.

But this is life or death, and I fight with everything I have, every dirty trick I learned in my years of evil, because this is for Bella and I know it. I don't care if I never leave this shell of a house, as long as she's safe. I pray she's long-gone by now, well on her way back to Mia's.

I need to give her time to get away.

Half standing, I slam my knee into his kidney and pull back, getting to my feet. If I can't beat him on the ground, then I have to take a chance of fighting him on his feet. My head's still swimming. I've been rocked hard, but I position my body in between my attacker and the door, praying it gives Bella enough time.

My opponent follows me up, and I throw a right jab at the middle of his shape, the smack of my fist connecting with something hard. A small success that I follow up with a flurry of punches to the same area.

He grunts, but in the midst of the flurry, I feel my feet swept out from underneath me, and I'm slammed to the floor, my head bouncing off the floorboards and making the world swim. I hear a creak beneath me, and I wonder if the fire-weakened structure can withstand much more.

A hardened boot heel slams into my gut, adding to the ache in my balls, and I curl up, protecting my organs and coughing as the hot metallic taste of blood stains my tongue.

"You're really a fallen angel now, Gabriel," the voice says. I look up, and like divine intervention, the clouds part for a moment, letting the moon shine through, the empty roofbeams letting the light in.

It's like seeing the devil come to life.

He's tall, with dirty blonde hair and wearing all black. And fucking night vision goggles. That's how he knew what moves I was making to counter me so well. I'm fighting blind in the dark, but for him, it may as well be daylight in the blackened ruins of Bella's house.

He grins, and as he does, I see the slight pull of a scar by his mouth . . . a scar that is as much his calling card as my good looks.

Fucking Jericho.

He kicks again, my head snapping back, and this time, it's *my* walls that are broken down, the world turning black once more.

CHAPTER 35

GABRIEL

*C*onsciousness returns in a painful pulse of red, from floating in space to achingly aware of the hard floor beneath my battered body. But I resist the pain, remembering what got me here.

Jericho.

Bella!

I turn over to my knees, and I lay my head on the floor, fighting back waves of nausea as my body reminds me of the abuse it's taken. I don't know how long I've been out. All I can do is pray Bella listened and drove like a bat out of hell back to Goldstone Tower.

But the gnawing unease in my belly knows she didn't do that. My princess wouldn't leave me, would instead give her all to save me because that's who she is, what she does. She gives everything to everyone while she's the one struggling or in danger.

The fear buoys me, helping me get to my feet even as the world continues to swim in lazy circles. Staggering, I make my way to the doorway, where I lean against the frame for a moment before my eyes start to cooperate and I can see straight again. With a deep breath, I step outside, my heart stopping in my chest at what I see.

Thomas's white truck sits in the driveway right where I left it, letting me know that Bella didn't speed away. More damning, though, is the open driver's side door, hanging wide like a one-winged avian harbinger of doom.

I already know it in my gut, but I run to the truck anyway. The truth won't let me pretend, though. Bella is gone.

The last vestiges of my illusion disappear as I see the nest of wires underneath the steering column and the keys still dangling uselessly from the ignition. He cut the wires . . . I'd left the door unlocked in case we needed to haul ass, but he'd used that against us, cutting the wires.

Jericho's good . . . and now he has her in his grasp.

I slam my fist into the door panel, denting it, but the fresh pain helps me focus. Reaching into my pocket, I pull out my Leatherman and reach further down the wires, finding what I need to hotwire the truck before climbing in. I drive back to Goldstone Tower as fast as the truck will go, but the elevator to the penthouse feels excruciatingly slow, even if it's a direct ride.

Stealth isn't a consideration now, I don't care if everyone from the security guards to the Mayor sees me. Only one man in town would have the connections to hire Jericho, and right now speed is of utmost importance. There's no telling what sick things Jericho is doing to my Princess even in this very moment.

"Thomas!" I bellow as I come off the elevator.

I'm typically a lone huntsman in my line of work, but I'm not so arrogant as to ignore the resources at hand. And I'll do anything to get Bella back. Especially since I have means as extensive and as dedicated as Thomas and Mia available to me.

Thomas comes out of the back wearing boxer briefs, with Mia hustling behind him. A quick glance shows me I've probably interrupted a little couple time, but I'm not here to compare swords with Thomas. Nor am I interested in Mia's body, although he shoves her behind him anyway. As if I'm looking at her when I have Bella.

"What's wrong?" Thomas asks me as soon as he sees my face. "What the fuck happened to you? Where's Izzy?"

"He took her," I snarl, my eyes clouded with rage. "That bastard."

"What? No!" Mia gasps in shock.

"It was a setup," I reply, nursing my aching jaw. "We were getting ready to leave when he jumped us. I told Bella to run, but . . ."

I haven't lost my cool in years, not since Jeremy's death, but I'm a hairsbreadth away from torching the whole fucking city and Mia's trembling like a fall leaf in a windstorm with what I've already said. Thomas stays cool and collected though, all business as he calms the situation.

"Sit, tell us what happened," he says.

I don't sit, needing to pace, but Thomas forces a small shot of scotch in my hand, saying, "It'll help." I toss it back and then manage to relay the story of us taking precautions to go check out Bella's house, how Jericho had been lying in wait for us, the fight and then the empty truck, with Bella nowhere to be found.

Mia gives off a single sob at the end when I tell them about the cut wires, the detail somehow convincing her more than me getting my ass kicked that Jericho is for real.

"What do we do?" Mia asks as she regains control of herself. "Call the police?"

Thomas and I lock eyes, and I know we're thinking the same thing. "No police," I reply, gripping the edge of the countertop. "I'll get her back."

Mia's eyes widen, looking from me to Thomas. "What? She's been kidnapped. We need to call the police."

I know that I'm about to piss off Thomas, but I need to make sure we're all on the same page here. "Mia, do you understand what I do, who I am? Because I'm going to get Bella back, and I do not want police anywhere near this when I do it. This is going to get ugly, fast."

Mia gasps, and Thomas' eyes are tight, but they seem to fully grasp my intentions now, which was my point. Thomas blinks his agreement and I continue.

"This man, Jericho, he has her now, under contract for sure. He's the sadistic type who enjoys his work and has no code other than completing a job. Bella will be like a shiny new toy to him, something to play with and test out her limits."

I swallow thickly, the thought making my stomach roil.

"You know him?" Thomas asks. "Personally?"

"No," I reply with a shake of my head, "only *of* him and his work. We're, well I guess you'd say we're competitors for the same contracts. But I'm careful about the jobs I accept. For Jericho, it's not about the money or making someone pay for a wrongdoing, it's about sanctioned brutality."

"And he's got Izzy?" Mia sighs, rubbing at her streaked hair. "What can we do?"

"I need your brains and your computers," I tell Mia bluntly. "I need intel."

Thomas raises an eyebrow even as Mia nods, her eyes setting firmly. "Not to put too fine a point on it, but he did get the drop on you. You sure you don't need help, backup of some sort?"

I shake my head, looking Thomas in the eye. "No. And this isn't up for debate, Thomas. I'm not taking you with me. While you might handle yourself just fine in a bar fight, you're dealing with a trained killer here. This is the point where guys like you *hire* guys like me. And I need to do this job alone."

Mia takes Thomas's hand, solidifying my decision. Thomas needs to stay here for Mia because to some degree, this is still about them, pawns being sacrificed to weaken the King and Queen. Thomas looks at Mia, then back at me. "I fucking hate this."

"I know. And I appreciate the offer, but I can do this. I just have to figure out where he took her."

"Then let's get to work," Mia says, her eyes narrowing as she disappears into the back. She comes out a minute later in some yoga pants and the same shirt before throwing a pair of sweats to Thomas. "My office will be faster."

Mia's basement office is a shrine to all things computer nerdy, and she puts her three displays to work, pulling data as quickly as she can type.

By the time the clock on the wall ticks midnight, we're looking over detailed maps of Roseboro, calculating possible hideout points where Jericho might've taken Bella. Mia's a machine, correlating tax records, population density, police coverage, and more, but even with all of that, there are simply too many possibilities.

"Seven," Mia says, hitting *Print* on her machine. "It's . . . it's the best I can do, Gabriel. If I had—"

"You reduced my load from thousands to seven," I reassure her. "If I have to, I'll—"

That's when we catch a break of the worst sort. My phone dings with an incoming text. It's my burner phone. Only one man, and Bella, have that particular number.

I open it and anger flashes hot and bright-white in my veins. It's a picture of Bella, her hands zip-tied to a chair, her head lolling to the side. Is she dead or unconscious?

"Fuck."

"What is it?" Thomas asks, his jaw clenching as I show them the picture and Mia cries out softly. Underneath the picture is an address, and I note with some satisfaction that it's on Mia's list of seven properties.

The final words are the only possible hope. *'Come and get her'* blinks on and off, with a grinning, laughing animated emoji.

He's enjoying this. The fucker is getting off on torturing her and taunting me.

I stand. "I have to go."

"It's a trap, you know that," Thomas says, surprisingly reasonable under pressure. "And you don't know anything about the building."

"I know, but this is my fault," I reply. "I have to save her."

Mia's brows crinkle and she wipes at her eyes. "Your fault? It's not your fault there's a fucking madman with a weird hard-on for hurting Thomas."

"I knew something was off about this contract from the beginning. It's why I delayed," I admit with a shake of my head. "I should've never taken her from the safety of this penthouse tonight, but I was weak. And while Blackwell wants to hurt her to get at you, Jericho is definitely taking satisfaction in doing this to me."

Thomas's voice is deep, controlled. "You said you didn't know him personally."

"I don't, but I can judge the man by . . . by the way he kills, if that makes sense. My guess is, Jericho's contract is for both Bella and me, because Blackwell will not take kindly to my defection from our deal. But either Jericho or Blackwell, or maybe both, want me to suffer. I was unconscious on the floor, Jericho could've just taken me out then, walked outside and double tapped Bella, and the job would've been done. But he didn't."

I imagine that scenario, my Bella splayed out in the grass, dead in the dark night, and pray that whatever Jericho's doing to her now doesn't make a quick and easy death a preferable, peaceful option.

I think about what I know of Jericho. Despite his sadism, and his reputation for cruelty, he's also known for his detailed planning and precise execution. It's why he's often hired to extract information, because by the time he's done having his fun, his victims will spill their guts just to get a final release from the pain he's put them through. Though sometimes he's hired simply for the torture aspect, no information needed, his depravity simply providing a painful death to the target of his contract.

Evil. That's the only word to describe him.

"Gabriel?" Mia asks, and I clear my throat.

"We're not friends, or even colleagues, but there's a certain level of respect given to other pros. By taking the contract against me, he's saying that I've betrayed the profession, and he'll want to back it up. But he wants to draw this out for his own pleasure, torment me by getting at Bella. That's the only reason he would've taken her and left me, to make it hurt because he's a cruel bastard. And once he's had his fun, he'll kill us both to complete his contract."

I say it matter-of-factly because if I'm going to make this work, I have to get in touch with the cold, heartless side of me again. Discussing hits for hire is par for the course for that part, even though this contract is as different as can be.

But Thomas and Mia look horrified at my casual discussion of death.

"Oh, my God, I'm going to be sick," Mia says, her hand covering her mouth. Thomas rubs her back soothingly.

"I'll be in touch as soon as I can," I say at the door. "Mia, if you can, I need you by the phone, ready to send me information."

"I can do you one better," Thomas says, reaching over and swiping a tablet computer from a docking station next to Mia's desk. "This is tied to her systems, a little gadget we worked up for business trips. She types it, it'll pop on your screen."

"Good . . . then I need any information you can gather in the next ten minutes," I reply. "Video feeds, traffic cams, anything. And

I'd suggest you stay here. If Blackwell is escalating, who knows if he still considers you off limits."

Thomas purses his lips, nodding. "I'm trusting you to take care of Izzy. You can trust me to handle Blackwell."

"If I fail . . . turn this place into a fortress," I advise him. "At least until you can get out of town."

The drive to the address Jericho gave me is quiet, the tablet beeping from time to time as Mia sends me information. I use every beep as a chance to separate myself, to shut down my humanity and to become the cold, relentless killer I know is inside me. My emotions close off, my heart slows, and my blood ices.

I become the Fallen Angel once again.

No . . . I must become more. Or is it less? More monster, less man, more evil, less salvageable.

Because tonight, I cannot stop. Not until Jericho is dead.

I only hope that I can come out the other side of tonight with Bella and my soul intact.

CHAPTER 36

ISABELLA

The first thing I'm aware of is the chill. It seems to be everywhere, on my skin, in my bones . . . even my hair feels chilly somehow.

I try to reach up, needing to wipe the tears leaking from the corners of my eyes. But when I go to lift my hands, they don't move and I realize I'm tied to a metal chair. I fight the restraint, but I can only wiggle a little bit before chafing my wrists. The same is true for my ankles. Blinking until I can see, I look down, seeing that both are bound with plastic zip-ties.

Shit.

"Hello?" I murmur, my mouth tasting like chemicals. My mind's fuzzy, but I have a vague memory of a cloth over my face and darkness.

I look around the room, trying to figure out where I am. I can't see much. The lights are so dim that I can't see the walls of the room, so I try again. "HELLO!"

The sound bounces off the walls, echoing and reverberating loud enough to make my ears ring. Well, at least I know that wherever I am, the room's not that big.

I wince, wishing I could put my hands over my ears, but all I succeed in doing is making my forearms hurt.

"It won't help you," a voice with a slight accent that I can't place says from the darkness. "You can scream until your voice gives out. Nobody will hear you. This building is a mile away from anything."

"Who . . . who are you? What do you want?" I ask, trying to keep the fear out of my voice, but the tremble is obvious.

The lights suddenly brighten, and I see where I am. Or at least, I see where, but that doesn't mean I understand.

It looks like an office, the sort of place you'd find in a mechanic's shop or something industrial.

I can't tell anything else because every surface of the room is covered in plastic drop cloths, the kind you get when you're painting a room and you know you're going to make a mess. Thick ones, too, slightly opaque clear plastic that covers every wall, the window, which I can tell is there only because a dim light shines through it, the floor, the door . . . looking up, I can even see the ceiling is covered in plastic.

The idea of being surrounded by so much plastic chills me to the bone, bringing to mind all sorts of images from the worst of the late-night horror movies.

But then I sense someone behind me, and slowly, a tall blond man, his hair neatly styled and his face looking cold and aristo-cratic, walks around me, coming to a stop directly in front of where I'm sitting.

He's dressed all in black, but where Gabe and I were wearing jeans and hoodies, this man is wearing slacks and a button-down dress shirt. And black leather gloves, filling my heart with a sick, desperate feeling of dread. He tilts his head, lifting an eyebrow, and after a moment, I realize he expects me to speak.

"Who are you?" I repeat.

"My name is Jericho," the man says. "And you're Isabella Turner."

He smiles, and another chill goes down my spine. It's the smile of a man who would have no qualms about ending my life. My heart stills in my chest because in his eyes I see no mercy, no humanity.

It's even worse than seeing Gabriel when he was ready to kill Russell.

"You amuse me," he says, but his face shows no sign of joy. "So please tell me, how did such a worthless thing happen to create so much drama? I don't understand it."

He brushes the back of a finger along my cheekbone, and I recoil, trying to get away. "No," I say, shaking my head. "Don't touch me."

From somewhere far away, I hear my name. "Bella?"

I can't pinpoint where it's coming from. It's muffled by either the walls or the plastic, I don't know which. But I know who it is.

It's Gabe! He's come for me. *Thank God,* I think. But then I see the glee on Jericho's face and I rethink my hope that Gabe can save me.

"Gabe! Run!" I shout, wanting at least one of us to get out of this and strongly doubting there's any way I am leaving this room alive.

Jericho turns back to me, his eyes alight, and I realize just how dead inside he looked before. But this . . . this look is so much worse. "Ah . . . he was a little faster than I anticipated. I'm not done setting the scene for him. Too bad, but we will continue this conversation later. Time to get to work."

I've heard the saying that if you love what you do, you'll never work a day in your life. Watching him hustle over to the desk, I suspect that's true for Jericho. He loves his work, as twisted and awful as it is. And I'll be the one to pay for that bloodlust. Me and Gabe, if I can't get him to leave me.

Jericho picks up something from a toolbox on the plastic-covered desk. At first, I can't see what it is, but then he turns and shows me, the anticipation part of the terror he's after. It's a pair of pliers, just like the pair I've used at The Gravy Train for helping Henry in the back with minor repairs, but these have sharp blades. He clicks them together, mimicking the movement with his mouth, teeth chomping at the air.

"What's that? What are you doing?" I say, my voice stuttering with fear and my eyes wide.

He doesn't answer, coming closer step by step, and I thrash in the chair. But he's got me trussed up tightly, with my feet off the ground, and the chair's hard to tip over. All I do is abrade my wrists and slam my shoulder blades into the back of the chair hard enough to make me scream.

Jericho grabs my left hand, and though I try to pull it away, it's locked in place by the zip-tie restraint. He runs the cold metal down the back of my fingers, sending shivers through my whole body.

"No, no, no—" I plead, not even fully grasping what he intends but knowing it won't be good.

"Eeny, meeny, miny, moe—"

My cry turns to a blood-curdling scream as Jericho, in a blur of speed, fastens the pliers onto my pinkie finger and twists it to the side.

The pain is instant and overwhelming. "Aaaaaahhhhhh!"

Tears run, and a new level of terror fills me. Fear of the unknown is one thing, but this is the first step of destruction in Jericho's plan, and the reality is beyond anything I've ever known. I thought I knew pain, emotional devastation from the losses I've suffered, and even physical discomfort from hardship. But this is sharp and bright and hurts so fucking much.

"Delightful . . . I love that sound," Jericho says conversationally.

He bends closer, as if inspecting his handiwork. I can't help but look too, even though I desperately don't want to.

I'm half-expecting to see my finger dangling loosely, but instead I find it's not there at all. Jericho cut it clean off from my palm and the room spins as I feel faint at the sight. Even through the dizziness, I swear I see the flash of Jericho's tongue as he licks his lips, delighted at the rivulets of blood running from the gnarled nub where my finger used to be.

"Bella!"

I hear Gabe, his footsteps pounding. My courage, telling him to go, evaporates in the fiery pain, and I look around wildly, trying to find him, shamefully wanting him to save me, help me, rescue me.

In a haze, I see Jericho's anticipation. He's ready, setting the pliers down on the desk and opening a drawer in order to withdraw a pistol. And for a split second, I can think clearly.

"No! Leave me, Gabe. He's going to kill us both. Please, I love you. *Go!*" I struggle against the chair again, trying to get free or at least away from Jericho.

A shot rings out in response, cutting off my words. It's loud and piercing, echoing in the empty space, but it sounds close. Really close.

Jericho grins, finally truly happy. "Showtime." His voice is robotic and cold, his countenance even more menacing as he inhales, spreading his shoulders wide.

He moves behind me and the plastic rustles. I look over my shoulder, and he's gone, disappeared into the space beyond the plastic room he's created for me.

"He's coming, Gabe!" I cry out, choking on tears and fear. "Run!"

My words are too late, though, as a pair of gunshots cuts me off. My heart's in my throat, terror that Gabe's been shot evaporating as I hear a scuffle start out of my sight. I don't know where they are because everything echoes, but I can hear the smack of flesh, the grunts as the punches connect, and the sound of their bodies banging against what I can only guess are walls and furniture outside the plastic.

My brain is a useless blob of jelly between my ears, and my chest aches from holding my breath until instinct takes over and I breathe again. I jerk against my restraints, and at first I think I've got nothing, but then I feel something . . . slip.

Blessedly, my mind focuses and I repeat the motion, wiggling my hand back and forth, to see what's giving way. The blood is helping my wrist slide between the plastic bracelet and the arm of the chair, lubing the tight fit a bit.

I've got the smallest space to pull my hand through and the thought of pulling my pained hand through that pinching gap already has me moaning in fear, but as I hear another thud from the fight outside, I put it aside.

I can do this. I have done some ridiculously difficult things in my life, been through hell and come out the other side, and can tackle any obstacle in front of me and conquer it. I'm a strong woman, and I won't sit here and wait for someone else to do what I can do myself.

And Gabe needs me.

Renewed, I don't thrash my whole body, but instead focus on just my left arm. I pull back slowly, lifting as I do to try and slip through the small space, but the only feeling I get is my wrist screaming as the nylon tightens like a vice around my bones.

I yank, twisting left then right, and the chair tips up again, this time almost overbalancing me to the point of falling over. But I'm so close, I can feel the increasing give in the zip-tie.

I think it through and fold my thumb across my palm, making my hand as narrow as possible. Taking a deep breath to prepare myself, I jerk hard and pain flares through me.

The chair falls from the force of my pull, crashing to the floor and knocking the breath out of me, and for a heart stopping moment,

I think I've failed. But then I realize my hand is loose, bloody and disfigured but free.

Oh, my God! It worked!

I can't do the same to my right hand though, so I look around. The desk, with its tools, is just four feet away, but it feels like four miles as I claw my way towards it, dragging myself by one hand, each grip on the floor making me grunt in pain. When I get close enough, I look up at the toolbox above me.

I grunt as I reach up, grasping for an edge of the metal box. With a yell, I shove the whole box off the edge of the desk, and the contents spill onto the floor next to me. There, right in front of me, is my salvation . . . a pair of wire cutters.

I shiver suddenly, wondering what Jericho had in mind for me with this tool, but I don't have time to ponder it now. Instead, I use the tool to cut my right hand free, and then both legs, and get to my feet.

I have to help Gabe, I think, pushing my way through the plastic in front of the door. It's still dim in the space, but outside, the office is more of a warehouse area with high tracks of faint yellow light.

I follow the sounds of their fight, grunted words becoming clear as I get closer.

"Should've just done your job, Gabriel," Jericho says. "She's just a contract."

"No, she's not," Gabe replies in a growl, like he's hurt. "She's mine."

I move closer, seeing the fight firsthand as they jockey for position. They're both bleeding, tangled in a pile on the concrete floor as they roll back and forth, short elbows and punches emerging from time to time to thud into the other's body before doing it again and again.

I want to scream for Gabe, but he doesn't need a distracting cheerleader right now. He needs actual help. I'd love to think he could handle this completely on his own, and the truth is, maybe he can. I've never seen him truly in action like this. But I can't stand by uselessly when the man I love is fighting for his life. And mine.

Seeing a broomstick against the wall, I grab it and risk getting even closer, ready to whack Jericho as soon as I get an opening. Suddenly, Gabe, who's on the bottom, elbows Jericho's neck, giving me an opportunity.

I wind up, swinging for the fences, and the broomstick cracks off Jericho's skull, shattering into three pieces but failing to knock him out.

Jericho turns his head, like some Terminator machine, staring daggers at me, and grabs the remains of the broomstick.

"Steel plate . . . skiing accident," he says, pointing to his head before tossing me aside. Gabe yells in fury as I go stumbling, but fortune smiles on me as I bounce off a water cooler and see a dark shadow on the ground. I bend down quickly and see if the spot is what I think it is. Thankfully, I'm right, and my right hand wraps around the cold metal of a gun.

Whether it's Gabe's or Jericho's, I don't know. But I check the safety and see the little red line on the safety, just like Saul taught me at the gun shop.

"Stop. Step away from him," I bark, praying my voice sounds more badass than I feel because my knees are seriously knocking.

Surprisingly, they shove off one another, actually doing what I said, Jericho getting to his feet while Gabe rolls to his knees, his hands out to me. Jericho, on the other hand, seems more intrigued than anything else.

"Come here, Princess. Let me have the gun," Gabe coos instead. "You don't want to cross this line. Trust me."

To be honest, that sounds like the best idea. Of the two of us, he's definitely better equipped to handle Jericho and a loaded weapon.

But as I reach toward him, Jericho lunges for us.

I don't think. I don't have time. Whether I'm the target or bait, I don't care. I just react in self-defense, my hand squeezing the trigger just like I was taught. Somehow, the pop of the pistol sounds quieter in here than it did when I practiced, and Jericho's body jerks once, twice, and a third time. He stumbles, his left hand going to the hole that's appeared in his chest, and he looks at his hand in total shock before he collapses to the floor.

"Oh, my God, did I kill him? Did I just kill a man?" I whisper as Gabe gets up and takes the gun from me, gathering me into his arms.

I can't . . . no . . . what? My mind fogs in disbelief, and the world starts to spin.

I can just make out his face, his eyes wide with shock, fear, or maybe anger? I don't know, but I can't focus to decipher it right now.

Instead, I collapse into Gabriel's arms as everything goes black.

CHAPTER 37

GABRIEL

I hope that waking up this time is a completely different experience for Bella. There are no zip-ties and chair, no Jericho and plastic. Instead, she's cocooned in the soft fluffiness of memory foam and Egyptian cotton, her head cradled on two down pillows that I've wanted to adjust but haven't for fear of waking her.

She makes a small noise, and I lean in close, worried she's in pain. Her lips twitch, and I can see she's having a nightmare, so I reach out, laying a hand on her forehead. "It's okay, Princess, I've got you. Welcome back."

She tries to make words come, but her throat seems to be scratchy and dry because she swallows a few times. I hold a glass of water with a straw in front of her and she sips gratefully.

"Not too much at first," I warn, and she slows down her gulps. "You've been out awhile . . . don't want to upset the stomach."

The bit of water eases her throat and she blinks, still a little groggy. "What happened? Where am I?" she asks, but then looks around. "Mia's?"

I grimace, focusing on her first question. "What's the last thing you remember?"

She blinks again, remembering, and I can watch the play of emotions across her face like a movie. The house, the fire, Jericho knocking me unconscious and kidnapping her. I see the fear, fear I had to be dead if I was letting Jericho take her, the fear she must've felt when she woke up in the plastic-covered room, the fear of seeing Jericho and me fighting.

And the gun.

"Did I kill him?" she asks tentatively after a moment. "There's a piece of me that hopes I didn't, that hopes I just hurt Jericho and we got away. There's an equal part of me that hopes I killed the fucker and that we're safe."

I nod slowly, stroking her cheek. "You were protecting us. You did what you had to do, Princess, and I don't want you to doubt for a second that if you hadn't shot him, he would've killed us."

I speak to her gently, unsure whether she feels guilty or remorseful over what she's done. Killing someone is not something to be taken lightly, and I can still remember vividly the first time I took a life.

There are times I wish I'd had someone I could trust to help me through the change it wrought upon my mind and my soul. So if I can be that for her, I will be.

She looks pensive, as if she's teasing through her thoughts, looking for any sign of doubts, and I can't read her expression to know what she's feeling. "Do you feel bad about the people you've killed?" she asks bluntly. "Any of them?"

I jolt, surprised at the question. "Bad is maybe too generic of a word. I don't feel guilty. They were all just like Jericho, not trained killers per se, but still people the world's better off without. I made sure of that. If I regret anything, it's that the situation ever came to that. I hate that they wasted their lives doing something that got them killed. I'd say I feel tainted, with a better perspective of what life should be. Does that make any sense?"

Admittedly, it's not the smoothest monologue in history. I've never tried to put my feelings about my work into words. It was safer to just keep it inside. I didn't have anyone to talk about it with, anyway, and was always able to justify my actions with thoughts of catching Jeremy's killers.

Even when the contracts moved beyond things that would help me with that mission and were more about taking out my anger on the world in a violent, destructive manner, I found some reason to make it okay on the surface.

Deep inside is a different matter. I know I'm damned and made my peace with that long ago.

"I know. I don't regret killing him, even if it was awful. Because the worst part of it all was the fear that he would kill you. He was excited about the idea, like a high he got from the anticipation, the torture, the experience of it all."

She shudders before continuing. "When he heard you, Jericho's face went from dead and impassive to hungry and eager. When you came in to rescue me was the only time he came to life. But, now what? Am I going to get in trouble?"

"I took care of it," I reply softly, knowing that even if I hadn't, I would have protected her. She would never have gone down for killing Jericho, even if I had to cop to it myself. In this particular case, though, that isn't necessary. "There will be no questions, no cops, and no one looking for Jericho. He was as alone in the world as I was before you. No one will miss him."

She frowns, looking down at the comforter. "That's sad."

Her words touch me. She can become strong and tough . . . but there's an inner essence of purity, of goodness, that will never be shaken. I swallow, my throat tight as her eyes lift back to mine.

"Do I want to know how you 'took care of it' or will that just give me nightmares?"

I lift one eyebrow, giving her a moment to decide for herself, and she shrinks a bit. "I don't want to know. At least, not now. Maybe one day."

I give her a soft smile, brushing her hair back and pressing a kiss to her forehead. "Anytime you want to know, I'll tell you everything. Or if you never want to know, that's just as fine."

Honestly, I selfishly hope she chooses the option of never knowing. There's no benefit to her knowing the dirty details of how I used Jericho's own plastic tarps to wrap up his body, minus one key piece. She doesn't need to know how I used Thomas's truck to haul Jericho's body out to the woods, where I implemented the same plan I'd originally had for Bella. The specifics of what I did won't give her anything but nightmares. I'd spare her those, as long as she trusts that I handled everything with the skills I've developed for years.

I made sure this body dump was my cleanest ever, with no possible signs of what happened, who did it, or where. One, because I want to make sure she is never implicated as the one who pulled the trigger, and two, because I want us to both get away scot-free so we can be together.

"What about Blackwell? Isn't he just going to send another hitman? This is never going to be over, is it?"

I wish I could spin her a tale of sunshine and rainbows, of happy endings and chocolate cookies. But I can't. "There's no way to be sure. To a logical man, he shouldn't. He went after you to try and get at Thomas indirectly since Thomas is too public, too well-protected. It was about the element of surprise. Now that Thomas knows, the costs of striking again is high, especially when Thomas is preparing for war. Blackwell has bigger fish to fry, the one he truly wants."

"Are you saying I'm a little fish?" Bella asks, trying to deflect her worry with humor. "The kind you throw back when you catch them?"

"Well, I'm not throwing you back, for damn sure. But I'm feeling like I'm the one hooked on your line." I lean in, kissing her neck before nibbling softly.

She pulls her hands out from beneath the comforter, beginning to reach for me, but stops when she sees the bandage on her hand. "Oh, my God, I forgot that part. Or blocked it out. My finger!"

She touches the thick white bandage wrapped around her palm and over where her left pinkie finger used to be. "It's numb."

"I'm sorry, Princess. Thomas had a doctor come in to clean and stitch it. The doctor said you'll be fine but need to take antibiotics for a couple of weeks. He gave you a mild sedative to do the stitches, that's why you were a bit groggy."

"Yeah," Bella says before she sniffles, looking at her hand. "I'm sorry. I know it's stupid to cry when things could've been so much worse. But it's my hand. I'm an artist, for fuck's sake."

I kiss her bandaged palm and then her right palm. "Bella, you're right-handed. You can write, draw, paint, and more. The only thing you're going to have problems with for the next few months is typing. I'm sure your geeky buddy will hook you up with some *Star Trek* voice typing program if you ask."

She rewards the silly joke with a watery smile, sassing slightly, "So you're saying I'm overreacting?"

"I am way too fucking smart to ever say that," I reply with a chuckle. "But what I am saying is that sometimes, we fixate on small things when the big things are scary. I just want you to know that you're okay, you're safe, and you're with me."

She snuggles into my arms and I hold her tight. "I almost lost you, Princess. I promise that will never happen again. I love you."

"I love you, too. I don't want to lose you either," she says pointedly.

I know what she's asking, if I can give up my mission to find Jeremy's killers for her. The danger and risks of going after the men who would take his life so casually could result in me losing my life.

Once upon a time, that was a reasonable loss. I would have happily died if I could take them out with me, one big blaze of glorious vengeance for Jeremy. But I can't do that now, won't do it to Bella.

She's lost so much, and for whatever crazy reason, she's chosen me as one of her people. I won't make her feel that loss again for any reason if it's within my power.

"I already told Mia to delete the data card," I whisper softly. "Jeremy will understand."

Bella blinks, stunned before she cups the back of my neck with her good hand, pulling me towards her. She lifts up to kiss me, and I can feel the heat building inside her the same way it is in me. Reluctantly I resist, looking in her eyes.

"Bella, you need to rest, recover. Your hand—"

"I can keep it off to the side," she says, biting her lip. "I feel okay. As long as you don't touch my hand, I'm good. And I need this. I need you, Gabe. I thought you were . . ."

Her voice cracks, and I roll her back carefully, pinning her beneath me with her arms over her head on the bed, out of the way. She instinctively spreads her legs, cradling me between her thighs.

"I'm right here, Princess," I say, grinding against her. "We're both safe, together."

She nods but her eyes still look anxious.

I reach between us, lifting her T-shirt nightgown up and her panties down before pulling my hard cock out of my boxers. There's no need for foreplay. That's not what this is. The reassurance she needs is that she's alive, I'm alive, and that she's still everything I need.

Right now, I need to remind her that she is mine, imprint myself onto her, no, *into* her very cells so she feels me even after my cock leaves the heaven of her pussy.

I push into her slow and steady, letting us each feel every inch as

I open her, spreading her soft folds and velvet walls, forcing them to conform around my thickness.

Each stroke is a vow.

Each retreat is a promise to always come back.

And as we come together, we pour our love, our hopes, and even our dreams into each other, along with our sticky cum, in beautiful and carnal bliss.

CHAPTER 38

BLACKWELL

"Sir, a package has arrived for you," my secretary says, her voice quavering. She knows about the extra security, although she doesn't know why. She just knows that I've placed a dozen security guards between the lobby and my door at various places, and each of them carries a gun.

I'm taking no risks when it comes to having two hitmen in town, both well skilled in their respective styles. Especially since I'm certain Gabriel Jackson would like nothing better than to get close enough to make me his next victim.

"Bring it in," I snap, not having time nor patience for her mousy pussyfooting about.

Three days.

After a deadline of two days, I've been waiting for three days since Jericho promised me my proof. Three days since I've had to place myself in this prison that's my own home and office.

"Sir, the package has specific instructions that you have to sign," my secretary says quietly. "Should I have them bring the box in here?"

A chill goes down my spine, and I force myself to slowly nod my head as a courier brings in a nondescript cardboard box. On each side are red stickers that say *Fragile, Handle With Care*, and the top is sealed with plain brown packing tape. "Sign here please, sir?"

I take the clipboard and see that the package is marked *Gift*, but there's no other information. I scribble my name, and the courier leaves like he wants to be anywhere but here, already ignored as I look at the box.

"Is that all, sir?" she asks, ready to go just like the courier.

"No. Open it," I tell her.

"What?" my secretary asks, shocked. "Open it?"

"Yes. Open it!" I growl. "Are you deaf as well as stupid?"

She swallows and shakes her head, taking the knife from my blotter and starting to cut the tape. Already, I can imagine an explosion, a bomb or something being sent by Gabriel Jackson. It's not his style, but my mind still wanders, contemplating scenarios.

Or perhaps this is finally my proof from Jericho?

The options are endless and therefore too unknown to open the box myself. But my secretary is disposable, with others lined up to fill the financially beneficial role.

"Oh, my God!" she screams, backing away. Her face loses all color. "Oh, God."

Before I can ask what's in the box, she turns, retching blindly before fleeing with staggering steps as though she's drunk. I watch her go, then turn my attention to the box which sits, the flaps open, the plastic that was used to pack the object inside exposed as well.

It's with almost a sense of inevitability that I cross my office, nudging one cardboard flap aside to look down into the plastic-wrapped face of Jericho.

There's a piece of paper in there with him, and my hand is steady as I reach in, unfolding it to see the typed note inside.

You once told me you prefer a body as proof, so consider this confirmation of death. And you seem to be rather fond of sending messages, so here's one for you. If you come after the people I care about, the Fallen Angel will have one last target . . . you. Besides, I think you have other things to worry about.

Underneath is a symbol that looks sort of like the letters V and A combined . . . but I know what it is. It's the symbol of an archangel.

It's the symbol of Gabriel.

Well played, Mr. Jackson. If I weren't angry with him, I might be impressed with his gall.

His implication that Goldstone is focusing on me should be a threat, but truth be told, it excites me. A worthy opponent for me to win against.

Let the games begin.

CHAPTER 39

ISABELLA

*I*t's been quiet for a few days, and as crazy as it sounds, I need to live my life. I refuse to be shut away in Mia's penthouse, no matter how castle-like it may be, any longer. There's only so many video games, so many hot tub baths, and so many rides one can take on a spin bike before your cabin fever gets out of control, and I've done all of this before.

It helps that Gabe has told me that I'm his new full-time gig. A protection detail, he calls it. I say he's my bodyguard when I'm feeling friendly, my babysitter when I'm a little on edge from the lack of fresh air.

Thankfully, he's agreed to let me out today, so I grab my backpack, double-checking that everything is inside.

"You ready, Princess? Your chariot awaits," he teases, flashing me the double-dimple smile I love so much.

He's been amazing, helping me calm down when I have a bit of a flashback or worry about what could happen next and using all of his imagination to keep me entertained in a myriad of ways when I'm feeling bored.

I'm not ashamed to say that Mia accidentally walked in on just one of those imaginative distractions yesterday morning. But being Mia, she just offered a hooting cheer and even clapped before closing the door. Thankfully, it'd been mostly my ass she saw, and nothing more . . . revealing. If she'd seen Gabe, the possessive bitch in me would've had to get her for that.

I lift to my tiptoes, and he stands tall, making me work for it. But I gain enough height to kiss him, rubbing a small circle with my thumb over each dimple. "Let's go," I say, ready to get my life back.

We take Gabe's SUV to the school, and I sit while he does a preliminary check of the parking lot before letting me out. It feels ridiculous. I'm not some celebutante fake royalty, but considering the outlandish story my recent life tells, I'll take it.

He opens my door, helping me out. "Which way first? I did a walkaround of campus yesterday, scouting weak security areas, hiding spots, and risk points, but I'd rather follow a spontaneous route to check in with teachers so that no one can lie in wait."

I waggle my eyebrows at him, adjusting my backpack just a little tighter to make my boobs stick out some more. "Talk security to me again. It's so sexy."

"Princess, don't distract me or I'll just throw you back in the car and fuck you right here," he growls, his hands still by his side as he maintains his control physically even as his voice slips a little. It's hot as hell, knowing that I can affect him while still driving him to such depths of dedication that he'll resist kissing me here. I'm sure he'll take it out on me later, though.

He continues. "And that wouldn't be safe for either of us because fuck knows, I'd be watching my cock slip in and out of your pretty pussy and not looking for threats." He knows exactly what he's doing, teasing and turning me on with his filthy promises.

My smirk is pure devilment, and my words are a purr. "I feel like you mean that to sound like a bad thing, but it sounds like a risk I'm willing to take."

It's not, and we both know it. Neither of us are gambling that big when the stakes are this high, but the tease is enough to promise later games.

Gabriel chuckles. "You're full of shit. But if it's a public fucking you're after, I'll shove you up against the penthouse window when we get done with our errands. Now where to?" he growls.

I grin, feeling like I won the verbal sparring and got a promised prize for tonight. "Fine, let's go see Professor Daniels first."

The meetings with my professors go surprisingly well. The first time I'd explained that I'd had a family emergency requiring some security measures that kept me off-campus had been awkward. But starting with Professor Daniels, I'm repeatedly assured that Mr. Goldstone had made it clear that he appreciates the university's assistance in keeping his inner circle safe.

My jaw keeps hitting the floor, shocked at just how understanding everyone is, but when I'm told I don't even need to turn in the assignments I'd missed, I balk.

No way am I going to let that fly. I've worked my ass off to get where I am, earning every single class with hours of slinging food and every single grade with hard work. I tell each of my teachers that I appreciate the sentiment but that I've done the assignments and want the grades deserved by the caliber of my work.

Everyone is willing to accept that, except for Professor Foster, but she's always a stickler, so I'm all too happy to take the late grade, since at least she lets me turn in the project I'd completed, albeit at a ten-percent penalty.

After completing the school check-ins, I have to do an even scarier one.

The Gravy Train.

"Martha and Henry are going to have my hide for being gone so long without a word, especially after unexpectedly going on a 'vacation' and leaving them stranded," I say with a cringe.

"I think you'll be surprised," Gabe says as he walks me across the parking lot.

He's right. When I go in, there is only love. Martha almost drops the tray she's carrying, and Henry runs out from the kitchen, still holding his spatula.

"Izzy, you'd better get over here and give me a hug!" she says, not giving me a chance as she wraps her arms around me on one side and Henry takes the other side. He's muttering something about me making his ulcer hurt, and I can't help but smile, having missed his grumbles.

Elaine stands back, waiting her turn, and then hugs me too once Martha and Henry let me go. Seeing my bandaged hand, she steps back, looking at it carefully.

"What the hell? We were betting he swooped you off to Vegas to get hitched, but this don't look like no wedding band."

She gives Gabe a hard look, but before she can consider fetching one of Henry's knives for Gabe's balls, I hug her again.

"No, no . . . it's fine. I am fine. Just a little drama, but I'm all good. No Vegas wedding either," I protest. "If that happens, I'm gonna do it right. In a real church, with you all there."

"And Elvis?" Elaine asks before calling over her shoulder, still eyeing Gabe. "Pay up, Henry. Told you our Izzy wouldn't get married without us."

"Fine." He digs in his pocket, pulling out a ten-dollar bill and holding it up for Elaine to take. She stuffs it into her apron pocket, earning a 'harrumph' from Martha. Henry shrugs and looks me over. "All right, then, girl. Tell us what you've been doing and what's happening now because my ulcer has been flip-flopping between worried and excited. Both hurt like the dickens."

I give them a very edited, very short version of the last few days, making the getaway seem like the vacation I told them it was from the beginning and then the stayovers at Mia's more girls'-

night-in than safety concerns. I can't mention Jericho or the danger. It wouldn't be safe for them or for me, really.

"We heard about your house," Martha says sadly as Elaine tells a customer to hold their horses and holds a finger up in the universal sign of 'in a minute'. "You okay?"

"It's almost a total loss, given the fire and water damage," I admit. "It was so old, it practically needs to be rebuilt. I'm just staying at Mia's for now."

It hits me as I finish—I'm homeless, for all intents and purposes.

Thank God for good friends. I've put them off so many times over the years when they've tried to help me, hidden how dire my situation was time and again, but when I need it, they step up to help without hesitation.

Gabe speaks up. "Doesn't matter," he says quietly. "I've already talked with a contractor, and even if it means a total razing and rebuild . . . we'll do what it takes." His eyes go soft, his gaze loving. "This beautiful Princess isn't going to be without her castle for too long."

My jaw drops. Henry smiles proudly. Martha and Elaine have matching shit-eating grins.

Martha whispers loudly to Elaine, "Told you he was one of the good ones."

I can't look at them, too hung up on the bomb Gabe just dropped. "What are you talking about? I can't afford to have some contractor rebuild my house."

Gabe brushes a thumb along my bottom lip, not giving a shit about the crowd watching the intimate gesture. "I was going to save this for later," he whispers in my ear, "but I couldn't hold back. It will be rebuilt . . . and it's not quite *your* house anymore."

I flinch at that, fiercely saying, "The hell it's not. I worked my ass off to keep Reggie's house, and it'll be mine until the day I die, even if I have to work my fingers to the bone to keep it."

His smirk is maddening until he continues, "I meant that it's not your house. It's *our* house, Princess. I know that's where you want to stay, and I want to stay by your side, so I'm moving in."

I blink, my anger dissipating instantly. "You want to move in with me?" I ask incredulously, giddy delight forming in my belly. Then, because I can't help but tease him, I say sassily, "I didn't ask you to."

He leans forward and whispers hotly in my ear, "Do I look like the kind of man that waits to be asked for shit? You're mine." Then he stands back up, gives me a look that dares me to disagree and declares, "I'm moving in with Bella."

I study his face, looking for any sign of uncertainty and find only love. I see my home, not the four walls I've always felt kept me in touch with my past, but my actual home in Gabe. A future for us. Wherever that may be.

He is my home.

But that he knows how important my house is to me lets me know, without a doubt, that he gets me. And with him having traveled for long years, I'll do whatever I can to make my house as much his as it is mine. And to hold his heart as dearly as he holds mine, in a safe haven.

"We're living together," I say, agreeing.

"Does this mean you're leaving us?" Henry asks cautiously and I wonder if he realizes he's rubbing his belly.

I shake my head, "Never. This is my second home."

It's been a long road, and I've been alone for a lot of it, beaten down by life again and again. But I have a good circle, supportive people who help me even when I don't want it, love me even when I'm too busy hanging on by a thread to give much back, and who would do almost anything for me.

I look to Gabe. Actually, he would truly do *anything* for me. Even kill. And rather than being scared by that, it gives me peace, hope, and makes me feel loved.

CHAPTER 40

GABRIEL

"*A* toast," Thomas says, raising his glass of red wine, and we all follow suit. "To a growing circle of family."

He looks around the dining room table, making eye contact with each of us, Mia first, followed by Charlotte, Bella, and lastly, me. Our fivesome has become rather tight-knit over the last couple of weeks.

Bella and I are both living in the guest room, but that's going to end when our house is ready.

The contractor showed up with a big fucking crew, and they've been working their asses off to finish ahead of schedule and earn a nice bonus. With Thomas paying for the rebuild as an apology for getting Bella mixed up in all this, I put up the rush order bonus, and Bella has decided to be okay with that after I'd promised her we'd christen every room and surface in the house.

And I plan to keep my word.

"To a day well-lived, a night well-slept, and a life well-loved. Cheers!" We lean forward, clinking our glasses to one another's and sipping.

After a few bites of delicious chicken and rice with asparagus, conversation begins again. The girls especially always have something to say, and Thomas and I have learned to have near-whole conversations with our eyes and eyebrows in response to their antics.

"But for real, I told my boss that I'd be happy to pick up his dry cleaning, but only for the next two weeks," Charlotte says, her voice tapering off in excitement, begging us to ask for more.

Mia's fork clangs to her plate as she realizes first what Charlotte is saying, "You quit your job!"

Charlotte nods, "I did. I'm so glad to be getting out of there, especially with all the nerves that every meeting was going to be a surprise firing squad of Blackwellian design. I've never been so happy to be the invisible girl at the front desk everyone ignores. But I got the business loan, put in an offer on the location I fell in love with, and I'm doing it. I'm opening my own bakery." She looks to Thomas, "Thanks again, partner."

Thomas shakes his head. "Nope, read that contract again. I'm not a partner and don't want to be involved in any way. I'm just a silent investor in a business owner I believe in. Especially if you add a delivery service for my orders. I'm seeing quarterly Bundt cake meetings at Goldstone, birthday cakes for the boys at Roseboro Boys' House, and some cookies for the veterans' monthly meetings."

"Deal," Charlotte says, and we all congratulate her.

Going by the few samples and trial runs of recipes she's brought by The Gravy Train, she's an awesome baker, and I'm looking forward to eating more of her creations. And being a taste tester.

She talks a bit about her plans for the space she's found, a supplier of Belgian chocolate she discovered, and then she turns to Bella.

"And I need to hire you to create my logo, business cards, menu boards, and whatever else I haven't even thought of yet."

Bella beams. "Really? You want *me* to do that?"

Charlotte rolls her eyes, "Duh, of course. You're the best graphic artist I know. You're also the *only* graphic artist I know, but don't let that dilute the compliment." More seriously, she says, "Just let me know the going rate, or maybe the friends and family discount rate?"

I lean over to whisper in Bella's ear, and she turns to me, a smirk on her face. "You sure?"

I nod, and she looks back to Charlotte. "My security detail has advised me that my fee should be . . . a weekly muffin and coffee for each of us when we stop by to visit."

Charlotte jumps out of her chair, throwing her hand at Bella and then me for a shake. "It's a deal, no backsies."

"I might be able to use the designs as a showcase for my final project too, if you don't mind? Two birds, one stone," Bella says thoughtfully.

Mia interrupts, sarcastically adding, "I'm sure your showing the bakery's logo and menu to a big group of hungry college students and professors will be a huge inconvenience for a new business owner. Huge." She holds her hands far apart and then moves toward her mouth like she's devouring a whole cake by herself. Her grin is visible even behind her hands.

"How's school going?" Thomas asks Bella, ignoring Mia's weirdness as she talks to the imaginary cake she's still pretending to eat.

"Good, turned in all the assignments I missed, even the ones Professor Daniels said I didn't need to." She rolls her eyes and Thomas laughs. "Everyone seems adjusted to my shadow here, and I've scared off all the girls who tried to talk and flirt with him."

The last part is growled, making me laugh as I remember Bella damn-near licking me to mark her territory when some blonde kept inviting me to her study group despite my telling her repeatedly that I'm not a student.

"Just maintaining surveillance on my most valuable possession.

Where she goes, I go," I say, resting my hand on the back of Bella's neck and rubbing small circles with my thumb.

Mia's accent appears again. "Newsflash—it's 2019. She's not your possession."

Bella's eyes lock on mine, and I can see the heat there mirroring my own. She doesn't break our eye contact, but she tells Mia, "Shut up, Mia. He didn't mean it in a bad way. And I've heard some of your stories, so you have zero room to talk."

Thomas clears his throat uncomfortably. "Before you two run down the hall to have sex in my guest bedroom, I did have something I wanted to give you, Gabe."

His all-business tone wakes me from the spell Bella is weaving around me. Reluctantly, I turn to him, one eyebrow raised and my other hand on Bella's thigh.

"Mia finished going through the information on the data card," he says quietly. "I know you asked that we ignore it, but we thought you'd like to know anyway."

I swallow, and Bella lays her hand over mine, squeezing it supportively. "And?" I ask both Mia and Thomas.

"There were two main names on the card you gave me. One, Joe Ulrich, you don't need to worry about. He's dead. But there was a full life history and background check if you want to see it."

"Dead?" I ask, lifting an eyebrow. "How?"

"Auto accident. His Harley hit an ice patch in Colorado and his head bounced off a Winnebago, with no helmet. The report includes pictures and the autopsy, if you're curious. Also shows there was a false bottom in his gas tank, and he was riding with two kilos of crystal meth, so nobody was really crying over his death."

I nod. "What about the other?"

"Steven Valentine," Thomas says, more cautiously than before.

"He's still around, changed his name though. Now he goes by Simon Bulger. You might have heard of him?"

I shake my head, and Thomas continues. "Butcher Bulger?"

I blink, surprised. "Yeah . . . head of the Devil's Forgotten Demons."

Thomas looks to Mia, who likely read the data card information first but is letting Thomas be the bearer of the bad news. "It looks like both were bikers before the incident with your brother. The intel says they might have been probies for the hit."

I scrub at my mouth, the five o'clock shadow rough under my palm as I think. "I don't work with bikers. They usually handle their own shit and don't have a need to outsource, but I've dealt with them a time or two. Before they allow a probie to get patched, they have you do a crime and turn the evidence over to the club to hold over you. So Jeremy's death . . ."

"I don't know," Thomas says with a shrug. "But Bulger's still around. The file included his last known whereabouts, but he's in the wind right now, hiding out with his motorcycle brothers as security to distance himself from recent club shit. The FBI wants him on a list of warrants longer than my arm."

"Thank you," I tell him honestly.

Thomas's head tilts and his face is carefully blank. "What will you do with this information?"

I pause, thinking how to say this even as everyone at the table holds their breath impatiently. "Before, my answer would have been easy," I finally answer. "I would have gone to war with all involved and left a river of blood behind me, retribution and revenge mixed with savage bloodlust, my reputation for preciseness be damned."

And still, no one breathes. "And now?"

"Right now, my only concern is making sure that Bella's safe and that Blackwell doesn't go fucking around in her life anymore. I have to believe Jeremy would understand that."

Bella's smile is sad but understanding. "He'd want you to live, not be dragged further into the dark. You've spent long enough there."

I give her a kiss, sweet with emotion and salty with the few tears she can't hold back, knowing that I'm choosing her over everything I've lived for over the past years. It's one thing to say I'll do that when the opportunity to make my brother's killers pay is a hazy, indecipherable possibility. It's quite another to choose a life with her when the other option is so readily laid out before me.

But still, I choose her, and I'd do it time after time.

Mia and Char croon in sync, "Aww, he loves her."

And I can't help but smile at the blush that washes over Bella's face. She's not used to being the center of attention, even with her friends. I think she's been hiding, to some degree, most of her life. She says she's been 'asleep at the wheel', just going through the motions like a hamster on a wheel because she had to keep on keepin' on or risk the house of cards she lived in falling to pieces.

But she's slowly relaxing into our new reality, where there's food in the refrigerator, the bills are comfortably paid, and she doesn't have to work herself to the bone just to keep her head above water.

I appreciate all the things her friends have done for my princess before I met her, sneakily helping when they could, checking in on her, and just generally being her best friends.

"You guys are second on my list because Bella cares deeply about all of you. Bulger's dropping down on the list to at least third."

It's a hard thing to say, but I'm a hard man. I have made decisions to end others' lives multiple times, but this time, I'm deciding to live mine.

I do think Bella is right. Jeremy would want this for me, would be happy I've found someone, and I daresay, I think he'd like Bella and the way she keeps me panting after her like a horndog.

Never thought I'd see the day, Jeremy says in my mind, miming a whip. *Pussy whipped fucker.*

I grin, mentally talking back. *Oh, but what a pussy it is.*

Even saved, I'm still no Prince Charming with sweet words, but Bella never seems to mind my dirty thoughts, especially when I share them with her.

Before I get a chubby at the dinner table, though, and sweep her off her feet to run to the guest bedroom, I try to focus back on the conversation around me.

I ask Thomas, "I'm doing my part to keep Bella safe, but you said you wanted some time on the Blackwell issue. Any updates or anything I can do to help?"

I'd truly wanted to kill Blackwell myself, rush into his fancy tower and take him out. Or wait for him to come out and kill him in the streets of the town he thinks he owns.

But the reality is, since I sent him Jericho's head, he's gone hermit, virtually living 24/7 in his tower, rotating between his office and his apartment there. And always with a full army of security. It wouldn't be the most difficult assignment I've ever taken on, but I don't trust Blackwell to not have some type of plan to sell me out if he were to disappear or die. He's a smart man, knows I'm here and gunning for him, so it would behoove him to plan accordingly.

So I've had to back off and wait in the wings while Thomas wages war in a very different style from my own.

Mia answers, "Definitely making progress. I've been doing a full analysis of Blackwell holdings and investments, evaluating which legs of his business hierarchy are most vulnerable, either financially or personally. I found several options for strategic takeover or flat-out destruction."

She begins talking in facts and figures, and I lose the train of her thought process around the fourth decimal point of a percentage of some company's quarterly profit-loss report.

Thomas smiles at her like she's reciting romantic prose or filthy sex talk, neither of which makes any sense to me because math is basically the ninth ring of hell to me.

Finally, he takes over and I understand what he's saying. "Long story short, I made a successful hostile takeover bid for Danver's Aluminum this morning. They're now under the Goldstone umbrella."

"And that matters why?" I ask.

Thomas takes his turn then, launching into some story about how his company had bid on the contract for Danver's years ago but had lost out to a Chinese consortium, effectively making Danver's go commercial instead of keeping their military contracts.

Mia found out that Blackwell has a considerable share in the company, likely directed their decision away from Goldstone, and was in fact double-dipping in profits by also holding a voting percentage of the corporation in China that buys the airplane parts. It's like a complicated version of a shell game, shifting monies in and out of the country and companies to maxi-mize the profit margin.

"But now, I own the majority of Danver's, and the first order of business is to cut all ties with foreign entities and reapply for the military deal," Thomas wraps up.

"Other than the contracts, this doesn't sound like you're waging war on Blackwell, but rather like business as usual for you," I argue. "We need to act quickly to keep us all safe."

Thomas's lips press together in a thin line. "I disagree. Blackwell has waged a years-long war on me and my company, going so far as sending in spies and trying to kill my family." He looks at Bella, who jolts at the label before her eyes soften.

He tells me, "Your style is swift, decisive, and that's warranted in certain situations. Hell, if you get the chance, take him out, for fuck's sake. But in the meantime, I need to play this smart, be methodical. Taking back a company that he actively worked to keep from me is a strategic first move, a sign of what's to come."

Thomas's voice has gone cold. "Blackwell will be destroyed one way or another, but his legacy, the thing he covets most, will also be decimated. That's what I want."

Char raises her hand like we're in elementary school, telling Thomas, "You realize you sound just as maniacal as he does, right?"

Mia defends Thomas. "But he's doing it for the greater good, not because he's an asshat in a tower with a narcissistic God complex. Like some Evil King of Roseboro."

Char laughs. "Fair point."

Thomas looks at Mia, and she sighs. "There is something though, Charlotte. We think you need security. Thomas and I already have it here in the tower, and take guards with us when we go out. Izzy has her own personal protection in Lover Boy over there who follows her everywhere she goes. Gabe is right that we don't know what Blackwell is plotting next, and the last thing we need is him coming after you the way he did Izzy."

Charlotte shakes her head, and though I already agreed with the plan to get her a guard of some sort, I let Mia and Thomas talk her into it.

Thomas adds, "The bakery building will have a top-notch security system, including cameras. But that won't keep you safe in the moment if something happens, won't protect you on the way to work and home, or anywhere else you go."

Though the rest of our dinner conversation has flipped between lighter and heavier subjects, this moment is what truly sets the tone. Acknowledging the elephant in the room with us, the very real risk looming over each and every one of us, but none more than Thomas. The pressure that responsibility adds to his shoulders must be back-breaking, but he withstands it like Atlas, only fighting to keep those around him safe from an unpredictable adversary he never saw coming and that will stop at nothing in his plan for destruction.

"I'll think about it," Charlotte yields. But looking at Thomas' eyes, I can see that whether Charlotte agrees or not, she'll have a protective detail. I make a note to give him a short list of possible options, good men that will blend into her daily life without notice, but can be deadly and decisive when needed.

Changing the subject, she adds, "And on that note, can I suggest we revisit the taste testing of my recipes? I have a Kahlua-infused chocolate cake with coffee frosting and shaved coffee bean garnish I'm dying for everyone to try."

Bella holds her belly. "Good lord, Char. I will never sleep again if I eat that."

But I tease, "I'll stay up with you and keep you busy, Princess."

The blush on her pale cheeks and the way she bites her full bottom lip tell me she likes that idea almost as much as I do.

CHAPTER 41

BLACKWELL

*S*illy boy.

He thinks he's making strides against me, playing at buying companies like this is some game of corporate Monopoly. As if hitmen are the worst I can sic on his pathetic life. Using the Fallen Angel had been a calculated move, and while I'm disappointed that play didn't come to the preferred conclusion, it was but one of my planned attacks.

The Golden Boy has no idea what he's up against, the depths I'll go to demolish him and insure my rightful place as the creator of Roseboro for all time.

Especially now that he can sense the target I've had on his back for years. I pray to any god that may be listening to a monster like me that the laser dot burns him hotly, feels weighty with the very real threat I wish to carry out.

He may not be a worthy adversary, not remotely on my level, but no one truly is. But as far as I'm concerned, the game just got interesting.

He's waging a war, thinking like the business man he has always been, from point A to B, with possible sidetracks under consideration. I'm plotting nuclear destruction of his entire existence, a devastation he could never fathom and could certainly not recover from.

And plans have already been set into action, I think with a pleased smirk.

My messy to his neat. My chaos to his order. My sovereign reign to his democratic leadership.

My strength to his weakness, the one he doesn't even know he has yet. But I'll be sure to remedy that. As soon as the last puzzle piece falls into place.

EPILOGUE

GABRIEL

I unroll the hose, pulling it to the front yard and setting up the sprinkler to water the newly planted sod and flowers. The house is looking good. It looks like a home where people are proud to live.

The door across the street opens and Mrs. Petrie steps out slowly, lifting her hand in a wave. Her lined face lifts. "You coming over here next, Gabe?"

"Yes, ma'am," I say, already heading out of our gate and crossing the street to hers. "I'll get your sprinklers all set up."

It's not a role I ever thought I'd be in—helper, friend, savior, especially not when my soul was destroyed so long ago—but it's growing back from the tatters, seeds taking root and blooming just like the rosebushes Mrs. Petrie begged me to plant because they reminded her of her own mother.

Shortly after I moved in with Bella, Russell came poking around again. He'd been high and more desperate than I'd ever seen him, and that's saying something. He'd fallen to his knees on the porch, begging tearfully for money, saying even a few bucks would help. At first, I'd thought it'd been so he could buy more drugs, but the truth had been so much worse.

We'd denied him, and then he'd gone after Mrs. Petrie. I'd defended her too, telling him to get off her porch. I'd intervened and protected the small group of people all up and down the street since I was the only thing Russell seemed to be scared of in his panicked mania.

He got desperate enough to rob a store in town, and his sins finally truly caught up to him, something I can understand and pray never happens to me.

Any loyalty the cops felt to Russell's parents had been worn away by his continued bad behavior, and they'd arrested him. Russell put up the last thing he owned as collateral for the bail and attorney fees, his house and the land the mill houses sit on. But before he was bailed out, he was killed by another inmate.

The typical thinking is that dead men don't pay debts, and Russell was in deep to his dealers and loan sharks. But the consensus is that they were more afraid Russell would rat them out to lessen his sentence, and the money and Russell were acceptable losses in that equation.

When he died, the land and Russell's house went to auction and I bought them for a steal. So now, Bella and I own the land for the row of mill houses, and we treat our neighbors properly.

The fees have dropped to a bare minimum, the sense of community has returned, and the homes are slowly but surely being updated and cared for. I help out where I can and act as landlord for Russell's house, which we've converted into a rental property after renovating it.

"All set, Mrs. Petrie. I'll be back in a couple of hours to shut it off and put everything away," I call out to her. She stays on the porch, not able to come down the steps very much anymore. When I come back, I'll be sure to sit with her for a bit and see if she needs anything from the store this week.

But for now, I go back across the street because my princess is sitting on her throne on the small porch we added. Okay, so it's more of a porch swing than a throne, but she looks regal in her purple tank top and denim shorts, one bare foot lazily pushing the swing.

I sit down beside her, throwing my arm along the back of the swing, and Bella snuggles in closer to me. I reach down and pet Vash, who's sitting in Bella's lap. The ornery cat has finally decided I'm an acceptable food-giver and will usually let me pet her as long as Bella is around.

Bella sighs happily, a soft smile on her face that makes me feel warm and fuzzy inside, which is a feeling I thought I'd lost the ability to experience. Her voice is music to my ears. "You saved me, you know. Hunted me down, woke me up, and brought me to life."

It's maybe a bit dramatic, but it's also a bit true. "Maybe, but you saved me right back, from loneliness and dark hatred, by bringing in your light and stubborn hope that everything would be okay if we just kept fighting for it."

"With a smile and a song, and some hard work," she says, then whistles cheerfully. I told her once that she reminded me of Snow White, with her dark hair and pale skin, and her endless optimism and kindness, even when life had been cruel and most folks would've fallen into bitterness, so now she likes to quote the movie to me. Thankfully, she doesn't sing the songs often. For a Princess, she's not the best with staying on pitch.

"I love you, Princess," I say, not her Prince Charming but the hunter who stole her away to save her. "Let's go inside."

I scoop her into my arms, Vash jumping down and following us like Bella is the damn Pied Piper. I carry her through the new cozy living room, with warm wood floors and cream-painted walls, to our bedroom. Bella had dreamed of a canopy bed, but the room is too small, so she'd settled on a scrolled iron headboard with fabric layered behind it.

I toss her to the bed before ordering her, "Naked. Now."

I follow my own command as well, and she grins, hurrying to beat me as she says, "I love you, too." Then she turns over,

345

getting on her knees and elbows, her hands gripping the ironwork. Her left hand is fine now, healed with a pink scar I always tell her makes her a badass, but mostly, she doesn't even seem to think about it anymore.

"Fuck, Princess," I growl, my voice rough as sandpaper as I look down the line of her curves, from her heart-shaped ass to her narrow waist, with her dark curls curtaining over her back. I kneel behind her, laying kisses down the bumps of her spine until I bite the apple of her ass.

She arches, pressing herself to my mouth, and I lick her, tasting her sweetness from behind. I use my thumbs to spread her slick lips open and dip into her, fucking her with my tongue the way I desperately want to fuck her with my cock.

I swirl around her clit until her hips circle too, chasing me and the pleasure I'm layering on her with my tongue, my hands, my words.

Finally, I give in and stay where she wants, flicking my tongue over her clit in rapid flutters and pressing two fingers along the front velvety wall of her pussy. Her cries tell me she's close, and I take her right to line and then . . .

Stop.

She whines, bucking her hips and begging me to finish her off. "Gabe," she says, turning the single syllable into at least three.

"I'm going to edge you, take you to the point where you're about to come over and over, but you're not going to come until you're impaled on my cock and I'm filling you with cum." I let every dark and dirty thing I want to do to her color the promise.

She nods, looking back at me over her shoulder with fire in her eyes.

I keep my fingers deep inside her and kiss my way back up the round globe of her ass, enjoying the way she wiggles in need, fucking herself on my hand. Flattening my tongue, I give her a long, slow lick along the crease of her ass before diving in and teasing the tight pucker.

She jumps in surprise, but the noise quickly turns to a moan. "Oh, my God, I've never . . . I didn't know." And then she spreads her knees a bit more, giving me greater access as she arches.

I lick her, then spread her slick juices up to her asshole, tracing the edges with both my fingers and tongue as I give her a chance to relax into it. I slowly start to push my finger inside her ass, lazily licking her clit to keep her climbing toward that peak I won't let her fall off of, at least not yet.

"That's it, Princess. Let me inside this sweet ass. One day soon, I'll fuck you here and claim you completely."

Her whole body clenches tight, and I retreat, smacking her ass. "I think you like that idea, don't you? Remember, you don't come until we're coming together."

Her breath is coming in harsh pants. "I can't, I need—"

"What? What do you need?" I'll give her anything she asks for, but I'm hoping I know her answer because all this teasing her has me on the edge too.

"You," she moans. "Please."

Thank fuck, I think, lining up behind her. I rub the head of my cock along her lips, covering myself in her cream and bumping her clit before I notch myself at her opening and slide in, one agonizing inch at a time. Any faster and I'd come instantly from her slick pussy taking me in, but the slow pace is driving us both mad.

I force myself to give it to her slow, but I succumb to the need for roughness, slamming into her so hard and deep, I bottom out with each individual stroke.

She cries out with each thrust, bouncing and rebounding off my hips, so I grip her waist, holding her in place. "I can't wait anymore, Princess. You ready?"

Her eyes meet mine, pupils wide with lust, but I can see the deeper meaning there. "Ready for anything with you," she says quietly, and her devotion to me is blessedly obvious.

How a soul as pure and sweet as hers can accept one as stained and sullied as mine, I'll never know. But I am so fucking grateful for it.

I can't promise her I'll never do anything wrong, anything violent ever again, but I can promise her that I will always act with her love and her future in mind.

So I slam into her faster, giving us both what we want.

"Now, Bella. Fucking come with me right now."

And we detonate, the two of us creating something beautiful, something neither of us thought we'd ever truly have.

Love.

Her, because she didn't trust the permanence of life.

Me, because I felt I didn't deserve it after letting my brother down.

But both of us were wrong. We deserve love. We have love. From and for each other.

EPILOGUE

ISABELLA

I don't know if I have ever been this nervous. I look in the mirror on the back of the door, even though I've already checked my outfit three times. It's not like it matters. No one is really going to see me, but it does matter. It's a sign of how important I'm taking this meeting.

So I look at my dark-wash jeans, low-heeled boots, and light-weight cotton shirt. The neckline is wide, showing my collarbones and framing the necklace Gabe gave me for passing my finals. I'd told him it wasn't necessary. I mean, I've passed every test I've ever taken without some promise of a material reward, but he'd insisted.

I swear, I half think it's a tracker for the rare occasion he lets me go out without him escorting me. But I don't mind. It's a beautiful necklace, and I love having him with me as much as possible, especially when there's still a question about what Blackwell's next move will be.

Gabe's head pops around the door frame. "You ready?"

I nod, biting my lip nervously.

"You look beautiful. He's going to love you. No worries."

I'm a bundle of nerves, and Gabe is as cool and calm as can be as we get into his SUV and he drives. I lose track of the turns, finally relaxing a little and singing along with his deep baritone to some old rock tune on the radio.

He turns through a metal archway covered in flowers, parking and coming around to help me out. We walk through the rows of stone, Gabe's hand in mine leading me. He knows exactly where he's going, like he's been here many times before.

And then he stops, and I look down, following his eyes.

"Hey, brother, got someone I want you to meet. This is Isabella Turner, my Bella. I think you would have really liked her." He speaks casually but switches in and out of both past and present tense. He probably doesn't even realize he does it, both living with Jeremy in his past and carrying Jeremy with him in his heart in the present.

I smile softly. "It's nice to meet you, Jeremy. I've heard a lot about you."

And there, under the bright sun and swaying trees, I listen as Gabe tells our story to his brother. He apologizes for not following through with his promise of revenge but finishes with the belief that he's doing the right thing, and Jeremy would've wanted that.

"Besides, as much as I love you, man, I love her too. And she's got something you don't have . . . a pussy that sucks me in like a damn vise."

I gasp, shoving at Gabe's shoulder. "What the hell! You were being all romantic and then you go and say something crude like that."

Gabe gives me the grin I love, slowly growing until his dimples pop and he's already halfway out of trouble. "That's how brothers talk, Princess. It's not like you thought I was some sweet Prince Charming."

He leans in, whispering in my ear even though there's no one around us in the cemetery. "And you wouldn't like me if I was."

"Fine," I say, rolling my eyes. "But you're my not-so Prince Charming, so let's keep the talk about my pussy to a minimum with other people."

He narrows his eyes. "That mean you're not talking about my cock with Mia and Charlotte either?"

I freeze, remembering how I'd just told them about our successful mission to christen the whole house. "That's different," I say, knowing it's not at all.

"Innocent, sweet, good girl, my ass," he says, but I giggle because he squeezes a handful of my ass as he says it.

I look to the rounded concrete engraved with Jeremy's name. "You see what I put up with from this brother of yours? But as much of a danger to my good name as he may be, I love him too."

A big wind blows through us, warm and swirling, and a white flower drops from a tree beside us. Gabe picks it up, moving to place it behind my ear, but I take it from his hand. Walking over to the tombstone, I lay it on top. "We'll be back soon, Jeremy. It was nice to meet you."

And then we go home.

Together.

PREVIEW: BEAUTY AND THE BILLIONAIRE

PROLOGUE - MIA

The darkness is complete, wrapping around me like an ebony velvet blanket, cool and textural on my naked skin. I can feel it on my goosebumps, the air adding to my trembling.

My body, exhausted from the last ordeal, still quivers as I try to find the strength to move. It's so difficult, the waters of sleep still tugging at me even as instinct tells me there's something in the darkness.

A soft shuffle of feet on the carpet, and I can sense him. He's here, watching me, invisible, but his aura reaches out, awakening my body like a warm featherlight touch on the pleasure centers of my brain.

Arousal ripples up my thighs, fresh heat shimmering with the memories of last time. I've never felt anything like him before, my body used and taken, battered and driven insane . . . and completely, thoroughly pleasured in a way that I didn't think possible.

It was so much that I don't even remember coming down, just an explosion of ecstasy that drove me into unconsciousness . . . but now my senses have returned and I know he's still there, measuring me, hunting me, *desiring* me.

How can he have strength left? How, when every muscle from my neck to my toes has already been taken past the limit?

How can he still want more?

My nostrils flare, and I can smell him. Rich, masculine . . . feral. A man's man who could tear me apart without a second's effort. His breath, soft but shuddering, sipping at the air, savoring the conquest to come.

Another whisper in the darkness, and the fear melts away, replaced by a heightened sense of things.

The moonlight, dim now in the post-midnight morning, when the night's as deep as it will ever be.

The sweat on my skin and the fresh moisture gathering at the juncture between my thighs.

He steps forward, still cloaked in shadow, a shape from the depths of night, ready for a new kind of embrace.

He reaches for my calf, and at his touch, I start to tremble. I should resist, I should say I can't take any more. He's already had his fill. What more can he want?

He inhales, his nose taking in my scent, and the knowledge comes to me, a revelation that I've chosen to ignore.

He wants me to be his. Not just his bedmate, not simply a conquest to have and to discard. He wants to possess me fully, to own me, body and soul.

But can I?

Can I give myself to such a man, a being whose very presence inspires fear and dread?

Can I risk the fury that I've seen directed at others turned back upon me?

His tongue flicks out, touching that spot he's discovered behind my right knee that I wasn't even aware of before him, my left leg falling aside on its own as my hunger betrays me.

My mind is troubled, my heart races . . . but my body knows what it wants.

He chuckles, a rumble that tickles my soft inner thighs as he pauses, his breath warm over my pussy. He scoops his hands under my buttocks, and I feel him adjust himself on the mattress, preparing for his feast.

"Delicious," he growls, and then his tongue touches me . . . and I'm gone.

MIA

The electronic drumbeats thud through the air so hard that I can actually feel my chest vibrate as I look at my screen, my head bobbing as I let the pattern come to me.

I've had a lot of people ask me how I can work the way I do, but this is when the magic happens. I've got three computer screens, each of them split into halves with data flowing in each one. I'm finishing up my evaluations, I've done the grind, and now I'm bringing it all together.

For that, though, I need tunes, and nothing gets my brain working on the right frequency as well as good techno does.

I can hear the door to my office vibrate in its frame, and I'm glad I've got my own little paradise down here in the basement of the Goldstone Building.

Sure, my methods are weird, and I'm sort of isolated considering that I'm in a corner office with two file rooms on either side of me, but that's because I need this to make the magic happen.

Frankly, I wasn't too sure if I'd be able to keep this job, considering the number of complaints I got my first six months working here.

Part of it, of course, is my occasional outbursts—to myself, mind you, and more often than not in gutter Russian so no one can understand me.

That, with the random singing along with my tunes, meant I was labeled as 'distracting' and 'difficult to work next to.'

But the powers that be saw the value that I bring with my data analysis.

So, as an experimental last gasp, I was sent down here, where the walls are thick, the neighbors are paper, and nobody minds that my singing voice is terrible.

It works for them, but more importantly, it works for me.

And here I've remained for almost six years, working metadata analysis and market trends, making people with money even more money.

Not that the company's treated me poorly. I've gotten a bonus for seven quarters straight, and I've always managed my own investments.

For a girl who still has a few years until she hits thirty, I'm doing well on the ol' nest egg.

But I'm pigeonholed. Other than dropping off files from time to time, I almost never see anyone in my day to day work, which I guess is okay with me. I've never been someone who likes the social scene of an office.

On the other hand, I can wear my pink and blue streaks in my hair and not have to see people's judging glares. And I don't have to explain what my lyrics mean when I decide to sing along.

"Another one for the Motherland!" I exclaim as I see what I've been looking for. This isn't a hard assignment, merely an optimization analysis for some of Goldstone's transport subsidiaries. But I prefer to celebrate each victory, no matter how small or large, with glee.

I swipe all the data to my side monitors and bring up a document in the center and start typing. I've already included most of the boilerplate that the executives and VPs want to see, the 'check the box' sort of things that my father would understand with his background.

After all, he is Russian. He knows about bureaucracy.

Finally, just as the Elf Clock above my door dings noon, I save my file and fire it off to my supervisor.

"In Russia . . . report finishes *you*."

Okay, so it's not my best one-liner, but it's another quirk of mine. While I'm as American as apple pie, I pay homage to my roots, especially at work, for some reason. It seems to help, so I'm sticking to it.

Heading to the elevator, I go upstairs before punching out for lunch and jumping into my little Chevy to drive to my 'spot', a diner called The Gravy Train. An honest to goodness old-fashioned diner, it's got some of the best food in town, including a fried chicken sandwich that's to kill for.

As I drive, I look around my hometown, still surprised at how big it seems these days. The main reason, of course, is tied to the dark tower on the north side of town, Blackwell Industries.

Thirty years ago, Mr. Blackwell located his headquarters here in the sleepy town of Roseboro and proclaimed it to be the bridge between Portland and Seattle. A lot of people scoffed, but he was right, and Roseboro's been the beneficiary of his foresight.

I've been lucky, watching a city literally grow with me. Roseboro is big enough now that some people even call this a Tri-Cities area, lumping us in with Portland and Seattle.

I get to The Gravy Train just in time to see the other reason that I come to this place so frequently for lunch wave from the window. Isabella "Izzy" Turner has been my best friend since first grade, and I love her like she's my own flesh and blood.

As I enter, I see her untie the apron on her uniform and slump down into one of the booths. Her normally rich brown hair looks limp and stringy today, and the bags under her eyes are so big she could be carrying her after work clothes in them.

"Hey, babe, you look exhausted," I say in greeting, giving her a hug from the side as I slide in next to her. "Please don't tell me you're still working double shifts?"

"Have to," Izzy says as she leans into me and hugs back. "Gotta keep the bills paid, and doing double shifts gives me a chance to maybe get a little ahead. I'll need it once classes start up again."

"You know you don't have to," I tell her for the millionth time. "You can take out student loans like the rest of us."

"I'd rather not if I don't have to. I owe enough to other people as it is."

She's got a point. She's had a tough life and has seen tragedy that left more and more debt on her tab, and student loans are tough enough without all the other stuff in her life.

And even though she always turns me down, I have to offer once again, just on the off-chance she'll say yes this time. "Still, if you need anything . . . I mean, I've said it before, but you can always come live with me. I've got room at my place."

Izzy snorts, finally cracking a smile. "You mean you want someone to stay up with you until two in the morning on weekends playing video games."

Before I can elbow her in the side, the bell above the door rings and in walks the third member of our little party patrol, Charlotte Dunn. A stunning girl who turns heads everywhere she goes with her long, naturally bright and beautiful red hair, she slides into the booth opposite Izzy and me, looking exhausted herself.

She settles in, sighing heavily, and Izzy looks over at her. "Tough morning for you too?"

"I think walking in the back and sticking my head in a vat of hot oil might just be preferable to working reception on the ground floor of Satan's Skyscraper," she jokes. "It's not like anything bad happened either."

"So what's the deal?" I ask, and Charlotte shakes her head. "What?"

"I guess it's just that everyone there walks like they've got a hundred-pound albatross on their back as they come in. No smiles, no greetings, even though I try. It's just depressing," she replies. "You got lucky, landing in the shining palace."

"Girl, please. I work all by my lonesome in the deep, dark dungeon of a basement," I point out.

Charlotte snorts. "But that's how you like it!"

She's not wrong, so I don't bother arguing, instead teasingly gloating, "And I get to wear whatever and work however the hell I please."

Our waitress, one of Izzy's co-workers, comes over with her order pad. "So, what can I get you ladies?"

"Something with no onions or spice," Izzy replies, groaning. "Maybe Henry can whip up a grilled cheese for me?"

"Deal. And for you ladies?"

We place our orders, and the three of us lean back, relaxing. Charlotte looks me over enviously again, shaking her head. "Seriously, Mia, can't get over the outfit today. You trying to show off the curves?"

"What curves?" I ask, looking down at today's band T-shirt. It's just a BTS logo, twin columns rising on a black shirt.

"Hey, you're rockin' it." Charlotte laughs. "It fits the girls just right."

I roll my eyes. Charlotte always seems to see something in me that I don't. Men don't seem to find me interesting. Or at least, the men *I* find interesting don't find *me* interesting.

Deflecting back to her, I ask, "How're things looking for you? That guy in Accounting ever come back downstairs to get your number?"

Charlotte snorts. "Nope. I saw him the other day, but it's okay. It's his loss."

She does a little hair flip and I can't help but smile. She hasn't always had the best luck with guys, but she never gives up and always keeps a positive attitude about the whole dating game. Her motto is 'No Mr. Wrongs, only Mr. Rights and Mr. Right-Nows.' Maybe not the classiest, but a girl's got needs, and sometimes it's nice to have an orgasm from a guy not named B.O.B.

We eat our lunches, chatting and gossiping and bullshitting as always. It's never a big to-do since we share lunch together at least once a week, if not more, but it's still nice to catch up. Izzy and I have been friends for so long, and Charlotte and I met in college. They're important to me.

"So, when do classes start up again, Izz?" Charlotte asks. "So you can, I don't know, get some sleep and not have fallen arches?"

Izzy snorts. "Too soon, I think. But if I can string together another two semesters—"

"Wait, two?" I ask in shock. "Honey, you're like the super-duper-ooper senior at this point. Seriously, some of the professors are probably younger than you by now."

"Hey, we're the same age!" Izzy protests, but shrugs. "You know, I had a freshman ask me if I was a TA the other day?"

"Ouch, that had to hurt," Charlotte says. "What did you say?"

"I pointed him in the direction of the student union and turned him down when he asked for my number. Seriously, I'm not sure if he even needed to shave yet. I don't have time to teach eighteen-year-old man-boys what and where a clit is!"

Charlotte and I laugh, and I punch her in the shoulder. "You'll get there in your own time, girl. But still, why the wait?"

"Mostly the internship," Izzy admits. "I can juggle classes and work, or internship and work, but I can't do classes, internship, and work. There's just not enough hours in the day."

I nod, understanding that Izzy has plans and dreams. But unlike most, she's willing to sacrifice and work hard to reach hers.

We shift topics, like we always do, until we've covered all the usual topics and my tummy feels pleasantly happy without risk of an afternoon food coma.

Wiping our mouths with our napkins, I glance at my phone, checking the time. "So, Char . . . rock, paper, scissors?"

"Nope, this one's mine!" Charlotte says, giggling as I lean into Izzy, preventing her from moving as Charlotte grabs the check and runs up to the counter.

"Hey! Hey, dammit!" Izzy protests. "I—"

"Should be quiet and let your friends pay for lunch for once," I whisper. "Or else I'll use my secret Russian pressure point skills on you!"

"Oh, fine, since you put it that way!"

Charlotte comes back, and she smiles at Izzy. "Chill, Izz. You bust your ass, and you've snuck us an extra pickle more than once. You're allowed to let me buy you lunch every now and then."

"We could all use some more *pickle*." Izzy chuckles. "Seriously, at this point, I'd settle for a one-nighter. No commitment, no issues, just a good old-fashioned hookup. As long he's well into his twenties, at least," she says with an eye roll.

"Mr. Right Now?" Charlotte asks, and Izzy nods. "Hmph. You find him, send him my way. I keep finding good guys . . . two months after they've met the girl of their dreams. Only single men I find are dogs."

"You've just gotta make sure you give them a fake number and a flea dip, and enjoy the weekend," I tease, though she knows I would never do anything of the sort.

"I'm lonely, but I've got rechargeable batteries."

We all laugh, and my phone rings. I pull it out, checking the screen. "Shit, girls, it's my boss. Says he's got a rush job for me to complete."

"How's he working out, anyway?" Charlotte asks as I finish my drink quickly. "And have you started working for The Golden Child yet?"

"Nope, I've never seen him except for the publicity stuff," I reply honestly. "He's the penthouse. I'm the basement. Twenty-four floors in between us. Anyway, I gotta jet, so I'll talk to you girls soon, okay?"

"Yup . . . I'm going to relax for this next ten minutes before I need to clock back in myself," Izzy says, stretching out. "Gimme a call later?"

I nod, blowing them a kiss, and head back to work.

THOMAS

Looking out over Roseboro, I feel like I'm looking over my empire.

Of course, I'm joking . . . but maybe not so much.

Twenty-five years ago, this town was just a suburb of a suburb of Portland. Though it was already up and coming, I'd like to think that over the past six years I've added my fair share to this place.

I'd finished my MBA at Stanford and set up shop in the growing town, watching the landscape change and cultivating the business interests that serve me best. Because I haven't just watched. I've worked my ass off to get Goldstone where it is today.

Still, I made sure to keep the competition in sight, literally.

My office faces the Blackwell Building, a one-mile gap separating the two tallest buildings in the city. It helps me keep things in perspective. I came to town because I saw potential, even if Blackwell had already created something big here.

But this place is too fertile for him to fully take advantage of. A rose that, if tended right, can provide more blossoms than any one man could utilize.

I watch the morning sun hit the black tower. I'll give Blackwell grudging respect. His design might be morbid, but it's also cutting-edge. All that black is absorbing the solar energy and using it for electricity and heating. The man was environmental before environmental was actually cool.

Too bad you'll never be that. You're just a wannabe, another young upstart who'll never stand the test of time.

I growl, pushing away the voice from inside me, even though I know it'll be back. It never really goes away, not for long. No matter how much I achieve, that voice of insecurity still resides in my center, ready to cast doubt and shadows on each success.

The soft ding from my computer reminds me that my ten minutes of morning meditation are over, and I turn back around, looking at my desk and office. It's nothing lavish. I designed this space for maximum efficiency and productivity.

So my Herman Miller chair is not in my office for lapped luxury, or for its black and chrome styling, but for the fact that it's rated the best chair for productivity. Same with my desk, my computer, everything.

Everything is tuned toward efficient use of my time and my efforts.

I launch into it, going through my morning assignments, answering the emails that my secretary, Kerry, cannot answer for me, and making a flurry of decisions on projects that Goldstone is working on.

Finally, just as the clock on my third screen beeps one o'clock, I send off my final message and stand up. Locking my computer, I transfer everything to my server upstairs in case I need it.

I see Kerry sitting at her desk as I leave my office. She's well-dressed as usual, her sunkissed skin and black hair gleaming mellowly under the office lighting, the perfect epitome of a professional executive assistant. While she works for me, she has this older sibling protective instinct. It's not often that I need it, but I appreciate her looking out for me.

"Need something, Mr. Goldstone?" she asks.

"Just headed upstairs," I tell her.

"Of course," she replies, her eyes cutting to her computer screen. "Just a reminder, sir, the governor will be hosting his charity event tonight at seven. I've already had your tuxedo dry-cleaned, and your car detailer called. Your car will be ready and downstairs by three this afternoon."

I give her a nod. Three's plenty of time. "I just sent you a list of other projects to work on, by the way."

"Of course, Mr. Goldstone. I was looking that over, and I got an email from Hank also, the team leader you assigned the Taiwan shipping contract to. He said that he's going to have to take a day off Friday, sir. His daughter's going to college this year, and he promised her that he'd drive her up so she can get settled into the dorm."

I stop, pursing my lips. "What is her name?"

Kerry taps her desk for a moment, searching her memory. "Erica, sir."

"Tell Hank that I understand and wish Erica the best, but if he isn't at work on Friday, don't bother coming in on Monday."

My tone has grown serious, and Kerry's eyes tighten, but she knows Hank is crossing a line. He should've given notice, especially when he's working a contract this important.

He's usually a good employee. But he knew his daughter was starting classes. No excuse for that.

No excuse for you, you mean. Failure just drips down from the boss's office down to Hank, that's all.

Leaving the twenty-fifth floor of the Goldstone building, I take the stairs up a level to stretch my legs. Not many people even know about this floor other than the executives. To everyone else, the Goldstone Building has twenty-five floors.

The twenty-sixth is mine. It's my penthouse, and while it isn't quite as large as the other floors, it's still six thousand square feet of space that's just for me.

I strip off my dress shirt, tie, and slacks, depositing everything in the laundry chute before pulling on my workout clothes.

Today's upper body day, and as I go into my home gym, I swing my arms to loosen up my shoulders. They're going to be punished today. Starting with bench presses, I assault my body, pushing myself to press the bar one more time, to get the fucking dumbbells up despite the pain, despite gravity kicking my ass.

Just like everything kicks your ass.

The finisher for today is brutal, even for me. The 300 . . . 100 burpees, 100 dips, and 100 pullups, in sets of ten, nonstop. By the time I'm finished, sweat pools on the rubberized gym flooring beneath me.

I have to force myself to my feet because I refuse to be broken by anything, even something as meaningless as a workout that's supposed to do exactly that.

Instead, I jump in for a quick shower and meditate for twenty minutes after. I need to focus because running Goldstone is a mental exercise.

Closing my eyes, I force myself to push all the responsibilities away, to let it all fade into the background.

I push away the flashbacks, the voice in my head, the memories that threaten from time to time, and imagine my perfect world . . . . my empire. My perfect Roseboro, deep red petals soft as velvet and eternally blooming, ready to be passed from my generation to the next for tending and care.

I know I can do it.

I *must* do it.

Changing into my tuxedo, I head downstairs to the freshly cleaned limo waiting to take me to this event. The Roseboro Civic Library is one of the newest public buildings in town, a beautiful hundred-thousand-square-foot building in three wings over two floors. The central wing is named for Horatio Roseboro, who founded the city in memory of his daughter, who died on the Oregon Trail, while the other two wings are named for the main benefactors . . . Goldstone and Blackwell. My only request was that the Goldstone wing contain the children's section, and they were more than willing to do that.

Tonight, though, it's the scene for a fundraiser for the governor's favorite charity. Governor Gary Langlee tends to ignore Roseboro most of the time—we're not his voter base—but when it comes time to get money, he'll go just about anywhere he can if someone will cross his palm with a little bit of green.

I arrive at just the right time, ten minutes before seven, in order to get the best of the press. I tolerate the leeches more than like them, but I do understand that the fourth estate has a purpose and a job to do.

And there are legit journalists who I respect. It's just the paparazzi and empty talking heads that I despise.

So I smile for the cameras, giving a little wave and shaking hands with our local state representative before heading into the foyer, where the party has already started.

"Ah, Thomas!" the mayor says, greeting me in that hearty way that really endears him to the locals. "I'm so glad you could make it."

"You know me, never pass up a chance to press the flesh," I reply, making him laugh. He knows I'm lying but thinks that I'm only here because of the press and good PR that Goldstone will get for tonight.

The reality is far different. While Governor Langlee and I might not see eye to eye on most public policies, I actually agree with the goals of tonight's event.

"I'm sure you'll enjoy yourself," the mayor says after a moment when I don't follow up.

Clearing his throat, he looks around. "If you don't mind telling me, Thomas, there's a rumor around town that Goldstone is looking into building a sea transportation hub in Roseboro. I'm not saying I wouldn't appreciate it, but if you are, I happen to know a man who's got about seven hundred and fifty acres just outside of town. It's county land, but I'm sure we could work something out."

That's the mayor . . . a good ol' boy to the voters, a sneaky deal-maker to those with money. The man would sell his grandmother's grave if it'd make him a buck.

Oh, like you've been such a good son.

"If we do move on such a project, I'll be sure to keep City Hall informed," I tell him with a smile that turns just a little predatory at the end. "But of course, I would do my due diligence on the property. No use wasting my money when it could be spent on a proper seaport instead of along the Columbia?"

The mayor blanches just a little, which is what I want. A tiny reminder that while he may hold office, I hold the funds that make this city thrive or fail. Or at least a large share of the finances that do so.

Leaving him, I do my best to 'mingle'. I know the faces. I've seen it all before.

A pat on the back here for a friend.

A backhanded compliment for the enemy whom you can't quite man up and call out in public. The icy stare from across the room at those whose families have somehow found the time to engage in feuds despite not having the time to make a difference in the world.

It's all old hat, and while some might find it interesting, I just tolerate it to get my goal here tonight done.

Finally, at nine o'clock, I can't do it any longer. I retreat to the children's section, which is relatively quiet in comparison, and I look over the newest books on the display.

"You know, I'm not too sure if *Long Way Down* really belongs in the children's section," a throaty voice says behind me, and I turn to see Meghan Langlee, Governor Langlee's daughter.

She's wearing a Chanel cocktail dress that fits her like a glove, highlighting a very fit body and a camera grabbing face. A former beauty queen like her mother, Meghan's parlayed her looks into a budding career as a political pundit.

"Actually, I personally insisted on it," I reply, turning away from her and looking at the books again. "While the subject matter might be a little dark and violent, the days of young people growing up needing little more than *The Andy Griffith Show* and reading Judy Blume are pretty much over."

"Hmm, well, I'll say my father would disapprove, but I understand what you mean," she says, stepping closer. "You know, Mr. Goldstone . . . mind if I call you Tom?"

"If you wish," I reply, sizing her up immediately. She must be up to something, she's coming on too hard, too boldly.

It wouldn't surprise me if she's been sent here on a mission. Her father's a weasel and would see no issue with using his only daughter this way.

She takes my arm, as if she expects me to suddenly escort her and be happy to do so, giving me a false coquettish giggle. "Ooh. I've heard your reputation Tom, that you're pretty *rigid* in your fitness routines, but wow, this tux is hiding a *beast* underneath all this worsted wool."

"Clean eating and good habits," I reply, already tiring of her and her lazily flirtatious innuendos. She tries to lead me back to the main wing, and I follow along simply to avoid any issues, but when she sees one of the press and starts trying to angle us in that direction, I pull my arm free. "Excuse me, Miss Langlee."

She looks surprised, anger hiding in her eyes. I doubt she's used to being denied. She reaches out and grabs my arm again, pulling herself close.

"Come on now, Tom. I'm sure we can find a little bit of fun."

I can't tolerate this any longer, and I pull away, my voice tight. "Sorry. I haven't had my rabies booster this year."

I walk away, cursing myself at that last crack. Turning her down cold? That's one thing.

But essentially calling her a disease-infested slut was probably too much.

"One of these days, you're going to piss off someone important," she says threateningly to my back. When I don't reply, she stomps her foot like a petulant toddler, loud enough to cut through the hubbub of the party as she calls out, "Bastard!"

Everything stops, and I nod, glancing back over my shoulder at her with a charming smile. "That's one of the things they call me."

I keep going, and as I pass by the governor, he gives me a dirty look. Reaching out, he puts a hand on my arm.

"You know, my daughter—" he starts, already conciliatory, which makes me think he knew exactly what Meghan's game was tonight.

I don't let him finish. I just shrug him off, ignoring the snapping cameras. I only pause at the door to reach into my jacket and pull out an envelope that I slide into the donation box.

It's unmarked . . . but that's just what I want.

Get the full Book on Amazon Here, or search for Beauty and the Billionaire by Lauren Landish.

ABOUT THE AUTHOR

Dirty Fairy Tales:
Beauty and the Billionaire | | Not So Prince Charming

Get Dirty:
Dirty Talk | | Dirty Laundry | | Dirty Deeds | | Dirty Secrets

Bennett Boys Ranch:
Buck Wild | | Riding Hard

*Irresistible Bachelor*s:
Anaconda | | Mr. Fiance | | Heartstopper
Stud Muffin | | Mr. Fixit | | Matchmaker
Motorhead | | Baby Daddy | | Untamed

Stay in contact! You can join my mailing list here. You'll never
miss a new release and you'll even get a free ebook!

37202381R00208

Made in the USA
Lexington, KY
23 April 2019